"RUN!" SHE SCREAMED. "RUN!"

Tarana cried out in her full priestess voice, her arm stuck out from her robe, pointing to the sky. "Godsfire!"

From between the clouds a rod of white-hot fire had been hurled and lay suspended in the valley air. Fire, without question it was fire, for the very air smoked where the fire passed through.

The mountains were scintillating, shimmering in the heat. The fire stream was engulfing the valley, creeping toward us. Its brilliance was of a stronger magnitude than I'd ever seen. . . .

Tarana's quivering voice broke the spell. "I will seek a vision now." She lifted her eyes to the godsfire. I thought her threshold of pain must be different from mine, but suddenly she collapsed, writhing in pain. "My eyes," she moaned. "My eyes." I think she would have gouged them out if we hadn't restrained her.

Then our fear was replaced with awe, and we stood staring at the brilliant mountainscape when . . .

GODSFIRE

CYNTHIA FELICE

A TIMESCAPE BOOK
PUBLISHED BY POCKET BOOKS NEW YORK

Another *Original* publication of POCKET BOOKS

A Timescape Book published by
POCKET BOOKS, a Simon & Schuster division of
GULF & WESTERN CORPORATION
1230 Avenue of the Americas, New York, N.Y 10020

ISBN: 0-671-44704-1

First Pocket Books printing June, 1978

10 9 8 7 6 5 4 3

POCKET and colophon are trademarks of Simon & Schuster.

Use of the trademark TIMESCAPE is by exclusive license
from Gregory Benford, the trademark owner.

Printed in the U.S.A.

The author gratefully acknowledges the cooperation of Bob, Erik, and Robert Felice during the preparation of the manuscript, and the assistance of Pam Haggart, her patient proofreader.

For Damon Knight, Edward Bryant, and Kate Wilhelm, who took me seriously from the start, my thanks

THE OCEAN

Wave-cut Cliffs

city Plateau

MORAINE

GLACIER

Evernight Mountains

To the King's City on the Coastal Plains →

Plateau

Badlands

B

Heoa's maps
are picturelike,
inked onto
animal skins
(which are
stitched together
by very fine stitches).

PART I
HEAO'S WORLD

Chapter 1

THE HIGHLAND winters have always been the fiercest in the realm; storms of stinging, icy rain, sometimes snow—which flatlanders don't believe in until they've wintered with us—and always enough cold in the air to build thick swatches of ice on the routes from the fishers' caves to the tops of the plateaus. Some fishers did brave the turbulence that the goddess Oceana set upon the waters, and with their belay lines holding them fast, they netted fresh kelp and fish, which they feasted on alone, for above them the cliffs were sheathed in ice.

An enterprising merchant, Baltsar by name, and an adventurer at heart, had rigged a hoist that raised baskets of fish and kelp from the fishers' caves past the ice-bound portion of the cliffs, to the plateau where the goods were counted and credited to the fisher below who had filled it. In this manner the tableland city, short on supplies after a war-filled summer, augmented winter moss-stews, which were our sustenance until the causeway to the lowlands was built in later years.

I first met Baltsar at his hoist, in my sixteenth winter. He was bundled in woolens and an oilpaper raincoat even though it was one of those rare winter twilights during which there was no rain. The mists from the warm sea below collided with the freezing plateau winds and swirled in an updraft that put layer upon layer of ice on the lip of

3

the cliff and on Baltsar's oilpaper coat. The slop from the buckets as he and a slave put their backs to the winch and then snared the basket with a gaff added to the wetness of the work. The basket was only half full, but, as his slave tossed fish into the packing cases, Baltsar dutifully counted the catch, marking his ledger with obvious pleasure.

"I thought that the catch would be good because the sky was calm," I said. Supposedly, Oceana's mood was reflected in the sky.

Baltsar, who was not startled by my voice, didn't even look up from his ledger sheet. "We had a large catch during the night," he said in an unpleasant fashion, "as you well know. No doubt you've just come from the marketplace and you saw my . . . " He looked up then and the scowl on his face gave over to surprise. "Oh, sorry. I thought you were . . . well, never mind. Did you come to buy fresh fish? I don't usually conduct sales here, but . . . "

"No," I said, "I didn't come to make a purchase."

He puzzled a moment, his eyes searching the shadow of my hood, then smiled. "Ah, you're Heao, Rellar's protégé." He glanced up at the sky, swirling with spuming mist. "The wind is strong and crystal clear. The sky will clear and, with luck, you'll see the skybridge."

He'd guessed my mission incorrectly, but it was not a wild guess to make of an academian. So I said, "I didn't know merchants kept abreast of Academe's endeavors."

Baltsar smiled. "I only keep track of the pretty ones."

"Indeed," I said, flushing despite my arched spine. Since the recent war, foreigners were viewed with suspicion. Merchants were a new class among us, landless offspring of lowland nobles, dissatisfied craftspeople, refugees from the land-grabbing campaigns, trying to make livings in less troubled lands.

"I didn't mean to embarrass you, but you are pretty, you know, despite your grisly profession."

"My profession, grisly! Listen to the usurer talk!" I was prepared to leave, but the man had the most mischievous twinkle in his eyes that I'd ever seen. Then the tip of his tail began to twitch. Without the smiling eyes, that twitch would have warned of battle, but now I realized it was an invitation to play. I laughed. "I'm sorry, I don't have time. I'm on my master's business."

He put aside his ledgers and walked away from his

4

work. "You are Rellar's eyes," he said. "Where does your master's work take you?"

I shrugged. "To the sea, by the old battlements along Prince Chel's stronghold."

"This is the sea," he said with an expansive wave of his hand. "And I can offer you more hospitality here than you'll find among fallen stones on a windy point. I've a mossy nest in that spire over there . . . "

His boldness was nearly frightening, yet there was no malice in his eyes and his tail was coiled casually around his ice-laden coat.

" . . . should you want to nap."

That's what I thought he was leading up to, and again I prepared to stamp away.

"I shall be leaving within a half-stick's time, but you're welcome to the nest."

"Oh," I said, hesitating. The twinight might remain fair, but winter winds and driving rains could blow in from the sea with little warning. It would be nice to have a retreat from the elements, since I was obliged to be near the sea at a high point. "All right," I said finally. I chose a rock to sit upon and pretended to be very interested in the sky.

"You're welcome," Baltsar said as he turned back to his ledger.

I ignored his pointing out my rudeness, ignored him, too, when he again put aside his ledger. Ignoring him was not easy to do, I realized, when he shed his raincoat and upper tunic, exposing his chest fur to me. The growth was handsome, even-colored, and smooth, close to the rippling muscles beneath. He dipped his hands in a wash bucket and splashed his face and chest, looking very much like a peasant in his woolen trousers. But the linen towel the slave handed him was streaked with perfumed oils, a fine distinction between commoner and patrician, but enough for sensitive noses no matter how pleasing the scent of fish.

Soon Baltsar was wearing a fresh tunic and a woolen cape, intricately embroidered with silver thread. He brought a pan of hot coals with a fine clay pot inside, set the apparatus near my feet, and signaled for the slave to bring cups. Another slave appeared, offering moss cushions, robes for our knees, a platter of spiced kelp, and a selection of three fresh fish. Baltsar delicately slit the belly of the choicest fish with his index claw, and, after a slave took away the entrails, he slivered the tender flesh for me.

5

He served the unexpected but most delightful meal as if we were seated in a noble lair instead of a merchant's rugged camp.

I speared a sliver with my eating claw and chewed gratefully. My master not being rich and I not being of independent means, I hadn't been able to afford fish for many months.

"You're smiling," Baltsar said.

"I often do."

"I know."

"How do you know? We've just met."

"Academe is important to me," Baltsar said. "They alone see through the temple's accusation of usury."

"Do pretty academians see best?" I said, trying to keep my tail from twitching.

Baltsar laughed aloud. "Actually, a certain blind old man sees clearest, but he's also a recluse who is difficult to find."

I sighed. "I thought my beauty had beguiled you, and now I learn you merely want my master's ear. Merchants are unscrupulous."

"Can you be bribed?" Baltsar said.

"No."

"That's what the rumor is, and I believe it," said Baltsar, selecting the smallest slivers of fish for himself. "Tell me what you expect to see when the wind finishes blowing away the clouds."

I glanced up. Over the sea the clouds were thin enough to see gray sky, but overhead the sky was still obscured. "If those clear, I'll see the skybridge, of course."

Baltsar nodded. "Yes, but why do you . . . why does your master wish to see it?" He seemed genuinely interested.

I shrugged. "Academe wants to learn."

"Learn what? The temple guardians were not interested in the skybridge until Rellar suggested we might learn more about the gods by studying it."

"Since you already know, why ask me?"

"Rellar is not usually given to religious pursuits, and I'm curious about his true purpose."

"I only know that I'm to scribe what I see on parchment—that is, if I see anything more than a black line across the sky."

"You're close-mouthed, too," Baltsar said. He smiled. "I expected nothing less. Well, I must go. There are still a few baskets of fish to be marketed, and my slave has them ready now."

I glanced at the slave, who was ready to hoist the carrying baskets onto his back, and I wondered how he was going to manage since there was more than he could carry. Merchants, it seemed, were usurers in more than one way. Even a slave's broad back had limits. But Baltsar shouldered one basket himself, and then he helped the slave with the heavier load. Once satisfied that it was secure, he turned to me.

"I used a map drawn by a young pathfinder named Heao when I had to find my way to the copper mines. Are you the same Heao?"

"If you used the canyon route, then it was my map."

"It was a fine map, Heao, except that a few rather tall peaks were not indicated."

"All unusually tall mountains are marked on my map," I said bristling.

"Not the distant ones," Baltsar said. His tail was twitching again and he was smiling. Why had he ignored my shaking tail while we ate? Why did he want to play just as he was leaving? Or was his playfulness involuntary—something he couldn't help from time to time? I considered that for a moment, wondering if I was pleased or affronted. My not having attained legal majority of seventeen years could mean he thought of me as a child and that the flattery was only a part of a private game of his.

"My maps are accurate," I said sullenly.

"Yes," he said quickly. "I wasn't disputing that. But . . . have you ever considered putting slaves' observations on your maps? In the lowlands, all but the meanest peasant travel with at least one slave, for they can see much farther than the human eye. Line-of-sight traveling is much faster, for the mark can be much farther away and there are fewer detours."

"You'd trust a slave with your path?"

Baltsar nodded. "They're much smarter than dogs, and if you treat them well, they're equally loyal. And they have certain physical advantages that I can use."

I nodded. "Such as carrying heavier loads and superior distance vision?"

"Yes. Slaves can see the sea from the top of the cliffs, so I know when to lower my baskets to the cliff dwellers. I'm surprised you don't have one with you today to help you look at the skybridge."

7

I looked up. The clouds were very thin and I could see the deep shadow of the skybridge through them, making a gray line from horizon to horizon. "I don't have a slave." He knew very well that the only slaves in our city were his own and those belonging to the occupational forces of the King-conqueror.

"There's a female slave in my nest who's too heavy with child to be of much use to me for a while. If she can serve you in any way, please call on her."

I nodded, curious with the idea.

"You're welcome," Baltsar said.

That time it was merely my distraction causing me to be rude. "Baltsar," I said loudly. He stopped, turned, and waited for me to speak. I left my rock seat and went to him.

"How did you know my name?" he said.

"Everyone knows the name of the city's most prominent usurer," I said.

"Must be my good looks," he said, shaking his tail at me.

I smiled, coiled my tail demurely about my waist, and said, "Thank you, Baltsar."

I really thought that, finally, Baltsar would turn the conversation to the usury charge, or perhaps to Rellar, or even to the temple, those three all being connected so far as he was concerned. But Baltsar just smiled, nodded, and departed.

I watched him and the slave leave. Then I returned to the fire. A breeze was updrafting from the sea and its dampness had matted the fur between my fingers. I held my hand near the fire and pulled at the offending mats until the fur felt silky again. A female slave, obviously the pregnant one Baltsar had mentioned, began clearing away the remnants of the meal. She was well bundled in woolens and I couldn't see her hair, which, aside from the pregnancy, was the only feature that distinguished her from the other slaves. Her pale, furless hands were unscarred and the skin covering the stubby fingers seemed clean. She moved the dishes deftly and silently, as if the camp were her master's kitchen.

When all but my cup and the teapot were stacked on her tray, she lifted her eyes to see if I would nod or frown. I noticed that her cheeks were plump and her doe eyes did not have the characteristic dark circles underneath. It was unlikely then, that she would have the

8

common slave name of Ring Eye; but she probably would have responded to the name, as most of them did. Her working without supervision made me even more curious. Was she called Industrious? Faithful?

"What are you called?"

"Manya," she said, stretching her lips back to expose her flat-tipped teeth, which I realized was an imitation of a human smile.

I laughed, at the smile and because her name was a human one, and Baltsar seemed more novel for having given it to her. Manya frowned at my laughter. "The merchant has a sense of humor," I said, comforting her. "Or are you his special plaything?"

Manya's eyes widened and she smoothed the folds of her robe over her balloon belly. She started to speak but bit her lip instead. I thought I saw something flash in her eyes.

"Are you shocked, Manya?" I said, wondering for the first time if a slave could be.

"No, I'm pained," she said. "That is a terrible accusation to make against a man who just served you a fine meal." There were tears forming in the round eyes and she bit her lip again. She took the tray and began heaving herself up.

I was dumbfounded. She'd spoken a cogent sentence in human tongue, responding in a fashion that suggested she understood the subtle nuances of good and evil. She was up and hurrying away from me before I recovered my wits. "Manya!" I shouted. "Come back!" Obediently, she came, her eyes properly downcast. "Leave the tea," I said.

Manya kneeled, set the teapot in the coals, and replaced the cup at my side. Her hands trembled.

"A man who beds with a slave is one kind; a man who doesn't is another," I said.

Her eyes blazed with—this time I could identify it— anger, but she held her tongue, no doubt wondering if she'd already gone too far with me. I was too fascinated to reprimand her.

"Sit down," I said in a gentle voice that I hoped was not patronizing, as well. I wanted to ask her if she had ever been bedded by a human. The city folk all suspected that the occupational forces were guilty of such bestiality, but much of that was because we were all too ready to believe anything evil of them. Anyhow, I didn't ask

9

Manya because I could see that she had feelings, and where there are feelings, there is pride. "Your master said you could help me see details in the skybridge. The clouds are nearly gone. Tell me what you see."

She tucked her knees under her, studied me for a moment, then said, "It's an arc from one horizon to the other. It seems nearly black and has no discernible features."

"You didn't look up," I said. "And it does have features. Even I can see that."

"You're seeing high-altitude clouds, lady," she said. "They are like puffs of smoke and they do not move very fast."

I scowled, uncertain whether clouds could be so high in the sky that I could not even tell they were clouds. I never suspected that clouds might have such great lift. "How many tall peaks can you see between here and the Evernight Mountains?" I said suspiciously.

"The front-range peaks are between here and the Evernights. I cannot see them at all."

"But you can see the front range?" I said, wondering. I could not.

"Yes. I can see the Five Brothers, the Crown, and, between them, I can see the great glacier."

I sensed that she was not lying, for surely she would be too frightened of a human to lie. I took out my parchment and stylus. "Turn your gaze to the city, Manya, and describe to me in great detail what you see.'

She did, and I began the first map, which was like a god's-eye view of the city. My true mission of that twinight would be accomplished in finer style than Rellar and I had dreamed was possible.

Chapter 2

IT WAS our terrible time, our being conquered by the low-land king, our own king reduced to a military prince, and our future uncertain. These things made us suspicious of the foreign merchant. Not only was he a lowlander and therefore suspect, but he was also without precedence. We had nobility, we had peasants, we had the temple and its guardians, and we had Academe, each filling a comfortable niche in our isolated mountains society. We didn't have merchants and we were afraid of changes. But we were making changes despite our fears.

"Did you count the new graves?" I said to Rellar as we walked past the temple courtyard. We were going to the merchant's camp at the palisades.

Rellar squinted in the direction of the graveyard and shook his head. The ever-thickening film in his eyes had been shortening his sight for years. "But I know there were fewer deaths this winter," he said. "The children were stronger, with fresh fish in their bellies." He looked at me to see if I would confirm his estimate.

I nodded, but he continued staring. "Yes, there were fewer this year," I said. "You'd think the citizens would have welcomed the merchant's invention and his ingenuity, since the fresh fish and kelp saved their children's lives."

"Illness was at hand, Heao. People, Baltsar's customers,

11

were not cheerful customers," he said gravely. "The few loose coins we had in our purses at the beginning of the winter storms are now in the merchant's hands. People wonder how much tax the King-conqueror will impose . . . and what will happen if they cannot pay."

The still-unimposed taxes were on all our minds. We'd been isolated from the King-conqueror's collectors because of heavy snow in the passes, but now the first warm winds of spring had billowed over the mountains. The fresh-water streams were gorged by runoff. The tax collectors would come soon.

"I think the people have begun to accept Baltsar," Rellar said thoughtfully. "You've surely noticed that only the temple guardians continue to grumble about him, and even they do not speak too loudly."

"How can they? The merchant puts fresh fish on every altar from each catch. Don't tell me the gods feasted on them!"

Rellar smiled broadly and his tail took on a jaunty angle. "He was clever, that one. He fileted the fish for the rich and took their coins. The heads and entrails he traded to the poor in exchange for pottery, trinkets, anything. He even traded for promises, and that's quite a risk for a foreigner."

"He is a generous man," I said, remembering the spontaneous meal Baltsar had served me.

"Clever," Rellar insisted. "To whom do you think the craftspeople will first offer their wares next year? To Baltsar? Or his competitors?"

"What competitors?"

"Next year he'll have them."

"Well, perhaps he was motivated by hopes of profit. Still, the children did not die," I said. "They coughed, but their bodies were sufficiently nourished to withstand the winter ailments. We had more deaths when we were a free people. The temple guardians keep strange tallies if they don't keep that one. They ought to publicly retract their accusations."

"It will take a while for the temple guardians to realize that for every coin spent on fish, a tither's life was saved. When those tithers have lived long enough to lay coins on the altars, then the guardians will remember how wise the gods were during this time."

I looked at Rellar, wondering if he was saying that our

conquest was the gods' will and therefore a blessed event, even if mortals were confused over the deed. But he pulled his hood close to his face, and I could see no special truth.

When we were well past the city, near the rocky palisades, I took Rellar's hand to lead him. He walked strongly and surely, trusting me implicitly. Soon we were at Baltsar's seaside nest. The hoist was gone, hidden, I guessed, but no matter, because the nimble fisherfolk were shouldering their own baskets. The ice on the paths up the cliffside had melted, so they were trading in the city without the merchant's aid.

Baltsar, wearing heavy traveling clothes, was overseeing the distribution of his accumulated goods into packs. Metalware clinked and baskets rubbed as he sorted and assigned wares into piles, which the slaves carefully packed. When he saw Rellar and me, he left his work and greeted us.

"It sounds as if your winter has been profitable, merchant," Rellar said. The work sounds had not stopped. Slaves continued their chores even though their master's back was turned.

"Not yet," Baltsar said. "The profit will be turned when I sell the goods in the lowland."

"And then you will have to pay taxes and you'll probably return empty-handed," Rellar said.

Baltsar laughed. "The king will leave me enough to acquire more goods so that he can collect more taxes from me next year."

Rellar enjoyed Baltsar's banter for a moment, then asked seriously, "How do you suppose the King-conqueror will tax Academe? We provide service and do not have much in tangible goods."

Baltsar looked thoughtful. Academe was as unknown in the lowlands as merchants had been in the mountains until the conquest. How could taxes be levied on Academe, whose income depended on wisdom spoken in the right ear at the right time? We wondered how the king would deal with such a nebulous commodity. "If I were king," Baltsar said, "I'd avail myself of Academe's services . . . assuming there are services of value."

"My thoughts exactly," Rellar said. "But if the King-conqueror does not have an accurate understanding of our services, he will not know how to levy a tax. He must learn our worth."

13

Baltsar, seeing the smile on my master's lips, was immediately interested. "You have a plan?"

Rellar nodded. "If you agree, Heao will accompany you to the lowlands and present the King-conqueror with Academe's tax." Rellar produced an oilskin packet from beneath his cape. The packet was of fine quality, sealed by Academe's crest.

"A map?" Baltsar guessed.

"Yes. The finest map in the kingdom . . . of only a small portion of his realm, but if he is as wise as is reputed, he will understand its value."

Baltsar took the packet from Rellar's hand. "I never heard of people setting their own tax, but I think you're wise to try. I'll deliver it." He was grinning at Academe's impudence.

"Heao must deliver it," Rellar said evenly.

The merchant's glanced appraised me quickly. "Your highest-ranking member surely would be more appropriate." His voice was low and sincere, but he seemed strangely ill at ease, as if simultaneously realizing that he should not be offering advice to an academian, yet knowing he was more experienced with the King-conqueror than these wise, but perhaps innocent, mountain folk. "She doesn't have her robes, yet," he added.

"But I do have my robes," I said. "I was invested last night."

The significance of my announcement, a robed academian who was still in her minority years, was not lost on Baltsar. He realized I was the only person my peers could send. The other academians were too old or were lame; many had died during the war. He weighed the packet in his hands, looked from me to Rellar, then nodded. "I hope you know what you're doing," he said.

"Trust us."

"I am," Baltsar said. "His Majesty is not one to trifle with." He signaled a huge male slave away from the packs. "Teon, please see that this woman is properly shod. She will be accompanying us."

"Yes, merchant," the slave said.

While Baltsar and Rellar continued to talk, I followed the slave and watched him dig into the supply packs for unspun wool, linen bandages, and leather casings. He slipped off my own fashionable boots and examined my foot bindings. Dissatisfied, he removed the bindings and rebound my feet with thin, loose-knit strips of cloth. Over that he distributed wool evenly, which was bound into place with another set of bandages.

"My feet look larger than yours," I said as the layers of fleece and cloth casings grew.

The slave laughed and looked into my eyes. That was the first time I'd ever associated the wrinkles in the skin by a slave's eyes with amusement. The movement of the furless lids eliminated some of the hideous white that lies exposed around the small gray irides. He was so close that I could see tiny black veins in his eyeballs and the gray muscle bulging at the inner corners of his eyes. Or were they glands? The crisp delineation between white and irides of the eyeball made his gaze seem bold. He resumed his work. His thick fingers were nimble and gentle as he knotted the bandages along the side of my leg in a neat row. When he fitted the overboot, he arranged the fold along the knots and laced it so the ties would not cause pressure spots along the bandage knots.

"Are they comfortable?" he said as he squeezed my ankle and instep. "They must not be too tight or you'll freeze."

"They feel fine," I said, flexing my feet every which way, "but my feet look like barrels."

Again he laughed, and skin formed a tri-cornered frame around his eyeballs. Guileless eyes. "We'll be walking through snow and over ice, and you'll appreciate their bulk then." He picked up the boots I had arrived in. "I'll put these in my pack."

I nodded and watched him walk away. The rigid, straight-backed spine and heavy steps of the slave Teon were regal.

He put my boots into his pack then put his arms into the straps. The load looked tremendous, but he lifted it easily. Baltsar and the other slaves were ready, too. I went to say farewell to Reller, and then we were on our way.

Our path across the citied plateau serpentined because the bridges across the ravines had not been rebuilt since the previous summer's battles with the King-conqueror's soldiers. I thought it a tedious trek, but when we set foot on the pass through the mountains, I longed for the spongy moss of the plateaus. We scrambled over wet, crumbling rock until we reached snowline Then the biggest slaves took turns kick-stepping footholds into the snow. Each step took us higher into the treacherous mountains.

The high altitude caused my breath to become more labored while the frosty air seared my lungs. The fur under my nose and around my mouth was frosted, and I had to tuck my ears under my hood to prevent them from freezing. My legs ached from the unaccustomed strain. As a child, I had endured greater hardships, trekking constantly with my nomadic tribe. But I'd been a city dweller for a long time now and I was badly out of shape. Still, it was a matter of pride with me not to slow the merchant's caravan, so I did not complain or beg for a rest. Instead, I wondered what shape my pride would be in when I could no longer summon strength to take another step and collapsed in the snow. Once, missing a snowstep, my foot skittered along crust, nearly plunging me head over tail down a steep slope. I glimpsed the dark lines of the tableland ravines and envisioned the fall that would have taken me into one of those abysses. But Teon, stationed behind me, caught my arm and prevented my fall.

"Just a little farther, mistress, and the merchant will stop to sleep."

Sleep! I hadn't dared to think of it. I'd missed a sleep period because of the ceremony the previous night at Academe's conclave and I longed for a nap. But I knew the warnings about sleeping in the mountains' frigid zones. Death warnings! Learning that the merchant, an experienced mountaineer, planned to take his regular nap eased my mind and gave me strength to take just a few more steps . . . and then a few more.

After a while I believed the slave had a different definition for "soon" from mine. "A little farther" was all the way to the top of the pass. When Baltsar finally called a halt, I sank into the snow, but Teon would not allow me to have my longed-for rest.

"This way," he said, hoisting me by my arm. He led and half-carried me into a rock niche where another slave was fluffing old moss.

Baltsar stuck his head around the rocks. "You sleep here, Heao." He winked at me. "The moss is last year's, but it's a lot better than the snow."

I realized that this area must have been the merchant's

regular stopping place, and, frankly, I didn't care that the moss was old. I sank into it, briefly worried over knowing that the merchant was probably sleeping in the snow, but I fell asleep before the worry overwhelmed me.

After I was refreshed by the nap, the trek took on a new aspect. Or perhaps it was the frolicsome method of descending the other side of the pass that cheered me. The snow was deep and the slope broad. Instead of walking down like civilized beings, we slid on our haunches like children on a winter picnic, covering great distances in a short time. The slaves had to be wary of their huge packs and the delicate goods inside, so their rates of descent were more controlled than mine. But they made better distance with their skill and experience than I did with my enthusiasm. Baltsar, caught up by my zeal, cavorted before me, urging me to greater speeds, challenging me to catch him.

I did. In the middle of a slide I caught him when he'd stopped to move a few paces to the right, and we tumbled quite a distance before getting under control again. The slaves were already at the bottom of the snowfield when Baltsar leaped away from me, charging down the slope with a triumphant howl. I followed, racing past him with a happy scream as his momentum slowed. I reached the waiting slaves before Baltsar. Delighted with my triumph, I stepped past the slaves and leaped onto the next slope. It was steeper and my speed was greater.

"Heao, wait!" I heard Baltsar shout.

I laughed, confident that I'd beat them all down this slope. Snow sprayed away from me as I shifted and my heart pounded because the speed was so exciting and the sounds of Baltsar's frustrated shouts were unheeded, except to fuel self-admiration. The way was clear, snow spreading before me for vast distances, and the sound of my body slicing through it was mingled with my joyful squeals. I could hear Baltsar futilely trying to catch up.

Suddenly something huge tackled me from behind, upsetting my momentum and thrusting me deep into the snow. My attacker was Teon. "That's not fair," I wailed good-humoredly. The slave was not laughing. His face was pale and his lips were thin. Then Baltsar reached us, halting his descent with a metal pick driven into the snow. His hood had fallen back, exposing his ruff, which was standing on end. His eyes were wide. If Baltsar's tail were not tucked into his pants, it would have been rigid with fear.

"There is a crevasse." Teon pointed downslope, sighed, and looked at his master.

"Another moment, Heao," Baltsar said, "if Teon hadn't caught you . . ." Baltsar shuddered and bit his lip.

"I don't see anything," I said defensively. I was feeling very awkward with their fear and foolish because my behavior had been childish. I hoped the danger had not been real so that I wouldn't have to feel awkward and foolish anymore.

Infuriated by my petulant manner, Baltsar took me by the arm, restraining me beyond what was reasonable while he led me downslope. Within twenty-five steps I could see it, yawning like a gullet, frosted and hard. "Oh," I said in place of an apology and thanks. Then I turned to go back upslope, but Baltsar's hand was still on my arm and he stopped me.

"We'll traverse and meet the others." His voice was clipped. Knowing he was overcoming his fear with anger, I didn't resist when he took a rope from beneath his coat and tied one end around my waist and the other around his own, coiling the excess length in his hands. I turned away so that he could not see my face.

Above us, Teon was kick-stepping his way back up the slope where he had left his pack. His progress was slow; the slope was steep and I'd glissaded quite a long way. High on the slope, the other slaves were navigating cautiously in short, controlled runs. Because of the angle of the pass, they were soon well ahead of Baltsar and me. Silently, we followed their trail for the rest of twinight, often not seeing them. I looked back many times for Teon, but I couldn't see him, either.

We'd been in the night camp, warming ourselves for nearly a stick of time before Teon finally arrived.

"Half a stick more and I'd have come looking," Baltsar said, obviously relieved to see the slave and pack.

"I knew you would, so I hurried."

Baltsar shook his head. "Thank you, Teon, but don't take risks. My eyes can see in the dark; yours cannot. I would not have abandoned you."

"The path was well traveled; I had no difficulty. I knew you couldn't be too far ahead," Teon said reassuringly.

Baltsar nodded, then gestured toward the cooking fire, relaxing for the first time since the trip began.

As the slave turned, I said, "Teon." He stopped and looked at me. His wiry facial hair was white with frost and he breathed heavily from his exertion—extra exertion for which I was responsible. But I didn't know what to say. When my hearth dog did something clever or amusing I'd say, "Good dog," but Teon, who had a quick mind, did not quite fit the category of dog. I smiled and cocked my ears at him.

For a moment I thought he did not understand, for he smiled and said, "You're welcome," which was hardly an appropriate response for the gesture that conveyed that I acknowledged him as worthy of my complete attention, however brief. And then I realized that he was deliberately giving the gesture more meaning than I put into it, chastising me for not being appropriately grateful to him for saving my life.

"Thank you," I mumbled. It seemed a strange thing to say to a slave. Then Teon smiled, erasing my discomfort. He turned to the cooking fire.

Baltsar was chuckling.

"What's so funny?" I said.

"I often wonder who is teaching whom," he said, nodding at the slave. "If you'd been an ordinary person, you would have assumed he was too stupid to understand our nuances and you would have dismissed him. It was nearly insolent of him to force your gratitude in that fashion."

"He deserved my thanks," I said, "but I was unsure of how to express it to one of them."

"Most people don't agree with you. At best, they treat them as pets."

"And at worst?"

Baltsar's brows raised and he shrugged. "You'll see soon enough. Slaves are common in the lowlands." He looked at me. "I plan to import some to the plateau. They'll take up the labor slack the war created."

"They're strong and *you* seem to make good use of them, but who in our poor province can afford to buy them?"

"Prince Chel and the temple guardians. Soon the others will recover and I'll take goods and promises in exchange for slaves."

His plan was timely. Chel was the hardest hit by the

King-conqueror's slaughter of our people. His quarries had been idle all winter for lack of adequate labor. Chel's father, our dead king, had sent the hearty land folk to detain the invaders while using his warriors to strike at the invader's flanks. Unfortunately, his own flanks were struck by yet another battalion of invaders, and our king with his soldiers fell before the onslaught. Prince Chel, commanding the king's personal guard, defended the city by demolishing bridges so that the invaders could not enter, but the city's perimeter was wide and Prince Chel's warriors few. The invaders climbed a ravine we'd considered unclimbable, and the city fell in only a few sticks of time. Prince Chel was left with wounded warriors and a field of dead laborers.

We knew the trampled fields of mushrooms and liverworts would not yield a harvest adequate to feed ourselves and the King-conqueror's soldiers for the long winter, and we were certain we would go hungry before our conquerors did. Then, at the last possible twinight, when the winter clouds were spilling the first freezing rain, the King-conqueror and most of his soldiers withdrew from the city, leaving a small occupational force to implement his will. Prince Chel came out of hiding and was given amnesty in exchange for governing the city's survivors. The occupational force *purchased* their food and supplies through Chel, who had to browbeat many people into selling, insisting that everyone must sell a portion of their personal supplies so that no single household would suffer disproportionately. The lowland coins were little comfort. We were accustomed to a show of might—at least, that is what we used when we conquered mountain tribes. We took their tin mines, we took their copper mines, we took their quarries, and generally we took them because a warrior prince or princess fancied them. The benevolence of a ruler who *paid* for his invaders' quartering made us suspicious.

I know Chel profited from handling the transactions because he was taken to task by the temple guardians for accepting fees for performing what the guardians considered his princely duty. But giving province princes a fee for handling royal affairs was the King-conqueror's law, and the guardians' censure was quickly aborted. So Chel, at least, profited, and he would be able to buy slaves.

"Yes," I said finally. "Chel has gold and silver, and he'll need to replace the dead quarriers."

"I thought so, too," Baltsar said. "You know him, don't you?"

"Chel? Yes. We grew up together." Baltsar was studying me, and I smiled. "Would you like me to arrange an introduction?"

"Was it so obvious?"

"Not on your face," I said. "It's just that I'm familiar with both your circumstances. Chel's not one to appear in the marketplace, and even if you've made deliveries to his stronghold, I'm certain a servant accepted the fish and paid you, not my friend Chel."

Baltsar nodded. "An ordinary person would not have picked that up."

It was the second time Baltsar had said I was extraordinary, and with the repetition I was beginning to believe he did regard me as special. Deliberately, I stared and cocked my ears at him. Teon interrupted before he could respond.

"What now?" Baltsar said irritably.

Teon was startled by his master's tone. "Her feet . . . they should be checked."

"I will do it," Baltsar said. Then, gently, he said, "Get some sleep, Teon." The slave left and Baltsar moved closer to me, taking hold of my foot. "Sometimes that one is overly conscientious."

I arranged the quilt beneath me, and then Baltsar pulled off the overboot. "It seems a strange time to sleep," I said, gesturing to the slaves. They had arranged themselves around the cooking fire, their backs to their packs for protection from the night wind. All but Teon were already lying quietly.

"They'll sleep nearly the entire night," Baltsar said.

"You're joking!" I stared at the sleeping slaves, who looked peculiar because they did not curl as they slept. Then, remembering their rigid spines, I realized they couldn't curl. I wanted to ask Baltsar if they got cold sleeping in such an abnormal fashion, but he was already answering my first question.

"No, I'm quite serious. They didn't sleep during twilight when we did, but they'll make up for it now."

"Surely you don't allow such laziness."

"I admit it's inconvenient, but their health seems to

depend on having nearly eight sticks of sleep every night."
He shook his head helplessly as he unwound the bandages
on my foot. "They are strange creatures but I've learned
the hard way that some habits can't be altered. If I deny
them the long sleep, or try to convert them to one stick
during twinight and one during the night, they become
stupid and clumsy. Later, they sicken. It's not profitable
to misuse valuable possessions. They are expensive. Besides, they are practically blind at night. I could lose one
in these mountains from just one misplaced step. Their
bones are brittle."

"But then we won't reach the lowlands for several
nights."

Baltsar nodded. "And we'll have to stop again before
we cross the badlands, and again in the plains."

I wondered how sleeping slaves survived in the wilds;
their ears did not track the night sounds, and their noses
did not identify scents in the air. It was as if the front
and the back of their brains were solidly asleep, leaving
them vulnerable to their environment. "Perhaps it isn't
so strange that they sleep so long," I said. "Since they
don't have night vision, they probably retreated to their
lairs to sleep. The forced immobility may have kept them
safe from predators when they didn't need to be moving
about, looking for food."

"In the wilds, you mean?" asked Baltsar. I nodded, and
Baltsar shook his head. "It's been a long time since these
creatures were wild in the sense that you mean. Their
habits don't resemble any domestic or wild animal that
I've ever seen. Their instincts seem survival-oriented, but
they are inadequate or else not completely understood.
Even their origin is a mystery."

"I heard that the lowland temple guardians were told
in a vision from the gods that a beast of burden had been
created and set down at the edge of the Evernight Mountains."

Baltsar was startled. Then he said quietly, "Yes, of
course." He unwrapped the wool batting from my foot
and unrolled the final layer of bandages with unusual
concentration. He stopped when the bandage was half
undone. "Don't believe everything the temple guardians
tell you, Heao. Not all of them are as righteous as they
appear."

I understood his hesitation. It was not wise to speak of

the guardians in anything but a supportive tone, especially to a mere acquaintance. I wound my tail around his still hands, as if we were close friends. "Temple politics were among the first lessons Reller taught me," I said. "After spending one season in our city, you must have noticed that we of Academe walk a very fine line between truth and heresy."

Baltsar's pupils narrowed to slits and the irides glowed silver, like the fire. "Most of Academe is old and very wise. I respect their knowledge. You're so young . . . "

" . . . that you thought perhaps I needed to be warned about guardians' duplicity, the complexity of their motives, and their single-minded aspiration to power? Thank you, Baltsar. I know your warning wasn't without risk."

"You are worth the risk. You're extraordinary."

How so? I wanted to ask, but I could not. And he, with his oddly formal way of speaking combined with a refreshingly unorthodox life-style, was he not extraordinary, too? I released his hands and shook my tail playfully.

Baltsar smiled. "Do you have your master's permission?"

Embarrassed, my tail drooped, for I realized what my age of peers understood was an invitation for close play, an adult, especially a foreign one, could easily mistake for a desire to nest. I wasn't even in heat, which Baltsar surely knew, but when people were removed from the scrutiny of temple guardians, the absence of biological aids restrained few people. But I didn't have Rellar's permission. I hadn't even considered asking.

Baltsar put his hand on my shoulder "I see by your dismay that I misunderstood. Please forgive me; I'd love to play with you. But first I'll finish this."

He gave his attention to the bandages . . . but he didn't really finish. He brushed my matted fur with his own lightly oiled brush, going much higher along my legs than was necessary. Petting and tickling with a fully grown man was more strenuous than the timid stroking with the boys I knew, and it was a lot more fun. It's surprising that our squealing didn't awaken the slaves.

Chapter 3

DURING THE night, Baltsar curled into his quilt and napped. My blood was still racing from being close to him and I knew I could not sleep. I took out my marking utensils and sketched the sleeping merchant's face. By the time I'd roughed in his features, I'd looked at him often enough to know that I would remember the shape and placement of a tiny tear in his ear, the way he brushed his facial fur to disguise a livid scar, the slant of his eyes, the clean line of his mouth, and the unruly whirl of fur on his neck. Then I put away the sketch, knowing I'd enjoy finishing it another time, a time when I wanted to recall Baltsar to my mind's eye. Dutifully, I began marking the path we had followed. I knew the general shape of the entire way between the tableland city and the King-conqueror's lowland city, for a friendly warrior had described it to the best of her recollection. Now I corrected her estimate of distance for the first twinight's travel, sketched in landmarks, and estimated altitudes and degrees of the slopes. When it was finished, it would be the first accurate map of the land between our mountain province and the lowlands.

Baltsar awakened before I was half-finished. "Aren't you weary yet?" His wide-open pupils were like pendants set in the glitter of his irides.

"Not yet." I started to put aside my work, but he took it from my hands and looked at the rough map.

"Ah," he said. "This is why Rellar wanted you to come." Shaking his head, he handed it back to me. "One like this is useless in the badlands."

"Why?" I said, dismayed. I hated useless projects.

"There aren't any durable features in the badlands. The runoff from the mountains erodes the bases of even huge hills. They collapse and are washed away. There is nothing but clay as far as the eye can see, mounds and gullies of mutable clay."

"But how . . . ?"

"I have Teon sight a distant peak in the direction of our travel. Then, if we lose our way, we simply climb up until Teon sees the peak again, and we head toward it."

"Is that how the King-conqueror found our city? With slaves' eyes?"

"I'm not sure," Baltsar said, stretching and flexing his claws. "I'm not privy to the King's Council, but it was Teon's eyes that helped me follow the warriors."

"Opportunist," I said.

He shrugged. "We walked in the badlands for nearly a twinight, fording many cold streams along the way."

"I hate to get my feet wet," I said, anticipating the disagreeable task with a shake of my tail.

"No help for it." He smiled sympathetically, then went to tend the fires. The slaves didn't even stir as he put another brick of peat moss in the flames. When he came back, he took off his boots and began unwinding his foot-bindings.

There was a seasonal dryness in the night air and the vague scent of sulphur, for this wind blew from the direction of the Evernight Mountains, where volcanoes are plentiful. It would have been a pleasant night for traveling. But not everyone can travel with only the wind for a guide, as I, with my nomadic heritage, can.

"I suppose we'll have to wait for the slaves to tend their feet when they awaken." I was impatient; the night seemed so long.

"No. Their skin isn't the least bit tender. It's probably tough because they have no fur. The worst I've ever seen on a slave's feet was a few blisters. You have to use a knife to lacerate their skin."

"They really are peculiar, aren't they? I used to think they just looked strange. I mean, it's weird to see a stocky, furless, but nearly human, form. And their eyes are like plates! Some of them seem so prominent that I believe I could knock them off with a stick!"

Baltsar laughed. "You'll forget their ugliness when you become accustomed to them. I don't consider them grotesque any longer."

"Oh, really?" I chided. "They walk as if they've swallowed broom handles."

Baltsar's feet were bare, so I took his brush to smoothe the fur on his legs and feet. I went no higher than was proper for a neighborly gesture, and I did it no longer than was proper, either. When I was finished, I put away the brush and retired to my quilt.

"You know, Baltsar," I said, "it occurs to me that we might gain time if we slept twice while the slaves sleep. If we skip our twinight nap, we'll be tired enough to sleep at first nightfall. Then we could sleep again just before they awakened."

"You'd change your sleep pattern to accommodate slaves?"

I shrugged and curled beneath the quilt. "If it's profitable, why not?"

I was nearly asleep when I heard Balstar say, "Academe could give a man of normal intelligence a complex."

I didn't bother to tell him that it had nothing to do with intelligence. We were trained to seek change and not wait until it caught us unaware . . . temporal puzzlers.

Just before twinight's first glow, Baltsar and I prepared food for the still-sleeping slaves. "I always thought that if I were wealthy enough to support servants, they'd wait on me," I said as I stirred the gruel. "And surely slaves, whose very lives depend on my caprice, will feel terror in their souls when they awaken to me waiting on them. Or don't they have souls?"

"Supposedly not, but you'll have cause to wonder from time to time." Baltsar had begun to rouse the sleeping creatures by shaking them and speaking loudly. I stopped stirring the pot to regard the slaves, who responded slowly, as if in a stupor, to Baltsar's noisy efforts. Their eyelids seemed puffy and there were creases in their cheeks from lying in one position for so long.

"If you treated me that way, I'd come up with claws bared," I whispered.

"If you slept that soundly, I'd fetch a healer," Baltsar whispered back.

The slaves went away to relieve themselves, returned to eat, then picked up their packs and started downtrail. A short distance from camp, I was shocked to see several urine marks in the snow. Baltsar, walking at my side, shrugged from embarrassment. "There are a few of them who refuse to practice public decency," he said.

"Gods, aren't they housebroken?"

"Yes. They will use sand pits when they're provided."

But I wondered if creatures that would leave spoors in snow could be trusted to cover their excrement in the sand pits. I vowed never to follow a slave into a privy, and I decided that if I ever owned one of the creatures, it would be provided with a separate sanitary facility.

After several twinlights of travel, the melting snows in the mountain passes gave way to rotten rock again, and that to mud, which was eroded by fast-moving water. The streams Baltsar warned me of were wider and deeper and colder than I remembered from my childhood, but there was some compensation, for the air warmed steadily as we continued to descend. Finally, I knew the wet leather was beginning to chafe me, and, fearing I would have an ulcerated leg before long, I asked Baltsar to halt.

"Teon, you were supposed to watch her," Baltsar said sharply.

Worriedly, the slave set down his pack and kneeled at my side to pull off the boots. "You didn't limp," he whispered. "You gave no sign of distress."

"I thought it best to stop before it came to that," I said, whispering also and wondering why he was being so furtive. He nodded and sighed. The adjustments to my leg-bindings were minor at that point, but Teon still seemed anxious when they were made. When I looked at Baltsar's irritated face, I understood. Teon had failed his master. "He couldn't have known," I said. "It was a trifling irritation."

Baltsar was doubtful, or perhaps he raised his brow to warn me against interfering between him and his slave.

"Well, he couldn't," I said indignantly. I was about to suggest that he examine my leg for himself when he walked away. I looked at Teon. "Touchy, isn't he?"

27

"Often," he said, "when he is fond of the thing . . . or person."

I couldn't restrain a smile at the thought of Baltsar's being fond of me. Yet, I didn't want Teon to feel any worse than he did, so I touched his cheek with my knuckles just so he would be certain that I wasn't mocking him.

"You have soft fur," he said, "and your touch is gentle." He squeezed my hand as a friend might do, then straightened and helped me up. After he shouldered his pack, we joined Baltsar.

"This is the bad part," the merchant said. "Here we begin depending on Teon's eyes."

Teon looked around. "I'll need a hill to make a sighting."

Baltsar gave Teon leave with a nod of his head, but I grabbed the slave's wrist. "Can you still see the mountains?"

"Yes," he said without looking up.

I looked behind us, but for me the sky and the horizon were one. There were only nearby gullies to be seen. "If we walked on a right angle to the sulphur winds, we could reach the sea before very long." Turning to Baltsar, I drew out my half-completed map. "I've heard there are smooth beaches in the low areas. Wouldn't they be easier to travel on than going through these badlands?"

Baltsar considered, his ears perked with complete interest. "Yes, but we wouldn't know when to leave the sea to strike inland for the city."

"I think I can tell when to turn," Teon said. "I can see the ocean from the mountaintops behind the city; surely I can see the mountains from the ocean."

"Will you recognize the right ones?" Baltsar said. "You'll be looking all the way across the plains."

Teon nodded. "There is a prominent saddle peak, and, of course, the one that smokes . . . "

"If the gods choose to make it smoke," Baltsar said. "Ah, well, if you feel certain, Teon . . . I suppose at worst we will walk to the downcoast fishing village before we realize we've overshot our mark. Anything that will get us away from these streams is worth trying."

Teon looked back at the mountains, then peeked over my shoulder at the map. "You could add a very large mountain here," he said, pointing to a place on the map where there was nothing, "and another here, and here, and . . . "

28

"Wait!" I dug in my bodice for the stylus, then hastily began exing the places he indicated. "Where else?" I said, trying not to notice Baltsar impatiently stamping one foot and then the other. With an adequate number of landmarks, I might be able to display more than one route on a single map.

"Teon," Baltsar said warningly.

"It's my fault," I said. Hastily, I put away the map and marker. "Loan me this slave's eyes and I'll make a copy of this map for you."

"Why? I know the way."

"Not the new way," I said. "We may be blazing a shorter trail, and you'd be the only person who knew of it."

"Me and whoever owns the other copy of the map." But I knew he was intrigued, for a shorter route could be important to him when other merchants began competing.

We walked, following Teon, who often glanced in the direction of the mountains. It was time for a twinight nap, but the merchant did not call a halt. I wished I hadn't suggested the new sleep pattern until after the journey; I was tired, and, despite our change in direction, there were endless ice-cold streams to ford. My fur felt like muck beneath the bandages. As twinight waxed, the air became hot. I threw back my hood and opened my cape for ventilation, but rain started falling, so I had to cover up again. The downpour became torrential; the sound of its splashing on the muddy foothills was often accented by thunder.

"Baltsar," I said, catching up to him and tugging at his cape to get his attention.

"Are you all right?"

"Yes, just wet."

"Civilized people are in snug lairs during weather like this . . . which is probably why people believe merchants are barbaric." He put a sympathetic arm around my shoulder and squeezed me reassuringly. "Even when it's only the skybridge overhead, and not rain clouds, carrying a heavy pack is the hardest work I can think of."

"Your pack isn't heavy," I said.

"I allow myself a few luxuries. Eventually I plan to have more, many more." He squeezed me again. His arm was heavy, but it was so comforting that I did not shrug it off. "This must be hard on you, Heao."

"I'm fine," I lied.

"I wouldn't have taken you if you weren't strong . . . and young enough for me to bully into continuing even when you were tired." His eyes were twinkling in the depths of his hood.

"I haven't noticed any bullying."

"Your pride has forestalled my need to use stern methods. You won't give in as long as I keep going."

"Are you tired?"

"Yes," he said, and he stepped up the pace to prove that he had no sympathy for himself. I put my arm around his shoulder. If I was going to carry his, he was going to carry mine, and if we dropped, it would be together. I fixed my eyes on Teon's heels, flicking steadily, easily. *He* showed no signs of fatigue despite his heavy burden.

Chapter 4

BEFORE NIGHT, Teon said he could see the ocean. When we camped, Baltsar and I could hear the distant sound of waves breaking on the shore.

The slaves started a cooking fire in the lee of some rocks, but before they'd even put on the pots to boil, Baltsar and I had curled beneath our quilts and fallen asleep. We awoke two sticks later, rain-soaked and stiff. The slaves were sleeping under a rain canopy, which was nearly as inadequate a shelter as the rocks, because the wind was strong, driving the rain horizontally. The packs, however, were snug, having been given the select location at the back of the canopy, near the rocks.

"Give me your coat," Baltsar said. I did so. He stepped over the slaves to hang it with his own near the fire. He motioned for me to join him, and, standing next to the fire, he helped me fluff my wet fur. Luckily, there were dry clothes in my little pack, so I hung my traveling garments, too. Baltsar changed, also, into a homespun tunic that did not confine his tail, as his traveling clothes did. The ruff along his neck and spine curved gracefully into the swoop of his tail, a posture some people never attained for lack of a worthy ruff. His shoulders were slim, hips and thighs powerful, as those of the fisherfolk who spent their lives leaping the ledges of the wave-cut cliffs of their homes. Baltsar's tail was excellently proportioned, and the dark fur, which was frosted with gray,

31

fluffed to incredible bushiness. I decided then and there that the bust I'd begun sketching the first night of the journey would have to be expanded into a full portrait.

"It's not really cold tonight," I said when I realized Baltsar was wondering why I was staring at him.

"It's always summer in the lowlands," he said, "or, at least, nearly so. Sometimes a cold storm comes out of the mountains, but as long as the wind is from the sea, it's warm."

"And wet," I said, I sighed as I picked at furballs between my fingers. "We're born during rain, live with rain, and we die in the rain, and we'd sell our souls to be dry."

Baltsar smiled. "Slaves talk of a place where godsfire burns the land dry."

"Godsfire on land!" I said, immediately interested. "Where? Not the Evernight Mountains." Those were not well explored, nor were they completely unknown. "They aren't mistaking volcanoes for godsfire, are they?"

He looked at me, no doubt thinking my interest was strange. "The old slaves claim their ancestors wandered into the Evernight Mountains in error. They say their true home was a dry region that is somewhere beyond the Evernights." He smiled at me in a patronizing fashion, which I didn't like at all. "And, as if that story were not fantastic enough, they say that before living in the dry place, they came from the sky."

"Well, maybe they did. It corroborates the temple guardians' visions of slaves having been sent down by the gods."

He said nothing. I already knew what he thought of temple guardians' visions.

"Tell me more about this godsfire land. Do they say the godsfire burns upon the land? Have they actually seen Flametender's hearth? Or is godsfire in the sky?"

"The sky?" Baltsar thought a moment. "I don't think they say where it is—just that the land is burned dry by it. Heao, why are you so interested in slave fables?"

I hesitated. The subject was heretic, but I trusted Baltsar. "Temple guardians say godsfire lies in a hearth at the end of the skybridge that is unimaginably far upcoast. They also claim that Flametender banks the fire each night. But from my observations, airglow seems brighter at the downcoast end of the skybridge just before night . . . as if the fire had been moved during twilight."

Baltsar shook his head. "You're seeing a mirage caused

by moisture in the air combining with the night winds." He rearranged our garments, spreading the folds so they would dry quickly. Our casual clothes were not much protection from the wet wind.

"I don't think it was a mirage," I said doubtfully. I was certain that godsfire moved through the sky and that our seeing the movement was obscured by the skybridge. But I was not willing to tell Baltsar of my belief, nor to tell him that my belief had been inspired by a dream-gift of the goddess Perspicuity. "Have you ever seen spring dawnglow?"

"Yes, I've seen it twice. The edge of Flametender's fire is visible on the horizon for several sticks of time."

"The god's signal for us to begin spring planting."

"But what good is a signal that is usually unseen because of spring storms?"

"I agree, Baltsar. Why would a god waste his time? The temple has never answered that question."

"You don't think it's a signal?"

"No."

"What, then? During spring dawnglow, the skybridge is silhouetted on the horizon by godsfire. It's so impressive that even I believe a god's hand is at work. I couldn't possibly see that far without the aid of a god!"

"I don't know the answer, Baltsar, but I know it's not a signal."

"Academe isn't so smart, after all," he said.

"No, but we are willing to question our world. That way we learn."

Baltsar stared into the campfire, shaking his head. "How does even a god carry fire from one end of the world to the other in a single twinight?" He looked at me, but I didn't answer. Even the changers are not always comfortable with change—at least, not changes that confound faith. Would Baltsar continue to consider me extraordinary if I told him that on a spinning, spherical world, Flametender would not need to carry his fire from one end of the skybridge to the other? Or would Baltsar think I was insane if I said that? I decided to settle for the extraordinary rating I already enjoyed. I kept silent.

The next twinight we walked along the edge of the sea. The thunderstorm had ended, but the sea was turbulent. Still, the shallow sand dunes were a great improvement over the muddy terrain we covered the previous twinight.

33

Baltsar was in great spirits, for we were obviously making good time.

"The only problem is," Teon whispered to me when I'd dropped out of line to pick up a few pretty shells from the beach, "that I can't see the mountains."

"Huh?" I said, dropping my latest find.

"The clouds are too low. The storm must have settled into the mountains. I can't see them."

"Have you told Baltsar?" We started walking, for the merchant was on a dune top, waiting for me.

"No," Teon said. "If I tell him, he'll return to the badlands route. I believe that if we continue on this course, we'll make better time."

"But, when shall we turn?" I didn't want to return to the badlands any more than Teon did, but walking aimlessly along the coast for an undetermined length of time was not appealing, either.

"When we see the first signs of humans, a dead campfire, a lost tool, anything, we will turn. Help me look."

I stopped. "You're not going to tell Baltsar?"

"I believe the sea route is fastest. I'm doing what is best for him."

"If he knew what you were doing, he'd be furious."

"Yes, he would."

"Why did you tell me?" I said, dismayed, for I realized that I would have to expose Teon to his master, or partake in the subterfuge myself. Neither choice was pleasant.

"Your eyes may see some sign that I would overlook, or you might smell something. If you don't help me, your map will merely illustrate a route already known to many warriors and slaves. Someone else may have already drawn a map."

"Mine would be superior."

"Neater, more detailed, but the same. Help me and you'll have something unique."

The map, tucked beneath my cape, was burning my breast. Rellar had not asked a new route of me, just a good map of the one that already existed. But I knew that an alternate route, especially a more convenient and shorter route, would greatly enhance the map's value. My master was not a wealthy man. I nodded to Teon. "I just hope this beach doesn't go around a peninsula."

"If we're wrong, do not say that you conspired with me," Teon said.

"What will he do to you?"

Teon shrugged. "I don't know. I've never been wrong before."

I did more than watch for signs. I counted our footsteps to the right and left whenever the beach zigged or zagged, meticulously adding and subtracting so that I'd have an estimate of the beach's angle to the mountains. I carefully sniffed the breeze, for often I can tell what land the breeze passed over by identifying the scent it carries. That, too, helped my sense of direction, and I felt confident that we were not walking on a peninsula. Near nighttime, I found a scrap of a fishing net, but that could have been washed up by the sea. Then I saw a damaged clump of straw that someone might have cut to fuel a fire. Teon, after I'd alerted him to the find, declared it was time to turn inland. Craftily, he hedged, reminding Baltsar that his distance vision was disadvantaged by the growing darkness. I insisted that we erect a trail-marker on the beach before we left it, and Baltsar agreed.

We walked after nightfall, for the ground was nearly flat and it was not difficult for the slaves to pick their footing. But as the slaves tired, the pace slowed, and Baltsar called a halt. I hoped the dawnglow would show clear skies, or at least high clouds.

But it didn't. A new storm was on us, and now Baltsar realized that even Teon could not see through heavy fog.

"It's one thing in the mountains where we know to stay on a slope or not climb out of a canyon, but this . . ." He gestured helplessly. "Did you know that your city would have been taken a year earlier if it hadn't been for fog?"

"There is a way to continue," I said. The merchant looked at me expectantly. "We walk only within our line of sight, leap-frogging so that our path stays straight."

Baltsar lowered his head, ears back, to have a conversation with himself. I waited patiently. Finally, he looked up. "I suppose that's better than waiting indefinitely for the weather to clear, and, after all, we do know the right direction."

I had the impression that Baltsar was regretting having taken the sea route, that he would be more comfortable floundering in the badlands, which, even if confusing, were familiar to him. I just hoped that Teon's arbitrary selection of what angle on which to travel away from the sea had been a correct guess. It did nearly tally with mine, but my methods were subject to mathematical error and the caprice of the winds.

"What if we've gone wrong?" I whispered to him at the first opportunity.

Teon shook his head. "I began counting my steps just as soon as I lost sight of the mountains. Our direction should be correct. That's why I needed you to look for the place to turn away from the sea."

I was surprised. I'd believed that trick was mine, taught to me by Rellar, who used it on a much smaller scale to navigate the city. Rellar's brain could tally long lists of numbers by simply seeing them with his mind's eye. I, a less-gifted mathematician, or perhaps just never before pressed into computations without concrete aids, wasn't certain my math was correct. I had serious doubts about a slave's ability, and for a long time I walked with fear in my stomach, for the slave's computation and mine matched.

Was it fool's luck, or was Teon a gifted trailblazer? I wasn't certain. But by nightfall there were many signs of human passage. When we made camp, it was beside a well-trod path. We were confident that during the next twinight, we would arrive at the King-conqueror's city.

Chapter 5

I NEVER quite understood if the crumbling hillock at the city's edge where Baltsar took us was his own, or if it belonged to the elderly person who occupied it. The old man was a relative, or at least a friend, from Baltsar's village, for the merchant had trusted him to safeguard awnings, rain canopies, fishnets, and other valuables during his absence. Teon unearthed those from a cache while Baltsar dispatched messengers to contact customers and friends, and another to petition the King-conqueror to give me an audience. Then packs were stripped and their contents appraised, sorted, and stacked, and slaves began digging up the rest of the dirt floor to reach carefully oiled tentpoles. I was underfoot. I retrieved from my pack the pretty shells I'd found along the beach, then slipped out of the hillock to explore the city.

The twinight was dim and a heavy rain was falling. Between thunderclaps I followed the sound of temple drums to the interior of the city, leaving the hillock district behind. I weaved through throngs of people dressed in homespun and hip-high muck-boots, which I quickly realized were practical garb. The alleys were not cobbled or planked, and in one place a butcher's gutter emptied into the mud. Eventually, I climbed wall-stairs of compressed clay to reach the aerial pathways on the roofs. That way was not much better than below, for the bricks were not kiln-dried and the bearing walls were slick. There was an unrepaired hole in the tanner's roof leaking water into paddle vats filled with hides. Farther on, thick smoke seeped out of the ground and backed up into the alley. Presumably, the tanner's smoke tunnel ran beneath. Obviously, the tanner never had heard of vent stacks, nor had his neighbors complained loudly enough to make him think of them. The people who scurried past me barely wrinkled their noses and were uncurious about the stranger burying her nose in her hood. I wished for the mountains' natural updrafts, for the foul-smelling smoke followed me quite a distance, even along the roof-tops.

During the final roll of temple drums, I descended to a street lined with warehouses fashioned from clay and straw, like the summer huts shepherds use as temporary shelter. No effort had been made to replace chinks that had worked loose or to rebuild walls that were washed thin by the rain. I nearly bypassed the temple, for it was indistinguishable from the warehouses. But there were peddlers in the muddy yard, selling fetishes and talismens, and a sharp-eyed acolyte was overseeing their trade to assure the temple of its rightful profit.

I entered the temple, intending to drop a pretty shell or two on Perspicuity's altar, but she was not represented. The earthy gods, Zephyr, Raingiver, Flametender, Oceana, and Terra, were prominently displayed, and a few of the popular war gods were tucked into alcoves along a leaking gallery. The representations were artless, the walls were bleak, and the floors were of hard-packed dirt, completely unlike my city's temple, which was rich with tapestries, paintings, and mosaics from dome to catacombs. Beyond the altar room was a dream chamber, into which I peeked. It was not pretty, either.

The dreamers' nest was occupied by a tiny child who was drugged beyond caring that the nest was foul and the chamber poorly ventilated. Spiced smoke ineffectively masked the odor of urine, indicating that dream drugs had been used excessively. A guardian, whose vestments were immaculate, gingerly stepped over clots of old moss to look at the child. A peer turned a noisy shutter-wheel that caused light and dark to flash alternately in the child's eye.

"You are overlooking details," the guardian said, her voice icily grave. The drugged and entranced child stared

at the light; his rheumy eyes gave no sign that he understood the words. The guardian pinched his ear to be certain that the trance was not too deep. His ear twitched
reflexively. Satisfied, the guardian said, "Look into your
dream again, and tell me everything you see." Her ears
were flexed toward the child, but her tail drooped indifferently. Clearly, she was not where she wished to be
or doing what she wished to do, a depressing attitude
for a guardian to assume during a dream. I'm sure she
didn't realize she had an audience, or she would have
behaved differently.

"I am leading you," the child said in a low monotone.

"Indeed," said the guardian, mocking the vision with her
tone. "Where are *you* leading me?"

"I don't know," the boy said.

Impatiently, the guardian's tail flicked. "Are you in the
city? In the mountains? Look around you, child!"

Dilated eyes rolled searchingly, and the child said, "I
don't know. The light hurts my eyes."

"The light?" She shook her head. "Again he talks of
light, yet that is only a small part of my vision." Then she
looked at the guardian who turned the shutter-wheel. "If
this sand-pit sprout is destined to be my guide through the
Evernight Mountains, it's no wonder I can't find my way
home."

"Perhaps his conscious mind is still aware of the dream-
lights," the other guardian said.

"Then you have not brought me a proper dreamer."

"But he recognized you and he has brindled fur, which
you said the pathfinder of your dream possessed."

The guardian put her hand on the shutter-wheel and
halted it, muttering about dreams, and fools, and patronizing peers. Then she left the chamber. The remaining
guardian glared at the child, as if he were responsible for
his visions . . . or lack of them.

I was disgusted because the child was too young to
know if he had an inspired dream or a fanciful one, and
even if it were inspired, he was too young to understand
the consequences of casting a dream with another human
being. At least the deed had not been completed, for
neither of the guardians had drugged herself and joined
him in the nest. But I wondered about the ethics of lowland guardians . . . even more suspect than our tableland
ones.

I left the temple without putting pretty shells on any of

the altars and followed the scent of conifer oil and untanned hides to the marketplace, where Baltsar intercepted me.

"I've been looking for you, Heao," he said breathlessly.

I smiled, pleased. "I was in the temple watching a dream being cast. The attempt failed, for the dreamer could not put aside his conscious mind." Baltsar looked at me strangely, and, thinking he was interested in hearing about the aborted dream, I hurried on. "The dreamer was a child, a very small child."

"Please, Heao. I have six slaves and several friends searching for you. My messenger took your request for an audience with the king to his stronghold."

"Yes, I know. I left the camp when she did."

"But she returned with a message that you've been granted an audience—now!"

"Now?" I looked down at my muddy boots and spattered cape. "Now?"

"Hurry back to the camp to change clothes. Then go directly to the stronghold. He's not likely to notice your tardiness, for he's gathered his warriors around him for a feast."

"Feasting during twinlight?"

Baltsar shrugged. "He does not like to be alone. Hurry, Heao!"

I wasted no more time with questions—I couldn't! Baltsar waved and disappeared into the throng of hawkers and patrons. I ran back to the camp and changed my clothes. Then, so that my boots and robes would not get filthy, Teon led me around the worst of the rutted streets, which were knee-deep with mud. The slave pointed out a well-guarded doorway; then he left.

The king's stronghold was a hollowed-out hillside, quite impervious to attack, very snug, but just a bit gamey.

I stepped gingerly through the doorway only to be surprised and startled. The King-conqueror was standing before me.

"Temporary quarters, I assure you," he said when he noticed my wrinkled nose. I unwrinkled it quickly. "My war minister fears attacks from rebels and insists on quartering his best archers with me. It's crowded."

The King-conqueror was a big, middle-aged man who looked capable of dispatching several rebels with one blow from the well-worn broadsword at his side. Baltsar's comment about his not liking to be alone seemed inconsistent with the king's rugged appearance. He was not a coddled nobleman. His clothes were cut from coarse cloth, and his sleek black fur was not perfumed. His slate-gray eyes had the sage look of a much older man, but they twinkled pleasantly. Unfortunately, his tail was scraggly, but it was to the king's credit that he carried it proudly. He had greeted me in an antechamber and graciously allowed me to sit with him at the hearth. I could hear sounds of merrymaking coming from deeper chambers, and the scent of wet leather and roasting snails occasionally wafted out of the poorly drafting flue.

"What do these mean?" he said, touching the flowing sleeve of my gown, obviously fascinated by its sheerness and generous cut. "You're not a temple guardian . . . or are you?"

"They signify my membership in Academe," I said, wondering if it had been wise to wear them. My attire put his to shame.

"Ah, yes, the mountain intelligentsia. I didn't see such pretty clothes when I was in your city."

"We wear them to celebrations and formal gatherings," I said.

"I don't imagine you celebrated your conquest, did you?" He smiled, so I knew he was joking, but I thought his jest was in poor taste. I shifted uncomfortably on a moss-stuffed cushion, and he passed me one filled with crushed mint leaves, then indicated that I might curl.

I mumbled my thanks and propped myself up in a leisurely fashion. When I looked up, I caught him staring at me, his eyes searching, as if my face or my form was familiar to him. To my great discomfort, he continued to stare for several heartbeats. Then he leaned forward.

"Tell me about the bridges your folk build," he said.

"Bridges?"

"Yes, the ones that span the impossible widths of your ravines."

"We suspend them from anchors on both sides of the ravines."

"With what? Rope would rot."

"We make our rope from braided wires."

And how is the wire extruded? Isn't copper too soft? What is an alloy? How do you get your fires hot enough to make an alloy? The King-conqueror was full of questions about the tableland city's construction. And I, a cartographer, was hard-pressed to answer him in the great

41

detail that he desired. My experience with bridges was limited to crossing them, and I knew even less of making brass and bronze wire.

"Who does have the answers?" he finally said, exasperated by my vagueness and ignorance.

"Other academians—the metallurgist, the architect."

"Then they must be sent to me at once," he said.

I squirmed uncomfortably and the movement enveloped me with the scent of mint. "They can't come," I said.

His brow shot up and his tail flicked angrily. His ruff was expanding when he shouted, "My orders will be obeyed!" The sage eyes were not twinkling now.

"The war took many lives," I said, trying to remain calm. His mood had changed so suddenly that I was uncertain of how to deal with him. He looked formidable. "Academe has been reduced to twenty very old men and women, myself, and a few novices and assistants. Some, despite their age, might make the journey when the mountain passes are completely free of snow. But just now the way is too hazardous and too trying for elderly persons."

He left his cushion to pace the antechamber, very agitated. "How many did they slaughter?"

It seemed to me that if he were really concerned, he ought to have checked into the matter before he left the tablelands. But I said civilly, "Eleven academians and eighteen novices died in battle."

"I told them to preserve the valuables," he said in disgust. "Eleven, you say?"

I nodded. "We are a simple folk. It's difficult to tell a peasant from a patrician if both are carrying swords."

"Simple?" He stopped midstep and stared at me. "Your people make knives harder than granite, raise dwellings taller than two tails that do not fall during earthquakes, fashion stoneware into fantastic shapes, and you call yourselves simple?"

I hadn't attached much significance to the crudeness of his dwelling or furnishings, because he'd said the quarters were temporary. Now I wondered if he'd told me a boldfaced lie, not wanting to be judged by his surroundings. Was he ashamed of what he was? "Mountain cities were isolated from the lowlands," I said demurely, "and our environment is harsh. We did the best we could with the materials at hand."

"Quite well, I'd say." He took a goblet from a set of utensils near the fireplace and tossed it to me. "That goblet looks like silver, but it's actually fashioned from something much harder. It's from your province."

I turned the goblet over to find the crafter's mark. It was indeed fashioned in the tablelands, but it was only second quality. "It's silver-plated brass," I said, looking up at him. "The woman who made this will be delighted to know you are pleased by her work. She was wondering how she could pay taxes, since she rarely deals in coins."

The king took the goblet from my hand, filled it with nectar, and then poured more into a clay bowl. He handed me the bowl. He reclined and sipped from the goblet. "You didn't come to speak of taxes," he said. His voice was gentle again, his tail relaxed.

"But I did," I said. My reply intrigued him, for his ears perked up. I smiled over the nectar, which was delightfully smooth and enriched by tingly tasting spices. "Not the metal-crafter's taxes, of course. Academe's. We wondered if you would be willing to accept this as payment." I put down the bowl and withdrew the map from my robes and handed it to him.

As if reluctant to break the seal, the king carefully loosened it with a claw. Then he spread the doeskin map on the hearthstones, scrutinizing my work.

My breath came in short puffs. It was a new-style map of my city that I'd made with the slave's help. It was like a god's-eye view, containing detailed expanses that the human eye could not see. Would the king understand that it was a factual representation and not just a fanciful picture? Would he grasp the meaning of the legend I'd used? Could the man even read? He frowned and laid back his ears.

"It's a map . . . "

"I can see that," he said irritably. "With this I wouldn't need a guide in your city."

I smiled, greatly relieved. "My city is so small that you probably wouldn't need a guide even without the chart."

"But what is this?" he said, running his finger over the border of the map.

"Gold leaf, pounded into the skin to beautify the map."

"Gods, woman! Must I drag every word out of you? I am not an idiot. Why did you choose fireballs to decorate this map?"

"I don't know," I said, completely addled. I certainly

43

had not expected him to be displeased by the *border!* "I
suppose I believed they were attractive."

He sat back on his haunches, rubbing the back of his
neck, as if suddenly in pain. His eyes narrowed and he
gritted his teeth. "Have you ever dreamed of fire?"

I was unwilling to answer, and I did not.

He sighed and shook his head. "Your silence betrays
you."

"I meant no offense. If I do dream, then the dreams
are mine to cherish," I said carefully.

"Or fear," he said gravely.

I shook my head. "I do not fear dreams."

"I do," he said. Then he asked, "How did you come
here, Heao? How did you arrive before even my own
aide?"

"In the company of a merchant, Baltsar, who is an
exceptional mountaineer."

He nodded. "Yes, I think I saw him in the corner of
the feast room. He no doubt squeezed an invitation from
a friend. I should have known he'd be atop the profits.
Did he tell you how much he earned from feeding my
army last summer? No? No, of course not. He's close-
mouthed, that one. Well, let's join the feast."

"The map," I said. "I could make you another with a
more pleasing border."

"No," he said. "It's fine. I need reminders like that
from time to time." He rolled up the map and tucked it
into his belt.

"Reminders of what?" I said, unable to restrain the
question.

"Of what it will be like to die in fire."

I shuddered. "Your dream . . . ?"

"Perhaps," he said. "Only time will tell if my fate is
sealed. If I drown . . ." He laughed, but the laughter
was hollow. "Come, Heao."

He led me through a labyrinth of narrow corridors to
a huge underground chamber that was crowded with
ranking warriors I was unprepared for the informality
with which they greeted their king, cuffing him lightly,
sometimes with a tail caress, turning their backs on him
to help themselves to nectar and food. Prince Chel's father, our dead king, observed temple-like formalities to
the extent that, when in his presence, I used to have the
feeling a god was in the room. The King-conqueror
seemed more relaxed with his friends than he had been

with me alone, and I wished I had known how to set him at ease. But I'd used the dead king's law as my guide, choosing my words carefully, trying to maintain a respectful, even subservient, attitude. I suspected that this man did not need formalities as governing tools, for I had been intimidated when he was angry, and that was a rare experience for me.

The king sought out Baltsar, who was wearing a spiderthread tunic embroidered with gold filigree. By the king's covetous glance, I was certain Baltsar would sell all the spiderthread he had brought from my city.

"Is this an accurate representation of the tableland city?" The king handed Baltsar my map.

The merchant unrolled it ceremoniously, displaying it for his neighbors. Necks craned and eyes stared, and, over the exclamations about the heights of the buildings, the domes, and the arches, Baltsar winked at me. Then he said to the king, "Except that all the bridges displayed have not been replaced, it is accurate."

"Their skills put ours to shame," the king said. I suspected he was referring to the buildings and not to the map's precision.

"Not their battle skills," someone said and drew a sharp look from the king.

"In time there will be fine cities like this all over my empire, and they will be filled with metal goblets and fine linens. And there won't be any bloodshed while doing it," the king said.

Those who had heard, as if genuinely battle-weary, nodded and smiled. A few seemed regretful but resigned. Silently, I wished he'd made his declaration of peace a year earlier.

"I want some of you to go to the tableland city as soon as possible to learn their building techniques. I'm certain Baltsar will be returning there within a few nights and would be pleased to have you along."

"Of course," Baltsar said pleasantly.

Several warriors volunteered to go and began discussing who would accompany them. Evidently the individuals involved did not believe the king intended that they become builders. And perhaps they were correct, for the king said, "Include young crafters who are not set in their ways." He sighed. "There is a guild of young masons downcoast and tunnelers from my old village whom I would send, but by the time they reach here, they'll miss the caravan. I'd guide them myself, but I'm afraid I'll be tending border skirmishes most of the summer. I wish I had more guides."

I knew a good map would serve the King-conqueror just as well as experienced guides, and I had a good map burning against my breast. Baltsar knew I had one, for he looked at me blankly. I hesitated, then fetched it out. The King-conqueror was, after all, my liege lord. "Would this help?" I said.

He took it and studied it. "This map doesn't appear to be finished," he said critically.

"It's not, but I could deliver a finished copy before I leave the lowlands."

"With a border of mushrooms or battleaxes, anything." He smiled wanly.

"As you wish," I said, also smiling.

"Yes, that would please me." He peered over the map at me. "I find myself wondering if you're as inventive in the nest as you are with your quill."

I laid back my ears as the front of my brain began jabbering to the back of my brain. Making an obscene gesture to a randy old warrior would be as satisfying here as it would be at home, but would I have spurned my dead king in such a fashion? No way of telling. Such a question was precluded by formalities in his court. The me directly behind my eyeballs looked at the king's tail for a clue, but it was motionless. The inner me screamed in frustration. I could destroy all Rellar's good intentions with one wrong word, leave him and Academe to the King-conqueror's caprice. Perhaps he would vent his anger on the entire province! Who knew how a scorned king would react? Or I could disgrace myself, which would also muddy my robed peers . . .

"Pardon, sire," Baltsar said quietly, "but the woman is still in her minority."

The King-conqueror's eyes widened. "Do they think I'm playing children's games down here?" He slammed down the map, knocking over a bowl of nectar.

A hush fell over the room and I imagined all eyes were upon me. "If they thought you were playing games, they would have sent you a courtesan, not a map."

I felt Baltsar's hand on my shoulder, his fingers pressed in warning. When I looked up, I saw that the silence had not been for the king's outburst, but for the entrance of a temple guardian. Her eyes were on me, burning humiliating holes into my forehead for having interrupted her ceremonial entrance. I recognized her as the guardian who had been tormenting the drugged child.

"Tarana," the king said.

I hated religious pomp, I never gave it an iota more of my observance than I could possibly get by with, and I felt no differently about it in the king's chamber. But he, mighty King-conqueror who had led a horde of warriors out of a remote hamlet to spill blood over three-quarters of the known world, arose, staring at the temple guardian with a timid set to his tail. He led her to choice cushions by the hearth, warriors parting like waves breaking on a rock to clear the way.

"Plan on her, too," a warrior whispered to Baltsar. "She'll want to prepare the temple for the king's arrival."

Sullenly, Baltsar nodded. He couldn't bully a guardian into walking longer than she wished, or was he upset because her presence during the journey would prevent our playing? I smiled at him and he smiled, resignedly and irreverently.

Chapter 6

THE WAY from the king's stronghold to the camp led us through the marketplace. Baltsar, noticing my trying to catch different scent levels and seeing me crane my neck to stare at the foodstands, decided that he was hungry. He purchased morsels of steaming snails and mint-flavored sweetcakes, and he shared them with me.

"The king gave me the impression this land was deprived of luxury," I said when I'd swallowed the last velvety crumb.

"It depends on what you call luxury," Baltsar said. "The city doesn't lack for food, and there are many bawdy houses. Physical gratification is easy here."

"The king is responsible for this environment—at least, I suspect that his city reflects his predilections." Baltsar nodded to indicate that I was correct. "Yet he's obviously devoted to the guardian Tarana, and temple guardians do not ordinarily tolerate physical excesses where they have the power to prevent them. The warriors sobered and departed just as quickly as they could, so I know she does have the power. But the king didn't seem to notice, or else he didn't care."

"He noticed," Baltsar said, "but he's not an ordinary man, and Tarana cannot use ordinary means, despite her favored station in his court."

"But which is his real life-style—the casual one he

shares with his warriors, or the serious one he shares with Tarana?"

"Both," said Baltsar. "He's tolerant and intelligent. He doesn't see the ways as being opposite poles. To him they are merely a continuum—like wartime and peacetime."

We walked for a while and I tried to admire the goods in the market stalls, but I couldn't really concentrate. "I must confess that after my meeting with him, my idea of how to please him . . . of what pleases him is even less specific than before I met him. He's . . . " I nearly said "moody," but I settled for "complex."

"Is judging him part of the reason Rellar sent you to him?"

"Only as an aside," I said. "Rellar will make his own judgment in time."

"Your master sees more without vision than most people see with it."

I nodded absently. "Usually a relationship between a nobleperson and a guardian is no more than an alignment of power. Somehow the king's relation to Tarana is different."

Baltsar began guiding me away from the market, his arm around my shoulder and holding me closely so that he didn't have to speak loudly over the cacophony of hawkers. "You're right. It is different. Our king is troubled by dreams. I've heard that he cannot sleep for hearing the screams of wounded children, that he fears the gods' vengeance for all the slaughter during his reign."

"A little late for conscience, isn't it?" I said coldly, remembering the dead in the battlefields of my homeland.

Baltsar shook his head. "He was never a cruel man. His helper-in-life was the bloodthirsty one. The king's only fault was his ambition. After the queen died in the tableland battle, the dreams nearly drove him mad, for the entire responsibility of the wars was suddenly his alone. He sought help from the temple."

"And the guardians, I suppose, told him he could redeem himself by mending his warlike ways?"

"Not quite," Baltsar said. "Though they do no violence themselves, the lowland guardians are not pacifists. Tarana encouraged further conquests, until she cast her dream with his. Together they saw the gods' wrath flashing out of the sky, enveloping the king in fire as the empire fell around his feet. And Tarana saw herself condemned to wandering in the Evernight Mountains."

"Which means . . . ?"

"Their destinies are entwined. Together they seek to change the fate of their visions."

"I've always believed that destiny is predetermined. Our purpose is to implement life-styles that embrace the greater good."

Baltsar seemed surprised. "I thought you were an atheist. Your attitude toward the guardians is so practical . . . and I'm certain I saw contempt in your eyes when Tarana entered the feast room."

I put my arm around him. "I don't worship idols whose greedy fingers were fashioned by artists, though, like you, Baltsar, I fill their fingers from time to time. And I don't need temple guardians to guide my feet through life. All that I need to serve destiny was given to me before I was born." He still seemed incredulous. "Do you believe in dreams?"

Baltsar shook his head. "I don't dream."

"I do."

Airglow swelled over a vast expanse of low-lying ground cover, enveloping the King-conqueror's city and the dense camps of warriors and refugees nearby. The distant horizon was a gracilescent line dividing the grays of the sky from the grays of the land, like a vein in strata. Aloft spanned the skybridge, unshortened by truncating mountains or mist or clouds. I clearly saw its base in the downcoast direction, silhouetted, it seemed to me, by godsfire.

"Volcano reflection," Baltsar said, barely glancing at the splendid scene. He was checking the manacles of slaves he'd purchased for resale in the tablelands. A crowd of warriors, their servants, slaves, and other chosen people who were to be our traveling companions were gathering at Baltsar's camp. Departure was imminent, and Baltsar had no time for me.

I left him and went to check my pack, which contained trinkets I'd purchased during my stay in the city and cold-weather traveling clothes. The plains were warm, but I knew that when we climbed the mountains, the way would be cool again, for in the highlands it was still early spring. I wanted warm garments at hand, so I rearranged the pack.

Seeing airglow was commonplace in the lowlands, but I was surprised that no one except myself was interested in glimpsing the light of godsfire as it curled around the base of the skybridge. Then I noticed that its light had captured at least one other spectator, the temple guardian Tarana. She stared, contemplating the light cheerlessly, as if it were a flaw in the panorama. Then she shuddered, turned away, and saw me watching her.

"Look at it while you can," I said. "You'll never see airglow this brilliant in the highlands." I fastened my pack and found her beside me when I stood.

"That would be a blessing," she said slowly, "but I shall see it again." Her face was somber, her eyes weary beyond what was right for a woman still young. She stared at me. "I know you," she finally added.

"Yes, I was at the king's stronghold."

She shook her head. "No, from before."

"Perhaps at the temple," I said. "I saw you in the dream chamber with . . . a child." I was certain my distaste for that episode was reflected in my eyes, but I couldn't help it.

"I didn't notice you. Are you certain we have not met previously?"

"I've lived in the mountains all of my life." I looked at her, wondering if she were one of the missionary guardians who came to the city from time to time, even before the King-conqueror. But I didn't recognize her.

Tarana's eyes narrowed and her tail flicked menacingly. "You are the pathfinder," she said accusingly.

"I am so called," I said, feeling my ruff begin to swell despite my will to keep it smooth. Her hostility was unexpected, my response reflexive.

Tarana shuddered, as I'd seen her do when she saw the bright airglow. "So, it has already begun."

There was no purposeful movement among our traveling companions. "What has begun?" I said.

The tip of her tail shook mightily. Her claws were unsheathed and her fangs were bared. For the first time in my life, I thanked the gods that our religious community was doubly cursed if they dared to shed human blood. I think that for a single curse she would have flung herself at me and ripped out my throat with her claws. My own tail flicked, saying, *come on if you dare.*

Then she won back her composure and said, "You are in grave danger, pathfinder. I have seen your face in my dreams, bringing down the gods' wrath upon the empire." She touched the fetish of Flametender hanging at her

51

breast, worrying it nervously. "You must put yourself at the temple's disposal. Then, perhaps, we can avert the evil that will surely fall upon you otherwise." Her voice was as patronizing as her words. Her eyes were cast with the righteousness that is peculiar to practiced guardians.

"If I am in your dream, Tarana, it's destiny. But I believe you've mistaken me for someone else. You are not in my dream."

I picked up my pack, but as I turned to leave I heard her gasp, then felt her claws digging into my shoulder. "What dream?" she demanded.

Instead of her being angry, I was surprised to see that she was openly frightened. Methodically, I pried loose her claws. "My dream is personal," I said.

"Cast your dream with mine!" she said, yet she was terrified by her own order.

I shook my head and walked away. The front of my brain was communicating with the back before I'd taken three steps. Temple guardians I'd known were disciplined people, their emotions difficult to read. They wore unnatural miens that left the secular community in a continual state of bewilderment as to the true intentions of religious words and deeds. Yet Tarana's malice had been unhidden . . . for a purpose? I wondered. Was it possible that she lost control for just a moment? Guardians were, after all, merely human, and facades crack under strain. I wanted to deny to myself that I, a rural citizen of little consequence, could strain a temple guardian's composure. But the front of my mind considered the dreams—mine, hers, the king's—and I gasped. The back of my mind didn't want to believe that my bright dream, which filled me with wonder and eager anticipation, could be linked to the dark and dismal dreams Baltsar had described.

Someone touched my arm. "What happened?" Baltsar guardedly gestured at Tarana, who still glared at me. Around us I noticed several curious stares.

I continued walking, whispering to Baltsar as I made my way. "She wants me to cast my dreams with hers."

Baltsar sucked in his breath. "What did you reply?"

"I said no."

"But hers is cast with the king's. He would be indebted to you."

"I have my dream. I don't need a king's debt."

"You're a stubborn woman, Heao, and perhaps a foolish one. Refusing an honor . . ."

52

"An honor? Indeed! Baltsar, you don't know what you're talking about. They want the light of my dream to make their black ones gray. What do you suppose will happen to mine? It will become gray, too!"

Baltsar wrinkled his nose. "What does temple hocus-pocus mean to a woman of your intelligence? It's harmless."

I looked at him sadly. He wasn't a dreamer. He couldn't be expected to understand. I just shook my head.

He seemed resigned to my not taking advantage of the circumstances, for he didn't argue with me. Then he said, "It's peculiar that your refusal made her angry enough to do battle."

"She was prepared to murder me before she asked me to cast my dream with hers."

"Before?" He considered that a moment, then squeezed my arm. "Perhaps it is better that you refused. If she had your dream, she might no longer have use for you."

"Having refused, what use can I be to her?"

Baltsar smiled. "As long as you're alive, she can hope you'll change your mind."

"I thought you didn't believe in dreams . . . or even in gods. Why so much concern over the fictitious fears of a guardian?"

"*She* believes, and I think the king does, too, and that can be as dangerous as if it were real," he said seriously.

I was not overly intimidated by any temple guardians, but my master had taught me to be cautious when dealing with them. Collectively, they had more power than aristocracy, and occasionally a single guardian, allied with a single, but powerful, nobleperson, could cause havoc. Baltsar continued looking at me, his eyes filled with concern. "I'll stay away from her," I said. He nodded then, much relieved. "And now that I have your undivided attention, I'd like to ask a favor. Can you send a messenger to the king's stronghold to deliver this map?" I pulled the completed map from my bodice and handed it to him.

Baltsar sighed. "Yes." The map seemed to be weighing heavily in his hand.

"It's not sealed. Look at it."

"I'm sure it's . . . "

"Please, look at it."

Suspiciously, he unrolled the skin and regarded the map. Then his eyes glittered. "You . . . "

"Teon helped me mark the way through the badlands," I whispered.

Quaking fur rippled along Baltsar's tail as he repressed a roar of laughter. "You're bold, Heao, and I love you for it."

He turned and was quickly lost in the crowd, but I knew his heart was bursting with joy. The beach route was still secret, and, for a while, at least, he would have a time advantage over all other merchants.

Chapter 7

I HAVE never believed that dreams were put into the back of a person's mind by a capricious god and thereafter waited to spring up full-grown during a nap. That smacks of prescience, which witches and wizards claim is real, but which I never believed in myself. It was plausible that the front of the brain, fashioned by the gods during incubation, would be gifted or not to use the data stored in the back of the brain. Consciously we react to our external environment. Subconsciously, we do some environmental shaping. To that extent our destinies are predetermined, and those people who cooperate with their subconscious desires are generally happier than those who deny or wrestle with them. The problem seems to be one of communication. Desires, unrecognized by the alert self, are often known to the back of the brain, but the information is concealed from the front.

By the time we'd returned to the tablelands, neither half of my brain was concealing information about my falling in love with the merchant. What was still fuzzy to me was how to find out if he felt the same. I rejected the idea of asking him outright. I was bonded to Rellar until the next anniversary of my birth, and until then I could not make arrangements or agreements without consulting him. If I consulted him, I would expose my intentions to my master, and if Rellar didn't approve, he could put my plans aside by making plans of his own for me.

I solved the dilemma by setting out to learn Baltsar's estimation of me by indirect methods. I brought Prince Chel to Baltsar's camp. Baltsar was surprised; I'd promised to introduce him to Chel, but it was implied that I would take *him* to Chel. We greeted each other on the cliff in a dreary rain that did not dampen Baltsar's enthusiasm and, I hoped, his pleasure in seeing me so soon after the tedious journey from the lowlands.

"My prince is nearly desperate," I said when the amenities were finished. "He has more orders to fill from his quarry than his laborers can supply. Each newly arrived lowlander is determined to order more than the last."

Chel, whose hand was on the back of my neck in a friendly fashion, sent a single claw through my cape and skin, an admonition for revealing his lack of bargaining position to the merchant.

My arm encircled Chel and I buried my fingers in the deep fur of his ruff. "The merchant is my trusted friend."

"But not mine," Chel said loudly so that Baltsar would hear.

Disappointed, I removed my hand from Chel's person. He had a bellicose nature. There was more than one scar along his chest that attested to childhood fights, yet the camaraderie between us persisted. I put my hands on my hips and looked into his hostile eyes. "The merchant is also desperate," I said. "He needs new quarters, but your quarrymaster won't take his order. Labor shortage, you know."

Slightly mollified, Chel flicked his tail casually. "Why didn't you say so?"

"I would have if you'd kept your claws out of my neck!"

The word "sorry" is not in my prince's vocabulary. Instead, his tail caressed his own neck in forgiveness. This gesture is peculiar to Chel. I believe he developed it late in life as a consolation for not always battling with his transgressors . . . for it was late in life that he learned he was, in truth, slow with his claws. He developed only a small measure of restraint while his friends developed prudence or speed. Let him get a hand on his opponent

56

and there was no escape; he was monstrous, strong, and merciless.

"Prince and merchant need one another," I said. "Why waste any time?"

Baltsar looked at Chel. "She's done something to us that cannot be changed. Let's get on with our bargaining." He gestured toward his lair in the rocks. Chel nodded and led the way.

Within the lair was a carpet of kiln-dried moss, a blazing fire, and a luxurious hearth rug set with three cups and sweetmeats. Manya, no longer pregnant, crouched in the shadows, waiting to serve should her master call.

As I removed my rain cape, I saw Manya smile at me and I winked in response. When I'd seated myself between Chel and Baltsar, I said, "May I see . . . what do you call an infant slave—a whelp, a fawn?"

Baltsar shrugged. "Infant slave, I suppose." He signaled to Manya, who arose and disappeared into the depths of the cave. She returned with a bundle of swaddling and knelt beside me to display the head of the infant.

"Oh, Manya," I said, nearly gasping. It was round, wrinkled, and didn't even have the redeeming growth of head hair that the adults have. Lumps of immobile flesh, its ears, protruded from the sides of the head. Curious, I unwrapped the swaddling, and, surprisingly, the infant began to awaken. I hadn't expected that, remembering the tremendous effort Baltsar had used to rouse the sleeping adults during our journey. And I was using care, as I would with any small creature.

It mewed for a moment, sounding very much like a baby, and then it screamed! Arms like sausages flailed wildly and it kicked aimlessly, trying to touch something firm. Instinctively, I turned it over so it could crawl and feel the security of firm ground beneath it. But the tremendous torso collapsed the limbs. It lay on its nose, unable to move.

"They don't breed true, eh?" Chel said, looking from the obviously healthy mother to the spastic infant. He thought he'd just found a new bargaining position, but I noticed Manya's face, somewhere between laughter and dismay at our confusion.

I picked up the squalling infant, swaddled it again, and held it close. "It's a normal infant, isn't it?" I said, delighted with my discovery of that fact. Its helplessness appealed to me. It has a sweet milk-breath and a pleasing scent on the skin, one which was universal to babies who don't need a diaper change.

"Teofil is hungry," Manya said quietly.

Chel wasn't as startled as I had been to hear a slave speak, but he did cock an interested ear.

"If I have your permission, merchant, I'll take this noisy child to another chamber to feed her."

Baltsar nodded and I handed over the child, reluctantly. I think that, given enough time, I could have quieted her. (It was a she. The genitals were not the least bit obscured by fur!)

"The infants are uglier than the full-grown beast," Chel said disparagingly.

"I thought it was cute, in its own fashion," I said. "What would one that size cost?"

Baltsar shook his head. "I can't sell the infants until they're weaned, and even then it's not wise to separate them from the mother . . . or the father, if he's known. The adults carry on so."

Chel nodded sympathetically. "The does squeal for nights when we slaughter the fawns."

"It's not the same. Most livestock can't articulate their anguish . . . nor will they give you slovenly service in retaliation. The slaves usually mate promiscuously, but occasionally you'll notice a bond form between two or three of them. I've learned that I get better service if I don't tamper with those bonds."

"You can send me feeding and mating instructions later," Chel said impatiently. "Right now, I'm interested in their work output and in knowing the limitations of those stiff spines and peculiar hands."

"I'd rather tell you of their advantages," Baltsar said. He'd poured tea and was handing out cups of steaming brew. Mint and ginger wafted past our noses. I sipped greedily; Rellar's cuisine was rather bland.

"All right, the advantages. I'll deduce the other from what you leave out," Chel said, unimpressed.

Baltsar sighed. "The big males can carry nearly their own weight for a short distance. All of them, male or female, can carry more than you or I over great distances. Properly loaded, they're tireless for an entire twinight. Their hands are, I'm sure you noticed, very broad, and their backs are powerful. They can swing a pick or an ax

58

with a handle as thick as your wrist, turn out two or three times the stone that your peasant laborers can during a twinight. My slaves work unsupervised, but that seems to depend on training and the slave's temperament. I don't boast it as a universal quality."

"I hear they hibernate nightly," Chel said, sipping the tea.

"That's true," Baltsar said, "but their superior strength more than makes up for the lost time. There are places in the lowlands where they're used exclusively in the fields, which frees the peasants for the king's work."

Chel frowned. "The king's work," he muttered, "everything is the king's work." His ears went back as he conversed further with himself.

Baltsar raised his brow fur, but he did not comment. Everyone was muttering about the seemingly purposeless expansion of our city. Without explanation, the King-conqueror's people continued arriving, sometimes in great clusters, such as the one Baltsar guided here, and sometimes in small family groups. They brought with them the king's gold coins, so the city was prospering. But people in authority, people like Chel, felt threatened. The newcomers were less responsive to his rule since they were commanded by a higher and more remote authority. And old-timers were looking askance at Chel, who was in the peculiar and uncomfortable position of recouping his personal losses without compromising his reputation as a leader.

Finally, Chel's ears came forward and he nodded. "I want the slaves. It's the only way. How much building material do you want in exchange?"

"It occurs to me that material from the quarry is at a premium just now," Baltsar said thoughtfully, "and until you have enough slave labor to meet the demands, delivery will continue to be slow." As Chel's tail flicked argumentatively, Baltsar spoke faster. "You own a building in the city near the marketplace that is unoccupied."

Baltsar's rush didn't completely prevent the argument; choice land was as much at a premium as building materials and builders. But in the end, Chel received eighteen slaves in exchange for the city site, which connected to caverns and cliff dwellings in an adjacent ravine. At his convenience, Baltsar could build a suitable dwelling, and

59

in the meantime the cliff dwellings were more spacious and amenable than his seaside cave.

While Chel was selecting his eighteen slaves from Baltsar's compound, Baltsar pulled me aside.

"In the future, don't be so straightforward with information about me . . . or about my clients," Baltsar said. He was a bit vexed.

"The time wasted in bartering is appalling," I said, "and so unnecessary. This way you both made good bargains in half the time it would have taken had you both not understood each was a willing participant."

"You don't understand," Baltsar said. "You took all the . . . the *fun* out of it."

Fun! I couldn't account for it with previous experience. Dickering in the marketplace was tedious to me, a terribly mundane task that one performed because the people in the market were mundane. My work, contemplating the shape of the world, using mathematical hypotheses as reference framework to scale the world onto a map, puzzling out solutions to problems in which the ordinary mind cannot even define the problem—now, that was fun! I laughed aloud at myself. "It never occurred to me," I said to Baltsar. "I won't do it again."

He nodded, somewhat perplexed by my laughter, but he accepted my words as sincere ones.

"When will you move your belongings?" I said.

"Just as soon as Prince Chel is gone," he said, still regarding me suspiciously. "Why?"

"I'm eager to visit you at your new quarters."

"When you do, bring your master," he said. "Through you I have become indebted to him . . . finding the new route to the lowlands, the map you made for me, even for bringing Prince Chel to me."

Bonding laws are very precise, so technically Baltsar was correct. "I acted out of friendship," I said, "but if you insist on calling my generous acts debts, you might wait until I've reached my majority to pay them."

"That wouldn't be entirely honest, would it?"

I shrugged. "I haven't been entirely honest with my master. I omitted details of the beach route on the template map I presented to him."

Baltsar's eyes were pleased, but his tail was repelled. "How awkward," he said.

"Only if you attempt to make payment to Rellar." I

shoved my arms beneath my cape; the drizzling rain was suddenly chilling me. "Just forget about them, Baltsar. Rellar is a gentle-tempered master, but he likes to think he is in control."

"And you like to think you are in control." He was frowning and had an admonishing set to his tail, as if I were a naughty child.

Irritated, I stamped my foot. "I am irreverent and wicked, but I am also in control. Give Rellar the gift if that will ease your conscience. When you do, consider how to renew our friendship. It may not be easy!" I set my tail in a lofty and defiant shape.

"I'll take that risk," he said thoughtfully. "You can't endorse straightforwardness while practicing concealment without losing something. Usually it's pride. Friendship goes beyond pride—at least mine does."

I nearly hurled words about how his pride in being honest with Rellar was of more consequence to him than mine, and which one of us deserved his loyalty? But Baltsar's pride was justified; he was a humble man spurred by something innate in his character to do better than was expected of him. My pride was something of a vice—not in my self-respect, but in my distaste for society's arbitrary judgment.

"I'm sorry," I said finally. "I regret involving you in my relationship with Rellar. Present him with your gift and give him whatever explanation is right for you. I'll deal with the results."

I felt his hand on my shoulder and heard him whisper, "You are a loyal friend, Heao."

"Good friendships always extract a price," I said, and I wondered what the toll of this man's love might be.

Chapter 8

I LIKED Baltsar's company and believed he liked mine. I trailed him, at times, with flimsy excuses such as needing to go to the copper mines or some mountain hamlet to verify a traveler's report of a better path, or a less steep climb, or . . . well, it didn't matter. He encouraged my company wherever and whenever I wished.

We played and even became close enough to curry one another's shoulders, he being the one to keep our attentions at a formal, friendly level. On my seventeenth birth anniversary, I gently insisted on currying his back.

"No longer a child, eh?" he said, sighing, trembling as my claws pulled nonexistent snarls.

I didn't answer. His underfur was fine and well rooted, the short overcoat sleek and shiny. I loved touching him.

He turned and put his arms around me, drawing me close, running his fingers down my spine. I arched my back reflexively, pushing my pelvis closer to him. As we sank into spidersilk cushions, I coiled my tail around his forearm to encourage him. Then I felt the fluffy end of his tail tickling my ear, saying, without words, *I'll play, but I won't copulate*.

"Tonight I don't need Rellar's consent," I whispered. "This is my seventeenth birth anniversary, and I'm recognized."

"I've always recognized you," he said, tickling me.

"I mean that I need only my consent," I said, just a bit too irritably for him to tickle me out of.

"And mine."

I stopped touching him, wondering how to interpret that remark.

"You're near your heat, aren't you?" he said. His fingers were on my spine again, making me arch. "Ah, really close, aren't you?"

"It's not just the heat making me want you."

"I know. I've dined with you while you've been ripe. If you didn't have control, Rellar would not have allowed that." He buried his nose in my shoulder fur. "You are mistress of your own body."

"And free to share it," I said.

"But I'm not free to enjoy such sharing."

"What? But . . . "

"Shh! Play. Let me please you."

With my body already inflamed by my heat and my mind determined to be intimate with him, I moved with his touches until the ultimate pleasure, even though he refused like handling. Then I sat curled in his lap, trying to ignore the hard fact that the enjoyment had been all mine. I couldn't ignore it, and then I felt silly. "I'd better leave," I said.

Baltsar saw I was uncomfortable and pulled me back when I arose. "Have some tea first," he said, gently smoothing the fur on my neck.

"No, I have to go," I said. I firmly left his lap and looked around for my cape, wondering where I'd left it. His quarters were cluttered with luxurious reclining cushions, down-filled bolsters, and deep-piled rugs.

"Heao," he said, still lying by the hearth, "Why so . . . ?"

I looked at him, and, just as I suspected, he was laughing at me. I found the cape behind an overstuffed cushion, threw it at him, and then reached for something more substantial to throw. But he was quick. He sprang from the cushions and stayed my hand before I could let fly with a bowl. "It was child's play," I said indignantly. "You diddled me like an infant, you disgusting . . . " I couldn't think of a word vile enough to fit my opinion.

He nearly broke my arm wrestling the bowl from my hand, and when he had it, he threw it against the hearth, chipping the beautiful marble inlay. "It's not child's play in adult hands!" he shouted. "You came to celebrate your anniversary with me. I was honored and I gave what I could to make the occasion memorable." He straightened to full height, and his puffed fur made him seem huge. "You are a terribly rude and spoiled child to make me feel as if I'd cheated you. You've always been rude, you know!"

"Me? Rude? You called me gracious when I whispered the right words in Rellar's ear about usury charges."

"He needed accurate facts. I made them available to you, and you did your duty to your master by delivering them!"

"Ah! Then you did use me?" I put my hands on my hips and dared him to answer. My tail shook from anger.

"Children can be used without their knowledge; women cannot. So tell me, Pathfinder Heao, when you whispered to your master, did you understand your reasons for doing so? I had no hold over you, no claim on your goods or your kin. Were you a lovesick child, doing my bidding? Or were you a cunning woman, creating a debt to be collected at a future date? Like the map!"

My tail was shocked still. "Neither," I said disdainfully. "I was my master's aide. I did him and the entire city a service." That didn't quite explain the map, but I already paid for that caper.

"That's what I thought at the time, but this evening has caused me some doubt." His ruff began to soothe. "Please, stay another moment and have tea with me."

I glanced at the door and shook my head.

"Please?" He started to touch my shoulder, thought better of it, then withdrew his hand.

"What's left to be said? I made a mistake."

Baltsar shook his head and gestured toward the cushions. "I don't know what the mistake is," he said. "Usually a polite refusal is sufficient between friends. Tonight is different. I know that now. Why?"

I allowed myself to be led back to the cushions. "I'm a responsible citizen now, I . . . "

"Not that," he said, reaching for the teapot, which was resting in coals at the corner of the hearth. "I know you wanted to copulate with me to . . . symbolize your seventeenth birth anniversary. I did something similar on mine. But when I said no, why didn't you accept what I could give freely, leaving us both with pleasant memories?"

"Because I wanted to ask something more, and when

64

you refused me, I couldn't." I put down the teacup, for even the rich spices couldn't lift my spirits.

"What did you wish to ask?" He looked at me expectantly while sipping his tea.

Well, why not? The situation couldn't get any worse, and the back of my mind was sending signals that there might still be hope. It wanted information, and I couldn't get that without telling Baltsar. "I wanted your permission to court you. Tonight was the first night I was free to do that."

"Oh," he said, "oh." He studied my face, realizing I was serious. "Courting with sex usually means . . . "

" . . . a trial before becoming helpers-in-life. Yes, that's what I had in mind."

"Oh." He set down his cup and smiled. "I'm flattered, but I must refuse."

"You already did," I said, "earlier."

"But now I wish to explain."

"What is there to explain? I was a useful little girl who was clay in your hands for nearly a year. Now I'm an annoying woman."

"Don't put words in my mouth," he said sharply. "You've been a woman since we first met. And I don't waste explanations on people who annoy me."

I shrugged. "Friends forever, eh?"

"You're impossibly stubborn, Heao. Be quiet and allow me to give you, my more-than-friend, an explanation of my seemingly inexplicable behavior. I *am* flattered. I never dreamed you would consider me. But now that you have, please remember who I am, what I am."

"Merchant. A fine match for an academian."

"Not everyone would agree with you, but I do, so that's unimportant. I mean the *kind* of man I am. I'm ambitious because there are things in life that I want. Among them are all the creature comforts I can afford . . . and that includes a courtesan, who will be arriving here in my lair before twinight."

"If she's a good one . . . "

"She is."

" . . . the province will notice her. They will also wonder if you're trying to imitate the royal houses."

"I am," he said frankly. "I like what they have, and I intend to get a good deal of it for myself, including the kind of respect they enjoy. I want to be one of the most prominent citizens in the tablelands."

"I'm pleased that you can afford to do this thing, and I believe you're special enough to accomplish what you wish. But what has the courtesan to do with our courting? I admit that my prestige is just budding, but in time . . . " I could tell by the look on his face that he had not over-looked reflected esteem by an association with me.

"I've given the woman a year's guarantee with an op-tion to renew if she's still agreeable at that time."

"Surely she wouldn't hold you to such a bargain if your heart were elsewhere," I said.

"No, I suppose she wouldn't. But there's you. You have taken Academe's robes and are subject to pressures from that career. You'll have worries that won't have anything to do with me. I want . . . "

Baltsar looked at me, embarrassed. I leaned forward. The man hadn't ceased fascinating me since our first meeting. "You want," I prodded.

He shrugged helplessly. "I want a courtesan as a wife —if not this one, then one who is agreeable to being a wife."

"Wife! I could never be one of those!"

"For sure," he said rather glumly. "I wish you could be. By the gods, I'd be proud to have you as my helper if . . . "

"If," I said, waving off further declarations. I'd never be gracious under all circumstances, polite, more than civil to just anyone—not even to him—all of the time. I wouldn't be less than his helper, a true and equal partner in life. Yet I understood; some men and women had such arrangements—one protecting and providing, and the other accepting vicarious living in exchange.

Baltsar arose, picked up my cape, and slipped it over my shoulders, his hands lingering, squeezing me. "More-than-friend," he whispered, "please be a part of my life. Don't step away from me because of tonight."

"That would be childish," I said. I hugged him, en-twined my tail around him, and buried my nose in the sweet scent of his perfumed fur. We held each other long enough for me to feel the stirring in his loins again. "The only thing that hurts now is that you're saving yourself for her." I sighed, tweaked his ear, then stepped away. The worry fell away from his face when he saw that I was laughing.

"It would have been unseemly," he said. "Courtesans are so clever in nest matters that she would have known she was getting only my second-best effort. How could I explain that on her first night in my lair?"

"The quicksilver-tongued merchant would have found a way if he weren't honest and scrupulous." I smiled and left. As I hurried down the rain-shrouded street, I glanced over my shoulder to find him watching me. "More-than-friend," I said, waving.

"More-than-friend," he called.

In Rellar's dismal dwelling, I labored over a map, fussing with lumpy sepia, cursing whoever it was who left the pot open.

"You," Rellar said, "you did it this very twinight."

"No!" I said, cursing again. "It was that slave-wench of yours."

"No, it was you. She doesn't touch your things. Manya is a good slave, well trained. I'm lucky to have her." He smiled wryly.

I groaned. Manya was the gift from Baltsar, and the map I was working on was one of several still due to Rellar, the penalty imposed on me for giving Baltsar the map without Rellar's approval. He had not been angry with me. He assumed that since I knowingly broke the bonding rules, I was prepared to accept the consequences. It would take me a great deal of time to complete the quantity he assigned.

"You came home much earlier than I expected," he said.

I shrugged, pounded on the sepia to break the lumps, and spattered my gown. I cursed again.

"Did you say something?"

"Yes—damn!"

"Before that. I commented on your being home early tonight. I didn't expect you until twinight."

"Oh? Why not? I've been working on your maps every night for forty nights. Why should this night be different?"

"When a woman forces her heat with herbs just before her seventeenth anniversary, it usually means she won't be home."

I looked up from my work. He was staring at me with his nearly blind eyes. "You knew."

"My nose isn't that bad," he said. "What happened?"

I told him.

"What are you going to do?"

"Nothing."

"Fah!" Rellar said. "You're lying."

"What's to do? The woman is a courtesan."

"She's perhaps three or four years older than you, not half as bright, and if you attained part of the beauty your childhood promised, she's nothing." He blinked solemnly.

"Baltsar had his chance. He chose her."

"He chose nothing. Baltsar is young and proud, but he's not stupid. He made a bad bargain. Give him time to see his mistake."

"Rellar, I can't be what he wants—a wife."

"He's a merchant, Heao. A merchant will always take something over nothing."

"Stop distracting me, Rellar. The back of my brain is plotting, and it doesn't do as good a job while I'm talking."

"I thought so," he said. "Well, come here. I'll scratch your back for you while you converse with yourself."

I shook my head, forgetting for a moment that he couldn't see me. "I'm nearly in heat, sorry, my friend."

"I'm too old to service twice in one night," Rellar said. "So, come on . . . your neck, at least."

I looked from him to Manya, sleeping on a rug near the hearth with the infant, Teofil, and wondered how any human could copulate with one of them. Not that it was physically impossible, but they were so grotesque. They were even worse without garments, with pale skin completely exposed. And for all her indignation when I accused her of copulating with Baltsar, she seemed to accept my master quite without protest. That she was fond of him was obvious, but the entire situation was most bewildering to me. I wondered if I'd ever understand slaves.

Rellar was holding out his arms to me, and finally I accepted his invitation. The minds flow when the body feels secure.

Rellar lies! He can service twice, but he has superhuman control. He merely comforted me.

Chapter 9

MOUNTAIN FOLK had referred to the tablelands as a city, though in reality it was a group of hamlets joined to a nearly centrally located temple by footbridges over deep ravines. Prince Chel's father more or less reigned over the entire tablelands, protecting inhabitants from attacks by bandits and hostile nomads in exchange for sustenance for himself and his warriors. He also defended the temple, for which he was handsomely rewarded, and he governed secular life when it needed governing.

Lowlanders continued arriving throughout the summer. They built homes, buying facing stones and marble from Chel's quarry and building bricks from the kiln people. Our masons and architects worked alongside imported laborers, showing them how to make the sturdy bell-bottomed foundations and the tongue sliding loose in the groove which prevented collapse during frequent earth tremors. Seemingly, structures grew overnight. The King-conqueror's warriors and their entourages of merchants and crafters filled them the next. Halfway through the summer, our rural community doubled its size to become, unmistakably, a city, and the vigorous expansion continued.

Tarana sent away guardians who were familiar to us and replaced them with lowland guardians and acolytes, and she added more until the sounds of their rustling vestments filled the temple. Temple drums were heard frequently over dinning rain and rolling thunder, making announcements on behalf of the King-conqueror, as well as orthodox ones.

Directly affecting me and all academians was the unexpected arrival of bright young people who were *assigned* by King-conqueror to academians as novices. We had always selected our own protégés, usually from sturdy peasant stock. Occasionally, a mountain child was brought to us by clan wizards or witches for consideration. Having come to Academe in the latter manner, I'd secretly hoped to select a mountain child as my protégé, for I believed my nomadic childhood was responsible for my uncanny sense of direction. But I hadn't planned on selecting *any* protégé so soon after taking my robes. They were a burden to their masters, who had to clothe and feed them. Suddenly, I had a ward, whether I wanted him or not.

I had just returned from the tanner's with a bundle of doeskins when Rellar flipped a gold coin into the air. My hand shot out and I caught it. "What kind of map must I produce for this?" I said. I set down the skins by my working place to examine the coin. It was minted in the lowlands and was heavy.

"No one wants a map," Rellar said. "Tarana sent it to you, and, likewise, one to me, on behalf of her dream companion, the king."

"They aren't trying to buy my dream, are they?"

He shook his head and began pacing. "That woman is crafty," he muttered. "The coins eliminate practical arguments for sending those boys away."

The two lads were gone at the moment, sent on errands that would keep them busy most of the twinight. "Is this a tutoring fee?" The concept of mentors being paid was new, but not unappealing, to me. I was still in debt to Rellar and was completely without funds of my own.

"The messenger called them gifts, but I believe calling them fees is the kindest interpretation we can put on it. I call it bribery."

"I need the coin," I said thoughtfully. The enlarged marketplace had a multitude of new and enticing imported goods waiting to be purchased.

Rellar glared at me. "Those boys, and all the children he sent to our peers, are practically grown. Their minds are set with lowland concepts."

"They are intelligent and curious," I said truthfully. "Obviously, they were selected carefully for their roles."

"Their loyalty will always be to the King," Rellar said, "and perhaps to the temple as well. We don't know how much influence Tarana exercised in their selection." Rellar bowed his head as he paced the length of the chamber. The mat was worn from years of his measured steps taken over the same obstacle-free course. He stopped with his nose nearly against the wall. There was a polished place where his tail brushed against the stones as he turned. "We shouldn't accept the coins," he said admonishingly. "If we do, what will prevent the temple from foisting acolytes upon us?"

"You're speculating on an event that hasn't even been suggested," I said.

"Don't believe that Tarana isn't speculating as well. By now she knows that Academe often undermines the temple . . ."

". . . through no fault of our own. We apply theoretical knowledge to our mortal lives, thereby improving our standard of living. They apply hypothetical ideals to our souls, thereby increasing our prospects for heaven on earth. If they'd look closely, they'd see that our goals are the same; only the methods are different."

Rellar stopped pacing. He seemed to look over my shoulder at the new batch of skins. "I am going to return the coin and send the boy away," he said finally.

By the set of his grizzled tail, I knew arguments would be useless. "When?" I said. There might be unpleasant consequences for his action, and I was living in his shallow cave and was still closely associated with him. Then, as I tucked the coin into my belt, I knew the time he chose was not important to me so that I could avoid the consequences, but so that I would be braced to share them with him. Academe had been forthright for too many generations to begin dealing in subterfuge at the whim of a new king.

"I believe I will wait until the king comes to the tablelands. I prefer dealing with him rather than Tarana."

"He's here now." It was Chel's voice coming from the doorway. He had approached so silently that not even Rellar noticed him. I wondered how long he had been listening to us. "A runner just arrived from the pass . . . a few sticks of time and he will be here." Nervously, my

71

prince shed his cape, which was wet with sea mist and rain. He came to me and placed a coin in my hand.

It was an unusually formal gesture. "What do you want of me?"

"Knowledge of the king," he said. "I am to be his host, since I have the only appropriate dwelling."

"An honor," Rellar and I said simultaneously. Prince Chel's stronghold was not the newest structure in the tablelands, but, aside from the temple, it was the most lavish.

Chel nodded, but he was distressed. "How shall I entertain him? What will I need for his comforts? What foods does he prefer? Does he nest alone?" Distraught, Chel leaned close to me. "You are the only person I can trust who has met him face to face. How shall I behave?"

Chel was extremely anxious, for he had retained his position of authority over our community simply because the occupational force leaders had found it convenient for themselves. The king could increase Chel's authority, or completely remove it on a whim. I handed the coin back to Chel. "Spend it with the merchant, Baltsar. His acquaintance with the king goes deeper than my single, brief visit to his court."

Chel shook his head, returned the coin, and then squeezed my shoulders affectionately. "I have another coin to spend with the merchant . . . after you have told me what I'll need to know. He could tell me anything, induce me to buy his entire warehouse. Please, my friend."

I sighed. I could point to hundreds of examples of Baltsar's honesty, but the suspicion of foreigners, especially merchants, was still strong. "You'll need nothing new, Chel," I said. "Your stronghold, with its spacious chambers, central heating, thick carpeting, and fine cushions, is better than anything I saw in his court."

Chel frowned, puzzled. "What?"

"It's true. Whatever you have heard of the lowlanders' greatness, it does not refer to creature comforts. They have armies, marvelous war machines, and unmatched ferocity. They boast about how straight their arrows fly and argue over which crafter makes the best ones. They excel in wrestling and enjoy acrobatics, but they know nothing about . . . peaceful pursuits."

Chel nodded slowly, believing me reluctantly. "What of entertainment? His nesting habits?"

"There was a noticeable lack of pomp in his court. He

72

seems to like people and relates to them very casually, though the usual customs prevailed when Tarana was present. I think he's afraid of her."

"Indeed," Chel said, immediately interested. He pressed back his ears and had a brief but furiously paced conversation with himself. Then his tail twitched and his ears perked up again.

"As for nesting habits, I can only tell you that I have reason to believe he's virile. Customs regarding nest matters seem to be the same in the lowlands as here."

"Is he afraid of all guardians, or just Tarana?"

"I don't know."

Again Chel was mesmerized by his own thoughts. I was curious, but I politely refrained from inquiring why Tarana interested him. He was not aligned with her, nor any guardian.

I waited until his ears came forward, then said, "That's all I can tell you, Chel."

"If it were anyone but you, Heao, telling me that the king is a simple man, I wouldn't have believed it," Chel said.

"Simple? No, not simple—the man is very complex. His needs are . . . straightforward, practical. His fear of Tarana is part of the complexity. Don't underestimate him, Chel." I smiled, then returned the coin to him again. "And don't let my robes intimidate our friendship."

Chel pocketed the coin. "It's not your status with Academe that makes me wonder where I stand with you."

I cocked my head. "What, then?"

"I assumed that when you reached your majority, you'd come courting."

He was too serious for me to let out the laugh that welled up. I swallowed until the tickling in my throat stopped. "You never hinted . . . "

He seemed pained. "Some things are understood between old friends."

"If that's so, you could have begun courting me."

"I considered that, but I suspect . . . the merchant . . . you." He stopped, uncertain of how to link Baltsar to me. The merchant's courtesan created a flurry of excitement in the city, making Baltsar's name a household word. And she enjoyed the excitement, created more by hinting Baltsar had considered her for his wife, though formal contracts had not yet been signed. If that were true— and, personally, I suspected that it was—fidelity was implied, leaving Chel wondering how to link me to the merchant. He knew better than to suspect me of encouraging adulterous behavior.

"If you have been investigating my activities enough to know that I frequent the merchant's dwelling, your spies also should have learned that I have business with him."

"Yes," he said, nodding, "I did so learn."

I became very irritated. Chel was behaving like a jealous lover, yet we'd never shared more than friendly slaps and tickles, except for some best-forgotten exploration incidents in our youth. I set my tail in a lofty position as he continued.

"That just made your not coming to call even more confusing."

"You arrogant brat!" I said. "Must it be I who comes to you?"

Chel smiled magnanimously. "I decided, no."

My tail sagged from shock. He *was* a jealous lover. I could see it in the glare of his iron-gray eyes and the set of his pensive tail. He'd sacrificed some of his peculiar pride to propose courting with me. "Oh, Chel . . . I'm sorry, but . . . "

His tail drooped involuntarily, and his eyes became hard. "The merchant?"

Secrets are very hard for me to keep, even my own. It's my nature to be straightforward as much as is humanly possible. I'd never had a secret like this before, yet there were few friends I cherished as much as Chel. If I lied to him, denied my affection for Baltsar, yet one night *did* court the man (as was still my fondest hope), Chel would know he had been slighted. Finally, I nodded. "Yes, the merchant."

Chel turned away, suddenly deep in thought. When he faced me again, his back was straight, his ruff full, and his tail coiled around his neck. "The merchant is a superficial man, Heao. He has affectations of royalty, but none of the innate qualities. His taking a courtesan instead of a real woman makes his affectation even more base. He's not worthy of you. If you could tell me that you will forget him . . . "

I shook my head. "Let's just say that I prefer to remain alone just now."

"Our courting can be for as long as you wish." That was as close to a plea as Prince Chel could bring himself, but he quickly got hold of himself. "I won't ask you again," he said harshly.

"I believe you," I said, shaking my head again.

Silently, Chel donned his cape, and stiff fur held the hood away from his face. His parting glance was neither sad nor contemptuous, his face already composed by a sovereign smile.

I stared at the empty doorway for a long time, hoping I'd done the right thing to preserve our friendship.

"You didn't tell him about the dream," Rellar said, breaking the silence.

"My dream has nothing to do with Baltsar or Chel."

"I meant the king's dream," Rellar said, "and Tarana's."

"There's already enough speculation about the king's dream," I said. "It's wrong to interpret dreams."

"Don't you interpret yours?" asked Rellar.

"No, I don't. I simply follow it."

"Where does it lead you?"

I didn't answer, and Rellar didn't repeat his question, knowing I would again refuse to answer.

Chapter 10

DESPITE HIS host's graciousness, which I suspect was considerable, the King-conqueror all but resided at the temple. It was located near the site he had selected for his own stronghold, and he enjoyed viewing the construction progress at odd moments. Court, if I may refer to informal meetings as that, was held at equally odd moments—while he was feasting, on walks between the temple and the privy sand pits, in the rain-filled marketplace, or while he stood on the bearing walls of the partially completed stronghold. He made himself available to the people at any location and at any time, still disdaining pomp, yet thoroughly enjoying luxuries.

When Academe sought him out, he was in Perspicuity's altar room prodding the floating representation of the goddess, watching the figurine pop up from the base into the cage that prevented the lodestone base and statue from flying apart. Prince Chel, Tarana, and several of his warriors were with him. Though his eyes were still twinkling with amusement, the entrance of twenty robed academians halted his play.

One by one we crossed the chamber to put gold coins in his hand. Rellar, among the first, stayed at his side while the coins clinked and the king's eyes lost their twinkle. I hoped Perspicuity exercised some influence in her own altar room.

"They are insulting you by spurning your generosity," Tarana said, incredulous. It was apparent there was no need for Rellar to explain that we were returning his gift.

Rellar ignored the guardian and addressed the king: "Academe is a self-regulating body whose philosophy leaves power in the hands of aristocracy, where it belongs. Returning your coins is a token of our self-restraint. We ask a token of your goodwill in return."

"I don't understand," the king said. His fists were filled with coins, which he carelessly handed to his companions, dropping many. "Are you accusing me of undermining Academe? Or is this insurrection?" He was plainly annoyed.

Rellar assumed a friendly posture, his tail at ease and his ears cocked. "We are unaccustomed to being considered unique, and your interest and generosity took us by surprise. Admittedly, most of us are extremely poor and we could put your coins to good use. But our poverty is relative to the general welfare of the community. When the community prospers, we prosper, which is as it should be. Do you not see that if we are rewarded in a different fashion, we could, in time, undermine your own power?"

For a moment the King-conqueror stared at Rellar. Then he threw back his head and laughed. "Gods!" he said. "You could, indeed!"

"But they refuse payment until their projects are complete," Tarana said immediately. She stepped between Rellar and the king. "They are too poor to feed their protégés. You desperately need trained people to spread over your realm if we are to change the future."

Thoughtfully, the king shook his head. "The vision you saw in the ritual fire of academian missionaries might very well change the future," he said gravely, "and the change might be as fatal as the one we already face. Academe is my most valuable asset to realm-wide prosperity without war. They have the knowledge to improve crop yields and to build easily defended strongholds. Their existence depends on their success in their endeavors, for if they are not successful, they are not rewarded. If I subsidize them, they will not need to be right. They could take advantage of everyone, anyone they choose—including me." He'd cunningly avoided mentioning that visions seen in ritual fires were known to be nothing more than temple stratagem. Secretly, I marveled at the king, a man who

77

dismissed chicanery from the very same temple guardian with whom he shared a dream.

As Rellar nodded, a satisfied shake of his tail escaped him. The king's understanding of his own danger was an important step to his understanding of ours. "Our protégés must be selected while they are small children. We need time to nurture their natural curiosity. The ones who aspire to knowledge, we keep as novices. The ones who are emulous, we return to the community, usually with a craft or trade."

The king looked over Tarana's shoulder at Rellar. "You do not approve of the students we sent, do you?"

"Approval has nothing to do with it. They are simply too old."

"It's an excuse," Tarana said, glaring at us. "They are bargaining because they see your need for Academe as your weakness."

"Even the blind can see our value to the king," Rellar said, finally addressing the guardian. I was sure he had hoped that the king would not allow her to participate in the discussion. Now it was obvious that she had equal concern in the matter and that the king respected her interest. "Most of us are working closely with the king's chosen representatives on projects that we know are templates for similar projects elsewhere in the realm. We are willing to impart knowledge in that fashion, for that is our duty, as well as our pleasure. But if there are to be more teachers when we are dead, they must be properly trained from childhood."

"You object to older children because they will not be influenced by your heretical beliefs," Tarana accused coldly. "The *Book of Raingiver* explains precisely how the god throws water from his barrel to the earth. Yet you claim water collects on the underside of the skybridge, just as water collects on the underside of a jar's lid, to fall accidentally as rain!"

"I never said it falls accidentally," Rellar said. "It falls when the droplets are a predictable size."

Tarana stamped her foot, and many of us in the chamber jumped. "Blasphemer!" she said. "You ridicule the gods!"

Calmly, Rellar turned his back on her to face the king, who was disturbed by the altercation. "Perhaps Raingiver specifies the size droplets must be before they fall, or perhaps he walks across the skybridge to jar droplets loose

78

I do know that rain appears to fall, not to be hurled, and I realize that at first such speculations seem heretical. But in all truth, I humbly seek an alternative to the humiliating sight of a god, laboring night and twinight, as he pours water onto the earth."

The tip of Tarana's tail was shaking, and she would have spoken again, but the king silenced her with a gesture and said to Rellar, "I will arrange for a forum of academians and guardians at another time in which you can debate with impunity." Then, over the murmurs of amazed academians, he said, "Now, confine yourselves to the topic at hand. I have a decision to make, and this digression is not helping me."

Rellar nodded obediently, then cocked his head. "Without even consulting her, I know the guardian believes that the outcome of any future debates between academians and guardians will be affected by your decision regarding the children you sent to us. The ambitious ones, who might become academians, will be eager to please a powerful guardian, or perhaps yourself, sire. If you wish to be patronized by Academe, order us to keep the children and the coins. If you seek truth and honesty, allow us to select our own protégés, in our own fashion, and in our own time."

"Sire," Tarana whispered, "don't listen to this pretentious old man."

"I am not pretentious," Rellar said sharply. "I take myself and Academe very seriously, even if you do not."

Tarana straightened up. "There is still my vision to consider, and the influence its fulfillment will have on the dream."

The king looked at her, then turned so she would not see his frown. Her reminder of their shared dream was not without effect. He paced over the inlaid marble floor, seemingly engrossed by the dazzling pattern. Finally, he stopped. "Build another vision fire, Tarana, for there will not be academian missionaries selected by me or you. They may select their own."

"Thank you, sire," Rellar said, his tail dipping humbly in sincere appreciation.

"Very well," Tarana said, her breath drawing her to her full, imposing height. "If you will not heed the fire-vision, which Flametender in his mercy sent to me to

79

avert disaster in your realm, then you must give me the pathfinder's dream. The future depends on it!"

"No!" It was the king who shouted. I was too stunned to speak. Everyone stared at him. He seemed more shaken than I by Tarana's demand. "No," he said more quietly. "I will not order her to cast her dream with me."

"You must. It's the only alternative. We cannot be certain that any of our plans will be effective until we see what precipitates the disaster." She looked at me, and he followed her gaze. My fur was rising from fear.

The king's frown intensified as he began to rub the back of his neck, his ruff swelling between his fingers. His eyes, pain-filled and ashen, met mine. "I will not order you to do this thing," he said slowly.

Tarana muffled a shriek of rage. "There is no question that she is the pathfinder in my dream!"

"I know it," he said. His ears twitched, as if he did not want to listen to Tarana.

"Even if she has only a small fragment, we must see it. Order her to cast her dream with ours."

He was grimacing from pain, but he shook his head.

Tarana threw back her shoulders. "Very well. *Ask* her." She glared at me through hate-filled eyes.

For a long time the king stood with his head lowered as he rubbed his neck, then his arm, as if the pain were traveling. Finally, he looked at me again, didn't speak, but the question was in his sick eyes.

"No," I whispered.

"He is your liege lord," Tarana hissed at me. "You are torturing him."

"Stop!" the king said. "I do not want her coerced."

"But . . . "

"Go away," he said wearily. "All of you, leave. I want to be alone."

Still angry, Tarana was the first to leave the altar room, her tail trembling with rage and insult. Rellar, Prince Chel, the other academians, and the warriors, all stunned by the confrontation, followed slowly. I stayed behind, watching the king lean against the wall for support, his hand clutching the back of his neck. Excitement was still surging through my veins, as if I'd not been saved at all. It had not occurred to me that I might be ordered into the dream chamber, drugged against my will, so that they might steal my dream from me. Now,

I wondered if he would relent some pain-filled night. I desperately needed to sort out some of the man's complexities. Finally, he sensed my presence, for he looked up.

"You didn't really want to be alone, did you?" I said quickly before he could order me away.

He stared blankly for a moment, then shook his head. His eyes were filled with agony.

"Come to the hearth," I said. When he did not move, I crossed the chamber, took his hand, and led him like a small child. The fire had waned to coals, so I fetched a few bricks of peat moss while he sat on the hearth rug. The flue sucked greedily at the added fuel and flames began leaping. The king, grimacing with pain, did not notice.

I touched his shoulders; the tendons and muscles felt like iron. Tenderly, I began to massage him with my right hand, prying his fingers loose with my left. "A muscle deep in your neck has knotted," I said quietly. "If I can get hold of it, I can press it out."

Slowly, almost reluctantly, he moved his hand to reveal a patch of unhealed scabs and oozing scratches in his thick ruff. Those did not seem to bother him. The pain was coming from deep within, where his nails could not reach. Carefully sheathing my claws, I probed the flesh, trying to work my fingers around his vertebrae. I knew the probing hurt, too, but he didn't complain as I worked my way down his neck. Finally, I found the knot deep in his shoulder. "Turn your head to the right," I said. He started to obey, then winced. "Move into the pain," I said, pressing harder so the lump of muscle would not slip away. It was like a rock, yet I knew it was not a foreign growth. I stood up to put my entire weight into my hands. I felt him straining against my fingers until, finally, the muscle straightened and slithered past like a silken cord. I eased my fingers out of his flesh. "Is that better?"

For a moment he wasn't sure. Then, as he flexed his neck and arm, he smiled, amazed and relieved. "How did you do that?"

"The healer showed me how to press knots out of my master's back. Apparently, he moves differently since he lost his sight, and muscles that once functioned in tandem were being asked to move separately. They could not because the muscle sacs had grown together, and so he developed stress spasms."

"I don't believe I move differently from the way I have moved in the past," he said doubtfully.

"Your stress is from a different reason. If you must think of your dream, you should learn to do it without tensing your muscles."

"You are observant," he said, pleased and amused that I'd associated his pain with the dream after only two incidents. "Tarana says the pain is sent by the gods to goad me into altering my fate."

"Nonsense," I said indignantly. "You had a muscle spasm that any competent healer could have integrated with your body. I merely separated two muscle sacs that had grown together so that the muscles would move independently, as they were meant to do. It shouldn't happen again for a while. But when it does, call the healer. He can probe deeper."

"Is he a wizard?"

"No," I said, groaning with the comparison. "If he cannot help you, you do not have to pay him."

"He's not a wizard," the king said, grimacing, probably from remembering fees extorted by a witch or wizard for fake cures and false promises. "You and your people continually astound me. It's almost as if this place were the legendary City of Refuge." He looked around the room, his eyes lingering on the peaceful but provocative altar.

I smiled. The wonders in the City of Refuge were often referred to in the gods' books. It was a place where humans lived in harmony, where anyone could find amnesty, and it was a place of hope. But, also according to the legend, the City of Refuge had been deserted eons ago and was encased in ice. "We might be their descendants," I said, half-seriously, half-jesting. "Have you seen the paintings in the catacombs? Some of those may be representations of the City of Refuge."

He nodded. "A few are . . . disturbing to me."

"The ones showing godsfire on the horizon? Do they remind you of your dream?"

"They are not the same, but . . . close enough."

"If you walk through the catacombs in an ever-widening spiral, the paintings seem to tell a story . . . one of an exodus from a warm, lowland paradise, through the

Evernight Mountains, until, plainly, the history of the tablelands begins."

He seemed surprised. "Tarana never mentioned . . . "

"It's an Academic speculation, though, quite surprisingly, it parallels religious history in some of the pictures. Other pictures are blatantly blasphemous, such as the ones that show godsfire completely exposed."

"It is strange when you consider they were painted on temple walls," he said, musing.

"The story they tell makes sense," I said. "Come, I'll show you."

He hesitated, involuntarily touching his neck, as if he feared that seeing the pictures might trigger the pain.

"Test what I have done for you," I said, gently touching his neck. "If the pain returns, perhaps Tarana is right. The gods are punishing you."

He arose, looking at me curiously. "Do I detect irreverence?"

"Not for the gods," I said hastily. "I become annoyed when humans postulate the reality of gods interferring in our lives. That infers a great deal of importance and regard for human beings, and more for some humans than others—like yourself, or Tarana, or me."

We walked through the next chamber to a staircase chiseled through the sandstone floor, leading to the cool, dry catacombs beneath the temple, where the paintings had endured for uncounted centuries.

"We are unique, Heao, or else we would not dream." He pulled his tail close to his body, for the way was narrow.

"I know a tanner who dreamed that his hutches were filled with albino does. When he learned that the herbist had developed a strain of albino ferns, he consulted with him. Together they applied mathematical principles to the tanner's breeding stock. Last spring, the tanner had twenty albino fawns. Next year he will have eighty, and his hutches will be filled with albinos. His dream was no less unique than ours. There have always been visionaries at every level in the social order."

"The destruction of the realm is not the same as hutches filled with albinos," the king said, shaking his head.

"No, it's not. But your dream is within your capabilities, just as the tanner's dream was within his capabilities."

83

As we followed a tunnel to the deeper chambers, I noticed that the king's ears were laid back; apparently, his two minds were conversing. Finally, he said. "That is a self-fulfilling prophecy."

"Perhaps all dreams are," I said, looking at his eyes to see if he believed me. He didn't deny it, and I wondered how to prepare myself for the changes his dream predicted.

We reached the central chamber, where my favorite picture of godsfire, lying on the horizon of an incredibly bright world, was etched onto the stone wall with chisel and paint. It was probably an imaginative representation, for the shrubs dwarfed the people and the flowers in the foreground were waist-high with blossoms as big as a slave's hand. And there were shadows in open fields, presumably cast by godsfire. The sky was the unlikely hue of white.

"This is, perhaps, the City of Refuge," I said, "which you notice is not a city at all. In such a land there was no need to shelter themselves from the rain and cold, and so the people did not."

The king frowned. "This is the very picture that has similarities to my dream. It's hell, not paradise."

I looked closely at the picture, which was in some ways similar to my own dream. I couldn't help frowning. "Sire, the characters are smiling, playing."

"It is just as they do in my dream. The instant before destruction, a bolt of fire casts shadows, which are strange to see out of doors. It happened so fast that people were caught completely unaware." He shuddered. "Let's go on to the next picture."

I led him to the first curve in the spiral, and I managed to refrain from commenting that even though he'd been upset by the picture and its similarities to his dream, he was not distressed by recurring pain. Tarana had not successfully conditioned him to that response, and I was pleased to know that he was not completely in her power. Eagerly, I began to show him the world as it had been and as it still was: changing.

He listened without comment as I described Academe's interpretations of the pictures. Great rivers of ice encroached on the City of Refuge, driving inhabitants deep into the mountains, which were still warm. The oceans receded and the ice grew, until several great glacial systems covered even the mountains. Then the pictures were confined to illustrations of the tablelands, its inhabitants apparently cut off from the rest of civilization by impassable glaciers. Then the glaciers began to melt, leaving behind new lakes and valleys, and in some places fjords, which were underwater. I reminded the king, perhaps needlessly, that we were witnessing the ocean's rising water level in our time, and that we might therefore assume glaciers were continuing to melt.

He nodded. "Missionary guardians have been coming to mountain communities for several generations," he said, "but it's been only a few years since real traveling resumed. And low-lying plains are still being consumed by the ocean. The place where I was born is underwater now."

The picture tour was over and we began walking upward. "To what does Academe attribute the coming and going of glaciation?" he said.

"It depends on whether or not Flametender's fire merely provides light during twilight, or if it also is responsible for heating the world," I said carefully. "If it is merely light, then I confess, I cannot even speculate, though there are academians who do have theories. But if godsfire also provides heat, then we can assume that during glaciation, less heat was produced, causing the world to freeze. I believe the skybridge blocks the heat."

"The guardians say Flametender banked his fire during the cold times."

"*They* claim godsfire is banked every night," I said disdainfully, "but I find it difficult to believe a god would trouble himself to do that. The premise is illogical."

"It's a matter of faith," he said reprovingly.

"No, it's facts and observations. At the beginning of twilight, airglow grows from upcoast. At the end of twilight, it retreats downcoast. Godsfire moves from one end of the skybridge to the other each twilight."

"How?" His eyes were twinkling, for he believed he had outwitted me. I could not postulate a god's unwillingness to bank a fire every night as a useless gesture and then postulate his walking over the skybridge with burning coals on his shoulders without knowing that that was equally useless.

I looked around me. Though we were still in the catacombs, we were closer to the more frequently used temple chambers. I saw and heard no one. Then I whispered, "The world moves; the fire is stationary."

"The wor——?" For a moment he looked at me with incredulous eyes. Then he threw back his head and laughed. "One thing I have learned for certain, my little, young pathfinder, is that if there are two equally satisfying solutions to a problem, always select the simpler one. Flametender banks the fire."

My ears burned from his laughter. "Above everything else, I hate not being taken seriously," I said. "I am an academian and a cartographer because I have demonstrated an instinct for understanding the lay of the land, how the wind blows, and the way the earth shifts."

"I do take you seriously, Heao," he said, though he was not affected by my haughty posture, "even if only because of your dream."

Slightly mollified, I smiled. "I didn't thank you for leaving it intact."

"You needn't bother. Admittedly, I find you fair and alluring, but it may be a diabolical fascination for your dream. If I don't see it, I can continue to hope that it cancels out mine."

I understood his logic. "Nonetheless, I am grateful."

"Would you misunderstand my intent if I said I'd still like to nest with you when you are of age?"

"I am of age, and, no, I would not misunderstand. But I hasten to add that I'm completely unskilled in nest matters, and I don't think I could please or be pleased by a man of your experience."

"An unsuccessful mating would sadden me," he said, "for I like feeling bewitched by you." He smiled in a very tender fashion, and he caressed my tail with his, and for a moment I thought he would offer to teach me. But, finally, he said, "Perhaps I'll ask you in the future."

"Perhaps I'll say yes."

Chapter 11

NEAR THE temple, the King-conqueror's stronghold took shape. The structure was clean-lined and graceful. Facing stones, meticulously selected for a uniform dove-gray hue, seemed to have the texture of fog. At the earliest possible moment, the King-conqueror and part of his entourage took up residence.

Then the vernal winds ceased. The air was still. Sea mists frothed upward, finally creeping over the rim of the tablelands, engulfing the city. Torches burned from the stronghold's lofty parapets, marking its presence with a ghostly glow. Just before the winter vortexes struck, the king departed for the lowlands, abandoning us to our harsh winter.

When he returned the following year, even more lowlanders accompanied him, and the city resumed the frightful pace that was becoming associated with him. At mid-summer, I gratefully accepted a request from Baltsar to lead him and Teon to a fjord I'd once described to him. He was looking for a likely seaport near the city, hoping to pioneer a sea route from the lowlands to the tablelands. I would have led him to the Evernight Mountains if it meant some time away from the madding crowd.

The twinight was fair. Rain clouds were moving swiftly toward the sea, but that landmark was obscured by distance and high mountains. Our path had taken us through canyons and valleys that lay on irregular angles, nearly useless as directional tools. Baltsar was completely lost, as were most people when familiar landmarks were out of sight.

"Are you certain you remember the way?" Baltsar said, for he knew I'd not been to this fjord since I was a child.

"I've led you to the copper mines on unused high trails, and to the coal fields by secret routes. Have I ever became lost?" I didn't wait for him to answer. "This is the way to the fjord . . . or, perhaps, to the Evernight Mountains. I get them confused."

"Heao . . . " he said crossly, indicating that he did not wish to be teased.

"There's obsidian there," I said.

"And showers of exploding magma," he said. But later he asked, "How much obsidian?"

Teon was grinning as we both looked at Baltsar. Was that gold I saw in the merchant's eyes? Yes, the glitter was unmistakable. "Does greed overcome the fear of hot lava?"

"I wish you'd differentiate between greed and profit in your mind," he said.

I shrugged, undaunted by his unreasonable moodiness. "There's enough obsidian to make an expedition worthwhile. I will take you, if you wish." Suggesting expeditions to Baltsar was a way of gaining Teon's services for mapmaking, and the only way to get Baltsar away from his courtesan for a length of time. "Well?" I said to penetrate his consternation.

"Not this year. I have too much to do."

To cover my disappointment, I stepped up the pace. Slave and man easily matched my stride.

Soon we reached the fjord, which was not the largest I recalled from my childhood travels with the mountain tribe, but it was the most spectacular. Its walls were nearly perpendicular to the sea inlet, and they were streaked with foaming waterfalls. Below, there was a narrow strip of land, which had been much broader when my people cultivated it one summer.

Using the route I remembered from my childhood, I led Baltsar down the cliffside. Teon, burdened by his pack and his clumsy body, followed at his own pace, clinging spider-fashion to the rocks. We quickly outdistanced him.

At the bottom, Baltsar walked to the water's edge and climbed onto protruding rocks. The sea lapped gently at his feet while he looked out over the calm bay. The flat surface was rippled in places from sea life curiously poking near the surface.

Idly, I walked on, passing a waterfall where I'd played as a child. The fresh-water mist engulfed me as I impulsively detoured and climbed to a pool where I used to fill my family's water jug. I'd made the climb a hundred times before I realized my foolishness. The water from the pool was no sweeter than the water that could be collected at the base of the falls. Time, distance, my efforts —nothing had changed it. As I looked back at Baltsar, I suddenly wondered if I were still being foolish. The merchant was still only my friend. Time, distance, and my efforts had not changed that, either. Saddened, I buried my face in my hands.

I felt his hand on my shoulder. "Do you still miss your family? Where did they go?"

I looked up to see Baltsar gesture toward the empty valley, misunderstanding the cause of my sorrow. "The plague," I said stiffly.

"I shouldn't have asked you to come here," he said regretfully.

"Don't be silly," I said. "They mean nothing to me." But he meant everything! I nearly screamed with frustration. Perspicuity had shaped my mind, given me the capacity to blaze trails and draw maps and love Baltsar. Either she or I was a fool. Just then I believed it was I.

By nighttime, Teon joined us at the mouth of the bay, his hands scraped and bruised from the long climb. "Is that the only route down the wall?" he asked me, unslinging his pack.

"No, but the others are steeper."

He looked at Baltsar, shaking his head. "We'll have to fashion a better way if my people are to carry goods from here to the city. We are not *cats*."

"Not what?" I said, not understanding the word.

"It's a word from my people's language. It doesn't translate." He went to the water's edge to wash his cuts. I followed.

"Why doesn't it translate?" I said.

"Cat is a legendary creature that walks where humans cannot."

"That seems paradoxical. I'm human and I walked down the wall."

He took off his tunic and deliberately splashed water over his face and chest, then seemed refreshed for having done it. When he looked at me, he wore a sly grin. "In my language we say 'human' where you say 'slave.' "

"Indeed," I said. "And what does that make me in your language? Slave?"

He shook his head. "Parahuman to some, *cat* to others."

"Well . . . " I sputtered a moment, trying to overcome my surprise. "Your translation is irreverent and illogical. We do not enslave even the lowliest human. If you consider yourself my equal, you would also consider escape and freedom to be your moral duty. You've had ample opportunity to flee."

"If you did once roam with a mountain tribe, perhaps you remember what it is like to be hungry and hunted," the slave said seriously. "I am more disposed to suffer evil while the evil is bearable."

"Stop it, Teon," Baltsar said. "Make a fire."

With a sour expression that Baltsar could not see, Teon turned to do as he was told. Baltsar approached me, saying quietly, "Don't allow slaves to draw you into arguments. It rattles their nerves."

"I don't think Teon was arguing," I said, "and, besides, now I'm curious."

"Certain disaster," he said dryly. "Heao, curious about slaves."

"Don't you think it's peculiar that slaves didn't exist until a generation ago? Don't you wonder where they came from?"

"The Evernight Mountains."

I frowned. "And what about the story of their having come from the sky?"

"The gods work in peculiar ways."

"Poop," I said. "How can you, an atheist, possibly believe that story? Did you hear him? He claims he's a man!"

Baltsar shrugged. "I indulge him."

"I won't," I said, turning back to the fire, which Teon had blazing by then. Baltsar followed. "Teon," I said, "tell me more of your language; teach it to me, especially the words that don't translate."

The slave looked at me, startled, and Baltsar protested immediately. "Heao, that isn't wise. The temple forbids . . . "

"Will you?" I said, cutting off Baltsar and changing what might have sounded like an order to a request.

Teon looked at Baltsar. I followed his gaze. My friend's ruff stood on end, his tail twitched, and his claws were bared. I hadn't anticipated a savage challenge from Baltsar, but, since it happened, I turned to see Teon's response.

Meekly, Teon turned to the fire, whispering, "I cannot."

Baltsar's ruff smoothed. "You're terribly presumptuous," he said, frowning at me.

"If he were his own man, he would have died on the spot." I smiled. "He is a slave."

"Of course," Baltsar said. "Are you satisfied now?"

I nodded, then glanced at Teon, who destroyed my satisfaction by scowling at me.

Late that night, while Baltsar prowled the mouth of the bay looking for a suitable place for a signal fire to draw in boats from beyond the shoals, I walked along the inlet. The leathery flap of batwings and buzzings of night insects had made me restless, yet I was unwilling to keep Baltsar company. I questioned my entire attitude toward the man, my love for him. I wondered if it were futile to expect more from him than he was willing to give. He was more-than-friend, and that was a responsible and respectable relation to have. Why couldn't I just accept and enjoy that?

"Pathfinder." I was startled by Teon's low-pitched voice, heard over night sounds where his footsteps had been silent.

"I thought you were asleep," I said.

"Obviously, I am not." For a while he walked beside me, hands on his hips, head hung as if deep in thought. Then he regarded me as closely as he could in the dense darkness, his pupils gaping through the irides like inkwells. "I was not willing to risk Baltsar's anger to prove myself to you. I'd have gained nothing, except a slashed chest."

"Then you did wish to teach me your language, but

91

you were unwilling to assert your human right," I said glibly.

"I don't need your respect. I *need* his trust to live."

"You're equivocating. *I* risked Baltsar's anger. Tampering with other people's property is not a friendly thing to do."

"He's too fond of you to be more than irritated, no matter what you do. My position is more precarious. Or can't you appreciate that?"

"Yes, but you can't claim humanity with your mouth while cringing like a hearth dog."

"Oh, yes, I can. I must! For the sake of my own sanity and my continued well-being, I must. We're not so different, Pathfinder. My compromises are just more obvious than yours."

"What do you mean?"

"I'm denied privileges. You are denied knowledge, because we must compromise to survive."

"I'm free to seek whatever knowledge I choose."

"Even godsfire?"

I stopped and stared at him. "What?"

The slave hesitated, then said slowly, "When we are alone, Baltsar speaks freely to me. He had added your curiosity about spring dawnglow and airglow to knowing of your dream. Did he guess wrong?"

I didn't answer.

He smiled wryly, and I thought the inkwells splashed over the whites of his eyes. But it was only his thick lashes, fluttering as he blinked. "All right, don't speak. You are afraid to incriminate yourself, just as I would not condemn myself earlier."

"It's not that," I said. "Dreams are very personal possessions, and hearing that he knows, that *you* know . . . " It was a bit frightening.

"We will not divulge your secret dream." The wry smile became more confident. I believe my tail was stiff from fear.

"Baltsar is my more-than-friend," I said, "but you . . . "

"Trust me, as I am about to trust you." We started walking again. "If you still want to learn my language, I will teach you . . . secretly."

"And if I tell anyone, you'll divulge the essence of my dream?"

"I didn't mean for that to sound as if it were a lever." Then he laughed. "Perhaps subconsciously I did; I'm not sure. I originally wanted to demonstrate that Baltsar has given me his trust."

"Which you just betrayed by telling me he knows the essence of my dream!"

"Your own secret is safe with yourself," he said, denying my accusation. "Mostly, I hoped to please you by letting you know he thinks of you often, talks of you. I don't think it's a betrayal to help his interests, even if he doesn't yet know what his best interests are."

"Are you saying he loves me?" Was Teon having fun at my expense?

Teon nodded. "I know the man very well. Love can be the only explanation for his behavior."

"What behavior?"

"'A few things shall remain sacred.'" His grin seemed more human, his eyes less strange when amused.

Feelings I had been trying to put aside just before Teon's unexpected arrival were causing my heart to pound in a manner I'd become accustomed to while thinking hopefully about the merchant. "Your assuming Baltsar's interests without his consent is neither fair nor right." But I was pleased.

"That's probably true, Pathfinder. Yet, it's a very human weakness to do such things on behalf of someone you love. Witness Baltsar preventing you from learning my language over your own protests."

"He's worried that temple guardians would find out."

"Of course, he's afraid for you. And I'm afraid for Baltsar's well-being if . . . " Teon paused, crossing his arms over his chest, looking at me with exaggerated seriousness. "I think you have the power to destroy him. Pursuing godsfire is dangerous to yourself and perhaps to those around you. Baltsar knows that, but I don't think he can resist."

"Surely my dream has not stood between us all this time," I said, aghast.

"Not in itself," Teon said. "He is a man with . . . ambition."

I shook my head. "He must know something more about the king's dream than he told me."

"No doubt," Teon said. If Teon also knew more, he was not going to tell.

"I'm going to join Baltsar," I said, nodding toward the mouth of the bay. "But before I go, tell me some words in your language."

"I trust you will keep this secret. My master has made his position clear."

"Trust is implicit in the deed."

And so I began to learn the mysterious language of slaves, beasts from the unknown.

With the site selected for a harbor and the plans made for his first nautical venture, Baltsar was especially light-hearted on our return to the city. I was glad, because except for the moments of tenderness when he thought I was sad over losing my people, he'd been uncharacteristically grumpy during the journey.

"Let's celebrate with a special brew of nectar," he said to me as we neared his home.

I'd celebrated with him before, learned I was uncomfortable with the courtesan fawning over him, anticipating his wishes before he could even name his desires. "No," I said. "I've neglected my work for several nights."

"Please," Baltsar said. "There is something I'd like you to see. Please?"

He usually did not wheedle me, so I suspected his motive was deep. I went with him to his home.

The something to see was a lack of something . . . someone. I sensed it immediately. The courtesan was gone! The smell of her was old, faded, and there wasn't a pot of herb tea waiting by the fireplace, nor a setting for two to be increased grudgingly to three when I arrived with him. Grooming cloths and vials of oil were not warming by the fireplace bricks in anticipation of a nesting ritual.

Teon took our traveling capes and disappeared into the mudroom.

"Something's different," I said cautiously.

"Just her absence." Baltsar guided me to the fireplace with a hand on my neck. When I sat, he sat beside me. His hand slipped from my neck to my knee.

"She didn't please you," I said, trying not to sound happy.

"She pleased me very much," Baltsar said.

I clamped my tongue between my teeth, resolved to keep silent until he explained why the courtesan was gone. But my tongue was too slippery for my teeth to contain. "I thought you two were going to become husband and wife, soon."

Baltsar spoke unfeelingly. "I paid the amount due her

for another year's service in exchange for her releasing me from my promise immediately."

I couldn't help touching him, full on his back, not caring if he scolded my boldness. "Would you be receptive to my courting you?" I said. "Or is it too soon? Is there sadness? I can't detect it, but perhaps my joy is blinding me. Please, speak frankly."

"It's strange," he said, moving into my touches, "but pleasure after pain is very sweet." Then his eyes were answering mine quickly, his hands matching mine in pleasure rounds. Finally, when we were holding each other very closely, he whispered, "If you're not too tired, we could go to the temple to declare as helpers-in-life . . . forgo the courting ritual. I'm tired of making up excuses for expeditions just to get you to myself for a few nights at a time."

I laughed. "I've made more useless maps this past year." Tenderly, I raked his spine with my claws, and soon I felt his teeth in my shoulder. "We can go to the temple later," I said. "Where's your nest?"

He sniffed deeply, sighed, and said, "My timing is poor." But he helped me to my feet, anyway, then he led me to the adjacent chamber, where the scent of crushed mint and sweet moss was heavy, heralding a well-padded nest. His fingers were tickling my spine, moving steadily downward. I was certain my not being in heat wouldn't matter at all. I was right.

PART II
THE YEAR OF THE DREAMS

Chapter 12

THE DRUMMERS' lexicon was an ancient book and revered, especially in the years following the land-grabbing campaigns. Dialects and neologisms often made communication difficult, but the temple drums were understood by everyone in the realm because the lexicon was universal and static. There was, however, room for individual creativity in people's names, and temple drummers have been known to differ when translating names to drumbeats. For instance, Baltsar was The Usurer, The Fishmonger, and The Monger. Prince Chel was known as The Scorpion or The Quarry Prince, and more recently as Prince of the Lake that was a Quarry. Occasionally, there was confusion because the twinight drummer thumped out messages about The Scorpion and the night drummer might use The Quarry Prince. But my name was the same to all drummers: Pathfinder, a distinctive, syncopated roll. So there was no mistaking who the temple's wrath was directed at when the drums rolled my name for the tenth night in a row. That Rellar's drum symbol, The Blind Academian, was linked to mine was little consolation.

Baltsar's ears flicked at the sound and he scowled, even in his sleep. I reached out to touch his shoulder, as I had done countless times in our life together. We were parents to a daughter, Mussa, little more older than I was when

Baltsar and I had become helpers-in-life. The twins had come several years later, and even more recently we'd spawned another infant, not yet even weaned. The bedding rustled, his ears tracked the new sound, and then he came awake with a sigh.

"When did you come in?" he said, uncoiling and stretching. His sleek black fur had always been tipped with frost-gray, and each year the frost in his tail and muzzle had thickened, giving him a distinguished appearance that he secretly admired.

"I came in just after you retired." I snuggled against his belly as he wrapped his arms around me. His teeth gently raked the scuff of my neck, then the deep fur of my cheek. The smell of bitter-root syrup on his breath startled me, and I turned to look at him. "No wonder you didn't hear me. When did you start using dream drugs?"

"Last night."

"Did you have pleasant dreams?"

"I didn't dream at all, but I did sleep, which is something I've rarely done lately. Unlike some people I know, I don't communicate with the back of my brain very well unless I'm well rested." He gave me a friendly pinch on the thigh.

"I haven't had any difficulty sleeping," I said, settling back. "My conscience is clear."

He held me tighter, and I knew that he was worried. "You've had ten twinights to clear up the misunderstanding with the temple. The drums tell me that you have not succeeded."

"Did you really expect Tarana to listen to reason? She ordered the shunning!"

"I hoped . . ." Baltsar said, and then he fell silent.

The lair was dark and warm, and we lay quietly until the drumming stopped. Baltsar's concern was more disturbing to me than the shunning, for I was confident that Rellar and I were innocent of Tarana's charges of heresy. The circumstances were admittedly difficult because, according to temple law, she was the only person who could listen to our denials, and she'd done that with stone ears. But there were other people who could speak in our behalf. Some of them were powerful in aristocracy and temple politics. But until their words had time to take effect, Rellar and I had to be patient.

I touched Baltsar's hand and wrapped my tail around his leg, not really intending to arouse him, but doing so, anyhow. He chuckled and moved closer until his body was snug against my spine. Then we heard the door in the outer chamber slam and the clattering of boots being discarded in the mudroom as the twins entered the house. Baltsar groaned as they shouted for us. Sashiem's head appeared above the threshold of the inner lair, where we were resting. His happy little face was wet.

"Look what we caught under the footbridge," he said excitedly. He held up a squirming moss lizard.

"Bring it here," we heard Drigal cry. "I've got the knife."

Sashiem dropped back to the floor, saying, "We're going to eat it. You can have some." Then he said, "Sema's awake." We heard Sema's lusty cry.

"I think I remember saying that I loved you so much that I needed children for the overflow," Baltsar whispered.

I nodded. "You said that three times, and I agreed each time." I got to my feet, giving him a bewildered look, and he replied with a tail shake of consternation. Both of us laughed.

When we joined the twins, they were in the slaves' kitchen, in the back of the house, arguing about how to dispatch their prey. Moss lizards are as long as a man's forearm, quite a difference from the finger-sized salamanders they usually snacked on during their play. Drigal's timid knife jabs to the horny skull accomplished nothing except to make the creature squirm frantically.

"You'll damage the hide like that," I said, taking the knife from his hand. "May I have the honor this time?"

They looked at each other. The desire to do things for themselves had come to them at an earlier age than most children, and they often rejected our parenting. But they were smart, too. "If we don't ruin the hide, we can sell it to the tanner," Sashiem said. Drigal sighed and nodded.

"Watch closely so that you can do the next one yourselves." I put the knife tip through the lizard's jaw and into the brain, killing it instantly. Then I skinned it, letting the twins help so they would get the feel of how much pressure to use and to learn when to cut and when to pull. They gutted and spitted the carcass themselves, then raced to the fireplace to roast it. I dipped my hands into a bowl of scented oil, then rubbed them clean on a soft cloth that was kept hanging on an ornate brass hook. The slaves would clean the mess we'd made of their marble-slab worktable with lye and water, neither of which I could bear to touch.

Baltsar was waiting for me in the huge formal den with the children, comforting Sema with a sugar teat and restraining the boys from putting too much coal into the fireplace. He gestured for me to sit by him on a moss mat covered with a thick carpet. Since the sheared pile was wool and not easily cleaned, it was not the best place to nurse a slurpy child like Sema, but Baltsar's lack of concern was typical. It seemed that he preferred to worry about things he had no control over.

"Would you like some refreshments?" he said, turning Sema over to me.

I nodded. "And you can fetch a cloth to put under Sema."

He nodded and left. Momentarily, he returned with the cloth and with a bowl of mushrooms to nibble while we waited for the lizard to cook. The twins left their places on the hearth rug to partake of the mushrooms, eating greedily.

"Didn't you find any salamanders tonight?" Baltsar asked. The twins rarely ate with us, preferring to forage in the ravines with friends.

Sashiem and Drigal exchanged glances, then silently stuffed mushrooms into their mouths. Since Baltsar continued to wait for an answer, Sashiem finally said, "We didn't go to the ravines. We caught the lizard in the gully in back of the house."

The matter might have been dropped, but for the fact that both boys' tails were drooping. "What's wrong?" Baltsar said suspiciously. "Was it a group hunt? Should you be sharing the catch with your friends?"

"We don't have any friends," Drigal said savagely. His eyes blazed and his tail stiffened.

Sashiem was a gentler child, and his tail continued to droop. He looked at me with great, sad eyes that were beautiful, like his sire's. "They know the law doesn't include us."

I wanted to reach out to them, but Baltsar did it for me, pulling them into his lap and whispering comfort into their ears. "Heao would not bring pain to you if it were in her power to prevent it," he said. "She has a duty not to compromise her beliefs because she is an academian. Can you imagine what this city would be like if Academe did not have to be right? Why, the bridges wouldn't have to hold our weight, and careless tanners might vent their smokestacks anywhere, instead of into the ravines, where the updrafts carry away the foul smells."

They nodded in unison. "Prince Chel would still have his quarry if he'd listened to the academians when they told him he was bound to strike an aquafer," Sashiem said solemnly. He looked at me from under his sire's arm. "They weren't very loyal friends, anyhow."

"Be prepared to forgive them, Sashiem," I said. "Even the best of friends sometimes make mistakes."

"Are you going to forgive Prince Chel for canceling the expedition?" Drigal asked.

That little one knew how to hurt. "It's not canceled," I said. "It's merely delayed."

"They say it's canceled because you cannot be the pathfinder while you're being shunned."

"It's true that Chel and I planned the expedition, but you cannot very well cancel something that doesn't really exist. We lacked financing before the shunning."

"Yes, but Prince Chel began gathering his aides. He even recalled Mussa."

"Your sister agreed to rejoin her prince without pay, for a time." Baltsar's eyes closed. "Her sire is wealthy enough so that she can afford to be generous." Baltsar gave them both a hearty squeeze. "I think your lizard is about ready."

The twins went to the fireplace to retrieve the meat. I said quietly to Baltsar, "It really isn't fair."

"You could end it," he said dryly.

"No, I can't," I said. "I really can't. Admittedly, Rellar and I were caught unprepared by Tarana's opposition, but it's important for the entire community to realize that slaves are more intelligent than animals. They are a species with a history and culture of their own."

"Oh, Heao," he said disparagingly. "They make up absurd stories to impress their own children and to frighten ours. That's not history or culture."

I shook my head stubbornly. "The stories are too consistent to be completely fanciful."

"I suppose you really believe that they once lived in grand cities beneath the sea and in other implausible places and that their ancestors could fly and move mountains with their fingertips."

"Not literally," I said, moving Sema to the other breast. "But I wonder if they might be the descendants of a lost

103

race from prehistoric times. After all, we only have a scanty pictorial record of the City of Refuge in our own history, and everyone believes in that, however vaguely. If the truth were known, I doubt that it would completely verify all the legends associated with the City . . . like the one that tells of our living in absolute harmony, completely without strife or warfare, and even without disagreeing about which god to worship. Nor do I believe that nature was so bountiful that people didn't have to work in order to eat. Yet, that's what our legends say. The real truth probably lies somewhere between the fantastic and what we know might be realistic human behavior, and that's probably the way it is with slave tales, too."

Baltsar grunted. "Your peers in Academe don't seem to agree with you and Rellar. If they united with you . . . "

That state of affairs simultaneously saddened and angered me. "They're being cautious. They have their own favorite projects that could be put in jeopardy by siding with Rellar and me. The king won't return for many months, and that leaves Tarana in command, you know. Our policy has been to lie low while he's absent."

"Why didn't you lie low?" Baltsar said irritably. "Why now?"

"I didn't pick the time," I said, equally irritated, "and you know it. Tarana found out and confronted us. Did you expect us to lie about our findings?"

"She's always snooping around anything that concerns you. You should have expected it and have been prepared."

"It seemed as if her entire attention was on the expedition. We thought she was going to oppose it on religious grounds, and for that we had made preparations. Rellar, Chel, and I worked out a comprehensive rebuttal for every religious objection to exploring beyond the Evernight Mountains that we could think of." I squirmed uneasily on the mat. "I was to have presented our case to a joint session of academians and guardians tonight."

"And now you cannot speak," Baltsar said. He raised his brows in a sarcastic fashion. "I'd say she put a stop to your expedition and to your radical ideas about slaves in one stroke."

I snarled, as much under my breath as I could. Baltsar was absolutely correct in his evaluation of the situation, yet I was not without hope or plans. I just needed time, but I didn't like his doubting me.

"The community has always grumbled about social change," I said, "but Academe used to be able to make people see reason. Why, you're a prime example! You were accused of usury until Rellar intervened. By the time the rest of the merchants came to the tablelands, the community realized that our agriculture and commerce needed to be directed toward an accumulation of gold. Academe parented a host of entrepreneurs who accelerated mercantilism, and people grumbled about that at first, too. We expect some balking until our ideas are proven.

"When I was a child, people prodded Academe for innovations to make their lives easier. They laughed when the first windmill failed, but it was a gentle laugh. When we finally succeeded in making a paddlewheel to grind conifer seeds, they shared our triumph," I said, shaking my head sadly. "Now we can give them neither inventions nor social change without being suspect. Have the people become so soft and spoiled that they resist change? Or has Academe outlived its usefulness?"

"Neither," Baltsar said seriously. "It's Tarana. A guardian has never had a stranglehold on a ruler before."

"The dreams," I said bitterly. "If they really want to transform their dreams into something less tragic, they should encourage change within the community."

Baltsar grinned slyly. "How do you know the dreams don't parallel the changes, that the changes are not what precipitates the tragedies?"

"Because they've suppressed so many changes, and stagnation hasn't changed their dreams! Academe used to operate for the benefit of the community, but the community no longer has the privilege of deciding what is a benefit and what is not. The guardian decides!"

"Except when the king is in residence," Baltsar reminded me. "I find that most of his decisions on disputes between Academe and the temple are very thoughtful."

I nodded. "But he's present only a few months each summer." I looked at Baltsar. "There's talk of Academe following him to the lowlands each year so that we can have the benefit of his consideration."

"We'd be separated most of the year," Baltsar said, dismayed.

"It's far from settled," I said hastily. "Tarana might

105

follow us, and then we'd gain little, except, perhaps, even closer scrutiny. Do you think she'd follow us?'

"I don't know. The tableland temple is still the finest in the realm, and apparently the oldest. Being the highest-ranking guardian here means considerable prestige for her. And many people believe the temple holds ancient secrets that the guardians have access to, though I'm not sure she needs that undercurrent of mysticism in addition to her influence on the king. Still, her only purpose in life seems to be in trying to shape the dreams, and she seems to feel that can be done only be keeping Academe under her control."

"That was never meant to be. Academe has a history of freedom."

"It could be worse, Heao. You could have a king who was stupid, or even more terrorized by fate than ours is. I don't think his position is an easy one, having to decide between the good of the realm and the damnation of his own soul. I don't envy him."

"I suppose not, but I can't help thinking of what life would be like if it weren't for Tarana. You'd be hauling goods up the side of the fjord with the aid of a fire engine instead of having to use slaves."

Baltsar shook his head. "Neering's crazy invention would take too much coal, even if the temple hadn't forbidden its use."

"You've been influenced by her lies, too! Baltsar, it takes time and experimentation to perfect new equipment. These thoughtless bans are completely unfair."

Baltsar seemed uncomfortable. "There are still many avenues of experimentation open to Academe. Merchants and fishers have begged for better boats. Reed vessels are ephemeral and they swamp during storms. Why can't you come up with a better design?"

"The problem seems to be in construction materials," I said, then stopped because he was trying to appease me and to change the subject. I shook my tail to let him know the ploy wouldn't work. "We were permitted to study the nutritional requirements of slaves and to sell the reports to interested citizens. We've been encouraged to study their sleeping habits, their vision limitations, and even their breeding capabilities. Why not their emotional and intellectual capacities, too?"

Baltsar was silent for a while because he knew there

was no reasonable answer to my question. "Well," he said, giving my ruff a friendly rub, "I need to go to the shops. The slaves will be awakening soon, and there is much to be done before tonight."

"I nodded absently. Each Decitwinight, Baltsar and other merchants and the owners of some of the city's more elite emporiums gathered to plan their caravans to the lowlands or to other mountain cities where they traded tableland products. Baltsar's exports and imports were based on sound judgment of supply and demand, and a fair amount of uncanny intuition was involved in decisions on items for which there were no precedences. He had prospered over the years, which was nice for me and for our children. Since causeways replaced the rugged trails through the hinterlands, few people needed to purchase my maps. Sometimes I worked for an academian peer, an architect who designed the causeways, but more often than not I worked outside of my ordinary talents, making a few coins on this scheme or that. That is, I did so until Chel began talking seriously about the expedition. I wasn't about to be thwarted. Not only would the services of a good cartographer and pathfinder be needed for the first time in years, but godsfire might lie beyond the Evernights, and if it did, I intended to see it.

"What are you going to do, Heao?" Baltsar said when he returned from the mudroom, his rain cape in hand.

"I'll stay with the children for a while; then I'll go into the city. We need salt, and I want to talk to Rellar about the conclave tonight."

He nodded, satisfied that I would not spend the twinight moping around the house; I hadn't in ten nights. Yet, each night since the shunning began, he'd been very solicitous, inquiring about how my time was spent and wondering if I needed anything. He smiled his farewell, then departed. I turned back to Sashiem and Drigal, who were beginning to argue over the lizard's heart.

"Fetch a knife to divide it," I said, then listened to why each believed the heart should not be shared. Even if they didn't think they still needed parenting, I knew better. It felt good to be needed, and it was easy to forget everything else while I was with the children.

Chapter 13

WE USED to make our salt by evaporating brine in flat pans over our hearth fires. In recent times, salt was imported in chunks from an inland village where tunnelers mined it from far below the surface. The cost of imported salt was about the same as the cost of fire fuel used to produce our own at home, but it was more convenient and more healthful to use. Many of us pump dry cave air through shafts into our homes, where we try to keep evaporative moisture to a minimum so as not to overturn the healthful effects of dry air. Homes without the benefit of cave air smell of mildew and mold, and their occupants sneeze and cough, and eventually their lungs rot.

But it was impossible to purchase salt, or any goods, while being shunned. When I approached the market stall, the salt hawker mysteriously looked through me to serve the customer just approaching. Then he looked past my left ear at another customer. When there was no one left nearby except me, he looked at the mud beneath our feet as he turned away. I could see the back of his head and his generous behind as he busied himself at the back of his stall, deaf to my voice alone. I suppose it was to my credit that he trusted me enough to turn his back, but it was annoying to realize that someone would have to be sent from the household to buy salt, retracing my footsteps. Ridiculous!

Empty-handed, I left the marketplace's thatch-and-canvas canopy, instinctively pulling up my hood against the rain as I entered the old section of the city. Stick and clay buildings with moss-thatched roofs were crowded with the simplest folk of the tableland city. Despite their comparative poverty, they were comfortable and satisfied. The old ones remembered twinights of starvation, plague, and pestilence, and even raids by savage mountain tribes. Now, a generation after the land-grabbing campaigns of the King-conqueror, the city was at peace and food was plentiful. Best of all, there was a wide variety of employment for the simple folks' strong sons and daughters in the military princes' and princesses' border guards, or as laborers for the wealthy merchants, farmers, and noblepeople. The poorer people in the city were content, and they even had pennies to leave at the temple altars. The merchants were content because business was lively. The farmers were content because even armies for defense consumed great quantities of food, which the land willingly produced. The King-conqueror imposed great taxes, and we all smiled while we paid them because there were goods and gold enough to keep us comfortable for a very long time, even after taxes. Only the slaves didn't smile very much, poor things, because it was upon their backs and with their lives that we enjoyed our comfortable standard of living.

My path took me across a roof that was reinforced with conifer branches and driftwood, then through a deserted courtyard that was really the top of a rocky hill. Below the hill was one of the many ravines that bisected the tableland city, and below the overhanging cliff was a cavern where Rellar lived. I climbed down chiseled steps and walked along a ledge until I reached the doeskin windbreaker across his door. I pushed it aside and went in.

Rellar sat before his hearth, cross-legged, naked, more frail in the nude than on the now rare occasions when he donned his robes to join Academe's conclaves.

"Heao," he said before I'd taken three steps into the huge chamber. Rellar's ears are more keen than most, more discriminating, too; Manya and Teofil are about my weight, and he keeps them shod and clothed even in summer. Though Rellar is blind, he's never mistaken my footsteps for theirs. He turned, his gleaming eyes fixed on me as I came to him, a comforting trick he's mastered: no drooping eyelids or blank stare, and no sagging chin. He often fools strangers. "Dry your cape, woman," he said. "Air out your body."

"I will," I said gratefully, for I was soaked, "but I'll need a bigger fire. May I?"

Rellar gestured to the peat bricks at his left. "You wouldn't need more heat if you would leave your clothes in the closet and discipline your body."

"I'm in enough trouble already without scandalizing the city by going nude," I said. I unhooked the laces and spread my cape over a tattered cushion near the fireplace and then stepped over to the stack of peat moss and selected two bricks. The tiny fire that Rellar nursed smoldered under the bricks, and the moss caught on, burning slowly and warmly. I stood to take advantage of the fire's full heat, holding the folds of my tunic away from my body with my tail so that everything would dry quickly.

Rellar moved back from the blaze. "Fur is enough to keep anyone warm," he said, disapproving.

"Not your fur," I said, trying not to laugh because he was so serious. Rellar was nearly bald.

He frowned. "Our ancestors did without clothes."

"If you're referring to the illustrations in the temple's caverns, and if those people are indeed our ancestors and not the figment of an artistic acolyte's imagination, then our ancestors lived in a much warmer world, not to mention drier." My boots had made a puddle, and I stepped out of it.

"Our world's becoming warm again, and that's a fact, not a picture on the wall. I remember when the glaciers' tongues filled the fjords and lapped at the sea."

"You do not," I said.

He shrugged. "Well, my granddam remembered, and that's practically the same thing."

"Did she also see godsfire rolling across the land?"

"No, Heao. Not even my granddam was that old. The exodus into the mountains occurred long before her time . . . if it occurred."

Forgetting my old master's blindness for a moment, I shook my head. No one who had seen the paintings in the temple caverns could accept all of them as being completely true; yet, no one could completely dismiss them, either. Among Rellar's favorites were pastoral scenes of unclothed men and women harvesting liverworts and mushrooms from the lush plateaus. Admittedly, the tablelands were once again flourishing with growth, and one couldn't

110

help wondering if the warm winds prevailing for longer periods of time each year had encouraged our recent bounty. Waning glaciers excited me, too, but only because their retreat opened passes to the largely unexplored Evernight Mountains, lighted eerily in places by erupting volcanoes. And beyond them? No one knew. Perhaps there was everlasting night, as the temple guardians claimed, a hell for damned souls. Perhaps it was heaven where the gods rejoiced in the warmth of Flametender's hearth, feeding reckless humans into the godsfire as we fed bricks of peat or chunks of coal into our furnaces. Actually, they'd be quite chilled if they depended on explorers for fuel, because expeditions beyond the King-conqueror's borders were rare. Our people had a history of sitting by their comfortable hearths and dreaming up ways to feed and clothe themselves with the least possible effort. Exploration of new lands was left to those driven from their homes by rising seas and earthquakes, and, with the exception of the King-conqueror and a few nomadic tribes, displaced people tended to resettle as closely to their old homes and as quickly as possible. Sometimes we were driven to far-off places by a lust for power and the need for conquest, or by our dreams.

"Academe and the guardians will be meeting tonight to discuss Chel's expedition," I said softly.

"How neatly you've shifted responsibility for the expedition to Prince Chel," Rellar said.

"He needs a new source of income now that his quarry is underwater. How else can he find it unless he explores? He stands a better chance of securing support for an expedition than I . . . especially now."

"Has the shunning caused you much difficulty?"

I crouched near Rellar, shrugging as I moved. "Only if you consider the inconvenience of being unable to make my own purchases," I said. "It has a funny side to it, too. My friends are embarrassed because they know that I'm right. They duck out of my path so that they don't really have to shun me." I laughed, then hoped my laughter didn't sound hollow.

"Does your family shun you?"

I looked at Rellar. The gilt of his irides were without flickers of amusement. "Of course they don't!"

"It will get worse, Heao, much worse. The temple has taken a very firm stand on slaves' inhumanity."

"A religious anachronism," I said, dismissing it.

111

Rellar shook his head. "Don't be confused, Heao. Freeing slaves is a political issue, not a religious one. The temple cannot change its position without losing powerful support from the aristocracy. Freeing slaves would cause economic upheaval."

I threw up my hands in dismay. I was much given to that gesture at the time. "We never suggested that slaves be freed," I said. "We stated facts about their intelligence and emotional levels, which are clearly human, though different. Did you say something to our friends and peers that I haven't heard? Why is slave *freedom* suddenly the issue?"

"The gods do not permit enslaving humans," Rellar said dryly. "Conquered people may not be bonded indefinitely, and mountain savages may not be forced into servitude simply because the King-conqueror's armies have more might."

"Only because it's not profitable," I said indignantly. "His Majesty cannot tax slaves, and slaves cannot tithe."

"Then you do understand the political issue," Rellar said.

"Of course, but my conscience won't permit me to ignore the truth just because it's profitable."

Rellar nodded. "The effects of our study mushroomed prematurely. Only Prince Chel is left to speak for the expedition."

"Chel's not eloquent, but he's forceful," I said.

"It's not enough," he said sadly. "It will take more than a military prince babbling about godsfire in boats to convince our peers and the guardians to ask the king to loosen his purse strings. This matter needs your authority or mine."

For a moment I stared at my friend's grizzled face. Then I said quietly, "Are you suggesting that we renounce our own words in order to speak in the conclave tonight?"

"The shunning will worsen, and if that doesn't work there are more direct methods of dealing with us."

"We're protected from imprisonment by our robes," I said. "As long as we hold our heads high and shake our tails at the temple guardians, tableland citizens will continue to feel shame. Eventually . . . "

He touched my hand, then held it securely in his. "My presence in the city is enough to keep the slave issue alive. It does not require us both. One of us should speak tonight. The expedition is especially important to you."

Rellar was universally respected, and shunning him was difficult for more people than shunning me. He had no enemies; he'd lived his life cultivating friends, yet he never used servile flattery or exaggerated deference to ingratiate himself. I couldn't claim the same for myself under all circumstances, but, then, Rellar had more patience than I with fools. Still, I wasn't without influence, either.

"I won't renounce my position," I said, "not even for the expedition."

"Perhaps for your life?"

"What?"

"The direct methods," he said. "Dead people are quickly forgotten."

I was stunned for a moment. "I can't think of anyone who would murder us just to have us out of mind," I said, carefully considering his words.

"I can think of many."

"Name one," I said.

"The guardian Tarana," he said without having to think. "She does not like people she cannot control. You have been the bane of her existence since you were a young woman."

"Our paths rarely cross," I said irritably. The woman had tried to make a national issue out of my refusal to share my dream. I knew Tarana hated me, perhaps she even feared me, but I was adept at keeping out of her way, at least until recently.

"Tarana's too smart to bloody her own hands," Rellar said. "But Prince Chel is a likely instrument; he can be manipulated into thinking we stand between him and the expedition, which is his only hope for regaining wealth since his quarry was flooded."

"No," I said, "not Chel. He's been my friend since we were children. And if that weren't enough, he needs my expertise to guide him safely through the Evernight Mountains." I shook my head. "Murdering us would make us martyrs, Rellar. They wouldn't want that."

"If the hero who stole fire from the gods had stumbled into a fjord and crushed his own skull instead of being downed by Flametender's arrows, I wonder if we would remember his deed."

I took my hand from Rellar's grasp. "I'm too surefooted to fall into a ravine and too fleet for anyone's arrows."

Rellar sighed. "You're stubborn."

"Just like you," I said.

He smiled at me. "I will come to the conclave tonight just to hear how well Prince Chel manages."

"With or without your clothes?"

"Hmmm," he said, "let me think about that. Garments chafe my skin and rub off the fur."

"Perhaps, but I don't think those tufts of hair you claim are fur will prevent your extremities from freezing if you walk naked in the snow."

"I suppose it isn't warm enough."

I laughed and turned to get my cape. "People will be relieved that you don't expect them to give up their clothes, as well as their slaves."

"Under the circumstances, they may never know what I expect."

I put on my cape, which was nearly dry, and patted Rellar's shoulder. "You needn't worry about Chel trying to convince Academe that Flametender carries his fire in a boat. That speculation was quite confidential and couldn't be tortured out of Chel in public. But perhaps I'll threaten him with exposure," I said, grinning. "If he's sufficiently motivated tonight, he can force Tarana and her guardian friends to reconsider the shunning. Chel needs us."

"He needs you," Rellar said. "I'm too old to go on an exploratory expedition."

"If they don't shun me, they can't shun you, either," I said as I walked across the cavern.

"Heao, stop!" I turned in time to see his thin silhouette arise. "You don't really expect to pressure Tarana through Chel because of his need for the expedition, do you?"

"Of course." I said it lightly because Rellar could not see my mischievous smile.

Rellar shook his head and I departed.

The twilight rain had hardened into sleet during my visit with Rellar. I used the sheltered concourse in the new section of the city, even though it was out of my way. We go to great lengths to stay dry. The King-conqueror roofed over the cobblestone path between his stronghold and the temple so that he arrived at his frequent devotional sessions dry. Then he raised roofs over the street to his favorite bawdy house, and to the forum, and even to the privy sand pits. With merchants and craftspeople following suit, it didn't take long before the city had roofs over most well-traveled streets. Beggars' children had a new livelihood as a result. They posted themselves at the city gates and offered to guard the umbrellas of landed countryfolk who entered to do business. It's well worth the pretty shell or quarter-penny to have your hands free; I always pay willingly. But, of course, one must exit the same way one entered, or else find one's umbrella for sale at another gate within a twinight. Since I'd entered at the main gate, that was the way I had to leave, which meant I had to endure averted eyes and lowered heads of merchants who were Baltsar's business associates and many of them my personal friends. Despite the bravado I displayed, it wasn't easy; I loved to gossip with friends and take advantage of an unexpected cup of tea, even when offered by a merchant who needed a sympathetic ear from Academe. I was gregarious by nature, and I missed the camaraderie and the patronizing.

Past the tentmaker's shop, past the alchemist's, and then I stopped seeing the people who worked with such intensity that they couldn't smile or nod. Tonight Prince Chel would insist that his expedition proposition be taken before the king, and by next twinight the temple drums would announce that slaves are human.

When I reached the gate, my umbrella was gone, and the beggar who'd taken my coin pretended he couldn't hear me.

Chapter 14

Since the land-grabbing campaigns, there was less danger of attack by mountain tribes, so the city expanded beyond the ancient borders. The population increased each year when the King-conqueror arrived to reside in his stronghold and worship at the kingdom's most ancient temple and to mingle with Academe. Unsavory characters thrived, and even though most of them seemed to disappear with the king's entourage each fall, the visiting aristocracy left their summer palaces well guarded by privateers. Under their watchful eyes, my walk from the city to Baltsar's rural home was uneventful, although wet without my umbrella.

Halfway between the city gate and the sea, a cobblestone path bisected the main road and wound its way up a hillside to the house I shared with Baltsar and our offspring. It was a showy place of white stone walls topped by blood-gray roofing tiles with inlaid gutters to carry drinking water to storage barrels. Thick moss and liverwort surrounded the structure so that the steady rains would not wear away the knoll. Behind the house was a network of footbridges leading to Baltsar's forge and casting buildings, where slaves and artisans produced the finest iron hinges, latches, andirons, knives, cooking pots, and even bronze finery.

I ran to the house, eager to have eyes meet mine again

and to feel the warmth of a smile. When I burst through the door, I startled the household slaves and met with disappointment. There should have been huge pots of honey over the fire to sweeten cakes, and the smells of baking mushrooms should have been filling the house in preparation for the Decitwinight feast. The slaves greeted me impassively, then returned to airing bedmoss over the ventilation shafts and setting the chambers to rights, as if it were any other twinight. I detected furtive glances.

Drigal and Sashiem obviously were not home, or else they would have greeted me like thunder. But Sema whimpered in her cradle near the fireplace as she kicked aside the swaddling. She bellowed, and Teon appeared from the back of the house, clucking to her in the slave tongue. He saw me and stopped. "I didn't know you had returned," he said.

"Just in time," I said in an irritable tone.

He thought I meant the child, for he smiled. "Sooner would have suited this one's demands much better." He picked up Sema, brought her to me, and exchanged the child for my wet cape. He ran his hands over my tunic to satisfy himself that it was not too damp to dry quickly by the fire, and then he took the cape to the mudroom.

I glared at the other slaves as I settled myself by the silvery fire, but it was useless to try to speak over Sema's lusty howls. Momentarily she was so angry she would not take my breast, and I had to fuss and coo until her anger gave way to hunger and she sucked. Then I looked at the nearest slave, one who'd taken the moss from Sema's cradle to dry by the fireplace. "Why aren't you preparing the feast?" I said.

She turned, one of the black-eyed ones whose gaze was disconcerting under any circumstances. At the sound of my voice, her eyelids opened wide, exposing great quantities of white around the round irides. She appeared witless, though I knew she was merely terrified. I regretted frightening her. "Fetch Teon," I said more gently. She scrambled and ran. So much for the persistent belief that most slaves aren't bright enough to understand our commands without a translator. Teon came in a moment. Before I could demand an explanation for the slaves' peculiar behavior and the lack of preparation for tonight's feast, he held out several message scrolls to me.

"These are regrets from Baltsar's associates," he said. "You and Baltsar will be dining alone."

Ordinarily, it was difficult to sustain anger while Sema tugged at my breast and the accompanying sensations nudged deep within my pelvis, yet I was overcome by rage. I flung the scrolls, scattering them over the mossrock hearth while shouting a contemptuous word. Teon reached out to soothe me, but I shied away from his touch. "Baltsar has nothing to do with my actions. He's my helper, not my parent or master. They're being unreasonable."

" 'Who in this world has more power over a human being—king or helper?' " Teon said. He was quoting from the *Book of Perspicuity,* and I wondered what kind of perverse inspiration had made me teach him to read.

"Neither," I said bitterly, "not in this issue."

Teon looked at me suspiciously. "Then you won't capitulate even if Baltsar asks you to?"

"No," I said, not hesitating. "Besides, Baltsar wouldn't ask."

Teon seemed pleased. He sat beside me, his thoughtful eyes meeting mine, wrinkle-skin fingers rubbing his chin. "But he won't be pleased." He gestured to the scattered scrolls.

"He'll be hurt, frightened, or angry," I said unhappily. "Which one?"

I thought, then said, "Mostly, he'll be hurt."

Teon nodded. "I agree. And I think we can ease his pain. Mussa was to have joined the feast tonight, wasn't she?"

"Yes." Chel had allowed Mussa to respond in his place since he was obliged to appear at Academe's conclave tonight. Our eldest child had been an aide to Prince Chel since before the ruinous floods in the quarry a year ago, and she had not sought release from her agreement with Chel, as many other aides had done when free spending had ended. Mussa's loyalty made me proud, for she'd not been properly serious while living at home. I think Baltsar and I spoiled her much of the time.

Teon smiled wryly. "Curious, isn't it?" he said. "Prince Chel is not a gracious man. Refusing the invitation would have been in character, yet he's sending a substitute who recently incurred his . . . um . . . disfavor. That's generous." Teon looked at me with innocent gray eyes.

I laid back my ears and wondered how much Teon knew about Mussa's blunder; probably everything, I decided. People tended to forget that the flesh lumps on the sides of their heads were ears. I wondered what he thought of a child of mine who had been foolish enough to trust the salt wind and Luck. I think even the twins, as young as they were, knew better than that. Chel had been furious with Mussa.

"I don't doubt that tantrum-prone child did something wrong," I said carefully, "but Prince Chel has chosen to overlook whatever it was in exchange for his life. All of them would have died if Mussa hadn't been able to bring them back to the coast after the storm drove their boat beyond the shoals." I shook my head. Chel's first expedition had been doomed before its start. I prayed the second was not also ill-fated.

"I repeat, the prince is not a gracious man. He mistreats his slaves."

"I think Prince Chel's contempt for slaves is well known," I said. "But he's also a brilliant strategist. He knows he needs me for his expedition. What better way to ingratiate himself than by accelerating my daughter's career?"

"By accelerating your career," Teon said, "or at least by supporting you in a time of need."

I shook my head and pried Sema's claws out of my breast. Thrifty Teon had cut off the mitts when she outgrew the garment so that she could wear it longer. He smiled apologetically as he handed me a cloth to put beneath her kneading claws. "Chel's strategy is sound. He can't afford to offend Tarana by supporting me outright. But I'm counting on him to find a reasonable compromise." I smiled triumphantly. "He must succeed if he wants the expedition."

"You've put a lot of faith in Prince Chel."

I touched Teon's hand. "I'm not blind to my lifelong friend's faults," I said. "But where he cannot further his own interests without furthering mine as well, I trust him."

Teon sighed, resigned to my logic. "As long as you trust him to send Mussa tonight"—he looked at me and I nodded—"then we can ease Baltsar's hurt. I thought a homecoming celebration for the girl would . . . "

"Excellent!" I said, seizing the idea. We hadn't seen Mussa since her return from the nearly disastrous expedition. "Is there time to make honeycakes? Baltsar is especially fond of them."

"We will make them," Teon assured me as he got up. "Leave everything to me."

I nodded and snuggled into the soft cushions. A slave like Teon was a luxury the rest of the world didn't enjoy, but I would have them share the peace of having an intimate household if they would only allow it. Who but Teon, slave, companion, and friend, would have known my greatest concern was for Baltsar? And who but he would plot to help me please my helper in life? I switched Sema to the other breast and napped. I was aware of the slaves' bustling in the huge chamber, and I knew when Teon took sleeping Sema from me to return her to her cradle. I think I mumbled a word of thanks when Teon threw a down-filled coverlet over me, and I was aware of Baltsar's arrival and I deliberately slept on, leaving the task of telling about the messages to Teon. The slave must have handled it tactfully, for no enraged noises penetrated my bliss.

Chapter 15

I WOULD have liked to dream on; the fantasies of sleep were more comfortable than reality. But, eventually, I felt Baltsar's hand on my rump.

"You can wake up now," he said. "Mussa will be here soon."

I sat up. Baltsar was wearing a white tunic embroidered with sky-gray spiderthread that complemented his deep-toned pelt. However, the twitch in his tail didn't go well with the regalia. I touched his hands. "I'm sorry, Baltsar. I didn't think your friends would slight you on my account. But events will move quickly after tonight. Our lives will normalize again."

"I wonder," he said grimly.

I stood up, drawing to my full height, my tail towering. "I appreciate your confidence, Baltsar," I said bitterly.

He knew I was hurt, but he didn't apolgize. His tail stiffened. "I've always admired your ability to manipulate your peers in a conclave and your unabashed flourish during court appearances. But I don't like your attempts to manipulate me!"

I glanced at Teon, who was arranging the dining carpets before the fireplace. He was well within earshot, but he was pretending not to hear.

"Don't blame him," Baltsar said irritably. "His tongue was as smooth as it always has been, and his impeccable humility adds an air of innocence that surpasses yours. It's taken me half a stick of time to remember he *does* understand the economic implication of the feast's cancellation. Then I wondered how small you two must think my brain is to believe I would be placated by your substituting one feast for another."

Teon glanced up and was momentarily bewildered to find Baltsar's eyes instead of mine. Slaves often find themselves treated as inanimate objects, and Baltsar, though not an unkind man, was inconsistent in acknowledging their presence. When Teon decided Baltsar hadn't excluded him from the altercation, he said, "My apologies, merchant."

Baltsar nodded. "I didn't think you'd let Heao take the blame."

"Having a feast for Mussa was my idea, but I didn't know whether or not Pathfinder wished for me to speak."

"Nor certain of what she wanted you to say." Baltsar shook his head, then looked at me. "Most slaves would have fled from the room to avoid confronting me. They are not able to accept the responsibility that goes with autonomy. Teon is an exception, and you've based your theory about slaves on a singularly cogent slave."

I was about to protest when Teon said quietly but firmly, "Pathfinder Heao is an unusual mistress. Most humans would have blamed me, whether I was at fault or not. It's an interesting paradox that you consider slaves bright enough to err in a human fashion, but too stupid to wait around for undeserved punishment."

For a moment I feared Teon had overstepped his bounds, but then Baltsar smiled in spite of himself. "Well taken, Teon," he said.

"Slaves," I said, "smart enough to make subjective judgments that keep them safe are already autonomous in a fashion. If merchants like yourself were to acknowledge . . ."

Baltsar stopped me with a wave of his hand. "I have reservations." He glanced at Teon. "Not about your intelligence or your abilities—I have many slaves who are superior crafters and ledger keepers, so I'm not fooled by temple claptrap."

Teon nodded gratefully. "You are a just master. Your directions are not ambiguous and chastisements are usually reasonable."

Baltsar's brow raised. "Usually?"

"There should be room for some difference of opinion in an egalitarian world," Teon said, smiling coyly.

Baltsar sighed. "But it's not egalitarian, Teon. The economics are not there. I'm not willing to pay wages to creatures whose services I can have for bread and board."

"Acknowledging slaves' humanity does not require setting them free or paying them wages," I said. "I had in mind some human rights, such as hearings before death sentences or maiming them as punishment."

"I shall never understand why you didn't state it that way," Baltsar said, shaking his head. "Many citizens deplore harsh and cruel treatment. You could have gained a great deal of public sympathy for that issue. As it is, you've been shunned. No one needs to listen now. Indeed, they cannot."

Frustrated, I sat on a cushion. "Tarana didn't give us time to explain why our study was important."

"All right, why?"

"Without acknowledging their humanity, *we* would not gain rights."

"What rights?" Baltsar said doubtfully.

"The right of owners not to be responsible for indolent or dishonest slaves."

Baltsar sat next to me, putting his hand on my knee. "If slaves are human, they must be freed. There is no middle ground. And since the aristocracy cannot exist without slaves, the guardians will not change their position."

"Their position is tenuous at best," I said, completely dissatisfied with his logic. "When slaves were captured in the Evernight Mountains, they made strange noises but could not speak. Now we realize those noises were a different language."

"*You* realize," Baltsar said. "You've taken the time to attach meaning to their mumbling. But just try to convince anyone else that there is more than one way to shape a word or communicate an idea. Even if you're right, they are set apart by speaking something other than the instinctive human language. And they don't have tails, so communication is never complete."

"The guardians know slaves have a separate language," I said. "If they didn't, they wouldn't pay a premium for communicators, slaves who can translate from human tongue into slave tongue."

Baltsar withdrew his hand from my knee. "A few have

the ability to learn our language. That proves nothing. My hearth dog understands at least twenty or thirty words."

"Baltsar, *you* know better! Everyone does. All humanity can't be willing to ignore what their eyes and ears tell them is true!"

"But they are ignoring you, Heao, and very effectively."

I sat glumly. "They won't after tonight's conclave," I said stubbornly. "Chel won't let them."

"Do you really know the prince well enough to be certain that he needs you for the expedition?"

I nodded, then smiled wryly. "Once we were close enough for him to ask me to be his helper-in-life."

"Why did you refuse him?" Baltsar said, suddenly curious.

"Because I didn't want to be that close to him."

"I can't remember why I didn't refuse you," Baltsar said wistfully.

I sucked in my breath, speechless.

"Never mind, Heao. I can afford to miss one caravan. You'd better change your clothes. Mussa will be here soon."

But at the appointed time, Mussa didn't arrive. I peered out the door, hoping to see her striding up the cobblestone path. I felt Baltsar's hand on my shoulder.

"Mussa is being less considerate than my associates. She's shunning both of us."

I wanted to deny it. Dozens of excuses for her absence came to my mind; each was lame. "You'll have her apology by twinight," I said angrily. Then I shouted over my shoulder for Teon to fetch my cape. I tapped my foot impatiently, and my tail trembled with rage. "Mussa wouldn't shun you of her own accord. Chel's responsible."

"I know." Baltsar shrugged and walked to the hearth.

"What does Chel expect to gain by this maneuver?"

"I don't know, but be careful, Heao. Chel may have lost his wealth in the quarry flood, but he still has power. He has been generous to Tarana and the other guardians."

"That power could end this matter. A whisper to Tarana . . . "

"He could, but he won't!" Baltsar's voice was rising. "He won't offend Tarana while he needs her influence on the king. You are the expendable one, not the guardian!"

"No," I said firmly. Teon appeared with my cape and I left, again feeling unsettled by Baltsar's doubt.

Halfway to the city gate, I heard footsteps behind me —heavy, splashing steps. There were no guards in sight, no safety.

"Pathfinder!" It was Teon. I realized I'd been holding my breath, and now I sighed in relief. "The merchant sent me after you."

"Come along, then," I said more easily than I felt. His company was welcome.

"Baltsar gave me this," Teon said, coming abreast and opening his cape to reveal a braided belt, sheath, and knife hilt. Each had Baltsar's distinctive design. Startled, I stopped. Teon gestured for me to continue walking.

We walked quickly; my mind was whirling. "Baltsar has a knack for turning small things into large ones," I said uneasily. "Witness one small fishing hoist becoming holdings so vast . . ." I tried to laugh, but I choked on the effort.

"That proves the merchant has an instinct for people," Teon said. He sounded worried.

"My instinct tells me I'll live through the night," I said with determination. But I hurried to reach the city and its numerous guards. I didn't dwell on my fleeing curiosity about the guards' behavior if an endangered citizen was also a shunned one.

Chapter 16

RELLAR WAS present, clothed, I am relieved to report. He and I took our usual places within the circle. Academians who usually sat near us crowded with their friends on the other side of the circle, except Neering, a brilliant academian who had only recently taken her robes. She planted herself by her fire engine, stubbornly having refused to remove it from the meeting chamber, even though the guardians had forbidden her to continue to work on it. She was, no doubt, armed with more well-researched arguments as to why the guardians should reverse their decision, and her efforts probably would be futile. Since she considered herself a devoted worshipper of Flametender, the guardians' refusals to allow her to honor the god with her machine had bewildered her. If they didn't capitulate, she would be driven to working in secrecy, just as most of the rest of us had been.

Since the guardians were late (as they usually were, to show their contempt for Academe, I suppose), the conclave began in the normal fashion. Our peers discussed the need for more storm pipes to carry excess water away from the cisterns. Water disposal was a problem. We couldn't empty it into the fields without washing away acres of liverwort and moss, and we couldn't dump it into the ravines, because in recent years lowland grapes were being cultivated on the rugged but warm bottoms. Piping the water to the sea seemed to be the only answer.

Academe was the city's problem-solver. It was not a tax-supported institution, but the king solicited our advice for tax-supported public works. Ideally, Academe in its advisory capacity was available to common people and king alike. But the king had a way of making his problems take precedence over all others; he didn't quibble about the cost of projects or about our fees, and he paid promptly. Since Academe had no legislative authority, he was free to reject our advice if he chose to. Yet, we were not without influence, for we were the economists, the mathematicians, the architects, the bridge-builders, the healers, the agronomists, the metallurgists, and the cartographers whose skills and knowledge were largely responsible for the King-conqueror's realm's unprecedented progress. He watched us carefully. The king knew he already had one co-ruler, the guardians, and he did not want another. Academe managed to survive while serving two masters, but at times I think we merely muddled through.

Finally, Prince Chel, Tarana, and a few other guardians entered the conclave chamber, with Mussa at their side. My daughter carefully avoided looking in my direction. I nearly got up to shake her, but Rellar sensed the sudden tenseness and asked me if Prince Chel had entered.

"Yes. Tarana and Mussa are with him."

Chel and Tarana joined the circle; Mussa stood aside, as was proper for an aide. I smiled at her, but she did not acknowledge me. No doubt about it—my own child was shunning me.

The moderator recognized Chel.

"I've come here to propose an expedition for scientific discovery," he said, smiling beatifically while holding his gorgeously groomed tail in a profound manner.

Mentioning science was a good way to get Academe's undivided attention. Tarana's presence and knowing she often affected how the king's purse was used made Academe's interest even keener.

"Science? Ha!" Rellar said loudly. "For military purposes."

A few of our robed comrades were startled enough to glance at us, but Chel merely frowned and continued.

"There are no maps to follow to upcoast cities that are

127

beyond our present borders. If we penetrate the mountains too deeply, we become lost; yet, we must do exactly that to get upcoast."

"I can't sneak past the upcoast sentries. Every logical route is guarded," Rellar said, mimicking Chel's voice.

Chel spoke louder and faster. "My recent attempt to open a sea passage resulted in fatalities for fifty of the sixty warriors who accompanied me."

Rellar grinned at the architect, who was seated in his customary place. "Your boat design was no better than previous ones. The craft disintegrated in the sea beyond the shoals, so I was unable to make a sneak attack by sea." The blind academian had captured every nuance of Chel's voice, and it seemed as if the back of the prince's mind guided Rellar's tongue.

Chel's tail was stiff. "There is a new orientation method, which, if successful, will open an overland route to the upcoast areas. The new route would expand trade and commerce."

"If my warriors and I could sneak up on their tenacious hamlets, we could take their copper mines and silver mines easily. Then I could supply metalsmiths throughout the realm and once again be wealthy!" said Rellar.

Rellar was not saying anything our peers couldn't surmise on their own, but invasion or offensive action of any kind was an inappropriate topic for academians, who devoted their lives to the science of living together. And during the past generation, the temple guardians had put great emphasis on peaceful co-existence, which was supposed to alter the visions of destruction in the king's and Tarana's dreams. Still, surreptitious military action, labeled defensive if it reached the king's ears, did occur. It was a fact of life that I accepted. But Rellar was a gentle person. Even if he didn't believe in dreams, he did believe in peace, and he would go to great lengths to preserve peace. His effort was successfully embarrassing Chel, Academe, and Tarana, and my heart was sinking. Chel needed some degree of success with my peers to gain Tarana's support and to overcome her doubts on the religious issues involved. She'd expended her personal fortune on his last expedition, and she'd be cautious before recommending another to the king. If she were convinced of the expedition's merit, her greed might then cause her to reconsider the shunning.

"I'll confine myself to explaining how this orientation

would be accomplished," Chel said. His tail twitched while he paused to see if Rellar had a different interpretation, but Rellar remained silent. Chel smiled. "It has been suggested that the rainshroud with which we are all familiar does not cover the entire world. It may end beyond Evernight Mountains."

Some of the guardians gasped at the thought of Raingiver having limitations, but Rellar began to speak again and they listened while pretending not to hear.

"I'm not capable of independent hypothesis, but my slaves speak of a rainless land, somewhere beyond the mountains . . . "

Chel leaped to his feet. "I will not be mocked by the beast-lover!" he shouted. "It was he who hypothesized the rainless land, and it was Heao who told me that if the skybridge were exposed, it could be used for orientation in lands where there are no maps. Rellar is trying to change the matter I brought to this conclave for discussion into one that will benefit himself. But I will not participate in an affront to the temple!"

Rellar smiled and coiled his tail around his neck, mocking the gesture that Chel always used. "I based my hypothesis on slaves' memories."

"Animal mysticism," Chel said scathingly. "A convenient corollary for a falling man who grasps at moss." He turned with a practiced flourish.

The door to our conclave meeting place slammed behind Chel, and my poor child had to open it again to exit. Tarana remained seated, smiling crookedly. I suspected her smile was for Chel's staunch loyalty to the temple over the slave issue. By ordering Rellar's and my shunning, she was treading on the spirit of the king's law that exempted academians from accusations of heresy. Shunning was not mentioned in the formal decree, but, until now, it hadn't been invoked. We didn't know how the king would react, for spring was still months away and he was in the lowlands. Next to his, Tarana's court was the highest in the land.

"You made it impossible for Chel to plead our case," I whispered to Rellar.

"You heard him, Heao. He's the guardian's man. We are nothing to him."

I shook my head. "If you hadn't told him about the slaves' participation in the hypothesis, he could have helped us. You embarrassed him."

"Do you think it's right to use the oppression of one people as a lever to release another? What gain?"

I had no answer. I'd not considered the expedition in those terms. Yet, I'd consciously used Chel's military ambitions to entice him into considering the expedition. My thinking did seem incongruous. The upcoast inhabitants were unquestionably human, yet I was willing to sacrifice their independence for slaves. I knew I had some soul-searching to do. I left Rellar to monitor the rest of the conclave and I quietly slipped away.

Teon was hovering in the eaves, his face frightened. "Prince Chel," he said, pointing across the marketplace, where Chel's tall silhouette was visible against the flickering street torch. "He's furious," Teon added.

"Did you think he'd murder me in front of twenty-nine witnesses?" Disdainfully, I pushed past Teon to walk through the marketplace. It was emptier than it had been at twinight. There was a noticeable absence of slaves, as there was every night. Slaves had difficulty selecting unbruised mushrooms and fresh moss in the dark, and most people resented the expense of supplying them with torches so that they could do their shopping chores. Consequently, slaves rested at night. Shopkeepers and merchants who dealt in mundane goods had taken to closing their shops during the night in ever-increasing numbers. Normal business would not resume until twinight, when slaves were up and working again.

Once past the marketplace, we walked along the deserted concourse, listening to the rain skittering over the roof. The wind from the sea was driving hard, and I suspected we'd be in the grip of winter before twinight's airglow. Suddenly an arm shot out from a doorway, pulled me, then released me to strike Teon. My slave fell with a clatter and a groan.

"Move for that knife again and you're dead!" Chel hissed.

Teon looked sick, determined to lose his life if necessary, but uncertain if that were required of him, for Chel made no menacing move toward me.

Satisfied that Teon would behave properly, Chel turned to me. "Stop this senseless crusade, Heao. I want you on my expedition."

"You end it, Chel. Talk to Tarana. She'll listen to you."

He shook his head. "She doesn't want the expedition

130

to take place. Anything to do with the Evernight Mountains terrifies her. If I could have convinced Academe to present it to the king as a public work, she'd be forced to approve it, or at least not to oppose it. But I cannot force the slave issue on her along with the expedition. That would be too much."

"Why? You are her patron, nearly as much as the king himself. If you make financial gains from the expedition, she'll benefit. She knows that."

"You forget that for all her political involvement, she is still a deeply religious woman. She would share the riches from the campaign I will launch against the up-coasters without so much as a tremor in her tail, but if we found godsfire there, too, it would shake the very foundations of her faith."

"Ridiculous," I said. "Godsfire is not waiting for her somewhere upcoast." But I wondered what it was like to be so rigid in faith that a scrap of fact would destroy a god.

"If only you would help me present the expedition to Academe . . ." Then, knowing I would not relent, he said, "At least give me your assurance that Rellar will stop interfering."

"I'm sorry, Chel."

His tail wrapped itself around his neck. "You'll never see godsfire," he said tauntingly.

Chel probably did not believe in godsfire—at least, not in my fashion. But he knew of my dream because as children we'd kept few secrets. It hurt to know that my friend would not help me pursue my dream, and it hurt to know I *could* pursue it if . . . I glanced at Teon, standing dismally nearby. I couldn't abandon him. I shook my head.

"Then I'll select another pathfinder and proceed," Chel said resolutely.

"Who?" I said scathingly. "Mussa?" By the stillness of his tail I could see that was who he meant. A chill went through me. "My daughter is not a pathfinder. Yes, she picked up rudimentary skills from me, but she never applied herself."

"She led us from beyond the shoals to safety when everyone else was disoriented."

"More luck than skill," I said carefully. "She's blessed by Luck, but he's a fickle god."

"Nonetheless, I will proceed with her."

131

I shrugged and stepped out of the doorway while suppressing a tirade of anger I wanted to vent. Though I'd never spoken of it, not even to Baltsar or Teon, I knew Mussa had blundered her way out of the open sea while Chel was delirious and incapable of giving orders. But for Luck, all would have perished. People always see Luck's good side. But for Luck, Chel would have been alert enough to realize my daughter had followed the wrong wind; even Chel knew better than to trust a salt wind! Ordinarily, Chel would have had Mussa in chains for stupidity! But the wind did eventually carry them ashore. And since a god's favor must not be scorned, and since Mussa was *my* daughter, Chel overlooked her mistake when he was well enough to realize what happened. Strange that everyone overlooked Mussa's turning her ankle when she reached the shore. So much for Luck.

As I walked away from Chel, I decided that I must out-wait him. My patience was more enduring than his. Chel knew that only I could keep track of all the subtle nuances of the wind; only I could measure a degree of change by feeling it along the hairs of my ears; and only I had ever smelled the strange winds that blew in from beyond the Evernight Mountains. He was trying to pressure me into renouncing my position on slaves in order to protect my child. Tempting. But any danger Mussa faced on an expedition with only fickle Luck to guide her, Chel would face, too. I trusted my friend to protect his own neck, and by association Mussa would also be safe. I would wait.

Chapter 17

THE WINTER crept toward spring, dragging its heavy burden, time. I longed for the sweet vernal winds, for soon after they appeared, the King-conqueror would, too. But the season would not hasten on my account, and so I endured.

The twins were practicing cyphering in ashes spread before the hearth for that purpose. Sema was on her belly, seemingly watching her brothers work, though her eyes had opened only nights ago. She was, I thought, seeing a haze of light reflecting in her immature eyes. If so, it was the first time I'd noticed signs of vision developing. Baltsar, of course, was not home. I don't believe we'd ever both been on hand to see our children take their first steps, or feel their first rain, or see their first sights. I suppose that's why it takes two to have children. There was not enough time for a single parent to enjoy all of a child's adventures. I made a mental note to tell Baltsar to watch Sema for signs of vision, turned back to the tapestry I was working on, then realized why I'd looked up in the first place. The rain had stopped.

"What's that?" said Sashiem, an ash-covered finger poised.

"Not what is," I said. "What's absent?"

"Baltsar?" Drigal said, idly finishing Sashiem's cypher.

"The slaves?" He looked up. "What are you two talking about?"

"The rain," Sashiem said, scrambling to his feet. Drigal was faster, and somehow, in the confusion of which door to head for and who would reach it first, Sema was miraculously untouched.

"It stopped!" Drigal shouted. "The rain stopped! Race you to the . . . "

Gods know where they were off to, but I was pleased to see them go. They had been devoting entirely too much time to indoor games, and when they weren't doing that they dogged Baltsar or me. Their pack of friends was still behaving in a cowardly fashion. Baltsar, too, was still being avoided, but he was putting the time to good use by completely reorganizing his warehouses and shops.

I tried to concentrate on the tapestry. It was a soft sculpture of the world of my dream, but it was fanciful in that the view I presented was the one that, perhaps, the gods saw from heaven. The world was a moss-like ball, stitched from fleecy gray threads. I'd paid considerable attention to darkening the limbs of the circle so that it appeared to be a radiant sphere, as if covered by airglow. Now I was encircling the globe with spiderthread, fashioning a translucent ring to represent the skybridge. I wasn't certain of what kind of suspension method to use on the skybridge, so for the moment it had the illusion of being suspended around the globe, as if by magic. The back of my mind was pondering over the eventual placement of godsfire. The pictures in the temple placed it on the horizon, cradled by mountains. Religious tradition placed it at the base of the skybridge, which rested its base on a flat world. But my skybridge had no base. The tapestry was irreverent, and I might have to be careful where and to whom I displayed it, but I enjoyed working on it. For the moment, diversion from my situation was what I needed.

I'd just finished the skybridge when Teon entered the room. "I couldn't sleep," he said. His eyes were alert, his voice clear.

I gestured for him to sit. He did, at my feet, luxuriously stretching out to catch the full warmth from the hearth, and then he began to sort threads from my basket. Half-finished, he stopped, leaned against my cushion, and stared at the hearth.

Except for the rhythmic movement of his breathing, it

was almost as if he weren't there at all. The back of my mind returned to its puzzle of where to place godsfire in the tapestry. Then I noticed Teon's jaw was clenched and his eyes were turbulent. Comfortable silence is one thing, but a bundle of muscle, coiled and ready to spring, is distracting. "What is it, Teon?" I said.

"You are . . . brave," he said quietly.

"What?"

His gray eyes became intense. "Brave. I know it's not easy for you to maintain your position on slaves' humanity while the entire city shuns you. I admire you for taking on the burden."

"But I didn't do it by choice," I said. "The matter was blown out of proportion and I was taken off guard."

"Do you regret doing it?"

I thought a moment. "I regret the consequences, but I can't deny what I know to be the truth, even if it would be more comfortable to do so."

"What will happen now?"

I shrugged. "I hope the temple will change its position, or that the king will overrule the guardians."

"You won't change your position?"

"I won't have to. Slaves have demonstrated their human quotient since they learned to speak . . . even before, if anyone cared to remember. The facts won't change."

Sema had crawled to Teon and was curling by his thigh to sleep. He rubbed her spine, relaxing her. "You have more faith in people than I," Teon said. "They see only what they wish—that our eyes are different from humans' and that we sleep in peculiar fashions."

"Physical differences are the easiest to explain to them and the easiest for them to accept. Some of your physical differences are valuable—your strength and the distance vision . . . "

"Few recognize that as an advantage," Teon said. "Slaves have few opportunities to use their far sight. Who but a mapmaker needs to see details farther than a stone's throw? Most point to our inability to see well in the dark and complain about the cost of providing us with torches."

I smiled at hearing Teon speak like the temple guardians. He was asking me for reassurances. "I suppose that's so, Teon. But those are not as difficult to overcome as your behavioral differences. It's the mysticism surrounding slaves that frightens most people. Where did you come from? If

135

you did come from heaven, why don't you believe in the gods? Your own tales tell of your coming from the sky. And why are slaves so stubborn about inventing different hues when, in truth, the hues are identical?"

He was frowning. "You don't believe the tales that we came from the sky, do you?"

"No, but I've heard slaves proclaim that they did, and they do it with pride."

Teon shook his head. "I don't think we did, either, but the belief persists among the old slaves."

"You're sensible in that matter," I said, "but you're far from perfect in others." When his frown deepened, I put down my needle and pointed to the threads he'd sorted. "Look at what you've done here. Why didn't you put these together?" I selected two threads of an identical hue from two separate groupings.

"One is . . . " He shook his head. "The word doesn't translate. It's . . . well, one is the magnitude of mushrooms, and the other is like the sky."

"Mushroom-gray, sky-gray. The only difference is in the selection of the word, and a preference for the description sky-gray dominates in the tablelands."

Teon shook his head. "They are not alike."

"But they are," I insisted. "I'm not berating you, Teon. I know there is a reason for your strange sense of order. I'd like to know what that reason is. Do you smell a difference in the dye? Is there some other instinct involved that you can't articulate?"

"No, I *see* the difference," he said firmly. "It has nothing to do with smell, or even touch."

I examined the threads. Both were sky-gray, or mushroom-gray, if you like. I held them to my nose, not to smell them, but to see if there were great variations in the filaments. There was none. I was certain they'd come from the same threadmaker's spool. "They are the same," I announced. I looked at my frowning, puzzled slave.

"Except for size and structure, they are *not* the same. Their appearance is different!"

I shook my head.

He took two more threads from my knee. "Are these the same?"

I smiled. "No. One is charcoal-black; the other is much lighter."

"Yet they are alike in that they are merely different magnitudes of the same hue."

"Well, yes . . . "

"This one is like spring leaves," he said, holding up the lighter one, "and the other is the hue of thick moss very late in the summer."

"Yes," I said, pleased with him.

"And this one," he said, taking a thread from my hand, "is like a mushroom."

"Yes," I said eagerly. Perhaps there was only some confusion in semantics.

Teon laid the three threads on my other knee. "No two are exactly alike."

I groaned. "Mushrooms, spring leaves, and sky are all the same magnitude, for all practical purposes. Only the one you refer to as moss-gray is different."

Teon sighed. "It's hopeless. I can't explain what you cannot see. Blood is black and moss is charcoal." He looked at the tapestry. "It started out so prettily, but now it's a nightmare, not a vision."

"Indeed," I said, dismayed. Such neat stitches. So much care used to shade the circle into a globe. I was perplexed.

"The shape is fine and the stitches are perfect, Pathfinder. But your selection of hues is garish: a world the magnitude of blood, the skybridge the shade of mud." He shook his head.

"I . . . "

"I know. You don't understand what I mean, nor does any human. Should slaves therefore ignore what their eyes see? It's difficult even to pretend."

"If you'll try, we can work out an understanding."

"No," he said, laughing at me now. "If I had never seen fire and you wanted to explain it to me, how would you proceed?"

I considered. "I'd probably first tell you that it's hot, like the springs near Chel's quarry."

"Good start," he said. "Now I have a vision of something that would comfort my body."

"I know slaves don't mind being wet, but the heat of a fire is too hot for comfort. If it touched your skin, you blister, as if from acid."

"Now I imagine that it's painful, but it's still liquid."

"But it's not liquid at all—more like air. It flickers and becomes one with the air. And it's not always painful. It can be comforting, too."

137

"It's like water, yet it's like air . . . painful and comforting—strange item," he said doubtfully.

I nodded, understanding. "But if I showed fire to you, you would understand. Why can't you show me the difference between these threads?"

"If my arms were made of stone, I could not feel the difference between water and air, pain and comfort. Your eyes are like stone."

"An impasse," I said reluctantly. "But now you understand why slaves do not seem human to my peers."

Teon stiffened and Sema was disturbed. "I've known the problem more clearly than you for my entire life," he said. He patted Sema's back until she closed her eyes again. Then he looked at me. "We try to use your words, but they are not there. We revert to our own tongue."

"But other behavior sets you apart, too."

"Such as?"

"Why don't you mate . . . civilly, neatly?"

"Pardon?"

"There is a great deal of promiscuity among slaves and the fashion in which you go about it . . . " Teon was watching me closely. Both of us were wondering how I would finish my sentence. "There is an inordinate amount of attention spent on one another's mouths. It seems very much like bucks sniffing the behinds of does in season."

"My nose is less sensitive than yours, Pathfinder. Slave women are not seasonal."

"But . . . "

"The pressing together of lips is a form of caress," Teon said seriously.

"Fah!" I said. "It's messy, and I don't want it done in my kitchen."

"What harm if slaves caress while they're waiting for the pot to boil?" he said quietly.

"Spittle in my food," I said, disgusted.

"Never," he said, shaking his head. "You've not watched closely enough. It's neither messy nor disgusting. It's very erotic. We like to do it, much as Sema delights in my petting her along the spine."

"Indeed. Well, it's a peculiar form of eroticism. There must be an odor from food particles left in the mouth, and spittle . . . ugh!"

Teon shook his head, but he didn't reply.

"Don't sulk," I said gently, touching his shoulder. "I

138

didn't mean to ridicule your mating habits. I'm trying to illustrate common reactions . . . our confusion."

"I wasn't sulking," he said. "I was wondering if a frank analogy would anger you."

"Of course not."

He turned to study my face for a moment. Then, apparently satisfied that I was sincere, he said, "When you and Baltsar mate, there is a great deal of touching of one another's bodies—the spines and other places special to each of you. Isn't that right?"

I nodded, then wondered how often Teon had seen Baltsar's playful advances, and mine. On certain occasions even I tended to forget the presence of slaves.

"And some touching places are so good that, despite the moment being inopportune, you do not want to stop."

"Yes, but mouths . . . " I protested, ignoring his patronizing smile. He had been watching!

"Lips are sensitive." Teon ran his fingers across his lips, then gestured for me to explore my own.

My lips were tiny compared with his, but they were sensitive, which is useful for keeping food in one's mouth. "Pressing them makes them numb," I said after another moment of experimentation. "And I've seen noses pressed, too, and those are equally sensitive. For a truly sensual experience, there can't be any pain associated with the feelings."

"Our noses are not so sensitive. Pressing them does not injure them, and, besides, they hardly touch. Pressing of lips and noses is just not all there is to it."

"What else? What happens to the spittle?" I touched his arm. "I want to know." I felt a bit like I had felt when I was a small child, sitting on Rellar's knee, asking him to describe copulation to me.

"Well, we . . . " He was hesitant, and I suppose that was natural. I would not have liked to explain more intimate details of Baltsar's and my mating, for, unlike Rellar, I felt those experiences were as personal as my dream. Yet it was important that I know and understand slaves' habits. If there were reasonable explanations for their behavior, I needed to know. Temple guardians were not completely stupid when faced with facts.

"Show me," I said insistently. "You said spittle is not a problem. I want to know why not."

Teon's brow wrinkled, and his eyes jumped nervously

in their sockets. "Pathfinder, wouldn't you find a demonstration rather like a buck sniffing . . . "

"No," I said resolutely.

He regarded me for a very long time. His eyes steadied, even became sly. "Are you willing to suffer to learn about slaves?"

"Stop it, Teon. Please show me."

"You'd have to cooperate," he said doubtfully.

"I will."

He moved Sema to another cushion, then knelt by me and leaned toward me. I smiled to encourage him and he laughed. His hand was on my cheek, tracing a line from cheekbone to lips. I tensed, and he shook his head reprovingly.

I wondered if I ought to touch his face in a like fashion, but then his lips were against mine, nibbling. I nearly pulled away because he tickled me so. Then my mouth buckled from the pressure of his, and at the same time I felt his arms encircle me, his hand coming to rest against my spine. I gasped, then stiffened; I suddenly wondered just how closely Teon had watched Baltsar. His hand was so close . . . but it didn't move. His palms flattened against my fur, and fingers stayed chastely still. Again I relaxed and tried to think of lips. . . .

Lips—not just the parts one sees, but also the soft, inner flesh, which usually rests against teeth, curled over mine. I tried to twist mine similarly, ludicrously aware that my face was contorted and probably grotesque to see. I felt his teeth scraping along mine, then the startling probe of muscle. He held me tightly when I jumped, then soothed me until I allowed him to cup his mouth more firmly against mine.

In a moment I understood. Spittle was a fine lubricant. Gliding, my tongue magnified his lips, his teeth, and the tip of his tongue. I felt a sexual stirring, which I hadn't expected, and I began wondering if this peculiar form of caressing was erotic, after all. Or was it Teon's fingertips, essaying the muscle along the side of my spine, which fanned my flames?

There was a problem with oral intimacy that I didn't know how to solve. How could I speak to tell Teon that if he didn't remove his hand immediately from my erogenous zone, he'd have the full force of my knee in his genitals? Or did I want to whisper that to be effective, he needed to touch my vertebrae, as well? Preoccupied with this dilemma, I stopped responding to Teon's tongue, and before propriety completely won over the playfulness in me, Teon's hand was on my shoulder and he pulled his face away from mine.

"I think you understand now," he said quietly.

His eyes were open and I realized mine had been closed during a moment of reflection. "Did you deliberately . . .?"

"Yes," he said. Then he arose and walked slowly over the glistening marble floor to his chamber door. "Good night, Pathfinder," he said, then closed the door between us.

Chapter 18

THE WARM vernal winds from beyond the mountains had been blowing steadily for several nights. The farmers began planting fields of mushrooms. Moss patches plumped and flowered, their tiny, straight stalks brightening the plateaus with lively shades of gray. Ferns uncurled along the cobblestones near our house, and I studied their growth with unusual interest; when the fronds were as tall as my ankles, the snow in the passes would be gone and the King-conqueror, with his court, could be expected to arrive any twinight thereafter. Then the torches on the battlements of his stronghold would once again blaze brightly, night and twinight. And with a blink of his sage eyes, he could end the temple's persecution of me and Rellar.

But the fern fronds were barely as high as my instep when I returned home from a walk to find Baltsar's slaves filing down the cobblestone path to the concourse, their arms and backs laden with clothes and cushions.

"What are you doing?" I said, bewildered. But no one would answer me. I rushed past them to the house, where the door was propped open to facilitate the exiting slaves. "What's happening?" I said loudly.

"I'm sorry, Heao." It was Baltsar, coming from the mudroom. His eyes were miserable, his tail drooping. "I thought you would be away for a few sticks of time."

I still didn't understand. "I came back early," I said, watching more slaves with more of his belongings walk between us and out the door.

"I cannot tolerate it any longer," he said. He would not meet my eyes, and then I understood. Anger surged through me.

"You tried to sneak away," I said in a shocked whisper, "without even a word."

"What could I say, Heao—that I am a selfish man who will not be beaten and broken by anyone? Would you understand if I said I cannot tolerate seeing my children being treated shabbily by their friends . . . that I cannot tolerate their despair? You've seen the anguish you've caused, yet you are unmoved."

I shook my head. "It's just for a while."

He turned away, his head hanging. "I can't abide it any longer, Heao. I swear to you that I have tried."

"It's not the children," I said accusingly. "You're afraid!"

"Yes."

"Of losing more profits."

"That, too." His voice was stronger. He turned and came to within an arm's length of me before he noticed my tail was twitching. "I didn't come lightly to my decision to leave you. I have a responsibility to my children that I will honor, even if you will not."

"Do you think my decision to endure the shunning was easy?"

"No," he said softly. "But from the very beginning, you have been unrealistic. You have never cooperated with Tarana, and that incites her fears. You came out publicly for slaves with complete disregard for the consequences. You've alienated the only champion you might have had, giving Chel no choice but to align himself with the temple. Their backs are to the wall, and so is mine."

"I am my own champion," I said, knowing suddenly that I was speaking the truth.

"I hope so," he said, "for there is no other—not even the king."

Frowning, I looked at him.

"You could have been his favorite." He sighed, knowing that what he said was completely untrue for me, for who I was. The king never ceased hinting that his nest might be a more exciting place with me in it from time to time.

"I'm still his favorite adversary," I said. And that was true, for if I would not spark his nest, I did, often, ignite his court.

"To whom he owes nothing," Baltsar said sadly. He gestured helplessly. "I put my faith in your knowing what you were doing. I kept asking for reassurance that you could make this thing work. How long will you persist?"

"As long as it takes," I said with determination.

He nodded. "I thought so."

The last of the slaves left the house and Baltsar moved toward Sema's cradle. Without hesitation, I ran to the cradle, reaching it before him. My claws were bared, daring him to take another step.

For a moment I thought Baltsar would fight with me. His eyes were strangely bright, as if fevered. But he turned and followed the slaves, leaving me and the child quite alone.

I could hear myself breathe, deep gasping breaths that rattled in my chest and seemed to echo off the nearly bare walls. The fire in the hearth roared and the heat became unbearable. I staggered and would have fallen, but for Teon appearing from someplace to catch me.

"I'm all right," I said, but I was not. He helped me to sit. I waited, still astonished by Baltsar's betrayal. I tried to gather my wits and compose my trembling body. I don't know how long I sat, but finally Sema's cries penetrated the vacuum in my mind, and when I turned to the sound I saw Teon watching me with deep concern.

He picked up Sema and hugged her close to his breast. He was devoid of smiles and his round eyes were somber, yet the sight of him clutching my child was charming, and somehow reassuring. I smiled. "I'm not beaten, Teon. I refuse to be."

"I know," he said, finally also smiling. "But the pain must be awful." He glanced at the door, which Baltsar had not bothered to close. A light rain was wafting in over the threshold, but there was no thick and valuable carpet there to get wet. "How is it that you can smile at me so soon? Into which mind do you put incidents like this?" He looked at me, wondering.

"If I worried consciously about all that has happened to me this winter, I'd go insane. The part of my mind

144

that I'm not always in contact with will take care of the worry."

I lied rather straight-faced, and my slave accepted the lie with a shrug. It would not do for him to know how angry I was with Baltsar and how helpless I felt. Streams of thought were pouring between my two brains, focusing on betrayal and desertion, revenge and endurance. Somehow, knowing that I'd been betrayed again strengthened my resolve. And anticipation of revenge, heretofore not considered by either of my minds, was a sweet feeling.

My strength returned completely. With Sema in my arms, I arose, then crossed the room to shut the door. I could tell by the scent that the breeze that wafted around me was a vernal one, yet I was chilled by it. I hurried back to the hearth.

Chapter 19

IT SEEMED as if I were dead. No one spoke to me or nodded in my direction when I flaunted my existence in the city streets. Worshippers in the temple hushed when I entered. Then I would be left alone with the statues and images. Perspicuity stood straight on her airy throne, offering no comfort. I was incessantly chilled, requiring winter garb while most people were beginning to use short summer capes and frilly tunics.

When I was home, Teon heaped the fire with peat bricks or coal, but my icy spirit was more powerful than my beating heart, and the cold lingered throughout my being.

I was breathing on my fingers, looking with grave dissatisfaction at the map I was making. Free of interruptions, this should have been a time of great productivity for me. But the marks I made on the albino doeskins that Teon had patiently stitched together were imperfect. I would press too hard on the stylus, and the sepia would blur. The hoarfrost-patterned border was an irregular width, and it could not be corrected. My mind distracted me, and I ruined the work. Loneliness was a crippling disease.

"Don't start pacing," Teon said when he saw me walk away from my work. He was stitching together more hides. A small stack was already prepared.

I began pacing, aware that he was watching me.

"If you won't work, you ought to groom yourself. Your

146

fur looks disgraceful." His words were chastising, but his tone was carefully polite.

I shrugged. "I haven't groomed alone for years. It brings me no pleasure."

He put down the hides. "Then let me do it for you," he said, clearing a place by the hearth. He'd stopped my pacing with the suggestion, and I stood, considering. "Come on. I've been grooming your children for years. I'm an expert."

Most of Teon's efforts to cheer me up had been unsuccessful, but the knots in my fur were uncomfortable enough to make me nod. I walked to the hearth, making every step fill a span of time, however small. Purposeful steps were a treasure.

I lay on the old hearth rug that Teon had found in a storage cupboard and pressed into use, along with some shabby cushions and rush mats. The huge room still seemed bare; none of the cubbyholes was padded, and the ornate wall hangings were gone. When Teon returned with my brush and grooming cloths, I fixed my eyes on the leaping flames and put my hand in his lap and let him begin. I was already dreading the moment when he would be finished and I'd have nothing to do again. He must have sensed my anxiety. He worked slowly, removing even the worst tangles without causing me to twinge. Or perhaps time was equally heavy for Teon to bear. Preparing food and cleaning up after just himself, Sema, and me occupied him very little. The grooming interlude was, I decided, a good diversion for both of us.

Or was it? My ears perked up when Teon put down the brush and began massaging light, scented oil into my fur. His ministrations were peaceful when he worked between my claws, or on my hands or neck. But when his strong fingers stopped massaging skin and soothing fur to probe along my spine, I knew, without asking this time, that it was deliberate.

Strangely, I was not angry . . . curious, perhaps. He was not expert in arousing a human, but his zeal was admirable. He was trying to be gentle, but his fingers lingered too long in places where he noticed I'd respond, even just a little. Still, he was close enough for my mind to fill in the pleasures he'd missed, and I realized that if I allowed him to continue, I could climax.

Part of me was repelled. I'd never considered bestiality before, not even while in heat. Another part of my being held me still beneath his hands, pretending that I was dreaming. Who would know? If I controlled the throes of pleasure that were approaching, even the slave would not be certain. I didn't have to acknowledge his presence or even his participation. My pleasures were few enough, I thought. If I could refrain from making a decision for just a moment longer, my body would have made it for me.

But Teon completely misunderstood my passiveness. I felt him press his engorged penis against my pubic area, and my sexual pleasure turned to rage. I turned and hit him across his arm and chest with my open claws. He leaped back, or I would have hit him again. His eyes were wide with surprise.

He knew better than to attempt any retaliation. Even though the house was remote and there was no one about to hear any skirmish, his far superior strength was useless against my speed and sharp claws. I could have cut him down to a mess of blood and guts in a moment. His eyes hardened as he backed away from me, and as the cuts I'd made began to bleed profusely, he covered them with his hand.

"You have always encouraged me to behave like a man," he said slowly. "You told me I was your equal in intellect and emotion. But you were wrong, Heao. I am your superior. I can love where you cannot."

He turned to leave, and I did not try to stop him. I was already regretful. Teon and I had had misunderstandings before, though never like this. I had treated him respectfully, and our trust had grown implicit in time. Our relationship was more nearly that of friends than master and slave. What use to me was an obedient beast? I needed his eyes to make my maps and his clever mind to keep order in the house when Baltsar and I were absent. I even valued his opinion on aesthetics, for he'd learned more about what pleased people over the years than I cared to know. I laughed ruefully. In his precarious position, he would need to know how to please people in order to survive. He rarely erred, and when he did, the errors were slight. Even tonight his calculations were only slightly awry. But if I'd allowed a true-friend to provoke my passions, would I have slashed my friend if he wanted to have intercourse with me? I knew the answer, but I didn't have to dwell on it, because, suddenly, I heard the clinking of mail and sidearms. Armed warriors were walking up the cobblestone path to the house.

I arranged my tunic and hurried to the door. Before I could pull the lever, Baltsar burst through, and behind him I saw several of his personal guards fan out around the house.

"You're intruding," I said coldly, but I was only half-nettled. I could tell by the set of his tail that he was not paying a visit. He was frightened.

He closed the door, looked around for the security bar, which we rarely used, saw it in the corner, fetched it, and put it into place. When he turned to face me, I coiled my tail around my waist so that it would reveal nothing.

"Apparently you have not heard the news," he said. He stopped himself from automatically taking off his cape. "Rellar is dead."

"When?" I said, stunned.

"Last night," he said. He shook his head at me.

Sadness was quick to engulf me, loneliness complete. I hugged my elbows and turned away from Baltsar, wondering how much worse my circumstances could be. It had been comforting to know that, even though my own family had turned against me, Rellar stood with me. His approval was important.

I glanced at Baltsar. He'd done me a kindness by bringing the news, but I wished he would leave. I didn't care to spar with him just now, and I knew my anger with him was too strong to resist much longer. I laid back my ears. He saw the gesture, then folded his arms across his chest and said, "Rellar was poisoned."

My hands fell open and my ears perked up. "Poisoned? How? By whom?"

"His slave, Manya, was accused."

"Manya!" I scowled. "Impossible. She was devoted to him." I walked to the fireplace, suddenly feeling icy. Manya and her child had lived peacefully with Rellar ever since Baltsar gave them to him nearly eighteen years ago. She had been his eyes after I left to live with Baltsar, and I knew they treated one another with great kindness. He used to nest with her, but I suspected that in recent years Rellar did not trouble her for such services. Even if

149

he did, I knew for a fact that she'd been willing from the very first. It was not likely to cause trouble between them now, but sex was the only area of discord I could imagine. Even so, I was pretty sure that it was my personal prejudices that brought sex to mind, not anything real. "I don't believe it was Manya," I said finally.

"Nor do I." Baltsar came to the fireplace and spoke low. "He died horribly, convulsing and hemorrhaging. He said her name."

"Of course—he would be calling for her."

"Tarana put another interpretation on it. She said he was naming his murderer."

I felt outraged and very helpless. My dear friend had been murdered, no doubt, but not by Manya. Blaming her, however, neatly prevented Rellar from becoming a martyr. Much as I hated to admit it, I recognized Chel's strategy when I saw it, and he intended that I know who was responsible.

"What will happen to Manya?"

We looked up to see Teon standing nearby. He'd changed to a winter tunic, which nearly covered the wounds I'd made.

"It has already happened," Baltsar said. "She was stoned."

Teon gasped, and then his fist clenched. "Teofil?"

Baltsar nodded. "Dead, also."

I have seen slaves collapse in grief. Tears run from their eyes until they are nearly blind and they fold in on themselves while making grievous noises. The process can debilitate them for just a few moments, or for several sticks of time. There were tears in Teon's eyes, but they did not fall. Then his face became an iron mask of hate, and his body trembled with rage. He did not move.

"Teon?" Baltsar was alarmed to see the slave behave in such a belligerent fashion.

Teon glared and would not answer.

"Let him be," I whispered.

Baltsar watched for another moment, then turned away, his ears alert for any movement from the slave. "You may be their next victim," Baltsar said to me.

I nodded. "That has already occurred to me. With Rellar dispatched and slaves discredited, the issue of slaves' humanity will die forever, if I cannot remind them of it."

150

"I brought guards . . . "

"Thank you. Now, please leave me alone so that I can think."

"Heao . . . " He looked at me through fear-filled eyes. Then, shaking his head, he left some plea or warning unsaid. As he turned to leave, he glanced back at Teon, who was still standing with his fists clenched. Baltsar approached the slave, curiously lifting his sleeve to expose three neat slashes. Teon stared at him silently with unrestrained contempt. "I can take him away with me," Baltsar said. No slave of ours had ever borne claw scars, and the fresh wounds testified to gross disobedience.

"That won't be necessary," I said. But I had cause to wonder as Teon's contemptuous glare came to rest on me.

Baltsar shrugged, then went to the door. He reminded me of the security bar by lifting it noisily and setting it down with a thud. This time he closed the door.

Silently, I replaced the security bar, returned to the fireplace, sat on a cushion, then idly began tracing the shape of the frayed spots. My minds were conversing, and my decision was made, in truth, even before Baltsar departed. But I was worried about Teon. I called to him, but he didn't respond. I knew that years of anger and fresh hurt were pent up in his taut muscles, and I also knew that one wrong word would unleash all of it against me. Yet I still had confidence in his fine mind, so I was willing to risk having to take him down with my teeth and claws. The second time I called his name, he turned his back and started to leave the room.

"If you don't halt immediately, I'll break your legs, cut out your tongue, and have you gelded."

He probably knew my threats were empty, but he stopped. His head drooped and his fingers clenched and opened rhythmically. Finally, he turned. "Why did you claw me?"

"I was afraid."

"Afraid? How can I hurt you?"

"I didn't want you to know how much I cared about you." I felt a tremor of embarrassment pass through my tail, but he didn't seem to notice. His jaw had a stubborn set and his eyes were like coals. "Why are you behaving like this, Teon. After all I have done for you, I surely deserve some consideration. I have been shunned by the entire community. My helper-in-life has abandoned me

151

and my children avoid me. I turned my back on the greatest opportunity to realize my dream that I will ever get in my lifetime, just because I believe in you. Now my best friend is dead and you dare to stand there and glare at me!"

"You're lucky that I don't have the power of my forebears. I would do more than glare if I could," he said.

"You're forgetting yourself. You are a slave and, even so, I have been your friend."

"My daughter is dead and you are responsible."

"Teofil?" Of course, Teofil, the back of my brain answered. "But you and Manya . . . "

" . . . comforted each other a very long time ago." He laughed sardonically. "Even that brief joy turns to poison for a slave."

"I'm sorry, Teon. Please believe me, I'm truly sorry."

"As you wish, Pathfinder," he said stiffly.

For Teon, that was a rude response, but I ignored it. "And I forgive you for . . . " Both of us glanced at the fireplace cushions, where the brush and clumps of knotted fur lay.

"That's your privilege." He rubbed his arm to remind me that wounding him had been my privilege, too. The sardonic laughter came over him again as he went to the fireplace. "You never should have encouraged me to think like a man. I want to murder your prince. I want revenge for my daughter's death."

"You'd never get near him."

"I know. Damn, how well I know. I feel so helpless." He faced me. "Why did you make me want to feel human? It hurts!"

"Please, Teon, please stop this. We have both suffered terrible losses this night. We mustn't turn on each other —we have no one but each other."

"My child is dead," he said stonily. "How can I ever forgive you for taking the only spark of joy that was mine?"

I couldn't respond. I knew that he did not mean me, personally, but he referred to humans collectively.

The glow from the fire silvered his silhouette as he sank heavily onto a cushion. "How do you think I feel, knowing that the only feeling I have left in life is for a furry *cat?*"

"I'm not much better off," I said heatedly. "You are merely a slave, and, aside from Sema, who has no thoughts on the matter, you are all I have left."

"I know," he said, groaning. "I know. I have felt your anguish with you."

"Truly? Or have you been kind to me because I have supported a bid for an end to slavery?"

He gestured helplessly. "How can I really know? Can you, who have never been a slave, possibly understand how important freedom is to me? I worship it and cherish it beyond anything else in life. And you . . . you are freedom to me."

I left the shadows to sit by his side, and after a moment he put his arm around my shoulders, fiercely daring me to deny our friendship. I could not, would not. He recognized his position and accepted it regretfully. For the moment I couldn't ask more of him. At the same time I was secretly drawing strength from him to face my own position. Finally, I was ready, and he must have noticed a change in my posture. He looked at me quizzically when I turned to him.

"You must take Sema to Baltsar and stay there until I come for you," I said.

"Why? What are you going to do?"

"I . . . have errands to run."

"Where are you going?" he demanded.

I breathed deeply. "To the temple where I will ask Tarana's forgiveness."

His comforting arm dropped to his side and his face contorted in anguish. "Oh, Heao . . . no." He choked back a sob and turned away from me.

"What else can I do? Rellar is dead. It would be suicide to continue struggling against Tarana and Chel."

"And a sin to die before you fulfill your destiny," he said bitterly. "Why couldn't you dream of freedom and justice?"

"There is law and order, but there will never be justice for everyone," I said sadly. I tried to touch his shoulder, but he shied away. "Take Sema."

"As you wish, Pathfinder," he said stonily.

"Teon," I said, grieved because he used those subservient words again that were alien in our relationship.

He shook his head. "I do not feel very much like a man tonight."

Chapter 20

JUDGING BY the great numbers of toads hopping over the cobblestone path, the night rain was warm and must have been warm for several nights. But even as I walked in the shadows along the edge of the causeway, I shivered as if it were winter. Trepidation. I wasn't afraid of doing my penance; that I would was a foregone conclusion as far as Chel and Tarana were concerned, and since I was making my way toward the temple I had to admit it was a well-devised plan.

Icy shivers. That's what it felt like to abandon a loyal friend to save my own hide, to compromise my ideals. The penance needn't be so bad. If I entered the temple quietly, no one would suspect my presence until the humiliating ritual was over. A few guardians and Tarana would be witnesses—surely she wouldn't use the public chamber.

I crept through back alleys under the shadows of eaves and shied away from every night-walker I met. Flying things shrieked in the darkness, drawing attention to my passing, and I imagined that fingers pointed and eyes stared, the minds directing them fully aware that I was bowing and scraping. Try as I might, I couldn't make a virtue out of necessity. I was ashamed.

Since our temple had no grounds, nosy peddlers were encamped on nearby roofs and in the foyers to sell fetishes. I entered the temple through a little-used portal that faced a rainwashed gully. Then I crept silently past the lightweight partitions, designed by Academe so that the walls wouldn't collapse on worshippers in the gallery during earthquakes. By the time I reached the lower, less public chambers, I knew I was being watched. I could hear the guardians' vestments rustle as they stepped out of a room before I stepped in, and I felt their presence behind me, closing in, urging me on. As I expected, I found Tarana in Flametender's altar room, where perpetual fires never consumed his stone-and-gem-studded altar. Academians knew that if the rocks were ever torn away, a gas pipe would be found somewhere in the rubble. But ancient artisans had concealed their ruse, and the pipe was still undiscovered, even after the installation of several new altars, each finer and more gem-studded than the last. Tarana forbade deep excavation. I think she liked to believe that the gas flowed out of the rocks themselves.

Tarana threw a measure of potassium nitrate into the fires, producing a flash of light and a cloud of black smoke. Then she turned to face me. I could see only the glow of her irides in the formless shadow of hooded vestments. Finally, my eyes compensated for the blinding flash and I saw her twisted smile and the contented sway of her black tail.

I pulled back my hood and my tail cocked proudly over my head. "I have come to repent," I said evenly, biting back the desire to add that my capitulation had been won only because she and Chel had stooped to murder. But there were established ceremonial forms and courtesies, and Tarana didn't tolerate improper or impious behavior. She was worse than Prince Chel's father.

The guardian looked past me and I heard vestments rustle and the soft padding of an acolyte's bare feet behind me. Tarana's lips curled up to reveal sharp white teeth, openly mocked me. Then the familiar calm washed over her features, and she said, "Follow me."

The caves beneath the temple were long, snaking out in many directions beneath the city and opening into huge chambers filled with stalactites and stalagmites. Despite the labyrinth-like confusion, they had seen centuries of use. There were chambers where natural ventilation did not stir the stagnant, unbreathable air, and there were crevasses bisecting some of the passages. I'd heard that recent earthquakes had opened a new crevase or widened one that had merely been a crack, but casual exploration had been discouraged by Tarana. Only children seemed disappointed that the once-public caves were denied to them. The rest of the community had all but given up dwelling in caves for more comfortable dwellings above the ground. As I followed Tarana, I realized that the rumor of a new shaft in the caves was true. We climbed down a rope ladder into a shaft, past an otherwise unnavigable overhanging lip, to a rubble-filled and irregularly floored chamber.

"What place is this?" I said, lifting my torch to see if the rubble hid the entrance to another passageway. It didn't.

"Did you expect a warm altar room for your contrition?"

That was only hope. More likely, I'd expected the public chamber, where the curious could gather to watch. I shrugged uneasily, then decided that since I knew the forms, I'd better get on with it. It even occurred to me to thank Tarana for keeping the ritual out of the public eye, but my tongue wouldn't cooperate. I assumed the proscribed posture, then waited for her to begin the opening chant.

"Give me your dream as a token that you are truly repentant," Tarana said, ignoring proper sequence.

The stones were cold and sharp beneath my knees, and grit clung to my limp tail. "I'd rather die," I whispered.

"A pyre of molten copper, and I'll have it out of your ashes," she said, equally low.

"I promise you that my dream will die the instant I draw my last breath. You will have nothing but pretty phosphorescence to look at in the copper slag." After years of evading her, I hoped she'd quickly realize I was telling the truth and stop bothering me about the dream. I wished she'd get on with the ritual.

She was silent for a moment, perhaps believing me. Then she pulled her robes close so that they would not brush against my ears as she walked by. Ordering a copper pyre was an appropriate penance for very grievous sins, but rather extreme for a repentant blasphemer. Fasting or flagellation, usually combined with exorcism and other forms of public humiliation, was more common. As I wondered which she would choose, I heard the sound of rope being pulled over stone. When I looked up, I was startled to find myself alone. The rope ladder was gone.

Petty games, I thought as I settled myself on a reasonably flat shelf of rock to await Tarana's return. But as my stick torch burned past the halfway mark, I began to fear that I'd been foolish to come to the temple alone. According to custom, we should be getting on with the sham of my penance or exorcism, whichever or both, if Tarana so chose.

Finally, a stick of time passed and the torch sputtered and went out, and I was in the absolute blackness that can happen only in a cave. I could feel my tail drooping before my eyes, but I couldn't see it. I strained to hear the rustling of vestments or footsteps coming from above, but there was only the distant sound of trickling water. I was so deep in the caverns that I couldn't even hear the temple drums. Then I wondered if they'd announced my presence. If they hadn't, Tarana would not be bound by temple formalities.

Eventually, I heard Tarana's voice drift into the abyss from above. "Are you ready to give me your dream?"

"No!" I shouted into the darkness.

Some time later her voice came to me again. "Can you smell the copper boiling, Heao?"

"If you really believed you could get the dream from my ashes, you would have murdered me, not Rellar," I said. But I was frightened. Each time I heard her voice, my heart pounded and my blood raced. Yet, each time I found the courage to say no.

The darkness was endless. Time became blurred. My milk-filled breasts ached and I was weak from hunger, so I knew I had been in the dungeon for a long time, but I didn't know how long . . . too long to believe that Baltsar had not inquired after me. Or, perhaps he did, and Tarana had lied and said that I'd not come. There was only Teon to tell anyone of my intention to come to the temple. Who would believe a slave? Baltsar might, but would he be brave enough to take issue with the temple on the word of a slave? I doubted it. He sneaked out of his own house because he was too cowardly to face me and throw me out.

Even the back of my mind believed that I had been stupid, or, at the very least, a fool for being too hasty not to plan the event that would put me in Tarana's power. I should have begged Baltsar to come with me, should have brought anyone who might be persuaded to come along—surely some of my peers in Academe. But, no, I was embarrassed enough. No doubt the back of my mind had secretly hoped to minimize my humiliation by keeping the incident as private as possible. The back of my brain confessed to that guilt and I groaned. But the sound of it was lost amid the echoes of all the groans that had preceded it.

Tarana must have continued coming to me, asking her question, but I was too weak to answer and too tired to care. I only wished I hadn't been so strong and healthy when I began the ordeal; then it would be over. I was quite resigned to accepting death as the consequence for foolishness, but I was wishful enough to dream that my deathbed weren't so hard and chilly. I became aware of a gradual shifting in position, as if going toward some end or purpose. Thoughts of death were pushed aside as I tried to understand where the puzzle would lead. I thought my eyes were open and I tried to close them against a steadily increasing light. But the light was not in the cave; it flooded from the back of my brain to the front, filling my consciousness with visionary brilliance. Thought process transported me into a world of gently rolling hills sprinkled with crystal. Roily silver clouds were dissolving on a mountain horizon, glowing like the lights of a million firesticks carried through the mist, and I felt a lifetime of satisfaction compressed into the time that it took my eyes to sweep over the fantastic landscape. Shadow people moved in the periphery of my vision, but I could not identify them; I wouldn't spare an instant of the vision to tear my eyes away from the brilliant landscape. I paid my cloaked companions little heed, then ventured forth, examining every golden twig I crushed beneath my boots, wandering farther and farther until I was quite alone, shadowless, yet casting great shadows on gold-flecked cliffs. I scaled the cliffs, eagerly climbing, as if the gods beckoned me from above. I ascended. I ascended into silver clouds and sailed breathlessly through light and air, following . . . no! I was not following—*pursuing* the gods themselves through the airglow of heaven and over the depths of hell. My heart pounded furiously as I tried to see and to define the vision, but the perspective reeled wildly, the faint haze of distance becoming mountains that dissolved into clouds. Rivers of black ice appeared, so close, and yet so far, and the heat of volcanic hearts spewed shimmering waves across my field of view, and, still, I pursued the gods.

Voices . . . shaking me. Would she never stop posing her question? "I'd rather die," I tried to say. The riddles of the dream were mine to solve.

"Drink! You foolish woman, drink! You've been reprieved!" It was indeed Tarana, and she was pressing a cup of warm broth to my lips. "Your life is charmed for certain," she said bitterly. "Drink!"

I think she cleaned me, too, before she allowed her acolytes to carry me to another chamber. I was given a bed of fresh moss and placed before a blazing fire, and food and drink were given to me every time I stirred.

A few nights later, when I was strong enough to walk without staggering, they dressed me in ceremonial veils and brought me to a public chamber. Everyone was there— Baltsar, Prince Chel, the King-conqueror, and my peers —and all of them were robed and looking very grave. Tarana entered and took an eternity to cross the room to her dais, where she finally made an announcement about my having fasted and something about her being satisfied with my good intentions. Now there remained the formal removal of the demon that possessed me and that was, hopefully, so weak from lack of food that it could be washed away easily. The front of my mind was too hazy to respond, but the back comprehended. I was saved. One of those persons standing in this chamber had interfered with Tarana on my behalf. I tried to determine which one it might be, but my eyes were playing tricks on me and all of them washed together. Perhaps the back of my mind did that to me, warning me to pay attention to the ritual going on around me; I was supposed to be a part of it.

The Divine Books allow for token washings—warm oils brushed over the fur. But they also allow for complete immersion . . . in cold, stinging water for stubborn demons. The water seeped through my undercoat and ravaged my skin. I gasped, and I nearly couldn't rise because the water made me so heavy. Finally, I came out of the tub, sputtering and crying out in agony. Fur was forced every wrong way and the air scraped like ice. Tarana stared, with her lips curled ever so slightly in a smile. I wanted to slash her eyes, but Neering, my peer in Academe, was before me, staring fixedly at a scroll from which she was reading:

" . . . and that humans have three fingers and an opposing thumb, and that four fingers and an opposing thumb are not human . . . and that humans have fur and tails, and that creatures having only patches of hair and no tails are not human . . . and that humankind's ears track distant sounds, and that their eyes see in darkness, and that any creature whose ears are immobile lumps of flesh and whose eyes cannot see except by the aid of a torch-light or twinight is not a human being." Without raising her eyes from the scroll, Neering then said, "Heao, will you swear to these facts?"

My mind reeled for a moment, trying to sort out events. I was still dripping, my flesh ached, and Tarana's grin mocked me. "Did this . . . definition of humanity origi-nate with Academe?"

Tarana's whiskers twitched.

My peer hesitated, then nodded, still not meeting my eyes, but her lips curled in a contemptuous snarl.

"Then I swear by it," I said, wondering how long they had worked on the endorsement, who coerced them to do it, and pitying my peers because they were afraid down to the last person.

I heard more than one audible sigh of relief, but I looked up too late to see who among my peers was wor-ried that I still might not repent.

"The demon is gone," Tarana said. She didn't sound the least bit happy despite the supposed triumph over evil.

Neering produced a huge towel from beneath her robes, smiling weakly and trying to hide her shame. For herself and our peers, I wondered, or for me alone?

Academians, guardians, and spectators filed out of the public chamber, leaving me alone in the silence to restore my fur. Since I was exhausted, the effort to peel off the sopping-wet veils and fluff my tail and soothe my ruff be-fore the dying fire took unduly long, but even I realized the loneliness was better than having to endure the mini-strations of an embarrassed friend or relative. When I was thoroughly dry, I donned fresh clothes, which had been left folded by the altar.

Prince Chel, Baltsar, and Teon stood outside the temple, waiting in a dismal but fresh-smelling rain.

"Heao, are you all right?" Baltsar said, stepping to my side and slipping one of my cloaks over my shoulders and squeezing me in a simultaneous movement, as if nothing had happened between us except a bit of separation. I turned my face from him.

"Of course she's all right," Chel snapped irritably. "A little weary, that's all," he added when I didn't bother to agree with him.

Teon, of course, was silent, standing quietly near

160

Baltsar, but his eyes nearly blazed with disgust for me. And Teon's eyes were the only ones I felt comfortable meeting, because they were the only honest ones near me. The weight of Baltsar's hand on my person was unbearable and I shrugged it off, stepping away at the same time.

"Come home," he said, but his voice sounded as if he spoke from afar. "At least for Sema's sake," he added when I gave him an impassive look.

"I have no milk," I said dully.

I would have kept walking, but Chel restrained me. He was too impatient to bother with amenities, let alone apologies, which wouldn't have occurred to him, anyway. "We have work to do, Heao," he said.

"What work?"

"The expedition."

There I was, still bedraggled by the temple ordeal, still dazed and just beginning to believe that I was really alive, and Chel would have me planning strategy to make the expedition a reality once again. But it was useless to be angry with Chel. He'd no doubt already forgiven himself for any anguish he might have caused me. "I'm too tired to talk of finances," I said.

"Finances? Oh, I forgot that you wouldn't know. We have financing for everything we need."

"We do?" In spite of myself, my ears perked up and my tail lifted.

"Yes. Baltsar has agreed to finance the expedition, so we need only to make our plans."

Slowly I turned to see my helper-in-life wearing a silly grin, shifting from one foot to the other, trying to look as if it were not extraordinary for him suddenly to become a principal in my dream.

"I've always been in the market for opportunities to expand my trade base," he said defensively.

I shook my head. "This one is too speculative for your taste."

He shrugged.

I felt certain that the agreement between my helper-in-life and my prince must be an interesting one. They'd never liked one another, their goals were always divergent, and their motives for the expedition would be different, too. I wondered how Baltsar had reconciled Chel's expectations of conquest with mercantilism. Then I decided that the two ideas might not really be that different.

"You will lead the expedition, won't you?" Baltsar asked hesitantly.

I sighed and nodded.

"You see how easy it was once you stopped that nonsense about slaves," Chel said, chiding and bitter over the delay I had caused.

"Oh, yes, yes, I see," I said. I saw Teon's eyes still sick with anger. I saw Chel's impatient eyes, ever darting through a sheen of lust that over the years had become a thin veil to hide his fears. I saw Baltsar's eyes, as love-filled as ever. But I had no pity for any of them, no understanding left, no reason to care. I pulled my hood over my head and walked off into the rain.

Chapter 21

I STAYED in Rellar's cave because it was out of the way, abandoned, and small, which suited my mood. His furnishings and supplies were gone, looted, I supposed, by beggars and thieves, and I could only hope that some academian had had the good sense to remove Rellar's inventions and collections and records before that happened. There were a few handfuls of food in the dirt-covered ice pit that the looters had overlooked, and there was enough coal dust and chips to build a small fire. I ate, and then there was nothing left to do but think.

I was allowed little time to brood. Baltsar and Chel found me by the next night, bringing with them a summons from the King-conqueror for an immediate audience with him. Wordlessly, I gathered my cape around me and stepped out onto the tiny ledge that lipped Rellar's cliffside cave. It was worn smooth by a lifetime of Rellar's footsteps and polished by eons of rain. Niches carved in the side of the ravine had been deepened only years ago to accommodate Manya's and Teofil's clumsy feet, and the indentations were glossy and darkened by oils left by the slaves' many touches. At the top of the cliff, I hurried across the rooftops. The two men followed, jewelry and swords clinking, their fine capes spilling rain away from crisp linen undergarments.

As he was wont to do from time to time, the King-conqueror received us in the antechamber of his nest. It was a cozy room with tiers of cushioned ledges so that occupants could settle themselves in whichever layer of air they preferred. I leaped for the highest, the warmest, where the cushions were scented with imported perfumes and where I had the advantage of seeing the entire chamber. Baltsar and Chel stayed in the cooler levels, rustling in layers of linen and spidersilk while the king finished talking to a chamberlad, who was stacking coal lumps in the fuel box, obviously flattered by his sovereign's attention.

The king hadn't worn the homespun and leather garb of a warrior for years, but he still dressed plainly, this time in a woolen shift and a black fringed sash. And he still retained the atmosphere of casualness in his court, with the notable exception of when Tarana or other high-ranking guardians were present. He had greeted us with his eyes when we came in, but to Chel's annoyance he continued his conversation with the boy. Ordinarily, Baltsar was extremely tolerant of the king's behavior, even though he tended to be more formal himself. But this time Baltsar seemed as impatient as Chel, and nervous, too. He kept looking at me from the corner of his eyes.

Finally, the king sent the boy away and turned his attention to us. "You are both looking well," he said to the men.

"Oh, yes, indeed . . . " Chel began.

"I assume," he said, cutting off Chel to speak to me, "that since you made it onto that ledge in fine form, no damage was done." Then he added, "Heao, you look awful!"

Though my garb might have been finer and my fur could have been smoother, I didn't think the king expected me to look radiant so soon after the temple ordeal. I thought that he was looking past my physical condition, but I didn't care to speak of the invisible damage; I couldn't have named it if I tried. "It was more . . . stringent than I anticipated," I said carefully.

He shook his head regretfully as he arose. "How are your plans for the expedition progressing?"

I shrugged helplessly, and Chel stepped from the sidelines to take over with an eager shake of his tail. "Everything is going very well. My best warriors are training with the new lightweight weapons." He drew his sword and handed it over to the king, hilt first. "The smith told me that you have not ordered one. I urge you to do so. As you can see, they are better than the old style."

"I have no need for swords," the king said, but he hefted Chel's and lunged experimentally. "Light," he commented. He bent the sword between his hands, testing the flex of the new alloy. "I wondered how long it would be before the weaponsmith began to use steel." He looked closely at the cutting edge, duly impressed by Chel's new sword. I'm sure he longed for one of his own, but disdaining the need for armaments had been his philosophy for many years. He was the king who was to be remembered as peacemaker. I couldn't help but see that he looked more comfortable with the sword in his hands than when he was unarmed. He handed the sword back to Chel reluctantly. "Be certain that your warriors only use their weapons defensively," he said.

Chel's practiced smile spread across his face. "Have I ever broken your sworn commands?"

"I don't know. Have you? The only battle news that reaches me is about hamlets full of farmers or tunnelers who mysteriously turn plows and picks into spears for the sole purpose of threatening my borders. The next thing I know is one of my warrior princes or princesses is overseeing the peace, taking a neat share of the mines or land for his or her trouble. I'm not a fool, Chel. You will remember that at least twice the true stories have unfolded, and the violators were punished."

Chel's intentions for the expedition were, at best, thinly disguised from the beginning, and Rellar had exposed him in Academe's conclave, if anyone cared to remember. Even so, he seemed chagrined that the king would allude to secret warfare. He demurred, muttering about his loyalty and having to protect the expedition from bandits and renegade slaves. The king listened, nodding occasionally, and when Chel finished he turned to Baltsar.

"You are the most unlikely financier for this expedition. What's in it for you?"

Baltsar was momentarily startled by the king's frankness. Indeed, even I was beginning to wonder why he summoned us. He seemed hostile, yet he could halt the expedition on a whim.

Baltsar's hands rose in an innocent gesture. "I am a

merchant. I have taken first rights to trade in exchange for financing this venture."

"Chel had to give you part of the spoils, eh?"

"Half of any *goods* we may find, as well as one of the two copies of the maps Heao will make of the path we take, will be mine," Baltsar said, nonplussed.

"A full partnership . . . in hell! That's what the guardians say you will find beyond the Evernight Mountains," the king said. His gaze turned from Baltsar to me. His eyes were as steady as his hand when it lifted the sword. "What do you say to that?"

I shrugged. "I may get my whiskers singed."

Everyone frowned at me.

"You are the only pathfinder that Chel would have on this expedition," the king said, strutting away from Baltsar.

I nodded. "I'm the best."

"Perhaps, but that's not why it must be you. You are the only one who is not secretly afraid to travel into unknown worlds. Could it be that what lies beyond the Evernights is not unknown to you?" His expression was sly.

"If you're asking if I have ever been there with my tribe, I have not."

"No, that's not what I meant. I speak of your dream. Perhaps the mystery of what lies beyond the Evernight Mountains has been revealed to you. Is that why you are unafraid?"

I didn't answer. He didn't expect one. He turned to pace before the fireplace, his ears back, listening to the back of his mind. Abruptly, he stopped. "Tarana will accompany the expedition," he said, casting his ears in my direction.

"As you wish," I said.

His scraggly tail shook with rage, and in a single bound he leaped to my cushion. "What's the matter with you? Why won't you fight with me?" he demanded.

I looked at him, not understanding.

"I said I'm ordering you to take Tarana along." He paused. Then he added, "Heao, do you understand what I'm saying?"

I nodded. The expedition was steeped in religious overtones—the skybridge, godsfire, perhaps even damned worlds. The guardians had been in a dreadful pother over Academe's speculations about the world for years.

166

What did the king expect me to say now that hadn't already been said?

"Are you going to agree to Tarana's accompanying you without any fuss?"

"Yes," I said. "I have no energy to waste on useless arguments."

"I've never seen you like this before," he said, picking up my chin and looking into my eyes like a concerned parent.

"She's tired, sire," Baltsar said from below.

"I can see that," he snapped, "but tiredness never stopped her from making a commotion before. I can't send her to change destiny while she's like this."

"Destiny?"

The king peered over the ledge and frowned at the two men. "I'll talk to Heao alone," he said curtly.

Chel and Baltsar moved slowly toward the tapestry-covered portal, reluctant to obey the implied command. For a moment I thought they would ask to be allowed to stay, but I think they noted the king's laid-back ears and the menacing sway of his tail, and they left silently. I stared at the tapestry until it settled, knowing that the king was waiting impatiently for my attention. I felt a perverse desire to sleep, and I put my chin in the crook of my elbow.

"Why can't you face me?" he said, dragging me up by the shoulders until we were nose to nose. "Did you finally give Tarana your dream?"

I tried to wiggle loose, but he dug in his claws and shook me, the narrow slits of his eyes angry and questing. "No," I said feebly.

The king sighed with relief and was immediately apologetic. His claws retracted as his grip on me gentled. "She said that you didn't, but when you behaved like a cripple, I thought she had lied. I couldn't imagine anything else that would sap your strength."

"I nearly died!" I said, suddenly feeling angry in spite of myself. "Chel and Baltsar pretend that my public chastisement was a natural turn of events that I should have expected and endured without resentment toward them, when either of them might have changed events if they'd only lent their prestige to my cause! And now you are dismissing everything except my precious dream. Doesn't anyone care about *me?*"

The king smiled. "Prince Chel's publicly denouncing Tarana as a liar when she denied that you were in the temple and Baltsar's barging into my nest during my first nap after my return to the tablelands to explain the situation to me and my intervening in temple affairs are three things I hardly call not caring."

"Each of you was concerned about your own selfish interests. Chel needs me for the expedition, Baltsar hoped I would come home, and you had to protect my dream. And you expect me to be grateful?" I shook my head. "None of you really cares how I feel."

The king finally released me, then leaped to the floor of the chamber to pace, the dilapidated plumes of his tail brushing against polished tiles. "Ulterior motives or not, you still should be grateful."

"Why should I be grateful that I was saved from wrongful death?"

"Tarana was within her rights to put you to death as the ultimate penance."

"But not to cast me into a dungeon and try to starve me into submitting to sharing my dream—that had nothing to do with the alleged sin. Do you know that she never even asked if I was repentant for having believed in slaves' human qualities? She aborted the entire ritual. I didn't know the exorcism was going to be performed until I stepped into the public chamber and saw everything set up for it. And I wasn't freed from sin or guilt by that ritual, either. I was punished for being a dreamer. It was a sham! And you permitted it!"

"I permitted her to save face, which cost you little since you have so damned much pride!" he shouted. "I need her . . . the entire kingdom needs her—and you have always known why. So stop this useless scolding for decisions I would not change if I could. Are you indignant because death nearly claimed you? Or is the true cause of your anger because, like a simpleton, you walked into the temple and endangered yourself just as surely as if you were a fawn racing to the slaughtering pen?" He stood in a shadow and all I could see was the glare from his eyes. "How could you be so stupid?" he demanded.

I cringed and tried to make myself inconspicuous, but even the depths of the cushions couldn't protect me from his awful accusations.

"Perhaps you have mind worms," he goaded. "Is that why you behaved so foolishly? Well?"

168

"No," I whispered.

"What was that? I didn't hear you."

"I have no excuse," I said more loudly.

"None? Really? You miscalculated? Heao, the brilliant academian, didn't think things through correctly? Do you mean to say that you made a simple mistake?" Slowly he stepped up the cushioned ledges until I could hear his breath in my ear. "Is that really it?" he said softly. "Making one stupid mistake has taken all the spark out of you?"

"Not by itself," I said miserably. "I'm heartsick because I believed in what I was doing. I still believe that slaves are intelligent beings."

The king made a warning glance at the portal and was about to protest, but I waved him off.

"Don't worry," I said. "I'm done with the issue. That's the last you'll hear of it from me. But doesn't it strike you as strange that Tarana did not use the proper rituals to deal with the matter? Only she and I, and now you, know that she put religious trappings on a scholarly declaration."

"Perhaps she hopes to leave you with unfavorable countenance before the gods," he said.

I shook my head. "Tarana is many things, but she takes her religious duties seriously. It merely proves that slaves are not a religious issue. She used . . . *mis*used her high office to lend support to certain popular beliefs about slaves, because it was politically advantageous. When it came right down to it, she used punitive and unsanctified rituals. How do you suppose I feel, knowing that I was right, after all? There are certain connections between slaves and my dream." I stopped and he looked at me expectantly, half-hoping and half-afraid that I would reveal some dream-essence in my excitement. "Well, suffice it to say that if I had not known my dream since before ever laying eyes on a slave, I might have thought I had been influenced by their legends and stories."

The king frowned. "Do you mean you've seen slaves . . . um . . . perform super-human feats?"

I smiled. "You've listened to slave tales, too?"

He seemed embarrassed. "Of course not. I don't even keep any in the stronghold. No, it's Tarana who has some vague notions about slaves becoming very powerful . . . perhaps a rebellion of some sort. It's a possibility that I guard against."

"And Tarana's behind it. I begin to see why she fought

me so hard," I said, musing. "She's trying to change the dreams by keeping slaves completely suppressed."

"We're always trying to change the dreams," he said seriously.

"Well, good luck," I said, flopping back against the wall. "You were right when you guessed that I was angry with myself for having lost control. I was too careless or too proud to consider all the alternatives before I went to the temple alone. By all rights, I should be dead; yet, I was rescued from my own folly."

The king chuckled under his breath. "One incident isn't proof of an inherent weakness."

"No, but I *was* rescued. Perhaps your timely return was preordained so that you could intervene, so that I would live to meet some other fate." I could feel my skin tighten and my ruff expanding even as I spoke. "I always believed that the dreams were speculations and projections of facts shaped by the back of the mind. I believed that it was the back of the mind's way of saying, 'Look, you have the potential to attain this goal. It's up to you to figure out the logical steps between where you are and where you want to be.' " I looked at the king, whose ruff was also expanding in fear. Talking of the dreams still made him nervous, even after many years. At least he had control over the pain that used to accompany his tension, thanks to the healer. "Every dreamer I met confirmed my theory, even you and Tarana. You are a warrior at heart, and the potential for a full-scale campaign against someone who threatens your realm is possible. I don't think it's unusual for a warrior to dream about a violent death."

"But it isn't merely violent, it's . . . unnatural. Fire from the sky . . ."

"Lightning," I said. "Your mind is complex enough to set you up between ungrounded lightning rods, or to conjure fantastic war machines."

"It isn't lightning," he said slowly.

"It doesn't matter," I said. "It symbolizes violent death, and that is enough. Trying to figure out every tiny facet of a dream will drive you crazy. It's the back of the mind's attempt to communicate a notion that won't be completely clear until the time is right. Tarana's dream is also symbolic. For all her apparent devotion to the gods, I believe that her faith in them is very fragile. She has single-handedly thwarted more academic investigations during my lifetime than all the guardians in the previous genera-

170

tions put together. The back of her mind is well aware that some scientific fact might one night shatter her faith; it naturally compels her to act defensively."

"Are you criticizing me for giving Tarana power?"

"That wasn't the point that I was trying to make," I said, "but it's no secret that all Academe feels hamstrung by her. We harnessed steam and know how to apply it in place of muscle power. We could replace many slaves with it. But Tarana isn't certain Flametender would approve, so projects are in limbo. We piped gas into our homes and for a while we were lighting and heating them cheaply. Then an earthquake destroyed the pipe connections and Tarana said Flametender and Terra were angry with us." I looked at him seriously. "We've had earthquakes in these mountains forever, and we will probably continue to have them forever. We had a contingency plan for shutting down the well in case of a quake, and it was implemented. Unfortunately, the pipe replacements were never completed because Tarana interpreted natural phenomena as the gods' wrath, so people didn't want gas pipes in their homes again."

"I didn't know."

"As with the so-called border-defense skirmishes, not everything reaches your ears in its true form. You are away for most of the year. If Academe told you everything that happened during your absences, we'd sound like tattletales and spoiled children. And, besides, it's Academe's policy to bend to the will of the community. In this last generation the community has become very religion-conscious. I don't think it's healthy for the balance between Academe and the temple to become heavily weighted on either side, and it wouldn't have if you had not let Tarana become de facto ruler during your absences."

The king drew up to his full height and the tip of his grizzled tail flicked. "Why do academians always digress?"

"We are chosen for our ability to see complete overviews, to pursue thoughts to their logical conclusions, to transmute ideas into reality, and to bring about changes. We are trained to discard one train of thought if another seems more productive."

"Well, I think you are all flighty and you need someone like Tarana to prick up your ears and keep your attention from wandering. Get back to the dreams. Is yours also a symbol of what you can achieve rather than a literal picture of the future?"

"Probably," I said. "In fact, one of the reasons that I am reluctant to discuss my dream in detail is because even I realize that what I have seen is too fantastic to really be true. The truth has probably been magnified or distorted by facets of my personality, perhaps even by cultural influences. Even so, the compulsion to discover the truth behind the symbols is overwhelming, and it is also a part of my personality—at least, that is what I thought. Now, I wonder . . ."

"You wonder if your destiny is, after all, fixed? You wonder if my intervention between you and death was more than a fortuitous coincidence?"

I nodded uneasily.

"I have lived with wondering if we were ever more than puppets, if our lives were purposeless since I first dreamed. After all these years, you've caught a glimpse of my fears. Wouldn't it be the ultimate irony to discover that in the end all the struggles and pain were in vain?"

The king sighed and his fingers rubbed the flesh beneath my ruff, comforting himself as much as me. I sat up to shake the tightness gripping my spine.

"I don't think we'll ever know, Heao," the king said sadly. "I once told you that I could end the suspense by drowning myself. I've considered it seriously, you know. I'm not afraid to die, and it would answer the question, once and for all. I haven't done it because I believe in myself, in my ability to rule, and because I haven't yet exhausted all the options open to me for changing fate, if it can be changed."

A comforting mind-set to keep his footsteps along the preordained path? I looked into his sage eyes and recognized the glint of courage and determination and the depth of sincerity. Even so . . . "I have to know," I whispered.

He shook his head. "Some things must be accepted on faith alone . . . unless you chose to deny your own dream."

"I can't."

"Then you'll have to accept the consequences, one of which is not knowing if you are your own mistress.

"Have you begun to see why Tarana's presence on the expedition is important?"

I nodded. "It's the only mercurial event to occur in years. It may change something, or put the dreams in a different perspective."

"Yes, but as you well know, Tarana resists change in spite of herself. I'm counting on you to be your usual forceful and willful self."

I smiled weakly. "A few moments ago you accused academians' flexibility as being a flighty trait. Suddenly it's a strength."

"That's a ruler's privilege," he said, wearing a tolerant frown. "Right now I'm wondering what I can do to restore your spirit so that you will be fit for the expedition."

"Don't worry," I said. "I am depressed right now, but what no one seems to understand is that I just need a little time to myself."

"Mmmm. I suppose, then, that it would be useless to suggest retiring to my nest with me."

"Quite," I said.

"How you have managed to elude me all these years is very mysterious," he said, tweaking my ear affectionately. "I ought to feel offended, or at least slighted, yet I am not. It merely leaves me puzzled about my relationship to you. One would think that, having known each other for so long, we would have defined the affinity we both know is there and have begun calling each other ever-friend, more-than-friend, or at least friend."

"It's never been a mystery to me," I said. "I always assumed that you avoided naming our friendship because you couldn't be certain of what role I played in your dream. I respected your hesitation, but in my heart I have always thought of you as more-than-friend."

"Thank you," he said, genuinely pleased. "Why don't you go now, before this desire to impose on our friendship completely overwhelms me?"

It might have been a hidden knife pressing against his woolen shift, but I think it was the shaft of something else. I left without further ado.

Chapter 22

MIST THAT had accumulated in the ravine during the stillness of night was being wafted away by a warm twinight breeze. Above me, the hazy image of a footbridge began to take form and I heard the distant leathery flap of a tardy bat making a rush for its cave. The twinight of the expedition had arrived.

Sashiem scooped the pile of snail shells into the flap of his sash. Then, noticing his brother's frown, he reluctantly handed over some of the shells to Drigal and me. Even though none was a pretty shell, I didn't refuse them. Booty from the night's hunt was the last thing I would share with the twins for a long while.

Drigal glanced up at the brightening airglow. "I think it's time to go, Heao."

I nodded happily. Anticipation for the expedition was already surging in my breast. Since I had given the twins permission to accompany the expedition until it turned off the causeway, Drigal was also excited. He smiled as he followed his brother, who had hurried ahead. I got to my feet and picked my way past a rotted tangle of grapevines. This ravine, the one below Rellar's cave, was too shallow to be warmed by the sea year-long, and someone had lost a sackful of valuable cuttings to the first frost by planting here. But decay of the thick, waxy leaves had provided excellent fodder for snails, which had provided a tasty feast for the twins and me.

"Race you, Heao!" Sashiem called, already making steady progress up the side of the ravine. Drigal was not far behind. I whooped a challenging response, leaped to the nearest ledge, and began climbing.

The nightly hunts with the twins and the other treks into nearby mountains paid off. I was in good condition again. My muscles responded without complaining and my lungs didn't begin to burn until I neared the rim of the ravine. I stopped for a while, panting and listening to the sounds of the boys' scrambling. When they were close by, I took a few final leaps and cleared the top, still well enough ahead of them to have made a clear victory. They came bounding over the edge, then collapsed at my feet, panting and laughing.

After they caught their breath, we walked to the temple, where the expedition members were gathering in the sheltered street. I was surprised to see that a number of friends and well-wishers had come to see us off. . .

Chel and Baltsar were checking the contents of the slaves' packs, working together as if they trusted one another. Chel's warriors stood a little to the side, packs at their feet, hands at their waists, or on the hilts of their swords, looking very brave as they said farewell to their loved ones. Tooled leather and well-waxed raincoats glistened when they moved. Even the slaves were well equipped. Baltsar had not spared the expense of also providing them with leather traveling clothes and sturdy boots. I saw Teon replacing supplies into his pack, which had been checked by the two citizens. His leather chaps were slick and dark from frequent use, but they were still thick enough to protect his legs from sharp volcanic rock. His boots were new, as was his rain slicker. I was glad to see him. Mapmaking would be easier with him along. But he was also in charge of Baltsar's household slaves, and I'd wondered, until I saw him with the others, if Baltsar would give him up for so long a time as the expedition would take. The slave took my footgear from his pack and approached me.

"Will you wear these now? Or will you wait until we leave the causeway to put them on?" The anger in Teon's eyes was gone, replaced with something I'd never seen before and couldn't identify.

"I'll put them on now," I said, not really caring, but wanting an excuse to look closely at him for a while

175

longer. We looked around, then walked to a place where I could sit while he worked. Teon's steps were quick, his back more erect than I remembered it, and when he kneeled to begin binding my feet, his hands were steady.

"You're looking well," Teon said after glancing around to see if any citizens were within earshot.

"I am now," I said. "Were you worried?"

He looked at me with guileless eyes. "Yes."

"Have you forgiven me?" I whispered, incredulous.

He chuckled under his breath. "Forgive is, perhaps, not the right word. Let's say that I have accepted what must be."

But acceptance wasn't the right description for the glint in Teon's eyes, and I wondered what inspired it.

Chel and Baltsar left the slaves and came to me.

"Hurry up with that," Baltsar said. "It's time for the blessings." His tail jerked toward the temple.

Baltsar was dressed in traveling clothes, too, and when his nervous gaze found the twins, I realized he was going to walk the causeway with us. The twins would be disappointed. Making the return trip to the city alone, but quite safely under the watchful eyes of the King-conqueror's patrols, had been the highlight of the journey for them.

"Where's Sema?" I asked.

"Neering is holding her," Baltsar replied. "I was hoping to see Mussa."

Chel gasped and his tail coiled around his neck. "She asked for the sea-watch . . . I granted her permission," he said, apparently just then realizing that his thoughtlessness would keep Mussa away from the city.

I shook my head and my tail twitched with disappointment. "Did she want to go on this expedition so badly that she couldn't bear to see it leave without her?"

"Worse than that, Heao," Baltsar said gravely. "The last time I saw her, I had the distinct impression that she felt you had cheated her out of an opportunity."

Chel couldn't control a laugh, and I glared at him until his expression sobered. "Well, you must admit that she's terribly naïve," he said.

"A condition we thought would improve in your service," I snapped.

Chel stiffened. "Are you implying that I have not done my duty by Mussa? Why, I did you a favor by taking her on. She wasn't exactly skilled in weaponry, you know."

"You've done me no favors in using my own child as a lever against me. And, even worse, you deceived Mussa while doing it. Chel, I've had a life full of your arrogance and your hurtful scheming."

"This is no way to begin the expedition," Chel said angrily.

"You should have thought of that before," I said.

"You said you would lead . . . "

"And I will," I said. "But I will never again help you save face or forgive you without your asking it." Teon was finished with my foot-bindings and I got to my feet, ignoring his ill-concealed effort not to grin. "I'm going to say farewell to Sema. You go receive your blessings. There's nothing in that temple for me." I turned on my heels and, carrying my tail as high as a flag, I went to find Sema and Neering.

The young academian was sitting on a stoop, dandling the infant. When she saw me, she handed Sema over, saying, "You must feel as if Academe has betrayed you along with everyone else."

The denial in Neering's words was provocative, but Sema stared at me, not really recognizing me with her eyes. Then her nose quivered and twitched, engaging me completely. I clutched her to my chest and she immediately began nuzzling, looking for my teat. "Sorry, little one," I said. I knew she'd either been weaned or Baltsar had found someone willing to wetnurse her, but I was a bit sad to think that she and I had been cheated from sharing that moment of her willingness to give up the breast. Still, she looked healthy and was full of friendly wiggles and happy shakes of her tail.

"The king ordered Academe to compromise to secure your release," Neering said.

I looked at her for the first time and saw the urgency in her face. "And you didn't want to argue until I was safe. Is that it?" The sarcasm in my voice was thinly veiled.

"Not exactly. We intimated that Academe might be very cooperative about providing a definition of humanity that was acceptable to the temple if Tarana were sent on the expedition."

I could imagine the healer, tenderly ministering to the king's taut muscles while planting a suggestion in such a fashion that the King-conqueror would believe, in the end, that the idea was his own. "And now you have a season to work on your fire engine without harassment," I said bitterly, wishing that for once someone besides Rellar or me would be left to deal with Tarana.

Neering's eyelids fluttered in embarrassment. "It need not be only one season," she said softly. "Expeditions are hard and dangerous. Some accident may befall Tarana."

My ears strained toward her, as if to hear the incredible words again. But Neering was silent under my gaze. My knees grew weak and I sank onto the stoop next to her. "Is Academe asking me to arrange . . . under the very nose of her patron, Chel?"

"He is the more experienced assassin, but we couldn't arrange enough profit to tempt him." Neering's eyes were very steady now, and I thought I saw flames in her irides, reflected, perhaps, from the fire engine in the back of her mind.

"Gods, you actually approached Chel, and he didn't report you to the king?"

"Innuendo is difficult to substantiate, Heao. By the same token, we believe that Chel will not interfere with . . . an accident, but we beg you to be cautious."

"Neering, I can't do this thing. I . . . I can't! It goes against every precept of Academe my master taught me."

"Rellar is dead," Neering said flatly, "and so much for martyrs. Change is a precept of Academe, too, and it is time to change."

It was the primary doctrine. Over the centuries Academe had changed the philosophy of humankind, transformed arts into sciences, but to change itself from knowledge-seekers to murders was to convert Academe's function from improving humankind to overseeing humankind. Having been disappointed in humankind's behavior since the beginning of the slavery issue, I wasn't able to dismiss the need for a good overseer like Academe, even if I were uncertain of the propriety of the means for bringing it about.

"What happened to the plan for academians to leave the tablelands?" I said wistfully. She didn't answer, and she didn't have to. Diluting Academe had never been a practical alternative.

Neering and I sat in the flickering torch light until the expedition members left the temple, shouldered their packs, and began to file off down the street toward the city gate. Tarana wasted a stolid stare on me while her acolytes fussed over her foot-bindings. Then she led them away, her pace decidedly slower than the people who had preceded her. Sashiem and Drigal left their sire's side to make their way to the front of the line. Baltsar, who was carrying a much larger pack than necessary for the trip the twins were planning, crossed the street to my side. I stared, realizing that his traveling clothes were new, too, as if he needed to be able to depend on them for quite some time. "Are you accompanying the twins, or me?" I said suddenly.

"I'm going on the expedition," he said quietly, as if it were commonplace. Then he turned to Neering. "I was counting on Mussa to look after Sema and the twins. Now, I'm not sure if . . . "

"I'll keep them with me," Neering said graciously.

"But, Neering," I protested, knowing that she planned to work on her fire engine and that projects were time-consuming. I was also just a bit wary about other sinister projects she might be involved in.

"It's all right," she said evenly.

"I don't consider myself bound to . . . to any decision in which I had no part," I said warningly.

She nodded. "Even so, you will know that your children are safe." She couldn't meet my eyes, and she was finally uncomfortable with the contents of the message Academe had sent her to deliver.

Baltsar hugged her in thanks, then chucked Sema under the chin and bussed her back with his tail. I made my good-byes equally brief. Then Baltsar and I trailed along behind the slaves, who were trusted to walk unsupervised until we left the causeway, well away from the city.

"Why are you going on the expedition?" I said huskily.

"There's obsidian in the Evernight Mountains."

"It has always been there."

"It's the only way I can think of to give myself time with you so that when the expedition is over you will come home again."

"It's easier to get a favor from Luck than to keep it," I said.

"Luck has nothing to do with it. I make my own opportunities."

"You're still betting against the odds," I said. "You're supposed to be my helper-in-life. You didn't help!"

He dropped back, momentarily stunned by my words. Then I heard him say, "I know you are a loving person, Heao. What I don't know is if you are also forgiving."

The set of my tail told Baltsar what a fool he was as I walked out from the street canopy and into a finely sifted rain. For the sake of the expedition, I'd spent a lot of time convincing myself that I could deal with Chel and Tarana in close quarters over a long period of time by plunging myself into the work at hand. I would use them for the expedition just as thoroughly as they had used me, and I wouldn't hide my contempt while doing it. If Baltsar wished to join them in the sand pit of my scorn, that was his business and none of mine.

Chapter 23

THE KING-CONQUEROR'S causeway bisected a huge glacial valley that had been piled with sheets of ice and snow when I was a child. Now it was covered with fields of cultivated moss. We walked in a steady drizzle that dribbled past flat gray stones and seeped between crushed rock piled high above the roadbed to assure safe and comfortable passage through the muddy sections of the fields. We passed mushroom grottoes, shepherds' hovels, and an overseer with a gang of slaves carrying sacks of rocks on their backs who were making their way across a section of the causeway that had been washed out by the torrential glacial runoff.

Far up-valley the glacier lay waiting for us, stretching from this valley to the black peaks in the Evernight Mountains. My plan called for us to travel on the mammoth river, which was not rushing, sparkling water, but ice. When airglow of twinight faded and refused to fill the air again, we would travel in the constant darkness of the formidable Evernights.

For now, we stayed on the causeway, even when it turned sharply and twisted through lateral moraine and led us to a series of narrow switchbacks cut into the valley walls to the top of the ridge. I wanted Teon to make a downward, cross-valley view of the glacier, and with his help I would sketch the signpost features to get us past the icefalls and crevasse fields in the steep, lower end of the glacier.

At the end of the switchbacks, the twins left us, barely taking time to bid Baltsar and me good-bye before they began plunge-stepping back down the slopes. The echoes of their shouts and laughter were with us for quite a while. Then we heard only the wind whistling past our ears. The expedition was finally on its own.

We followed the knifeback ridge until night; then we made camp. When I retired, I found Baltsar in my night canopy. I snarled and started to withdraw, but he grabbed my arm.

"Surely you don't object to saving some slave the unnecessary burden of carrying an extra canopy," he said.

I frowned and shook off his hand. "Let me know when you've finished napping," I said. "I'll be awaiting my turn by the cooking fire."

"Heao . . ."

But I flung the flap shut in his face with my tail and stamped off to the fire. I'd rather have shared a canopy with Tarana. She, at least, was celibate and would ignore the scent of my heat. I must admit, though, that I felt strange sitting by the campfire alone. I've always enjoyed the special spark that a woman in heat brings to any social gathering, even rugged ones like this or at remote construction sites, to which I was no stranger. But I had slighted Chel when he started the light-hearted banter over our meal; then his warriors were too put off to pick it up, and the meal wound up being a rather dismal affair. And now, sitting with my maps spread across my knees, with only the sound of rivulets of water dripping off the canopy and the occasional hissing in the fire to keep me company, I wondered who was suffering more from my wrath.

My people have always avoided glacier crossings because even a slight rain turns the snow-covered glacier into a sea of ice that few people can navigate. Our crew was no exception, and we wasted a twinight while everyone but Baltsar, Teon, and I, who were familiar with ice-and-snow traveling, practiced using crampons and ice axes. Tarana mastered the skills quickly, and, until we encountered our first hidden crevasse, we had a difficult time making her understand the need for safety precautions like walking in a line and far apart from one another. Thereafter, she dispersed her acolytes, lest their

182

weight send her crashing through a snowbridge, which might have suited Academe, but which, if nothing else, would reflect unfavorably on my skills and abilities and didn't suit me at all.

I had planned to lead, since I was the most experienced in recognizing crevasses, and, being the lightest weight, should I have the misfortune to fall into one of them, I'd be easiest to pull out. But as long as Baltsar was there, he and I took turns out in front, with Teon holding the belay rope for each of us. But it was I who fell into a hidden crevasse, and Baltsar helped Teon pull me up.

"There's something to be said about the caution that finally comes with age," Baltsar said, looking with approval at the silvery coils of rope as I stood shaking off the cold of the ice cavern. I remembered the other crevasse, the one Baltsar and Teon had saved me from so long ago, but I didn't give him the satisfaction of letting him know I remembered.

We proceeded. The others followed in our footsteps, unroped, except when we had to cross ice bridges. Then we took turns with the limited lengths of rope. Progress was necessarily slow, but it was too treacherous to be monotonous. The night camps continued to be dismal because I was still irascible. I didn't seem to have any control over my peevishness. Baltsar and Chel, for once, were glad for one another's company.

Once we got above the rain and into the cold, upper reaches, where the warm salt wind did not blow, snow fell in thick, clumpy flakes and the glacier's slope was less steep. Our passage was nearly like walking in any snow fields. We neared the Evernight Mountains in the span of only thirty twilights, more quickly than I remembered doing it with my tribe, which had preferred ranging alongside the glaciers in the mountains to dealing with the crevasses and ice falls. I was quite pleased with my causeway of ice and snow until we reached an impasse where hot lava had pierced the glacier, causing the ice to twist and wrench and split into gorges that even ropes could not span. We retreated, fighting our way over every tail-length of hills covered with granular snow until we reached the slopes of the offending volcano. Then we walked through moraines of hardened lava, uneasily watching the reflection of a magma-filled cone in the clouds above us. Even with our first live volcano behind us, total darkness loomed ahead, and anxiety struck everyone silent. Finally, Tarana called a halt.

The air was thin and cold and the snow was powdery. Walking over the sharp, windswept lava slopes had made short work of her boots which were fashioned from a too-soft leather. She held up the shredded leather for all to see. "I have another pair, of course," she said, "but they will last only as long as these did." It was a thinly veiled command to turn back.

Chel was nonplussed. "We have proper leather in the packs. One of the slaves will fashion you another pair."

Tarana looked at him so warily that I wondered if she had wind of what Academe had asked him to do. Or perhaps she was merely perplexed because he was not being solicitous of her, as he had been in the past.

"We can afford to take the time, Tarana," I said, forcing a gentleness into my voice that I did not feel. I was as eager to go ahead as she was to turn back, our supposedly intertwined dreams arousing divergent desires. "I'd have called a long rest tonight, in any case."

"I'd rather push on as soon as the boots are done," Chel said, but I shook my head.

"Our supply of meat can stand replenishing, if your warriors are quick enough to catch lizards."

Coming up behind Chel, Baltsar stared off to where the darkness of the Evernights was truncated by another volcano, but his mind easily filled in what his eyes could not see, and he shuddered. "There won't be anything to catch once we reach the darkness."

"Are you certain there is twinight on the other side?" Tarana said, looking balefully toward the way we would go and wistfully at the place we'd come from.

"That's what we've come to find out," I said. She frowned.

"Will we be out from under these clouds soon?" Chel asked, taking advantage of my marginal civility.

"I don't know," I said honestly. "We'll be traveling against the prevailing winds, and I hope their birthplace will bring us clear skies and an excellent view of the sky-bridge."

Tarana's acolytes were gathering around her, making ready to build the canopy right over her. I knew her to be a physically strong woman, but she'd insisted on having every comfort that could possibly be carried on a slave's back. The rest of us carried small packs filled with our personal gear, but Tarana's possessions had been distributed among her acolytes so that she could walk unburdened. She had displayed a decided lack of spirit for the expedition; however, until now, she had not actually dragged her heels.

"Well, since we must stop, let's make use of the time," Chel said to his warriors. "Leave your packs and we'll go hunting."

"That's what I said," I said, refusing to allow him any credit for my idea. But Chel merely seemed perplexed as he dropped his pack at my feet. His main attention was on his warriors, and he was gone with them before I could press the point.

"Perhaps you would consider going with me to look for obsidian," Baltsar said to me.

"Are you afraid to go alone?"

"Yes."

I resisted a scowl, but refusing meant staying in camp with Tarana, so I agreed. I led Baltsar upslope, where we would find places swept clean of snow.

"I don't really want to look for obsidian," Baltsar said before we'd gone very far.

"Well, I really do," I lied, pushing past the group of sheltering rocks he was eyeing. "And keep watch for lizards. It wouldn't hurt for us to add to the larder." He followed me for a while.

"You'll do anything to get out of talking to me, won't you?" Baltsar said bitterly as I hurried past yet another comfortable resting place.

"Yes," I said. "If we do talk again, it will be at my convenience. Just now I have the welfare of thirty people and twenty-five slaves to consider."

"It's heartening to hear that I'm so important to you that you feel I deserve your undivided attention . . . eventually. But I can't believe that I've not had it . . . to some degree, at some time, during this trek."

My ears folded against my head and I growled a warning. Baltsar dropped back to sit among the sheltered rocks, then deliberately scared a lizard I had spied by throwing a rock. Even though the creature was sluggish with cold, it reached the safety of a deep crack in the rock.

"You'll wish you paid more attention to the hunt when we run out of food," I said.

"Until now I've been a cooperative member of your

precious expedition, but, unless you come over here right now, I will harass you at every chance I get."

I nearly laughed because his threat was as empty as the one I'd made to Teon when I needed his attention. "Tarana has been behaving in a reasonable manner because she has seen Chel kill. She's useless to him now and therefore cautious. I should think that you'd be cautious, too, since he already has what he needs from you." I leaped off in hot pursuit of a lizard that wasn't really there, and as I moved, I wondered. Was I afraid to talk with Baltsar? *Oh, yes, indeed,* answered the back of my mind. But I cut myself off before I could hear things that would only distress me. It didn't work. *You love . . .* I fell over my own feet and wrenched my shoulder, which was a good way to keep my mind where I willed it. The pain was engrossing. I limped back to Baltsar. He saw the agony in my eyes and his features softened as he opened his arms to me.

I shook my head. "I hurt myself," I said.

But that just made him all the more tender and supportive, and it brought to his mind dozens upon dozens of other times in our life together when he had been strong when I needed him to be strong, and he recounted them, all the way back to the camp, and he continued to talk during the whole time he ministered to my shoulder. I resisted the temptation to be moved by his recital of love until he tucked me into a down-filled traveler's cocoon and he said, "You were never the kind of woman I wanted to share my life with, and I don't think I'm the perfect mate for you, either. But I'm trying to help where I can because, in spite of everything, I love you."

"And you want me to forgive you when you can't help?" I said bitterly.

"It's no more than I've always done for you. The only difference is that I've always known you were not given to the kind of helping I wanted from a woman, and you've just realized my shortcomings."

I turned to look at him and winced because my shoulder ached. Considering everything, we were an unlikely pair. Had we been thrown together by the gods so that Baltsar would be on hand to finance the expedition that would fulfill my dream? And if that were so, why wasn't I content to be rid of him, now that his resources had been put to the purpose the gods intended?

186

"I wish you had been a dreamer, Baltsar," I said. "Then you might understand what has happened to me."

"But I'm not," he said slowly, "and I may never understand."

I sighed, closed my eyes, and turned away. I knew he wouldn't leave the canopy, and I didn't have the heart to chase him out. I kept still as he pulled out his own cocoon and curled up next to me. His presence was comforting. If he were a part of a convoluted plot of the gods, it would have been simplest for them to allow him to grow disenchanted with me and for me to set him aside once he had done his part. This way, with the long haul of the expedition before me, I would continue to be troubled by Baltsar's presence. Baltsar was strong-willed and he wanted me to be bothered by our relationship, or lack of it. In that he had succeeded, not the gods. I smiled, feeling a bit more at ease with myself than I had since making a fool of myself at the temple.

Chapter 24

I WASN'T able to carry my pack when we were ready to move on again, so Teon added it to his load. When we finally reached the treacherous terrain in the Evernights, where everything was as black as pitch, only human eyes could spy the way. Some of Chel's warriors walked in the front of the line with me, but most brought up the rear to be certain that none of our slaves dropped out into the darkness.

The wind was true, which was a blessing when we couldn't see the glacier anymore. Volcanic rock is not stratified the way our coastal mountains are, and so the lay of the land did not help me keep track of our direction. I had to depend on the wind and the back of my mind's relentless calculations to compensate for updraft and other wayward currents. The others sensed my preoccupation and left me alone, even Baltsar, who continued to share my canopy in silence.

After endless camps in total darkness, we awoke to the sight of distant airglow. It was none too soon to find twinight again. This time our supplies were dangerously low. We moved our camp and hunted for several twinights before resuming our trek again.

Tarana was visibly relieved to have come through the Evernight Mountains, at least the first time, without having lost her way and being left to wander, as she had seen herself in her dream. But she didn't speak of her allayed fears. And I was disappointed that *no one* had the grace to mention that Academe had been right when we said the darkness didn't go on forever; nor did they even express relief that demons and monsters hadn't even threatened us, much less devoured us. But they expected too much; even though we had made it safely through the Evernight Mountains, rain clouds still covered the sky. They were becoming impatient for their first glimpse of the skybridge.

Finally:

"How much longer?" Chel said, glancing up at the thick clouds. Rain streamed off his waxed hood and the wet fur on his face was momentarily blanched by a flash of lightning.

We had been traveling through a boisterous storm for several twinights and the Evernight Mountains were far behind us. I tried to ignore the wet sop of batting in my boots as I said, "Patience, Chel."

"That's what you said the last time I asked."

I shrugged, and Chel scowled in disgust and dropped back to walk with Tarana, leaving me to lead the way down the muddy slope. Below us was a valley, thickly overgrown with the strange foliage we had been seeing for several twinights: lace-leafed trees whose branches twisted upward, as if reaching for the sky with weird arms instead of clutching the ground, as our conifers did at home.

Airglow dimmed and faded as we reached the valley floor, and I called a halt for the night. Drenched and tired slaves erected the rain canopies and started the cooking fire with charcoal from our small reserve.

"Why not turn back?" Chel said as we huddled near the sputtering fire for warmth.

"The rain," I said.

Even Baltsar looked up at me in surprise.

We had eaten and the slaves had retired to their canopy, leaving us humans alone. When I saw Chel and Tarana exchange puzzled glances, molten silver firelight reflecting in their eyes, I stood up to leave. Though I was only half dry, I was eager to depart before they finished examining my response. But Tarana stayed my departure with a single finger and a black frown.

"When we left the Evernight Mountains, we expected to be using the skybridge to navigate," Tarana said, fixing her narrow, accusing eyes on me. "The rain clouds are ever-present, as you can plainly see."

"This rain's worse than back home, and we don't have the sea or a familiar peak . . . not even that horrible glacier for reference," Chel said. They were reasonable words, but irritably spoken. "We haven't even glimpsed the skybridge since we left home."

Tarana's acolytes watched me through slit pupils, their irides like hot coals in the depths of their hoods; they were eager to see the expedition end. Their guardian's comfort was difficult to assure without the city's conveniences at hand. Chel's soldiers seemed less interested. If not pleased with the expedition, they were at least accustomed to hardship. But their prince was plainly disenchanted. We'd traveled too far for a practical campaign to follow our path, and the skybridge was still obscured.

Chel and Tarana were watching me, and, sighing, I sat down. "Even though we can't see the skybridge," I said, meeting Tarana's gaze, feeling Chel was beyond appealing to with any kind of reason, "I believe we've walked out from beneath it."

Tarana's eyes widened and she shivered. The acolytes shrank from my words. But Chel merely laughed and said, "Then we'd be walking in the embers of the godsfire. This land is no god's hearth." He pulled soggy blades of foliage from the ground, then tossed them into the fire, where they sputtered before burning. It was not like the moss and lichen ground cover of home, but it was not cinder and ash.

"You're right," I said, "unless, of course, the god's hearth is not on the ground, but up in the sky."

"Bah! You've spent too much time in slave quarters," Chel said.

I glared at him. "It's bad manners to speak of the *transgression* for which I suffered. It would be wiser to remember that I'm the only one who can lead us back to the tablelands and the only one who can lead us forward. We're going forward, to our goal, so stop sniveling and cooperate."

He looked stunned. Momentarily gratified, I continued in a more civil tone. "You think we'll never see godsfire, but I think we will."

Chel frowned at me. "At home the glow of godsfire always lies on the horizon, not up in the sky."

"So it would *seem* if the world were curved," I said.

"Locating godsfire is as much the mission of this expedition as determining if the skybridge could be used for navigation."

"Fire in the sky is a whim of Academe," Tarana said nervously. "The temple never sanctified that hypothesis."

"Tarana's right," Chel said. "If we had walked out from under the skybridge, godsfire would be overhead now." He pointed out at the black night sky. "Those are clouds, Heao, not smoke. So . . . "

"So why waste more time?" I said. "You can't prove the fire isn't in the sky simply because we haven't seen it there. It might be above the clouds."

"Oh, Heao," Chel said in his most disparaging tone.

"We must know where godsfire is before we can be certain of where it is not," I said hurriedly. "We've come so far. Why not go a little farther?"

"Our supplies . . . " Chel began.

"You see to replenishing them. I'll go on with Heao for a while," Baltsar offered. He shrugged, seemingly embarrassed. "Perhaps the rain will stop and we'll see the glow from the godsfire, just as we do at home."

"Rain is life," Tarana said, "and you would have it stop." She shook her head reprovingly.

"I've seen light bending around the skybridge. It does end, and if we're not out from underneath it, we must be close." Chel was shaking his head. "Why, Chel, I remember a time when you and I watched it together, speculating on whether Flametender's hearth was on some distant land or held upon the sea in a marvelous vessel. We wondered if kelp could be burned. We wondered how far Flametender ranged in his vessel. We wondered if he sailed around the skybridge or under it to the opposite side of the world during winter."

The rare sight that once captivated Chel only made him shrug indifferently now, but Tarana was instantly alert; speculating on the gods' activities was more improper for military princes than for Academe. "It fits so well," I said, directing my words to Tarana now. "The tales the slaves tell to their children describe a duskglow that heralds winter in these lands."

"Duskglow," Chel muttered. "If there is such a thing, we could see it as plainly as we see the spring dawnglow."

"Our view could be truncated by mountains, or even by

191

the skybridge itself. We seem so close to one edge, but the other is difficult to resolve."

Tarana was frowning at me. "The brains of animals are unreliable," she said, "subject to mass hallucinations. They cite supernatural mysteries to justify their incomplete memories because they have but one brain. Such creatures are different from other animals only in possessing the gift of speech. But speech alone doesn't make humankind, Heao. Remember that. It was your own Academe that defined the attributes and aspects of humans, and a person must possess each and every one to be considered human."

I was not prepared again to risk being shunned by suggesting slaves were human, but I could not fail to use the most convincing reasons for continuing. "It's time to end slaves' nonsense! If they saw something that they can't articulate, humans should discover what it is. Academe has scientific observations to support its speculation about the possible curvature of the world. It's coincidence that our reputation has lent credence to slaves' superstition. But if this expedition shatters the mysteries surrounding slaves and silences secular citizens who are confused by the apparent similarities of the two positions, we will have gained much."

Tarana grunted and leaned forward to whisper; the acolytes leaned to hear. "I've heard citizens say that Flametender *carries* his fire across the skybridge, depositing it on the opposite side for winter . . . to keep the heat away from us, I suppose, and to ensure heavy snow in the mountains." Tarana sneered, glancing at the slaves' canopy to see that they were all out of earshot, then continued. "Do they think he balances burning brands on his shoulders, or on his head?"

The insult was so subtle that stupid slaves might believe she'd joked at the god's expense. Or did she whisper because she did not wish to tarnish the fragile godhood of humankind in the eyes of slaves?

I smiled tolerantly. "Of course, if there is truly a movement of the fire from one quadrant of the skybridge to the other, there are far more reasonable explanations of how Flametender accomplished it than his carrying it," I said. Tarana could not hide her bewilderment, but it was Chel who voiced the next question.

"How else?"

I shrugged. "He might hurl it across heaven with his

godstrength, or perhaps he swings it in a basket tied to the end of a rope. I leave speculating the hows of the gods' activities where it rightfully belongs," I said. I nodded to Tarana, then bowed my head humbly to hide my irreverent grin.

Tarana straightened up and her acolytes leaned back. "Well, there's no time left for speculation. Prince Chel is needed at home for the realm's defense, and my place is at his side." She smiled at Chel, not recognizing that I, too, had obligations in the city. It was typical of the guardian's contempt for Academe, contempt for family loyalties, and even for physical love. But Tarana had never known those, so she would not acknowledge them. She was living evidence that we *can* be more blind than slaves in the night. The arrogance of ignorance, oh, how I despised it. I knew my longings for time to set things right between Baltsar and me were real. So couldn't the visions of slaves also be real, even if incomprehensible to us? Who has ever seen a god, anyway? I don't think Tarana would have wanted to even if she were capable.

Tarana looked into the campfire, staring unblinking until I couldn't see her pupil slits at all. "I will seek a vision to guide us." she said.

Two acolytes moved forward and removed her traveling garment while a third produced Tarana's ceremonial veil from the folds of his garment. I almost groaned aloud. With the acolytes so curiously prepared, I knew my arguments had been unheard. Tarana used my dissension to set the stage to make an irreversible decision about the direction the expedition would take the next twinlight. Chel probably plotted with her. She must have been pleased to learn he needed her again. I would have preferred that they simply dig in their heels and refuse to continue. But as it was, I had to watch the scrawny woman, poised unnaturally by the fire, for several sticks of time, breathlessly hoping beyond hope for a glimmer of truth from the flames. The acolytes chanted and tended the fire, throwing potions and lotions that caused great white flashes of light and thick black smoke to liven the monotony beneath the rain canopy. Baltsar, Chel, and I became restless, but we sat respectfully. I did, truly, admire Tarana's endurance. I shifted sleeping feet, legs, and buttocks a dozen times before she stirred from her trance.

She replaced her traveling garment and accepted a drink offered by her acolytes before she spoke. Then, still trance-like, or at least in her most serious manner, she said, "I saw the glow of spring."

My heart leaped with excitement.

"And the place from whence I saw it was the palisade overlooking the sea, near Prince Chel's stronghold."

Chel took advantage of Tarana's breathing pause to scramble to his feet. "We'll have to hurry in order to see the glow," he said, delighted. "I'll give my warriors their orders."

"Perhaps it's not *this* spring she saw," I said, looking around, wondering when the warriors had sneaked away. "Perhaps we have a whole year to explore." But Chel did not hear me, nor did Tarana.

Just like the King-conqueror, I've had cause to question the guardians' fire-visions; they become complicated and obscured in symbolism that is generally explained after the fact. But this one was so simple that it was beautiful. I had no doubt that Tarana would fulfill the vision, this season, exactly as she described. I'd probably see it, too, wondering if just one more twinight would have given me facts to know instead of leaving me with a shattered dream. Unlike the king, I did not have the prerogative to set aside a guardian's fire-vision.

Chapter 25

DOWNHEARTED, I left the camp and walked to a distant knoll, listening to the squeak of the wet foliage and the sucking sounds of mud pulling at my feet, getting wet all over again. I didn't seek shelter; I just let the rain drizzle over my hood and run down my face like slave tears. At the top of the knoll, I stood looking at the campfire light. Someone left to follow me, Prince Chel or Teon by the size of the silhouette. I turned away, not caring about that person, and I fixed my eyes on the dim and distant mountain ranges, which I would never cross. They were clay-gray, gray-spotted with iron-gray, and striated with charcoal, rain-shrouded. They should have been fringed with silver if, as I believed, godsfire were near. Was it possible I was wrong? Perhaps my wish for an orderly world caused me to envision a godsfire that swung back and forth over the skybridge like a pendulum. Perhaps I was not a true dreamer at all. I shook my head. I had difficulty picturing Flametender building a fire to cause dawnglow only once a year, signaling his stupid subjects that planting time was at hand. It's pure arrogance to assume a god would perform great physical labors to duplicate the blessings of other gods, and I, for all my willful ways, am not arrogant with the gods. Curious . . . oh, yes, very curious. I grieved to know I would spend the rest of my life without seeing godsfire, without knowing if Flametender's hearth were on the ground or in the sky.

I heard the foliage squeak against leather soles and felt someone standing at my elbow. Teon; Chel would have hailed me from the bottom of the hillock, demanding that I meet him halfway.

"Pathfinder," he said, "do you need me?" His voice was almost obliterated by the rain. He had retained a proper slave attitude under all circumstances during the expedition, but I was tuned to the low and gentle pitch of Teon's voice.

"No," I said. "I didn't come up here for mapmaking." I had little enthusiasm for cartography at that moment. Unless we saw godsfire with our own eyes, it was unlikely that anyone would ever follow my new maps. They led nowhere.

"I brought your utensils," Teon said, opening his rain-soaked poncho to show me the oilcloth packet of markers and parchment.

I looked at Teon's strange pupils, dilated into such large round circles that they all but effaced the gull-gray irides. Strange, too, because the irides did not reflect nightlight. Yet I could read those eyes as plainly as I could read Baltsar's. Teon was sad for me. I touched his shoulder, then took the packet from him. "My friend," I said. "Better to work than to brood." I seated myself as comfortably as I could on the wet foliage while Teon wordlessly converted his poncho into a tarp so the parchment would stay dry as I sketched. From time to time he'd look at the sketch, but he didn't suggest any details for me to add; the rain and dark put his superior distance vision to disadvantage.

When I finished, I rewrapped the utensils, handed them to Teon, and he slipped the poncho over his head. He extended his hand to help me up, but I refused, patting the ground beside me. "Sit here," I said. "I don't want to return to camp just now."

Teon glanced down the hill at the campsite. "It's all right," I said. "Chel's not concerned about slave security anymore."

He sat down. "The slaves say we're turning back at twinight."

I sighed. "It's true."

He shook his head with disappointment for me. "I believe the rains would have ended soon, that we would have seen the . . . the godsfire. This is not a land accustomed to

196

so much rain. It's only bad luck that it's falling during our journey."

"Or slaves' poor memories as to how frequently rain truly fell in the deep range," I said tartly.

Teon frowned impatiently. "Explain the difference in animal life—no frogs or toads or snails, and this abundant bladed foliage in place of moss and lichen. There are more trees than we've ever seen before. You've noticed it, too."

I was suddenly impatient with Teon. Could I have nothing my way this night? "It's not so different from the lowland plains," I said.

"You should have been a temple guardian, Pathfinder. You could take comfort in the dogma, never having to consider that the world may not be as you like it."

I bit off another slurring comment and sat silently for a while, trying to hold back renewed grief. Then I said, "I've failed to change the dogma, failed to make them even question it. The expedition is a failure, and I must accept it as mine. It's hard to do. It hurts, and I lash out when I'm pained. I'm sorry, Teon."

I felt his hand on my shoulder, comradely fashion. I moved closer to Teon because the warmth of his touch penetrated my wet clothing, and I needed comforting desperately. He held me, and he did not speak for a long time.

At home, my hearth dogs crowd close to me when I'm sad because they are bewildered and need reassurance. I no longer believed that when my slave touched me in a friendly fashion he was behaving similarly. I looked at Teon; his face was relaxed, yet thoughtful. There was no bewilderment in his expression. When he saw me regarding him, he frowned.

"My people say the skybridge is a ring around the world," he said. "We used to believe the ring's shadow was cast on a land of refuge where godsfire could not burn us. Our belief in the ring persists, but the stories change; this dark world is a place of bondage."

"Progress is a kind of bondage, too," I said, sharing his bitterness. "The more land my people till, the stronger grows our aristocracy and temple guardians. We need them to build bridges and causeways and to defend our city walls. I envy the simple nomadic life of my ancestors. If I were still a nomad, I would go on at twinight to see the godsfire, even if it took my whole life to find it." My longing for shattered dreams was very real. I did want to go on.

But Teon shook his head. "A nomad is guided by its belly, Pathfinder, not hypothesis." He paused, grinning wryly for a moment, then, suddenly serious, he said, "Two of the slave women are pregnant."

"Not the girls Chel's been bothering, I hope."

"It doesn't matter," he said. "Chel can't tell one from the other, and two are pregnant."

I doubted that Chel had begat any halflings on the girls. I'd heard rumors, but had never seen any myself. "I must be the only one who sleeps," I said, then sighed because I sounded foolish and lonely.

"Will you interfere in the disposition of the halflings' mothers?" Teon asked thoughtfully.

"If Chel were not involved, I'd try," I said. "But Tarana will side with him and my protests would be weightless. He won't suffer the embarrassment. He'll destroy the girls as soon as he notices they're pregnant."

Teon nodded. "We assumed as much . . . so perhaps it will be better if those women do not return with the expedition."

I looked at him in surprise. "How nice for the children, who will then not lose their lives. But the mothers will have a hard time of it. They're city girls, athletic and strong, to be sure, but . . ."

"I do not intend for them to be alone," he said quietly.

I put my head in my hands. "Oh," I said, finally understanding the glint he'd had in his eyes when the expedition began, and his perfect behavior during the entire trek. I guessed then that he'd followed me up the hillock to say farewell. "By law I should alert Baltsar and Chel." I'd mumbled through my fingers, but from the stir in his body, I knew he heard.

"A stronger bond in your heart will keep you silent," Teon said.

"Perhaps I have enough burdens for one night. Perhaps I don't want any more."

"Tonight you need to know I believe you've always been sincere in respecting my autonomy," Teon said quietly.

I felt a desperation inside. I could not say, Teon, have I been a kind mistress? I could not apologize for enslaving him and his people. All that was patronizing; Teon only wanted my respect. I would accept the burden. Teon knew that. And when my anguish passed, I realized we'd not said farewell. Such words were too painful for us. I stayed at his side, not wanting to return to camp, where the fire glowed senselessly cheerful.

Sometime during the night the rain stopped. From time to time I saw a slave arise to feed the fire, and sometimes I'd hear a night creature call. And too soon, it seemed to me, I saw the air was brightening and twinight was upon us.

"We'd best go back, Teon," I said reluctantly.

"A moment," he said. He was staring across the valley, seeing details in the distant mountains that my eyes could not perceive. Perhaps he was planning the best path to take with the two pregnant girls. I did not follow his gaze because I didn't want to be able to suggest a direction of pursuit to Chel. I dug my heels into the wet ground and hugged my knees. "Now," Teon said finally, adding quietly in final deference to the role he'd played all of his life, "if it suits you, Pathfinder Heao."

I nodded and we got up. I walked slowly, for the air-glow wasn't strong and Teon was having difficulty placing his feet. How sad it was that they could use only half their lives. Would Teon be able to hunt enough food for the three of them during twinights? Without benefit of city lamps and well-made torches, what would they do at night?

The camp was stirring. Slaves were packing feather-beds, cooking breakfasts, and holding washing bowls for Tarana, Chel, and Baltsar. It seemed more animated than usual. But why not? They were filled with the joyous anticipation of homecoming. They were not unfulfilled. Godsfire lay on the horizon at spring, where it always lay, always would lay. How comforting consistency was to them. How baffling to me that it would be there only a few months every year. How mysterious was its disappearance. My brain was as different from theirs as my eyes were different from slaves'.

I heard Teon gasp at my heels, and I turned to see if he'd harmed himself. "We are out from beneath the sky-bridge," he said.

I stopped. I wanted nothing more than for him to be correct. But I knew the world would be drastically different without the skybridge overhead, and it was not: no silver, no whitening of the flora.

"Look, Pathfinder, there—beyond the mountains."

I looked to where he pointed but saw only airglow, the lightening that marks twinight. In my heart I knew that dim glow was diffracted light from godsfire, bending over the rim of the skybridge, but I was alone in that belief. Airglow—the same airglow that always followed night.

"There's a rainbow," Teon whispered, "very faint, very dim."

"A what?"

"It's what we see when moisture is between slave and light source," he said. "The word doesn't translate into human tongue; 'various magnitudes' is inadequate."

"It doesn't translate because it's a mystical word that has no substance," I said automatically. But I frowned and stared off into the gray distance. "I see nothing but airglow," I said.

"The clouds behind the mountains are like blood," he said with great excitement.

"I can't see clouds behind the mountains," I said. "I can barely see the mountains' silhouette."

He looked at me, exasperated. "Poor creature," he said, and then he shook his head and smiled, so I was not nettled. I entered the camp.

"A good sign, Heao," Chel called from across the camp. "The rain has ended." He laughed, then waved his tail toward the sky to show that the world was still the same.

I shrugged, turned away from him, and found Baltsar's hand on my shoulder in sympathy. Teon went to prepare our breakfast, glancing over his shoulder at the mountains all the while. All the slaves were looking toward the mountains, furtively. Tarana, busily supervising her acolytes and overseeing her slaves' packs, did not notice. But Chel did. He looked at the mountains, studied the airglow for a moment, then snarled at the nearest slave. Shaking his head, Chel resumed his breakfast. I accepted the cold meal Teon offered me and began eating, too.

Suddenly Tarana cried out, in her full temple voice, "Godsfire!" Her arm stuck out from her robe, pointing to the sky.

Chel leaped to his feet, upsetting his plate, and I ran to his side, Baltsar and Teon following.

From between the clouds a rod of white-hot fire had been hurled and lay suspended in the valley air, impaling rocks with its shaft, brightening them with the magnitude of bendable iron. Fire, without question it was

200

fire, for the very air smoked where the fire passed through. Tarana and her acolytes huddled, and as they did the rod of fire widened. "Run!" she screamed. "Run! Flametender throws fire!" But none of us moved.

The mountains were scintillating, shimmering in the heat of godsfire, and it seemed they would be consumed. The fire stream was engulfing the valley, creeping toward us, spreading right and left. Chel looked at me, his face fearful and his oval pupils narrow slits. "Perhaps we should retreat," I said anxiously, knowing the warrior prince would be reluctant to make such a suggestion.

Teon spoke. "It's light, Pathfinder, not fire. Smell the air. The wind comes from the mountains, but it does not bear smoke." Teon's eyes glittered, and his round pupils were smaller than usual.

Chel snorted angrily. His hand was on his knife hilt, and for a moment I feared that because he could not slash at the swelling fires, he would slash at Teon. I motioned the slave away.

"It could just be light," Baltsar offered, but I wondered; this was not gentle fireplace illumination. Its brilliance was of a stronger magnitude than I'd ever seen, save in the white heat of a forge. This fire was so hot that the valley's wet foliage didn't prevent its spreading. Still, though there was a smoke-like haze, this fire did not consume.

Tarana was trembling. "We can't escape! The clouds are parting and it's falling out of the sky!" She looked askance at me, as if I'd summoned the fire.

"It is light," Chel said more hopefully than with conviction, and as he spoke, the light reached us.

When it touched our eyes we cringed and turned away, Baltsar's arms coming around me protectively. Tarana moaned and Chel cursed. I may have whimpered without knowing, for the light hurt my eyes. But, gradually, we became aware that we were not being seared by flames but bathed in a great light. When my eyes became accustomed to this new phenomenon, I glanced at my companions. Their pupil slits were thinner than I believed they could become.

"The light of godsfire," I said, breathing hard but relaxing a bit, "coming from the sky."

Chel nodded and Tarana frowned.

Our fear was replaced with awe, and we stood staring at the brilliant mountainscape. The clouds, even though distant, were resolved by the bright light, edged with silver as they pulled apart, letting more light fall onto the ground. The source, we could now see, was a fat ball climbing up out of the mountains. And, surprisingly, when it topped the peaks, it didn't tumble into the valley but slowly rose into the sky. Such a miraculous event renewed our fear, but by then we were too bewitched to do anything but watch—the white sky, the silver, lighted valley, the black and charcoal shadows of the mountains. Finally, we watched the last of the super-illuminated clouds blow away. And we saw the skybridge, arching from one horizon to the other. It was awesome now because we were not beneath it and we could see the rim, bright and crisp as the edge of a blade. In the distance, beneath the skybridge, we could see our homeland—dim, lackluster, forever separated from godsfire's absolute magnitude, cast in shadow by the skybridge. I felt gratification swelling inside. I nearly shouted with joy, for this was the light that filled my bright dream.

Tarana's quivering voice broke the spell. "I will seek a vision now," she said. As her acolytes moved shakily toward Chel's breakfast fire, Tarana stopped them. "I will use the godsfire."

She knelt and there was a moment's delay while an acolyte went to fetch Tarana's ceremonial veil. And that's when we realized the slaves were gone, all of them. Chel and his warriors scattered, heads high, searching the valley for sight or scent of them. Baltsar followed. I nearly smiled; I knew we'd been bewitched by the godsfire long enough for them to be well away. With their superior vision, they probably watched us, giggling behind their hands at the wise masters who were awed by light. All except Teon—I think he must have laughed out loud. I liked to think of Teon laughing.

Tarana's devotions were not long delayed by the slaves' disappearance. She donned her veil, outstretched her arms, and lifted her eyes to the godsfire. My admiration for her ability to sustain her trance-like pose increased. My eyes were comfortable only when I avoided looking at the light source, and, always one to prefer comfort to pain, I looked to the right or left of it, squinted or made a shadow over my face with my hood or hand. I thought Tarana's threshold of pain must be different from mine, but then I noticed muscles twitching in her nose. She seemed about to sneeze or blink when she finally gained control of all involuntary responses. She stared at the fireball, and stared. Her brow twitched and her ears laid flat on her skull. Many moments passed, and still she stared. Suddenly she collapsed, writhing in pain. "My eyes," she moaned. "My eyes."

The acolytes and I were at a loss as to what to do but comfort her. She struggled and groaned despite all our ministrations. I think she would have gouged out her eyes for their betrayal if we hadn't restrained her.

Chapter 26

THE FIREBALL moved through the sky, nearly perpendicular to the skybridge. At the apex of the skybridge, it did not skitter on the downhill, but moved as slowly and steadily as it had when it was traveling uphill. Baltsar and Chel returned when godsfire was near the horizon. The prince was an angry, frustrated man, and all were more exhausted than I have ever seen any people, gulping water in unbelievable quantities, wiping at body dirt of a kind they were unaccustomed to—specks of foliage and earth caked onto their fur by sweat. As I helped Baltsar remove the disgusting filth with a wet cloth, I felt his unnaturally hot flesh. Then I realized my own ears and hands were hot, yet I knew this heat was not from fever. "We've been burned," I said.

"Light doesn't burn," Chel said, rubbing his chest with handfuls of water.

I held out Baltsar's bowl of cleansing oil to him. "The tips of your ears are blistered, Chel. The light from the godsfire burns."

He touched the ears and felt the bumps. "This is demon's land," he said bitterly. He cursed the slaves. "We'll never find them. Without landmarks or maps, we don't dare range far beyond this valley."

I didn't remind him of the signpost in the sky. He would think of it soon enough himself. "Perhaps they'll come back when it's dark," I said. "You know how afraid they are of the dark."

Chel shrugged, not believing. "Can she travel?" he said, nodding at Tarana, who lay crumpled beneath her canopy.

"No," I said. "She's mad with pain. She thinks it's the damnation of her dreams."

Chel scowled as he glanced at the searing godsfire, which nearly lay on the horizon opposite from where we first saw it. "That's not in her dreams, and these are not the Evernight Mountains."

"Any place is ever night to her blind eyes," I said quietly.

As he realized what I said was true, he stiffened. "Whose dream are we trapped in?" Chel knew Tarana's dark dream from years as her patron. And from our childhood he was recalling glimmering moments, fragments I'd revealed to him of mine. "Without the slaves to far-see for us, are we doomed to wandering this forsaken range?" He was aghast.

"Fear not, my friend. I can lead you home again. My maps are true, and with them we have no need for slaves' eyes."

"Your dream, then?" The lesser of two evils, perhaps, but Chel snarled to think of it.

I shrugged. "She never was in mine. Mine lies before me."

Satisfied, Chel started toward the cooking fire, following the scent of a hearty broth the acolytes had been brewing. He hesitated, then turned to me. "I'm glad this vicious, blight-carrying light is not the light of your dreams, Heao."

"Oh, it's the same light, Chel, most assuredly the very same." He waited for me to say more, but I would not. Then he shrugged and went away.

He was not impressed with discovering godsfire; it was of no strategic use to him in our homeland. His ally of last night, her useful vision, was simply a burden now, a cause for delay. None of us would see the spring dawnglow at home this year if we did not begin our return journey with haste. Guiltily, I realized that Tarana's misfortune was my blessing. I could study and record the phenomenon of the godsfire during Tarana's recuperation, which would be longer than my companions would willingly have allowed.

That night, while we ate, godsfire finished its trek across the sky. I was uncertain if the world rose to greet it, or if it had a nesting place in the distant mountains. I only know I felt light-headed while watching it. Splendid. The valley dimmed to a familiar darkness, but not to the black of night in our homeland. The level of illumination was closer to the diffused airglow of twinight. The skybridge was brilliant with silver, only partially lighted, but its arch was complete. I longed for Teon's eyes to add detail to the sketch I was hastily making; my dinner was forgotten.

"You were right, Heao. Godsfire is in the sky. Flame-tender banks it now," Baltsar said. "There are sparks in the sky resulting from his poker."

When I looked away from the skybridge to where Baltsar pointed, I started. The sky was filled with embers and it seemed as if they would shower down on us, but they did not. I exhaled a sigh and heard Baltsar's laugh.

"Just sparks," he said comfortingly.

"Or window lights from heaven itself," I said.

Chel stared skyward, pondering the tiny lights for a moment. "Or more godsfires," he said, "very distant ones." Then he laughed nervously, as he often did at serious speculation.

I wondered. More godsfires?

"Your half of the expedition is successful, Heao. Academe will praise you . . . though I don't think the temple will have kind interpretations."

Chel, shortsighted Chel, was not thinking in terms of new lands for our people, not considering that orientation in this part of the world would be easier than his wildest dreams of using the skybridge in our shadowed, rain-shrouded world. But I did not say this to Chel, for even if he is shortsighted, his mind is quick, and I was worried about Teon. Baltsar gave me a stolid look and I know that he, too, was deliberately keeping quiet. I smiled in gratitude.

For several nights, Chel and his soldiers searched for the slaves, sleeping in the shadow of rain tarps during the blistering lighttime. I refused to waste the god's brilliant illumination, and I wandered through the valley and in nearby canyons, marveling at the fresh detail of a well-lighted world. I tracked the fireball through the sky, being careful not to look directly at it, noting its position every time it rose and set. Those places were always identical, as if it were stationary and the world rotated beneath it.

In my wanderings, I arranged my hood so that my ears were shaded. I suffered no burns, but at times lighttime was filled with oppressive heat. One of those times, I retreated into a shady canyon where a fast stream ran, cascading over smooth rocks and sending a fine, cool mist into the air. I sat in the comforting dampness, listening to the sound of splashing water, and, when I closed my eyes, I dreamed of my own rainswept home. I saw the king's eyes widen with amazement when he saw the sketches I'd drawn of the skybridge from this new angle, shaded with painstaking strokes to illustrate the brilliance of the light it reflected at night. Then I pictured myself with Baltsar, at ease, and . . .

"Heao." Not the deep voice of my helper.

"Teon!" The stream's noise had muffled the sounds of his approach. My eyes flew open, alarmed, yet anticipating. Grinning, Teon squatted next to me. The hairs on his arms and legs were lighter than usual, and his skin was dark and ragged. "You're burned," I said, touching the wounds.

"No," he said. "The burns toughen the skin and then it only becomes . . ." He shrugged. "It doesn't translate . . . darker. There is no pain."

"Why did you come back, Teon?"

"To see you smile, Heao. The skybridge is there." His thumb jutted to his left, but we could not see the arch because the high canyon wall foreshortened our view. "And the sun, the godsfire, is there." His other thumb jutted to the right, but we could not see godsfire because we were in shadow.

I smiled. "But for Tarana's misfortune, I'd not have had time to study these wondrous sights."

Teon's brows raised. "Tarana?"

I told him. He was not much perturbed by the news.

"Heao, are you not troubled by the bright light?"

"Not unduly," I said. "Actually, I rather like it." For a moment I couldn't tell if my revelation disturbed him or pleased him.

"Well, then," he said finally, "since you can indeed dwell in the real world, stay. This is a plentiful land where a bit of knowledge could turn simple gatherers into farmers."

"You have the knowledge, Teon."

"Together we could do more, and you could see the

cloudless sky every *day*." He used the slave word for
twinight, and I sensed that it was right.

Once I'd asked for nothing more than to see the skybridge, edge on, and to know if godsfire lay upon the
ground or was suspended in the sky. Having seen, I was
still unfulfilled, my dreams incomplete. Godsfire climbed
out of the mountains every dawn and nestled elsewhere
every dusk. How did it travel during the night, or did the
world move? When winter approached, would it disappear, just as it did in my homeland? Would it fall from the
sky? I saw no pendulum, no stem, no rope. Would I see
Flametender himself come to attend it if I stayed? But I
shook my head. "I can't stay, Teon. The others need me."

"They might not make it back if you stay."

I thought it was a question. "Yes, and I have affairs to
tend at home." I squeezed Teon's hand. "And there is my
helper to think of."

"You love him," Teon said. Then he stood up and our
hands no longer touched. Did he still misunderstand our
friendship? His face seemed pained. "I think you will be
back, Heao," he said. "Your eyes can see here in the real
world as well as mine. The maps no longer lead to nowhere."

I nodded, knowing it was true.

Teon drew up to his full imposing height; his jaw was
tight and his hands fisted. "Your people will come, too."

"Teon," I said, "did you come here to learn if we were
sufficiently intimidated by the light to stay away? Do you
think Chel will return here with an army?"

I could tell by his eyes that I'd spoken his mind, and I
knew in the back of my mind that he was right. Once the
expedition returned to show my people the way, they
would . . .

Suddenly I was frightened. I felt Teon's presence behind
me and didn't know when he had moved from my side. He
could kill me with those big hands, and my companions
could be picked off one by one. My people would never
come to the lighted world if the expedition did not return
to show them the way. My ruff was swelling as I turned,
but Teon grabbed me like a naughty child, his huge fingers
seizing my scruff and tail, keeping completely out of reach
of my claws and teeth. My kicking feet uselessly struck
air. I cried out.

"Stop, it, Heao! Stop struggling!"

Anguished because my struggling was useless, I waited

for the final blow. His fingers dug into my flesh. "I should kill you, you know," he said. Then the ground was beneath my feet, my tail free from his grasp, and I twisted to look into his eyes. There was no malice there. Was there ever? Had I seen fear or anger just a moment ago? Then his eyes hardened again. Disgusted, he threw me aside.

I scrambled, but didn't flee. He stood, looking at me.

"If you're going to come back, then you'd better see what you're coming back to," he said bitterly. "I have found your gods."

"What do you mean?" I said, smoothing the fur on the back of my neck with my hand.

"Gods," he said. "They can be nothing else. They fly and they eat rocks." Then he smiled sardonically. "But you're in for a surprise, Heao. The gods look like me."

Chapter 27

TEON WOULDN'T allow me to return to camp, even though I promised to tell only Baltsar that I was going on an excursion. I knew he and Chel would be worried when I didn't return by night, but there seemed no help for it. I couldn't resist my desire to see gods, and perhaps heaven itself. And I couldn't help remembering the slaves' tales and stories of their ancestors who had godlike powers. My curiosity had to be satisfied.

Teon led me over a high and rugged pass, deeper into the lighted world than I had ventured before. When he pressed on past nightfall, I knew why Chel's patrols never found a trace of the slaves. They had scaled the worst-looking mountain, then foraged along the edge of a raging river when they reached the other side of the pass. By night, the way was partially lighted by the eerie reflection off the skybridge, but even under the best of circumstances, Chel, through ignorance, would have judged the way to be too hazardous for brittle-boned slaves. And Baltsar, who was always one to minimize risks, probably would have agreed. Teon laughed when I commented on the difficulty of our trek.

"Have you forgotten the walls of the fjord that I climbed with you and Baltsar? My people may be slower than *cats*, but we are not clumsy."

"Not when you don't want to be," I muttered, wondering how many times the expedition had circumnavigated steep terrain because Baltsar and Chel feared losing the slaves if we climbed. And climb we did, after a full sleep for myself and a partial one for Teon, out of a vertical river canyon onto a forested plateau.

I had considered the foliage in the valley to be dense. Certainly it was more dense than any I had encountered in my life. But on the plateau the trees were taller than several tails and their branches were so broad they formed interlocking umbrellas. The earth was covered with an acrid-smelling layer of rotting vegetation through which very little grew, making passage in the forest very easy. Occasionally, we'd encounter an opening in the trees filled with tangled undergrowth, which we detoured. Soon I was hearing thunder-like noises, and though clouds were gathering in the bright sky, I knew the sounds were not thunder. Teon noticed my ears perking.

"It's them," he said. "They make trees fall." He glanced at one of the trees, with its trunk thicker than a slave's shoulders, and he shuddered.

"Let's go on," I said, trying to stop the back of my mind from wondering how to fell trees the size of these without getting killed in the process.

Teon nodded and started walking again, but his steps were more slowly paced than before, and his nervous eyes sent out darting glances through the forest gloom.

Without warning, a screaming god skimmed the treetops. The shock of its passing knocked us to our knees. Despite the ghastly noise, I looked up to see a metallic flash and a trail of vapor before it disappeared. Shaken, I got to my feet. Teon was staring at me through wide and frightened eyes, waiting for my reaction. I smoothed my ruff and raised my tail from between my legs. "It was . . . wonderful," I said, hoping that my voice would not betray me. My curiosity was overwhelming, but if Teon were too frightened to continue, I knew that I would stop, too.

He breathed deeply. "It didn't seem to notice us."

I shrugged. "Perhaps we're insignificant." I liked the concept of being anonymous to the gods. It fit my lifelong precepts.

"How many spiders have we stepped on during our lives without noticing?" Teon said. But, with head raised and fist clenched, he stepped off into the trees.

Finally, Teon deemed that we were as close to the gods as he had come before. He hoisted himself into the lower branches of a tree, then climbed from limb to limb. I used the clumpy bark as handholds and footholds, and I wrapped my tail around branches for additional balance. We raised ourselves to a vantage point. Teon didn't have to point. I could see the gods quite clearly.

A swath of land was devoid of trees; I knew that it was not a natural clearing. Uprooted trees and boulders were heaped so high along one side of the clearing that they formed a towering blockade. Nestling on the flat, raw earth were huge metallic blisters and cubes that gleamed, even though the light of godsfire was now dimmed by clouds. For a moment I wondered if the metal things were the gods themselves, for even at a distance they were wonderful to behold. Then I noticed tiny shadowy figures in the clearing.

"You see?" Teon whispered. "They are straight-spined and tailless."

I shook my head. "We're not close enough," I said, squinting. "But sometimes I hear . . . " I stopped talking and strained to hear what I believed was shouting between the great groaning and thunderous clangor. The clearing sounded worse than if the blacksmith were working in the miller's shop. Some of the geometric-shaped metal things were attacking the trees, heaving and hoisting. "The gods are noisy," I said. "They do a lot of shouting." Occasionally a sound, a part of a word, seemed familiar.

Teon cupped his hand to his ear. "I can't hear anything except falling trees."

"Let's go closer," I said.

Teon gave me a wild-eyed look, which could have been fear or surprise, but he followed me to the ground. We darted from tree to tree, cutting down the distance between the gods and ourselves.

At the edge of the clearing, we hid behind some underbrush and spied on the gods. They did indeed look like Teon, and their clothes were uniform. It was difficult to distinguish one from the other except by the darkness or lightness of their hair. They numbered only two or four, depending on whether or not I counted the same ones twice.

Then we heard screaming from the sky and we scrambled beneath the bushes, and not a moment too soon. The strident-voiced god-thing fell slowly through the air, its breath rattling the foliage and filling our mouths with grit. With a whine, it settled on the ground before us and qui-

212

eted. When I looked up I stared into flat eyes as big as shields, and I was certain we'd been discovered. But the god-thing didn't move against us. Its belly split and two gods leaped out. They didn't move against us, either. They stood, one leaning against the god-thing, the other with hands on hips, talking to each other.

" . . . just can't depend on the beacon anymore or you'll be off target."

"I spent the whole week tearing up the wrong damned section. Why the hell didn't that old crone have the beacon fixed?"

"It was earthquake damage. We can't get a replacement until the atmospherics clear up. Meanwhile, you'll just have to work harder. Don't try to use the beacon with your rangefinder, and forget you even have a compass. This isn't Earth. . . . The compass doesn't work."

I looked at Teon as the exchange continued. His eyes were wide. "They're speaking slave tongue," he whispered, amazed.

It was, indeed, the slaves' language, and though they spoke it badly and with horrible accents, we both could understand. I dared to move enough to push some leaves away from my eyes so I could see them more clearly. One began binding the god-thing to stakes in the ground with slender lines while the other looked on. Suddenly their voices were furtive.

Teon peeked through the place I'd cleared to see what they were doing. Then he ducked down quickly. "They've seen us. They're coming this way."

He was ready to run, but I knew that by the time we crawled out of the underbrush, they'd be upon us. I was probably more nimble than they, and I considered finding safety in a tree. Then I remembered the uprooted trees on the far side of the clearing; but I discarded that hasty plan. As Teon moved to flee, I touched his shoulder. "Be calm," I said as much to myself as to him. "I don't believe they are gods at all." Teon swallowed back his fear, and as I straightened up through the foliage, he did also.

I hoped to impress them with my boldness. If they were gods—I couldn't completely dismiss that possibility —they might admire my courage. Gods are said to be impressed by pluck.

The pair halted and stared. Both had dark hair, cropped close to their heads like caps. They wore smartly tailored gull-gray garments and glittering boots. I

213

searched for a difference in their apparel, found none, and surprised myself to discover that I depended on outward show to set one apart from the other, even if only initially. Finally, I realized that despite both having hairless faces, only one was female.

"What the hell . . . ?" she said, backing off a step.

"I don't know." The male's voice was calm and low. "What's that he has with him?"

"Strangest goddamned cat I ever saw." And as the male took a step toward us, she added, "Careful, Sergi. It looks wicked."

He edged closer, anyway. He certainly did not seem annoyed by us, as a god might have been. His expression was definitely one of curiosity. "Maybe they came out of Shadowland," he said to the female softly, perhaps for our benefit.

I smiled at him. His description of my homeland was accurate, coming from one who lived in the light of godsfire. I fancied him to be a quick thinker, perhaps, therefore, a leader, too, so I directed my response to him. "Yes, we came from the mountains that lie in the skybridge's shadow."

"It talks!" the female said, stepping back warily. "Sergi, watch out for its teeth!"

The male ignored her outburst. "Who are you, fellow?"

The female interjected something in rapid, frantic tones that sounded as if she'd accuse me of having fleas or asked Teon if he had collided with the mountains while making a loud noise.

"Huh?" said Teon, completely bewildered.

The male continued to edge closer while Teon and I tried to move back, but we were prevented from doing so by the bushes. The male stopped and stretched out his empty hands in what I hoped was a gesture of peace.

"Where do you come from?" he asked slowly. "Where do you live? How did you get here?"

Teon smiled then. "Shadowland. In a cave near the sea. I walked."

"You walked from the Shadow Sea?" He sounded impressed. I squeezed Teon's hand to give him confidence. He nodded. "Come on out," the male said, still speaking slowly. "We won't hurt you."

Teon drew back when the male extended his hand, and he looked at me. I shook my tail bravely, indicating

214

that we should go forth. Together we extracted ourselves from the bushes as gracefully as we could. Then we were standing right next to the male. He smelled as sweet as honey, and his gray eyes were as steady as Teon's. The female stayed back, seemingly aloof, which was fine with me; I didn't like her smell, which was like smoke from sour moss or a cowering slave. As we stood regarding one another, it began to rain.

"I'm Sergi, and I want to help you," the male said, wiping the first raindrops off his nose.

Gods simply do not offer to serve, and I relaxed, finally certain that he and his companion must be mortals. "I am Heao, the pathfinder," I said.

Sergi's gaze traveled from Teon to me. "You must be a hell of a guide."

I wondered if he thought we were from the spirit world, and while I hesitated before replying, his attention returned to Teon. "What a journey you must have had. There's nothing left of you except skin and bone. But don't worry, you're safe now. We have food. We'll get you back to the settlement."

The female joined us then, her hands shoved into slits in her garment, head bent against the increasing rain. She gave me wide berth while her eyes appraised Teon approvingly. "What's your name?"

"Teon."

"Well, Leon," she said, pronouncing his name in the inimitable slave fashion, "I think I have the best kitchen in the camp. The chummery can't offer much more than soup, and Sergi's rig doesn't have a kitchen, so why don't you . . . " I recognized some of the rest of the words she used, but they seemed out of context. And I didn't miss her loathing glance at me. "Come on, Leon," she said. Too cloying. Teon froze.

"We're very curious about both of you," Sergi said, gently interposing himself between the female and us. "We have food and shelter. We can talk comfortably." He gestured to the metal things in the clearing. Dwellings? My mind reeled.

Water was running down his brow and cheeks and his hair was already plastered against his skull. He glanced toward the clearing again, but he did not urge us as the female had done.

"Do you suppose they mean to harm us?" Teon said in human tongue.

"What did you say?" the female said, frowning and stamping water off her feet. When she looked up at Teon, she smiled.

"We have come in peace," I said, having to speak louder than the overwhelming rain sounds.

Sergi nodded. "That was understood, sir." This time he looked longingly at the silver structures. "The rigs are warm and dry. The others are already inside."

"Are those your dwellings?" I said, following his gaze.

"Temporarily," he said. "They're jerry buildings—construction shacks."

"It looks as if you're dismantling the forest," I said, wondering.

"We need a clear space in order to build permanent dwellings."

"So much space?"

He gave me a patronizing smile while nodding. "The energy plant and some industry will occupy most of this site. Adriana is . . . will clear another site a few kilometers from here with the aerologger." He nodded casually at the flying thing. "The other site's to be farmland for refugees from the coast. The ocean has risen and driven them from their ancestral land-grants."

I glanced at Teon. "Kilometers?"

"Distance measurement," he said. "About a stick's walk on level ground, I believe." He put his hands on his hips, then wiped rain from his brow, better to see the silver machine behind the strangers. "Is that flying demon merely a tool?" A wry smile was wrinkling the corners of his lips.

I stood silently for a while, pondering the problem of invisible leverage that allowed the magnificent aerologger to uproot trees. Now that I knew what I was looking for, I saw grapplers suspended on weak-looking chains hanging from the underside. The tensile strength had to exceed wrist-thick braided wires that we used on our bridges at home. The magnitude of the project was nearly incomprehensible. I swallowed with some difficulty.

"Leon, how old were you when you were lost in Shadowland?" Sergi said suspiciously.

"I've never been lost," Teon said indignantly. "I can read Heao's maps as well as anyone, and I've a good memory for landmarks."

"You've lived in Shadowland all your life?" Adriana said, incredulous.

"Yes."

"But there's nothing there! No plants, no animals. No one could possibly . . . "

Sergi was waving off her protests. "No wonder you hesitated, Leon. Don't be afraid of all this. We're your people. We won't harm you." He smiled and his eyes looked sincere. His empty hands gestured, as if to remind us that he was weaponless.

Teon glanced nervously at the aerologger and Sergi followed his gaze. "It won't move without . . . Didn't your parents tell you about construction equipment? Any machines? The city?"

Teon didn't answer at once. His eyes moved from the aerologger to the glittering dwellings and he breathed deeply, as if simultaneously proud and awed. Finally, he looked at me and said in human tongue, "I'm going with them."

I knew he realized there was a risk, despite Sergi's assurance of safety, but surviving in the wild mountains with the other escaped slaves was certain danger. I did not need to take the same risk. I could slink back into the forest and return to Baltsar, Chel, and Tarana, and with them eventually make my way back to the tablelands. But I didn't even glance at the forest. I was transfixed by the awesome size of the clearing, by the enormous aerologger, and by wonders yet unknown. "I will stay with you for a while," I said to Teon, "at least until I understand how they make the aerologger fly."

Teon smiled and touched my shoulder. "I knew I was right to bring you here." I coiled my tail around his wrist and nodded. Sergi and Adriana watched us, perturbed by the exchange in human tongue. Teon's hand dropped to his side. "We will go with you now."

Chapter 28

THE HEAT in Adriana's dwelling was stifling to me and Teon, even after we shed our outerwear. We looked bedraggled. Our tunics were damp and they clung, making the accumulation of trail dirt chafe and itch. Sergi and Adriana peeled off the gull-gray clothes to reveal a skin-thin layer of sleeveless shirts and short pants. Both were barefooted and seemed comfortable in the heat as they conferred in a corner of the strange room. Adriana's voice was definitely strained, and Sergi's tone was patronizing—for her benefit or ours, I wondered.

Teon and I stared at our surroundings, wondered why they'd put legs on the cushions and how they'd made parts of the walls transparent and what purpose the array of finely crafted cubes, cones, and cylinders, shelved along one wall, served. Those hissed and whirred as if they had lives of their own. Bubbles of flame-like substance drifted in the cones, and firelight flashed over the face of a cube, sometimes lingering and dancing along the surface in intriguing patterns.

Before I could question them about the strange lights, Adriana and Sergi presented us with plates filled with steaming food, prepared I know not how, or when, or by whom. My back had been turned only half a moment, and in that short time they'd filled their hands with plates.

It pleased me, though. Offering food was a civilized and friendly gesture.

"I hope it suits you," Sergi said, putting two plates on a table in the corner of the room. He glanced at me, smiling. "Some of it is of off-world origin."

Adriana placed two more plates on the table, then pulled up a legged cushion and sat on it. She gestured for Teon to sit next to her, leaving me to sit at the far side of the table, next to Sergi. The cushion was soft beneath my rump, but the hard back that the others leaned against prevented me from resting my tail comfortably. Finally, I wrapped it around my waist.

Our hosts used knives and other utensils during the meal, and Teon tried to imitate them, getting good-natured assistance from Adriana. I noticed that her eyes avoided contact with mine, and there was a glimmer of disapproval in them when I began to eat in my accustomed fashion, spearing portions with my index claw.

The food was not to my liking, but I forgot it after a while because I had to concentrate on understanding Sergi, who talked during the entire meal. Evidently, he was trying to solve the puzzle of Teon's origin and discover who his ancestors were, since they were obviously like species. I listened carefully.

He studied Teon as he pushed food into a pronged utensil with his knife. "I don't think there's been a transport crash in Shadowland since pioneer times," he said, "which means you could be as many as seven generations removed from the survivors. I suppose that's enough time for people to forget their true origin."

He seemed doubtful, and I was even more skeptical. "Teon's kind have been with my people only for seventy seasons," I said. "At most, that is three or four generations. Ranging lowland warlords discovered them in the Evernight Mountains, groveling for food in the tundra."

"Evernight? Do you mean in the umbra of the planetary ring's shadow?"

I thought about that. It seemed to me that the sky-bridge, which Teon had also referred to as a ring, was too far for the umbra to touch the ground, yet I knew that it was a good and reasonable explanation for the night blackness and for its being much longer than it was wide. As a child, I had trailed its edge with my tribe. Finally, I nodded. "There are volcanoes everywhere, but nowhere are they as plentiful as in the Evernight Mountains."

Sergi nodded. "We're talking about the same place." He looked at Adriana. Didn't the transportation commissioner ban all public conveyances from trans-shadow flights in the last century?"

"I wouldn't know about that, and I'd ignore it if I did. No one tells me where I can or cannot take my equipment. I'm not afraid to take on that black girdle," Adriana said, looking askance at me. Then, stabbing some food on her plate and shoving it into her mouth, she continued. "You locals know less of what's going on in your world than outsiders like me. You should have been pushing to the equator twenty-five years ago. That's when the last piedmont glacier receded into shadow. You should be taking advantage of the warm phase. It won't last forever."

Sergi frowned. "Even if flights weren't officially forbidden, trans-shadow flights stopped . . . probably because it's cheaper and safer to develop resources outside the shadow than to fight the navigation and atmospheric problems at the equator." Sergi looked at me. "Lodestone deposits, cloud cover, and sunspots," he said seriously. I didn't understand, and I think he knew it, but any explanation he might have offered was interrupted by the outer door's opening to admit two more people.

A blast of cool, moisture-filled air swept over us and I sucked in greedily, hardly hearing introductions. One of the newcomers was addressing me, but the person spoke so rapidly that I couldn't understand.

"What?"

"Talk slower," Sergi suggested to the newcomer.

"When I looked through the field glasses, I thought I saw a tail," he said loudly, but slowly.

"I do have one," I said, deliberately speaking softly as I unwound and wound my tail for his benefit. He smiled in appreciation while peeling off a garment from his torso. This one was not gull-gray, as Sergi's and Adriana's had been. It glittered, very much like their boots. Curious, Teon held out his hand, indicating that he wished to see the garment. The newcomer handed it over with a smile. Teon ran his fingers over the fabric, puzzling, then handed it to me. It was as light as spidersilk, but more dense, and when I looked closely I realized the fabric had no woof or warp. "This can't be an animal skin," I said, astonished.

Adriana laughed aloud. "It's made from magic," she said.

I dropped the garment and shied, half-expecting it to leap after me.

"Adriana!" The newcomer's tone was sharp.

"He wouldn't understand if I explained the process, anyhow," she said churlishly. Then she gave me a look that would be considered contemptuous if done by a slave. When Sergi frowned and Teon fidgeted, I decided the expression had nothing to do with slavery, but that it was common to the species. My ruff swelled.

"Adriana," I said, hoping I'd pronounced her name correctly. Her pupils gave a pulse of recognition. "You have made two mistakes. First, you assumed that I am a male. That's understandable because you have never seen my kind before, and my external genitalia are covered by my garments. Presumably, you cannot distinguish male from female until you've seen both. Your second mistake was in assuming that I cannot distinguish trickery from rudeness."

Adriana seemed surprised, but she did not apologize. Then her face became blank and she looked at Teon. "How would you like a steaming-hot bath?"

Teon laughed, deliberately trying to relieve the tension in the air. "I would like that, but I wouldn't care to run through the cold rain to get to the hot spring."

"I have a built-in hot spring in the next room," she said. "Come along and I'll show you."

Teon barely hesitated before following her. I've never understood slaves' attraction to hot water, but I'd often indulged their desire for it, and I did so now, too. I was glad for any excuse to be rid of Adriana, which left me with the more charming host and the two newcomers.

"She sure doesn't waste any time," one man said under his breath.

Alarmed, I looked at Sergi. "Will she harm him?"

"No. She'll probably scrub his back."

That seemed a friendly thing to do for him, but I could tell that Sergi and his friends disapproved. I cocked my ears in the direction that Adriana and Teon went; I heard water gushing, but no sounds of distress. In fact, I think I detected giggling, and the sour moss smell was fading.

"How'd the hot-shot from Earth shape up this afternoon?" said the older of the two as he sat in Teon's vacated place.

221

Sergi nodded agreeably. "Better. Once she knew the rangefinder signal was out of calibration, she knew what to do. It really wasn't her fault; no one told her it was malfunctioning."

The old man hissed through his teeth. "She knew about the earthquake just like everyone else. Yet she's the only one in camp who didn't bother to check damage with me, and you can't tell me she's just independent." He shook his head. "She won't even stay in the same room with me."

"Oh, I don't think the bath thing had anything to do with *you*," Sergi said. He glanced at me, then hastily added, "Leon needed one . . . I mean, after such a long journey and . . . " Sergi shrugged uncomfortably. "It's a bitch having to work with the beacon that way, but I guess there's not much we can do about it until sunspot activity settles down and we can restore communication with the coast."

"I'll see what I can do with it myself, tomorrow," the old man said, "if you really think that's all that's bothering her."

"Sure it is, Joan. She's good at her job and . . . " He looked at me. "Sorry, Heao. We have some internal problems, but we don't need to discuss them now."

My tail rippled in sympathy. Then I realized they probably didn't understand the nuance, so I nodded. "I didn't catch your names," I said to the newcomers.

"I'm Joan. This is Hanalore."

Again, both were smooth-cheeked, but the taller one, Hanalore, had big breasts and her pelvis was smooth under the tight, short pants. I decided that Hanalore was female. She reminded me a bit of Manya with her dark, doe eyes and silent, pleasing way of moving. Joan was wiry, with narrow shoulders. He was old and wrinkled, and his hair was white and wispy. I thought his face looked wise. I was pretty sure he was a man, for his breasts were as flat as mine. I nodded politely at them, then turned to Sergi.

"You've mentioned sunspots twice, and I didn't see any markings on godsf——the sun," I said.

Sergi smiled and leaned forward, speaking an aside to Hanalore and Joan. "We're dealing with an intelligent and curious native," he said.

Joan nodded eagerly. "Discovering you is an exciting event for us, Heao," he said.

I didn't remind him that it was they who had been discovered. I smiled, genuinely pleased, and said, "For me, also."

Sergi sighed and relaxed. He was obviously at ease with Hanalore and Joan and me, now that Adriana was gone. "Now, for sunspots. Well . . . "

I wished I hadn't asked. That godsfire was a ball of flame was crystal clear to me. I've always known that. That it boiled and erupted was also understandable, but the part about the boils sending out invisible forces to disrupt other invisible forces that were used to carry messages farther than a person could walk in fifty nights was incomprehensible. They tried to demonstrate; the hissing things along the wall were the messengers, but they wouldn't move. They screeched in protest when Sergi touched them, and I covered my ears from the assault. Sergi silenced the messengers, then apologized.

"There are ways to get around the problem. We use landlines, but they're pretty hard to maintain in remote areas because of the earthquakes."

"Earthquakes are a constant source of harassment for us, too," I said, grateful to be able to turn the conversation to something I could understand. "We've learned to use light and malleable materials whenever possible, and we use flexible joints when we can't. They're less likely to collapse."

"We must have been a great help to you," Sergi said.

For a moment I was confused. Then I realized he was referring to his kind—Teon and the other slaves. "Yes. Discovering your species was fortuitous. Without them, we might not have been able to implement Academe's finest ideas. The mills . . . " I shook my head, remembering the impossible weight and bulk of the millstones, muscled into place by brawny slaves.

"I can imagine," Joan said, nodding happily. "You have probably experienced a great deal of progress. It must have been baffling in the beginning."

"I wasn't there myself; still, I doubt it. Academe has always been very progressive, and people were accustomed to seeking our advice. Of course, there are always factions . . . internal problems." I glanced at the door Adriana had closed between us. They nodded in understanding. "But our King-conqueror has provided an atmosphere that favors innovations, at least some of the time."

"The anthropologists are going to scream when they

223

hear that primitives have been tainted by humans," Hanalore said, more to Sergi than to me.

"I hadn't thought about them," Sergi said, "but I have been wondering if we'll be found in violation of the Non-interference Act, which prohibits colonizing planets with sentient natives."

"God, what a mess it will be," Joan said, running gnarled fingers through his hair. His eyes widened in mock horror; then the laugh lines in his wrinkled face deepened. Sergi and Hanalore seemed to share his amusement.

"You have a law that prohibits this meeting?" I said, gesturing to them and including myself.

"Yes . . . no." Sergi chuckled. "To tell the truth, Heao, the law didn't foresee this. The authority that prohibits cohabitation also establishes that there is no one to cohabit with before they give permission to colonize. We can't figure out what they're going to do when they realize their own survey teams gave them bad information. We've been here a century in excess of the probationary period, and we've accomplished considerable development along the coast. Some people can trace their land-grants right back to Colonial times."

I began to see the problem. "How is it that your marvelous survey machines did not notice us?" I said. "We have many cities . . . "

"Which, I assume, are all in Shadowland, where there is constant cloud cover, turbulent air, not to mention the weird magnetic force lines and lodestone deposits that make ordinary atmospheric navigation extremely difficult. And the planetary ring is so close in that the cheapest orbits are hazardous, so there's never been much satellite reconnaissance in the equatorial zone. I suspect they just didn't expect the most hostile region of the planet to warrant close examination."

"It sounds to me that this authority you speak of has some decisions to make, and that it may need to examine its operating policies," I said, not sharing their amusement.

"Well, they aren't going to evacuate a million people," Joan said, "at least, not until after the next election. Damn, I'll probably die without knowing what's going to happen!"

"Are you ill?" I said, dismayed, for I liked the old man.

"Oh, no. It's just that the Board will deliberate for years on a problem as sticky as this one, and then it will be years before a decision reaches us . . ." His voice trailed off as he saw my perplexity. "Does anyone feel up to explaining space travel, light-years, or the politics involved?"

"To a cat?" It was Adriana's voice coming quite loudly from across the room. "That's very funny."

Joan nearly snarled, but Sergi put his hand across Joan's chest and shook his head.

For my part, it was easy to ignore Adriana as Teon entered dressed in alien garments. He looked very refreshed. His hair was clean and fluffy, his beard trimmed neater than it had been in months. He was looking at me, no doubt to see what I would say at seeing him dressed like a god. I shook my tail playfully and laughed, and as he came closer, I sniffed deeply. "You smell like Sergi," I said, "just like honey!"

"A scented soap of his," Teon said, looking very pleased with himself. "The garments are his, too." He turned to Sergi. "Adriana said you wouldn't mind since you'd never seen the need to reclaim them from her closet."

Sergi shrugged, seemingly with some embarrassment.

"Mmmm," I said in appreciation as Teon sat near me.

"Heao, you should have been there. The water was . . . well, what the water was doesn't translate properly. You would call it muddy, but it was pretty," he said in a patronizing fashion, "like the rainbow."

Adriana was inexplicably agitated as Teon continued to describe the bathing process to me in great detail. Sergi, Hanalore, and Joan exchanged furtive glances.

"We ought to get some sleep. You must be tired, too, Heao," Sergi said hastily.

I was, but I was too exhilarated to admit it.

"You can have my rig. I'll bunk with Hanalore and Joan in the chummery." They nodded in agreement. "And I'll give you your first lesson in astrophysics in the morning," Sergi said. "All right?"

I looked at Teon. "I'm staying here with Adriana," he said. Then he added in human tongue, "You won't be afraid to be alone, will you?"

"No. Anything is better than being out in the rain, bivouacing under a bush."

Hanalore and Joan were already at the door. They seemed eager to leave. Likewise, Adriana seemed happy to see them go, anticipating, I believed, having Teon to

225

herself again. Sergi lingered a moment after I'd stepped into the rain, whispering to Adriana. "You don't seem to realize that Heao is not Leon's pet. Her species is intelligent."

"Don't be suckered, Sergi," she whispered. "I've encountered mooncalves before."

"You don't mean that mutant group back on . . . but you can hardly compare Heao to a cult of unfortunate . . . freaks!"

"I was right about them, wasn't I? They stole my land and tried to kill me."

"But the Board said . . . "

"The Board coddled them, moved my ass right out of Sol System to get me out of the way."

"I don't care what your opinion of mutants is," Sergi said, finally becoming angry. "Treat Heao with consideration or . . . "

"Or what, Sergi? I've as many rights around here as the rest of you, and I don't take orders from you."

"Nor anyone else," Joan muttered under his breath.

I didn't think his kind could hear the furtive conversation over the rain sounds, and his reacting to their talk left me wondering if I'd been underestimating their hearing all this time, or if I were, once again, fooled by slave duplicity.

The door slammed and Hanalore and Joan tried not to notice. We walked across the muddy compound in silence. I was glad that Hanalore's and Joan's behavior more closely resembled Sergi's. I'd have been at a loss in deciding between Sergi and Adriana as the norm without them to tip the scale. And without knowing, I probably would have preferred a drippy bush to the strangers' hospitality.

Chapter 29

I watched the lights of the tree-eating machines most of the night, my curiosity heightened each time the lights moved. But I couldn't make out what they were doing through the rain, and I was too intimidated by their awesome size and their terrible noises to investigate. Before dawn, the rain ended, and soon thereafter the machines stopped their gnawing and growling and their operators returned to the chummery. I left Sergi's rig at the first tentative light and crept into the forest and circumnavigated the clearing, stopping occasionally to pick mushrooms and fat grubs from beneath moss-covered logs.

Godsfire made the wet world sparkle, as if it were covered with precious gems. Pools of water were like molten silver with slags of cloud reflection, and the trees dripped crystalline droplets. The skybridge seemed crisp and white against the ever-brightening sky, dwarfing even the nearest peaks and belittling the clearing.

Finally, I reached the place where the trees and boulders had been. There was nothing left of them but a hill of chips and a pile of sand, and the ground was gouged with knee-deep ruts, tracks of the machines. I sat on the chips, which were damp and full of life-smells, while I surveyed the products of progress or destruction, I knew not which. It depended, I supposed, on one's point of view. I could picture the King-conqueror estimating how long it would take one of the machines to eat its way through the ramparts of certain stubborn mountain hamlets, and I could see Baltsar sacking the chips and carrying them to market.

When I heard the aerologger whine, I looked up to see it rise and begin to fly. I started to flee the worksite, lest it not notice me and drop a tree-mountain on me, but the aerologger sailed out over the forest, magnificent in flight, disappearing quickly. Later a small round machine buzzed over the clearing toward me, and when it got close enough, I could see Sergi and Joan through its transparent top. The machine settled and stopped; then Sergi got out.

"Joan and I are going to check that beacon this morning. We thought you might want to come along," he said. "It will give you a chance to ride in a flyer and see what the world looks like from the air."

I stood up, immediately excited and frightened. "Can we go up to the skybridge, the planetary ring?" I said. "Legends say there are messages written on it by the gods."

He laughed at me. "Heao, do you have any idea of how high the planetary ring is? All we have here is ground equipment and tropospheric flyers, which operate only in the lowest part of the atmosphere. The air gets thin above the clouds and gradually fades into space. It takes special equipment to get up there. Even if I had a shuttle and could take you, I guarantee there aren't any graffiti on the ring. It's nothing but dust and debris from a broken-up moon." He laughed again and I was both embarrassed and disappointed. "I'm sorry. I promised you a lesson in astrophysics this morning, and I think it will be time well spent. We must seem very powerful to you, but we do have limitations. A lot of them are strictly economic . . . I know you won't have any trouble understanding that part."

The embarrassment faded and I smiled. "Teon will be interested, too," I said.

"He already left with Adriana in the aerologger," he said regretfully. "It's hard to say no to her."

Especially for someone like Teon, I thought, who was unaccustomed to refusing any requests. "I'm sorry she doesn't like me," I said.

"Well, she's the only one who doesn't," Sergi said graciously.

"She seems to like Teon." We started toward Joan and the little flyer.

"Adriana likes anyone who will warm her bed and be . . . " He checked himself and glanced at me nervously. "Leon's a nice guy, but he's kind of . . . easygoing."

It troubled me to know that Adriana might take advantage of Teon, yet I couldn't think of why she would want to, unless she were an adventuress. That kind found pleasure in unexpected things, and to these people, Teon and I must have seemed exotic.

"Hop in," Joan said cheerfully. But I noticed that Sergi did not hop, and I copied his carefully placed steps.

Sergi strapped me into a rigid seat, then fastened himself in like fashion. The transparent canopy flopped down over our heads, then snapped into place. The flyer began to buzz, but not as loudly as it had when I was outside. I felt a strange vibration through my seat, and then we lifted and the ground fell away.

For a second, I thought it was the end for me, Sergi, and Joan, even for the flyer. Like a projectile, we were thrust toward the towering trees, but as I opened my mouth to scream I luckily opened my eyes, too, and I saw that the treetops were already beneath us, looking very much like a carpet of moss. In moments the clearing was only a dim patch and the world became a mottled gray thing without depth or features.

We flew like the wind itself, through clouds (which were nothing more than swirling fog) and sunshine. I settled back to watch Joan's hands moving over the controls and to listen to him whistle in tune to the flyer's drone.

"Those are the Needle Mountains below us," Joan said, pointing through the canopy. "Some of the tallest peaks on the continent are in that group. They don't look quite so impressive from up here, do they?"

"I can't see them," I said. "I don't have distance vision."

Sergi reached into a pouch and pulled out parallel cylinders and handed them to me. "Try these field glasses," he said.

They were black and smooth and cool to the touch, but I couldn't imagine what I was supposed to do with them. I turned them over.

"Um, Sergi," Joan said with a meaningful glance.

"Oh, like this, Heao," he said. "Turn them on with

this toggle, left for normal, right for infrared. Left, just now, then look through here." He raised them to his eyes, demonstrating. "Squeeze the lens casing until you have the proper adjustment."

I took the field glasses and looked into them. I discovered mountains, ravines, and carpets of forest inside. Momentarily, I realized I was looking through the instrument, not into it, and that every time I shifted my field of view I had to squeeze the lens casing to refocus. But each time I was able to see a new part of the world with great clarity. It nearly was like looking at one of my maps, more encompassing, and without legends to fill in between landmarks, but the scope, the vastness of the world, was as I'd always represented it.

"We're coming up on the beacon," Joan said, and we began a rapid, breathtaking descent.

Joan set down the flyer in a mountain meadow, below the lonely pinnacle where the beacon tower stood. The faint tang of volcanic ash was on the breeze when the canopy was opened, and I wondered if the wind were heralding a storm, as a wind from the Evernight Mountains would come before the storms in my homeland. When we left the craft, Sergi led the way along a faint trail in the tundra to a switchback track that had been carved out of the mountainside. Patiently, I walked the broad road with them, though I easily could have cut corners by scaling walls and leaping rocks. The faint scent of their machines, which must have followed the rock path once, lingered in stains on the roadbed, like spoors in the snow. Like slaves, my companions didn't notice the scents, not even when a downdraft brought the strong aroma of Sergi's honey-sweet soap.

"Adriana and Teon are already at the beacon," I said to them. As if on signal, Teon hailed us from above and Adriana stepped into view beside him, her arm encircling his waist as they peered down at us. She saw me and drew closer to Teon. The downdraft suddenly brought the stench of cowering slaves, and I knew it was not Teon's fear I smelled.

"Wonder where she parked?" Joan said, waving briefly.

"Probably on the ledge," Sergi replied.

Joan stopped to stare at Sergi. "I wouldn't put a flyer there, let alone an aerologger."

Sergi smiled wryly. "She handles that rig as if it were a part of her. She's good, Joan. The mess last week was a fluke. She knows her job, and she's very thorough. How may other riggers have bothered to come up to check the beacon? She's not getting paid to do that."

"Neither am I," Joan snapped.

I suspected another comment was on Sergi's lips, but he didn't say it. He just smiled again, an easy, knowing smile, and left Joan to mull his words.

Joan and Sergi were breathless when we reached the beacon, and they sat, sipping flavored liquids from clear flasks they'd carried in their shirts. Adriana ambled behind Teon, who was having difficulty in restraining himself from running to my side, happy to see me after the night's separation.

"Did you ever imagine . . . ?" he said, gesturing broadly to the sky. "The speed, the height . . . when we swooped so fast, I nearly had an orgasm."

I laughed, and shyly confessed that I, too, found flying very sensual. Then, noticing Joan's puzzlement, I added, "We ought not speak the human tongue in front of our hosts."

"You mean parahuman tongue," Teon suggested, his eyes glinting.

"That depends on your point of view," I said, perturbed. He certainly was getting uppity.

Sergi offered me a drink, and though I was not very thirsty, I accepted so that I would not have to continue the discussion with Teon. Adriana turned away when Sergi drank again, after me.

"Here," Joan said to her. "Have some of mine."

Adriana shook her head. "I'm not thirsty."

"Saliva doesn't cause wrinkles," Joan said, but Adriana made no move to take his flask, so he put it away. Suddenly dour, Joan looked at Sergi. "Let's get after that beacon."

"It's operating correctly," Adriana said.

"It's ten klicks off!"

"Easy, Joan," Sergi said, interposing himself between Joan and Adriana, reminding me of the way he'd stepped between Adriana, and Teon and me. "What did you find, Adriana?"

She crossed her arms over her chest. "The laser's operating fine, but the electromagnetic shielding has been compromised. Something's shorting the shields, but I couldn't get at it. I didn't want to use my laser blade, because it looks like the outer skin can be unbolted."

"Copper shields?" Sergi asked.

"Corroded copper," Adriana said, nodding.

"The quake probably jiggled something loose and it dropped between the shields. Doesn't take much . . . a bolt or a piece of wire would break the isolation between the shields."

"That would do it," Joan said reluctantly, "and put a lot of hash on the line." He looked at Sergi. "Let's take a look."

They checked the equipment in the little kits on their belts, and, between them, they were satisfied that they had what was necessary to make the repairs. They approached the tower of girders upon which the beacon perched. Access was via a slender ladder that stretched into the sky, nearly to the edge of my vision. Joan and Sergi started up, climbing hand over foot, heavily and slowly.

"Do you suppose they'd mind if I joined them?" I asked. I'd never seen a beacon before, or even a tower the likes of the one before me. I was eager to examine their method of fastening the girders. I saw no sign of braided wire ties.

"You're not permitted," Adriana said flatly.

"But, I went up with you," Teon said, surprised.

Adriana pretended to be engrossed in watching the climbers ascend, and she answered absently, walking away from us at the same time. "There are things you don't understand . . . industrial secrets, the risk of sabotage."

"But . . . "

I touched Teon's arm and brushed his neck with my tail to silence him. "I don't understand, either, but there's no sense in forcing a confrontation with her. Sergi and Joan are very amiable."

"I've tried to explain to her that you are not like the other *cats*," Teon said, answering in the human tongue. "But it's to no avail. Your . . . difference unnerves her"

I looked at Adriana, so straight-backed and sturdy in her stance. The sour-moss scent still oozed from her pores, even though she looked brave and sure. My own people don't have a fear scent, yet I believed I'd encountered similar behavior among them, Chel and Tarana foremost in the number of people who feared any person not in their peer group. I wondered if I might change Adriana's opinion of me, perhaps attenuate my strangeness by finding a common ground to share.

Teon followed Adriana, touching her shoulder and speaking softly in her ear. I thought I detected the muscles in her shoulders easing for a moment. Then, winking to her over some private joke, he left her alone. She smiled after him, then turned her gaze back to the two men in the tower.

I walked in small, measured steps toward her, my ears flat, my minds conversing at a furious pace. We both were female, but that, I was certain, was not anything she'd care to identify with me. However, Teon trusted me, whatever my species, and Adriana trusted Teon. Therefore . . .

My foot dislodged a tiny stone and Adriana whirled.

"Why are you sneaking up on me?" Her hand was already in the little tool kit at her belt, holding, I could guess, the laser blade.

I stopped and pushed back my hood with empty hands as I replied. "My step is merely soft—the tender leather boots are the cause, I believe. Haven't you noticed that Teon walks softly, too?"

"He doesn't sneak up behind me."

"Oh, but he just did, and you recognized his touch instantly. I know what that is like. He is a comforting friend, very sensitive to the needs of people around him," I said. Adriana's eyes were puzzled now, her muscles tense under the slick garments. One hand was poised at her side like ballast, yet her posture was not overtly defensive. Mostly the fear scent betrayed her deliberate calm. Without that, her hatred might have remained as much an enigma to me as it was to Joan. Since Adriana didn't comment about my remarks, I decided to expound. "During all the years Teon lived in my helper's lair with me, he was loyal and faithful. He has a quick and discerning mind, and he pleased me above all others."

For a moment her eyes widened, as if shocked. Then she recovered. "Is that why he is scarred with claw marks? Or is clawing him your method of assuring his loyalty?" She turned away, walking quickly at an angle that kept me in the periphery of her vision, yet put as much distance between us as the rocky summit permitted.

From the base of the tower, where he was lounging and watching the two men climb down, Teon observed Adriana's hasty departure. She waved him along, and, with a puzzled glance at me, he trotted after her. I watched them disappear over the far edge of the pinnacle, disappointed that I'd failed to make her reconsider me even for a moment. Perhaps it was pride that made me think I, a stranger, might succeed where Joan and Sergi had failed. It certainly wasn't humility that made me dismiss my failure rather quickly by deciding that Adriana was an extreme case in any species.

As Sergi and Joan approached me, we heard the whine of the aerologger from below the ledge, and an instant later we saw the silver missile make a line toward the distant camp.

"She didn't even wait to see me eat humble pie," Joan said, watching the dust settle.

I laughed. "We have a stew in which unsaying is the main ingredient," I said.

At ease, we walked the rock-carved road to the meadow where the flyer waited.

Later, as we floated out of a bank of clouds and over a forest plateau, Joan pointed into the distance. "Just about home," he said.

I raised the field glasses and saw the clearing directly ahead. Joan was not off so much as a degree.

"How do you know your direction of travel?" I said. "You can't feel the wind inside the ship, and you can't detect its origin by smell in here, either."

"Some places you can use the compass," Sergi said, pointing to a circling dial, "but you have to be able to compensate for all the distortions. Takes too long, too complicated to do in your head, and this region isn't as well mapped as the coastal areas are. Here we use the range-finder, the beacon we just repaired."

"I like to use familiar landmarks, and I can always get a direction heading off the sun. When you're born and raised on a planet that rotates on a nearly perfect right angle to the sun, you don't ever need a compass," Joan explained lazily.

"But you couldn't see godsf—— . . . the sun when we were in the clouds," I said.

"No, I cheated in the clouds and used the beacon," he said with a chuckle. "But you can't always depend on that—even when they're not broken, there're plenty of places where there just aren't any. Riggers like Sergi, here, have to stay within beacon range or they get lost."

Sergi laughed good-naturedly. "I do all right," he said.

"Do you mean that the beacon signal is limited in its

234

distance?" It was difficult to imagine invisible communication as having any limits. "But what limits it?"

"Well, the planet is curved and . . . " Joan's gray eyes twinkled. "I think it's time for that lesson, Sergi."

I don't think that Sergi could have fit all that he explained on his thumbnail. He couldn't even get it all on the back of a parchment map! He claimed the nighttime sparks that we saw in the sky were distant suns, godsfire if I pleased, and that each of those suns had a distinct personality. The sun in our sky, he said, was particularly disruptive of signals his people used ordinarily on other worlds for communication and navigation. They hadn't been in contact with their homes for weeks, and they didn't expect to reestablish communications for several more weeks. They were temporarily isolated, but they were well compensated for any inconvenience it caused them.

I was not satisfied by the flight; it only raised more questions about tools like field glasses, and the world's shape (which was round!), and the strangers' knowledge. Sergi and Joan were very patient with me. When we returned to the construction site, they showed me how to operate a machine that produced miniature light-visions of anything I wanted to see—a holopedia, they called it. The machine also spoke, describing the origin of the current manifestation being viewed, then went on to illustrate practical application, or to give other interesting details. I found *cats* by accident and was appalled that my people had been likened to those frozen-faced beasts. They were impassive, and their stiff tails conveyed only the most rudimentary information, and they walked on all four legs (no hands!), looking more like aged does than people.

I punched keys at random, but if I wanted to see something specific, Sergi or Joan located it for me. I couldn't comprehend their categorizing system, which was apparently based on an order of sound that once had been random but that was now in general use throughout many worlds. When I found maps, I memorized the coordinates.

I thought Teon had supplied me with an extensive vocabulary, but I was wrong. Often Sergi or Joan had to paraphrase an entire article for me because I didn't understand all the words the machine used. Despite the language gaps, I was learning exciting things about strip-mining, fabulous wealth hidden beneath the planet's crust, and a lot about the people who stripped away mountains to get at the planet's riches.

In the evening, Hanalore brought food for us from the chummery, and afterward, while the two men rested, she assisted me at the holopedia. I sensed that all of them were as intrigued by me and my people as I was by them. We often digressed into comparisons between their ways and ours, their tools and ours, their government and our aristocracy. Finally, they yawned and begged off, alluding to obligations and responsibilities they needed to be fit to meet when godsfire, the sun, next arose.

Then I was alone in Sergi's rig again. I coiled up on a legged cushion called a divan. The back of my brain was overloaded with stored words, and they were called forth each time I looked around the dwelling—plastic walls, synthetic-fiber carpets, radio, the whimsical communication device, fine tuning, channel selector, dwelling monitor, octophonic sound system, lasers, holograms . . . the list was endless. I dozed for a while, then heard the whines and growls of the heavy equipment. I got up, pressed my nose against the transparent wall—*window,* the back of my mind supplied—and saw huge lights pushed by dark shadows toward the other end of the clearing. Closer in I noticed someone walking toward me. Judging by the gait, it was Teon. I hurried to open the door, luckily remembering the sequence of maneuvers on the first try. I was beginning to feel confident that magical things were nothing more than applied cleverness.

"I knew you wouldn't be sleeping," Teon said.

"Of course not, but you ought to be."

He shrugged. "It was too hot to sleep," he said. He glanced back at Adriana's jerry house, looking very perturbed. I thought I sensed relief in his face when he closed the door.

"What's wrong?" I said.

"She . . . " But he caught himself quickly and shook his head. "Nothing. I thought you might like some company."

We sat together. He still smelled like honey, so I moved closer until my shoulder touched his. The tenseness in him ripped through me like a shock wave.

"Only today did I learn what an imposition sex can be when two people are not of like minds," he said softly.

"I was never free to learn that before; there was never enough time to call my own. I'm disgusted by my memories of what I tried to do to you."

"But still sad that we are not mutually agreeable?"

He smiled wryly. "Perhaps, but wiser now. I know that desire in only one, no matter how overwhelming, is not enough."

He got up and paced, finally stopping in front of the window. "They're powerful, Heao," he said in open admiration. "They're pulverizing trees tonight, and tomorrow they will cut down more. Then they will start to build, and more people will come." He sucked in his breath. "Adriana showed me some holographic displays." He looked at me, and my tail thumped and waved to indicate that further explanation was not necessary.

I felt tiny and insignificant just remembering the size of their eastern city, the bizarre shapes of the buildings, the sheen of polished metal, and the throngs of people with wonder and magic at their fingertips. The back of my mind tried to compensate by supplying pictures memorized in minute detail—the remains of a clifftop city that had fallen into the ocean during an earthquake, and another of crop tenders half-covered by sea water, rusting in what once had been farmland. But the tragedies were not comforting. They merely reminded me that, if the aliens couldn't hold back the sea or prevent earthquakes, they would build another city and raise more crops, farther from the earthquake epicenter, nearer to Shadowland.

"In the morning," Teon was saying, "I'm going to ask if they will shelter me and the rest of the runaways until we can fashion something of our own."

"I don't think they will refuse you," I said. "They have plenty to share, and they're generous—even Adriana."

Teon's eyes clouded at the mention of Adriana's name, but he nodded slowly. I stepped to the portal and watched with him for a while. The far side of the clearing was flooded with light, as if godsfire itself were shining. "They can't see in the dark, either," I said, smiling because that weakness seemed so trivial now.

"To think that I am like them!" Teon's eyes hardened and I believed that he was thinking of all the humiliation he had endured as a slave. Guiltily, I turned away. He didn't try to comfort me or to ease my conscience.

Finally, he came away from the portal, sat on a divan, and leaned back. In a moment he closed his eyes and fell asleep, leaving me to contemplate alone. I listened to the wrenching and gnawing sounds of the equipment. Even muted by distance and by the walls of Sergi's rig, they were great sounds, representing awesome power. And within the cozy room there were soft noises, too, coming from the heating system and the communication instruments. I listened to them, naming the sources and forming the sounds of new words in my mind and reevaluating the meanings of words I thought I knew. Later I went to the holopedia console and dialed the coordinates of the planetary maps, copied as much as I could understand, then put the new map with the one that had been steadily thickening the pocket in my cloak since I left the tableland city.

Most of the night passed with me reviewing the slave tongue and in reevaluating slaves and the abilities my people had suppressed in them. Perspicuity, forgive me! I thought I was wise to recognize their intelligence and that I was noble to believe in them. But I'd underestimated so badly that for the second time in my life I felt like a fool. Before dawn, I curled up on the floor and took a nap.

Chapter 30

GODSFIRE'S BRIGHT rays streamed through the window and awoke me. Teon was already awake, running the water in the bathroom with such force that it splashed and gushed.

"I freshened your cloak," he said, returning.

And he looked fresh, too. The honey smell permeated the room. He had helped himself to more of Sergi's clothes, their darkness setting off his fair hair to gleam like sunshine. He wore his own boots, which had been cleaned as much as the rough leather would allow. I scratched at a knot of fur under my arm, uncomfortably aware that my own gear was still mud-stained.

The cloak at least looked better, but it was wet. Teon hung it up to dry, then produced a brush. "Use it," he said. "I can clean it when you're done. Sergi will never know." For a moment his hand lingered in mine. Then he turned away and I was left with the brush in hand.

I sighed. My fur was admittedly motley after the journey and the rain, and though I don't like to use anyone's brush without permission, this time was the exception. The knots under my armpits and between my fingers ached. I used the brush, quickly but vigorously, then returned it to Teon, who freshened it with scented soap and water. He'd barely finished when Sergi knocked on the door. We giggled as we opened it, glad to have shared the clandestine use of the brush and pleased that we were not caught.

"You must be hungry," Sergi said. He left the door open for Adriana, Hanalore, and Joan, who were about twenty paces behind him. The morning breeze was fresh and not too cold.

"I thought I would go into the forest to forage," I said, remembering the terrible taste of their food.

"Didn't dinner agree with you?" Sergi said, suddenly concerned.

Adriana entered just in time to hear him, and she laughed. "Doesn't anyone have cat food?"

"Jesus Christ, Adriana!" Joan looked angry enough to hit her.

"Let it pass, Joan," I said, instinctively reaching for his arm. They were both like Chel; he in temper, and she in tact. She was looking at me with unmasked hate, and I wondered what I had done to increase her wrath. Teon avoided her gaze when she turned to him.

"Don't you have supplies, Heao?" Joan asked. "Surely you didn't come all this way without sustenance."

"My supplies are back at camp with my friends," I said.

Joan gave Sergi a smug smile. "I told you that two was an unlikely number to survive a two-hundred-kilometer trek through Shadowland mountains."

"*My* friends probably have accumulated enough food to share with you, Heao," Teon said. He was standing with his arms folded across his chest, looking at me without compassion.

Sergi and Joan looked at him strangely. "Where are *your* friends?" Joan said.

"Hiding in the forest," Teon replied.

"Hiding? From us?"

He shook his head. "They're hiding from her friends." He indicated me.

"Huh?"

Teon looked impassive. "We've talked a lot about people, yours on one coast and Heao's on the other. But we haven't talked very much about my people, or about why I am here."

"Maybe you'd better tell us now," Sergi said quietly, sensing Teon's urgency despite his stoic posture.

He did, and I stood in their midst, feeling very uncomfortable. Plainly, they were shocked and displeased.

240

"Slaves!" Sergi nearly choked on the word. "And I thought the survivors brought the natives out of the Stone Age. Whew!"

"And Heao is your mistress?" Joan said. His eyes were as hard as iron.

"Was," Teon corrected. "I am my own master now." He was, too. In his splendid clothes, he looked like the master of his own fate, and the way he'd just taken charge of the alien gathering proved nothing less.

"Wait until the Board hears about this," Joan muttered, shaking his head. Then he looked up. "They'll have to be rescued."

"If you agree, I can bring them out of the forest now," Teon said.

"Of course," Joan said sympathetically, "but I meant the others back in Shadowland."

I must have gasped, for suddenly they were all staring at me.

"You didn't really think we'd allow our own flesh and blood to languish in slavery, did you?"

"I hadn't considered . . . anything," I said haltingly.

"The damned, filthy . . . for Christ's sake, why didn't you smash in their skulls while they were sleeping?" Adriana shouted. She was trembling with rage.

"They don't sleep very much," Teon said dryly. "And if we did, where would we go?"

"You've been harboring a slavemonger!" she said to Joan.

"In all fairness, I remind you that Heao does not condone slavery. She is my friend, and a wise one," Teon said, putting his arm on me protectively. It was a gesture common to Baltsar, strange but much appreciated coming from Teon. Adriana blanched to see it.

"Pretty gusty to walk in here all high and mighty, knowing all the while that our people are slaves," Joan said.

"Not really," I said. "When I agreed to accompany Teon to your camp, I didn't know that slavery would be an issue. But since it is, I'm glad I'm here. I don't think I can justify slavery to you, since I've never been able to justify it to myself. But perhaps I can explain some things; at least you may understand how it came about."

"All right," Joan said, being deliberately calm. "Explain!"

I sat down, hoping that they would, too. Their kind

were clumsy risers, and I thought that if I had to, I could sprint for the open door before they could gain their footing. Teon sat next to me to show that for all the travesty of slavery, he was still my friend. Until that moment I never appreciated just how good a friend he was. Adriana could not be expected to behave in a civilized fashion under the best of circumstances, and now Sergi, Joan, and Hanalore seemed equally angry. Slowly they sat.

"When slaves were first discovered, my people thought they were animals."

"That's ridiculous!" Adriana said, leaping to her feet.

But the others glared her down.

I continued, explaining as I went along about the temple guardians and the economic structure of our society. It took me a very long time, but in the end they had a complete picture of the King-conqueror's realm.

"You're right, Heao," Sergi finally said when I was finished. "It doesn't justify it, but we do at least understand how it happened."

"Your people are going to go through a hell of a change when we come in there to remove our people," Joan said. That seemed to give the old man some satisfaction. His eyes lost their hardness.

I knew that they could probably overwhelm my cities, if they could ever find them. But if their navigational problems had been nearly insurmountable for more than a century, they might continue being that way . . . at least, for a while, perhaps long enough for me to return and prepare my people for what would inevitably follow. For the nonce, I did not respond to Joan's declaration.

"Rescuing them would be in violation of the Noninterference Act," Hanalore said, then added quickly, "not that they wouldn't violate it under these circumstances. But it . . . "

". . . will take time," Sergi said, finishing for her "What a predicament! The whole Act could go down the tubes. Technically, we've interferred with the natives for several generations. They'll never be the same, whether we pull out or stay."

"Oh, come on, Sergi. We'll stay. At this point the natives are an internal problem. The Board won't touch it." Joan seemed very sure of himself, and Sergi nodded tentatively.

"There's a practical solution," Sergi said thoughtfully. "After rescuing our people, we could leave the natives to themselves. That wouldn't be difficult; Shadowland has its own natural border, which we aren't even interested in penetrating."

"Indeed," I said, bristling. "By your own admission, you have been trespassing for years. It seems to me that *we* should decide what will happen next. Perhaps my king will command that you limit yourselves to the eastern coast!"

"It isn't for him to decide," Sergi said, patronizing me.

"Isn't it? From what I have learned, our cultures may be different, but our ideas of right and wrong are strikingly similar. We got those values from our social organizations."

"You don't understand, Heao. We have had experience with these things. The people with the higher state of technology always absorb those with a lower state of the scientific arts. Reserving Shadowland for you would be for your protection."

"You're speculating," I said. "It remains to be seen who has the higher state of civilization. Besides, no one in this tiny construction camp has the authority to make decisions about my people."

"She's right," Joan said, finally smiling again. "I think I'll see some action before I die, after all."

"You'll hear from us again," I said carefully. "An emissary will come."

"You can be certain that we will be prepared to declaw it," Adriana said, brushing past Sergi to stand next to Teon. "Come on, Leon. Let's go get your friends." She took his arm to usher him out the door, but he slipped out of her grasp and stood looking at me. He knew that I no longer felt welcome and that I would leave.

"It's time to part again," he said, obviously dismayed.

I nodded. "My presence would only alarm the other sla—— . . . people. I have learned many things and have you to thank for the knowledge. I don't have adequate words . . . "

"What's going on?" Sergi said, and I realized we'd been speaking in the human tongue.

"Heao is going back to her camp now," Teon said. "Her people are waiting for her."

Sergi nodded slowly. "How far is your camp? Perhaps I can take you there in the flyer," he said. He seemed a bit uncomfortable, as if he regretted our differences because he admired me.

"It's not far, as your flyers travel," I said, pleased because I could think of nothing more perfect to convince Chel and Baltsar of the aliens' power than for me to arrive in one of their flyers.

Teon was grinning. "Is there room for me?" he said.

"Aren't you going with Adriana?" Sergi asked. I hadn't noticed when Adriana slipped out, but she had, no doubt nettled by Teon's hesitation.

"It might be awkward," Hanalore added.

"For Chel and Baltsar," Teon said, the grin widening. "But for me . . ."

Both men could use a little humility, especially Chel, but it didn't give me pleasure to know that.

"Let's take one of the aerologgers," Joan said. "There's enough room in them to ride in comfort."

I turned to fetch my cloak and spied it lying askew near a chair. When I put it on, I slipped my hand into the inner lining to reassure myself that my map and the one I'd copied from Sergi's holopedia were there. But they were gone. I shook the cloak.

"What's the matter, Heao?" Teon said.

"I carried the map," I said in human tongue.

"Yes, I left it in the pocket," he replied.

"It's gone." I felt sick. I didn't doubt for a moment that any one of them would recognize the map to be just that. I was too good an artist, and each of them was too smart to be confused by my legends for very long. Yet, I didn't recall any of them being near the cloak. I looked at Teon. "Are you sure you didn't take it?" I said suspiciously.

He stiffened. "I can draw my own map if I choose to do so."

I nodded glumly. I had forgotten that Teon could show them the way through Shadowland to the tableland city with as much accuracy as my map. Hadn't he described every distant peak to me and watched as I recorded every one? I laughed ruefully. It hardly made a difference as long as Teon was alive to show his people the way. I understood the urge he'd felt when he attacked me in the canyon, but I knew I was as incapable of murdering him as he had been of murdering me. "Never mind," I said when Teon started to search Sergi's quarters. "I have another back in camp."

Chapter 31

TEON AND I led the way across the clearing to the aero-loggers, our heads down, staring at the long shadows preceding us across the dry lumps of dirt. Dust motes swirled up from our feet. Dust! Not fog or mist or ice crystals.

The sunlight gave spark to the curls that tumbled over Teon's bronze forehead. I envied him, knowing that each night would end in a sunlighted dawn.

We heard a hoot and looked up. Adriana was standing in the hatch of her whining machine, beckoning to Teon through the shimmering air. He stopped and scowled, then turned his back on her to head toward the other aerologger, giving hers a wide berth.

Adriana's aerologger screamed and lifted, sending a thick cloud of dust and grit boiling through the clearing. I buried my face in my hood, felt Teon pull me against his chest, and heard Sergi curse through a series of coughs. By the time the air had cleared, Adriana's aerologger was out of sight.

"Thank you, more-than-friend," I said when Teon released me. He stared as Sergi opened the hatch and helped me into the aerologger's broad belly.

"Finally learned to say no, eh, Leon?" Joan said, climbing in after us, cheerfully brushing dust from his clothes.

Sergi laughed mirthlessly. "Now is when you really have to worry," he said. "She doesn't give up easily."

"You ought to know," Joan said, his eyes twinkling wickedly.

Teon hardly heard their banter. He'd seated himself next to me on a bench by a window, barely paying attention as Joan strapped us into a protective web. When Joan left us, Teon sat stiffly. There was an armrest between us to be shared, but our hands did not touch.

"More-than-friend," he said softly, "I did not take your map."

I nodded, realizing how seriously my ex-slave perceived his new status and how very strongly I felt about it, too. I was very much aware that the aerologger would speed me back to Baltsar and that these moments with my friend were final ones. Even the sight of the clearing falling away as we soared into the sky couldn't subdue the wretched longing I felt in my heart.

We sailed over the treetops until the land dropped away to form a great river canyon, where we followed white, rushing water to its source in the high country. Up and over the rugged escarpments Teon and I had climbed, and within a half a stick of time—about a third of an hour, the back of my mind converted—we approached the valley where the expedition had last camped.

Sergi set the huge machine down far enough away from the little camp so that the air barely disturbed the canopies. Even so, my companions could hardly have overlooked our approach. Through the window, Teon and I saw them standing by the canopies, terrified, acolytes praying and warriors with swords drawn. I unfastened the restraining web.

As soon as the hatch opened, I hailed the camp with a whistle. Baltsar answered with one of his own, and, when he saw me step out, he started walking, disregarding Chel's and Tarana's protests. I resisted an urge to run to him and waited by the hatch. I wanted him to come close to see the greatness of the flyer that had borne me back to him.

"Heao?" he said, slowing. His ruff was on end.

"I'm fine," I said. His keen eyes were darting from me to the splendidly clothed strangers, and when he finally spied Teon, Baltsar's jaw slackened.

"These are Teon's people," I said. "The slave legends are true. His people can fly, and they did come from the sky, and . . . " He seemed incredulous and very leery.

"It's not magic, Baltsar, nor are they gods. They have a very advanced technology."

My helper-in-life is not often at a loss for words, but he was then. He had been too pragmatic to believe in slaves' tales, and now the back of his mind was racing to catch up with hitherto disregarded thought lines.

"Christ Almighty!" Joan said, climbing down from the aerologger's belly behind me. "Will you look at the size of that broadsword?"

My prince was approaching cautiously. Tarana, ears casting and tail stiff, followed a few paces behind, two trembling acolytes whispering furiously to her as they helped her find her way. She stopped, but Chel continued. I stepped past Baltsar. "Chel, sheathe your sword. These people will not harm us."

He hesitated.

"Chel, your sword is a puny and ridiculous affront. Can't you see how powerful they are?"

My heart was pounding furiously. These people were unarmed and they were slow-moving. Chel's grip on his sword was firm. He scowled.

"They're slaves," he said, but his voice revealed awe.

Quietly, I began to explain again, in more detail this time, and I was aware that Baltsar was listening closely, too. Only Tarana held back, seemingly outraged by the words she was hearing. I caught the sound of Teon's voice from time to time, translating for Sergi, Joan, and Hana-lore. "They're offended by our enslavement of their people," I said finally, my voice very low.

"And I am offended by their invasion of my world," Chel said, his tail coiled righteously around his neck. But as he stared at the former slave and the construction engineers, he sheathed his sword. "And not a warrior among them," Chel added, offended even more grievously because there was no one of acknowledged rank for him to take down.

"This is a time for observation," Baltsar said quietly, "not for confrontation." His ears came forward as he finished the conversation with the back of his mind. His tail assumed a pleasant set, but I sensed that it was held there by sheer willpower.

When Sergi came to us, the two men held their ground, eyes wide with amazement. It was difficult for them to dissociate Sergi's shape from servitude, but no slave ever talked to them in the animated tone he was using, or postured so casually, and ended up with one hand stuck out in front, as if to receive something.

"He's greeting you and introducing himself," I said. "His name is Sergi."

"Tell him our names," Chel said almost reluctantly.

"It's our custom to shake hands when meeting in friendship," I translated for Sergi. Baltsar forced a smile and took Sergi's hand briefly, but Chel could not bring himself to touch the furless mitt.

"Baltsar, you should see the inside of this machine," Teon said, speaking for the first time. "When the time comes, you'll want to import some of their materials."

"And pay them with what?" Baltsar said irritably. He'd already realized they could hardly be expected to trade for inferior commodities. If they could tool and polish a machine like the aerologger, they wouldn't be interested in hand-wrought ironwork or fish.

Teon smiled. "You'll think of something."

Baltsar looked at me. "Do you think it's safe to go inside?"

"Yes. All of us must," I said, looking pointedly at Tarana. "It's our duty to report as much as we can to the king and as accurately as possible."

But Tarana pulled away from us, muttering, "Abomination." Her sightless eyes were glazed with fear. Chel had no patience to waste on Tarana. He turned and strode to the aerologger, with Baltsar accompanying him.

I looked at Tarana for a while, amazed that this sniveling woman was the same one who had held all Acaddeme in her merciless grasp. Her ears tracked me as I approached her.

"Abomination," she said. "You are an abomination, Pathfinder."

"Me?" I finally laughed and the acolytes shrank behind their mistress. "I didn't make godsfire; I merely found it, Tarana. And it hasn't harmed anyone except you, the one who would have kept our people in darkness for all time. If ever there was a sign from the gods . . . "

She gasped and laid back her ears, the front and back of her mind in a furious debate. Leaving the guardian of humankind's pathways thus engaged, I hurried to the aerologger just in time to hear Chel suck in his breath as he saw the vast work area inside, the flashing control panels, the cushioned consoles, racks of special equipment, and supplies for which he had no names.

As Baltsar and I followed Chel into the aerologger, we heard the sky scream with the approach of another. Involuntarily, Baltsar and Chel trembled.

"Now, what's that woman up to?" Sergi said, leaping on board to go to the control panel. He pressed buttons and moved dials. The equipment hissed and crackled. Flexible ears flattened against the noise. He looked at me apologetically, then spoke into the transmitter. "Adriana? Hey, Adriana, you're causing problems down here. Move your craft out of the area."

"Who's he talking to?" Chel asked me, and I explained again about the whimsical communication device, stopping for a moment when Adriana's aerologger shrieked by at low altitude.

Suddenly, Joan shouted from the hatch, "Sergi, she's making another pass and her laser warning is on! Warn her off!" She scrambled inside, with Hanalore following.

Sergi dived for another switch and the panel lit up.

"Still coming!"

"Dear God . . . "

"Gods . . . "

Coming in low over the valley the screaming machine slowed perceptibly. Even so, its wake of turbulent air was strong enough to collapse the canopies and send warriors and acolytes running headlong, every which way though the valley. Then the aerologger touched down, careened over the grass, and came to a stop. Before the high-pitched whine of the engines had died down, Adriana scrambled out of her hatch and came running toward us. An angry greeting by the three engineers was cut short by at low altitude.

"I thought so," she said accusingly, staring at us from the hatch. "A friendly tour, is it? Don't you realize they are our enemies? Do you want them to build their own flyers so that when we come to battle them we can meet on even terms?"

"They've done nothing aggressive."

"You should be putting the fear of God into them, not amusing them."

"There's no reason to believe they will be enemies."

Her eyes flashed dangerously. "They're barbarian slavemongers, not visiting dignitaries. Damn it, Sergi, hasn't it occurred to you that they might be lying about the purpose of their being here? Did you see what I routed

249

back there? About twenty of them with swords, and they've several armies back in their cities."

Sergi seemed surprised. "I don't think . . . "

"We have our lasers," she said urgently. Her hand moved quickly into her tool kit, then reappeared with the laser blade clenched. Involuntarily, I made an alarming sound. I didn't know the range of the blade, but I'd seen what it could do to solid rock, and I feared it.

In the flick of a tail, Chel associated my gasp of fear with the appearance of the thing in Adriana's hand. He unsheathed his broadsword and poised to strike before I really saw him move. But Adriana saw, and Sergi saw, and their response was instantaneous. Sergi may have been raising his arms only in a gesture, but he stepped between Chel and Adriana. He was too close to Chel, and my prince lowered the sword into Sergi's skull the same instant that the laser blade came on. My prince crumpled over the construction engineer as the smell of burned fur and flesh filled the aerologger. Baltsar had drawn his dagger and growled at Prince Chel's assailant, but Hanalore was the hero who kicked the laser blade from Adriana's hand as she prepared to turn it on the rest of us.

For a stunned second Adriana stood holding her hand, looking at Sergi's distorted face. The blood-matted hair nearly masked the wound in his skull, which nothing that lived and breathed could have survived. Then she fled before anyone had the presence of mind to stop her. I stayed Baltsar's hand before he could lunge mindlessly at Joan and Hanalore, or Teon, who stood trembling off to the side of the battleground. Baltsar tried to push me aside with a mighty roar, but I held firm.

"No!" I shouted. "No more killing, Baltsar! The danger is gone!" Frantically, I looked at Joan and Hanalore. I prayed that they, too, had not fetched out weapons. Perhaps they didn't carry laser blades, or maybe they believed they could have the blades out and in use before Baltsar could leap on them. Whatever the reason, they were watching me struggle with my mate, waiting to see if I could bring him under control. Baltsar relented when he realized there were no more threatening gestures being made, that Hanalore and Joan were standing slave-like, passive. He sheathed his dagger, but his hand remained on the hilt.

For a moment we stared at the carnage at our feet,

still watching when we heard Adriana's ship lift off. I saw Chel's tail tremble, and with a hopeful heart I kneeled to turn him over. He moaned. Half his stomach and most of his chest had been laid open and seared. Even though the wound was nearly bloodless, it took only a glance for me to know that he was mortally wounded.

"Chel?" I said softly.

"Whose dream am I in?" he said, confused and hurting.

"Your own," was my sad reply. I smoothed his sticky ruff and tried to pull his tunic over the gaping wound.

"What have you done, Heao?" he groaned. "Why didn't you give me a fighting chance?" His tail tried to lift from the floor, but suddenly it was lifeless.

"Chel?" I knew he could no longer hear me, and I let Baltsar lift me to my feet.

"It was an accident," Joan said, moving slowly and cautiously, mindful that while Baltsar comforted me with one arm, the other hand was on the hilt of his dagger. Not a broadsword, perhaps, but with his ruff so high, he looked as much the warrior as Chel ever did. "A dreadful accident, but an accident just the same," Joan said, horrified. He looked at me imploringly.

I nodded, agreeing, then in low tones translated Joan's words to Baltsar.

"The other one may come back," Baltsar said, still watching the two aliens suspiciously. "We should be prepared."

Quickly I explained my helper's fears to Joan, and they turned to locate her ship on the radarscope. We watched uneasily. Teon, recovering his composure now, pulled something over the bodies, then came to stand with us.

"Nowhere near us," Hanalore said finally, pointing to a spot of light on the scope. "She's headed straight for Shadowland."

"She's going to destroy the cities," Teon said, his fist clenching as his voice tensed. He looked at me. "She knew about the maps. She could have been the one." He gestured helplessly. "I shouldn't have offended her."

"What map?" Joan said. Teon told him.

"Maybe she'll get lost," Hanalore said, half-hoping, half-fearing.

Joan shook his head. "Anyone who can set an aerologger down on a fifteen-meter-wide, windswept ledge would probably think Shadowland storms were a game."

"Let's follow her, Joan," I urged.

251

"We shouldn't," Joan said. "The Board may pull our contracts . . . " He looked out the window to the depths of Shadowland, where storm clouds hovered and lightning streaked the darkness. Then he nodded. The hatch snapped shut without anyone having touched it, startling Baltsar. As the ship gently lifted and nosed its way toward Shadowland, I sat down beside Hanalore, concentrating on a shape and a bleep displayed on a lit screen. If only the swirling mists, turbulent clouds, and confusing continental divide would protect our people a while longer.

"Have you delivered our entire realm to the enemy?" Baltsar said, amazingly calm as he stood behind me.

"Perhaps we'll catch her," I said miserably as I looked at the engineers huddled over the control panel.

"And then what? Do you think they'll strike at one of their own?"

"I don't know," I said.

I turned away from him then, determined to help Teon with directing the engineers as much as I possibly could without my map for reference. I wished for the feel of the wind along the hairs of my ears, and to smell the bucolic scent of volcanic air, and to see the lay of the land. My last wish was granted. Between the infrared scopes and the radar, I could see the land, after a fashion. Hanalore and I conferred hastily, directing Joan onto what I hoped was the true path to the umbra where the great glacier began.

Chapter 32

JOAN TRIED to avoid the worst of the Shadowland storm, but it engulfed us despite his evasive action. Streaks of lightning made crazy patterns on the infrared scope and the instrument panel hissed and crackled. The powerful aerologger plunged and soared like a reed boat on the waves while we clung to the webbing, wondering when Luck would become bored with lifting us over mountaintops and keeping us out of the way of volcano caldrons.

Joan was sweating over the controls, and his wispy hair was curling into damp clumps. "Which way, Heao?" he said urgently.

But I didn't know. The winds aloft were different from winds along the ground. The only smell was that of the aliens' perspiration. Cloud formations that I thought were mountains perished before my eyes. Distance as I measured it was meaningless to Joan; a twinight's walk to the edge of Shadowland, three twinights to cover the ground between there and the last volcano we had encountered. But the aerologger did not need to angle off into an easily walked canyon, or ascend the hip of a volcano, or veer off to avoid unclimbable escarpments. The aerologger flew straight until the volcano lighted up the scope, covering the distance of four twinights' travel in time increments that were unrelated to ground travel. Then it, too, veered off to avoid the storm, but the maneuver was unsuccessful. We were hopelessly lost.

"Can't you get above the clouds?" Hanalore asked Joan.

"What the hell do you think I'm trying to do?" Joan said irritably.

I sensed that the aerologger was gaining altitude, but this piece of equipment was, I knew, designed for low-altitude work. The clouds seemed to spume upward endlessly.

Finally, Joan made the ship climb above the huge storm. The horizon was screened by a blanket of dark clouds, but we could see the rays of the sun bending at the edge of the skybridge, demarcating Shadowland. Greatly relieved, Joan pointed the ship's nose toward the far edge of the skybridge and we flew onward.

Hanalore, Teon, and I watched the hot glow of volcanoes on the infrared scope, and finally we saw the dark of the great glacier that ran like the black river of my dream from the continental divide nearly to the sea, where the tablelands lay. We dropped down through the buffeting clouds and skimmed along the highway of white ice toward the city, following . . . no, not following, *pursuing* my dream to its climax.

Baltsar stared through borrowed field glasses, stunned by the swiftness of our journey. "A season," he muttered, "it took us nearly a season's time to travel this far." The tip of his tail was twitching.

A season to travel through the shadow of a planet's halo, but an impossible journey only a generation ago while fire and ice clashed and fought for sovereignty over the last of the winterlands. Ice was foredoomed, losing the battle as the planet's warm phase continued to melt the glaciers to a fraction of the girth they had enjoyed centuries ago. Volcanoes thrived in the land of steam, ash, and monstrous winds, accelerating the glacial melt by adding carbon and other particulates to the atmosphere that trapped godsfire's heat like a pane of glass. Shadowland was the only place where glaciers still leveled mountains and collided with volcanoes, and the rugged girth might never see perpetual summer, as it would had it been the equator of other planets these aliens knew. Even the highly energetic star that godsfire was could not compensate for the planet's wobble, a highly predictable phenomenon, according to the aliens' holopedia, which would

254

thrust the entire planet into another ice age, as it had time after time throughout the ages. The distant ice age didn't worry the aliens very much. They'd dealt with many on other worlds, or abandoned them if the ice was too severe. But my people had nowhere to go, and they didn't even know what the future held in store for them. I wondered what the King-conqueror would say when I told him. Did he even have the capacity to worry beyond the future of his terrible dream?

"I've got Adriana on radar again," Hanalore announced. "She's well ahead of us. Looks like she knows where she's going, too."

While our ship accelerated perceptibly at Joan's command, he prodded, thumbed, and flipped switches at the console. "Damn," he said. "I can't even get her on the laser-com. The clouds are too thick."

"The radio?" Hanalore said, but Joan shook his head.

"Look!" Joan said, pointing out the front of the cockpit. "What's she strafing?"

I strained to see even as Baltsar turned the field glasses in that direction. "The causeway!" he said, gasping. "The king's causeway . . . like mushrooms . . ."

A few moments later we flew over the steaming ash of stones and rock, heaved and sliced as if by a monstrous blade.

"She's using full power," Hanalore said.

"Testing," Teon said quietly, "to see how well it will work on a city made of stone and iron."

"More speed, Joan," I said through clenched teeth. "The city will be high, Joan. Over the pass to the right."

"How high are those peaks?" he asked.

"About a day's climb." He shot me a worried look. "About a kilometer," I said, converting quickly.

"She's already there," Hanalore interjected as we climbed. "Making a pass." She looked up. "She's dropped off the scope."

"She has to get in close," Teon said. "She has to work beneath the clouds in order to see what she's doing. Come on, Joan. Hurry!"

The old man did not reply, but his lips tightened to a thin line. He was tense over the controls.

As we watched, the fertile valley of the causeway was left behind and the black slopes of the peaks known as the Five Brothers loomed before us. We slipped between them, and then the city was below us, and Adriana's ship was visible on both radar and infrared.

"Lots of people down there," Hanalore commented, looking at the slightly delayed computerized refinements on another scope.

"I've got her spotted," Joan said eagerly. "She has her floodlights on."

Through a mist, we could see the lights from Adriana's ship splashing over the countryside, filling ravines and jerking up the hillsides of landed nobles' estates. As we followed at low altitude, I could see my robed and hooded countryfolk staring up at us.

"She's looking for something," Joan said breathlessly. Before our eyes, Adriana's laser struck a bridge near the city gate; it crashed soundlessly into the ravine below, its brass suspension wires cleanly severed. Her ship meandered on, lazily it seemed, over the densely populated plateau that housed the temple, the marketplace, and the King-conqueror's stronghold.

"Try the laser-com now," Hanalore said. "The fog isn't so thick here."

Joan reached for the microphone, then spoke urgently into it. He thumbed the switch when Adriana didn't answer. "She must be receiving," he said angrily. He spoke again, then set the instrument aside in frustration. It slipped to the floor, but Joan didn't care. Working in such close quarters to the city's buildings required his complete attention.

I picked up the laser-com to replace it in the cradle, but my eyes were locked on the scene before us.

Adriana was, perhaps, confused by the rain shelters over the streets and alleys that tended to eliminate building delineations—that is, until her lights flooded the gold-covered dome and crystal inlaid arches that housed the main gallery.

"Not the temple," I prayed aloud.

Abruptly, Adriana's craft moved, circumnavigating the temple and swinging its light over the rooftops of neighboring buildings. The edge of the light caught the rear buttress of the king's stronghold, and the craft swerved from its circular path to a line between the temple and the stronghold.

"No doubt about it," I said. "She has the maps. That's the king's residence she's heading for."

256

"Are all his troops garrisoned there?" Joan asked grimly.

"No, only a small personal guard. The building is filled with his advisors and their families."

"Jesus!" Our ship lurched as Joan turned the controls. "She pointed that laser at us!"

No harm had been done other than to upset Teon's and Baltsar's footing, but the beam ripped through rain coverings and fragile cornicework in the city behind us. Flames flared briefly, but there was little combustible material to perpetuate fire in the street. Joan cautiously changed course so that the King-conqueror's stronghold was between us and Adriana. He glanced nervously at Hanalore. "Do you have the lasers ready?"

Hanalore nodded, fingers tensing on the levers.

"I'm going to edge around the building. Be ready . . . " Joan made the ship hug the wall to cut down the angle from which Adriana might see us and fire on us again.

We were all aware that Adriana had moved boldly to the front of the building, for her floodlight beam was wide, giving away her position.

"Why doesn't she fire?" someone asked. But no one had breath to answer.

Suddenly we accelerated into the light, cutting across the beam and abreast of Adriana's ship. Instinctively, I turned away from the light source and my frantic eyes beheld the stronghold, lighted as if it were made of silver. The residence torches in the battlements were drowned in the flood of alien light. To my horror, I saw the King-conqueror, standing on the stones of the battlements, his arms raised in defiance, his robe wind-whipped around his body. And for an instant I shared the night terrors of his dream, waiting for the other light, the one that would strike him dead as surely as a bolt of lightning. He must have seen the carnage Adriana already had wrought on his city of progress and enlightenment and known that the godlike fire of destruction was the moment of his dreams. There would be no ignoble death in a drowning accident to end his fears, only flames, searing, and consuming fire to end his reign. Yet the tip of his battle-stiff tail shook with challenge, and I nearly believed I could hear him roar for the god-thing to come close enough for him to engage with tooth and claw. He did not believe in the survivor guilt with which Tarana had tried to intoxicate him. He'd never sacked or crushed wantonly;

257

warfare was a means to forge, organize, and preserve his kingdom for the future, and he was willing to face the gods themselves, royally enraged at their lack of comprehension at his intent. He would do battle with them, even at the instant of what must have seemed to him like the truth of his haunting dreams.

But Adriana was no god, nothing more than a creature crazed by primordial fear—a fear reinforced by something in her past, learned from sad experience. Caused by the gods? I wondered instantly. Was even this alien mortal merely a tool of some greater power?

"No!" I screamed. "We are not puppets!" I brought the microphone to my mouth, shouting, "Did you think that leashing Teon to your bed made him less a slave just because you loved and caressed him? You're no different from a goddamned cat! There is no freedom for those who deny freedom to . . . "

The light bathing my sovereign disappeared instantly and I could not see him or his stronghold. Our ship shuddered, and as I staggered I realized Joan was grappling with the controls. Adriana's ship was visible through the cockpit portals. Part of the underbelly, including the floodlight, was cleanly sliced away. Despite the damage, it soared upward, leaving a trail of smoke.

"Got her," Joan said. His voice sounded bitter, not at all triumphant.

"Why didn't she fire?" Hanalore said, again, I suddenly realized. "She had plenty of time."

Joan ran his fingers through his hair, then wiped his forehead with the back of his hand. "I'll follow her," he whispered, already trailing the line of smoke that angled up and out toward the sea.

I looked back to see the torches in the battlements flickering like tiny stars, and then the distance and the mist shut their light. The stronghold was safe. Why had Adriana hesitated? Had she looked at her infrared and seen how many people were in the stronghold? Had she noticed the absence of weapons in my sovereign's hands? Or had one of those marvelously engineered switches malfunctioned? I looked at Teon. He was staring at the laser-com, still in my hand. Then our eyes met and we knew.

"Pull up! Pull up!" It was Hanalore's voice, but it was not Joan he was shouting at. A trail of smoke and vapor was angling from the cliffs at the edge of the city down to the sea, preceded by a speck of silver. Then there was no more smoke, nothing but the frothing sea, and that calmed quickly. In a few minutes we could not tell where the aerologger had plunged into the sea. Dismally, we circled.

"What have we done?" Hanalore said. Her voice was nearly hysterical. Joan shook his head and touched Hanalore comfortingly. His flesh was ashen against the gull-gray sleeve.

"She left us no choice," Joan said resolutely. But Hanalore said nothing.

"Make them let us out," Baltsar said when the circle over the sea spiraled and brought the tableland city into view.

Yes, I thought. Let us go home now that our destinies have been fulfilled. I have seen godsfire and even pursued the gods through heaven and over hell. Now I want to see my children, smell the salt wind, and put my feet down on the wet stones of the city's streets and walk where I will. I want to see my sovereign greet me without death and destruction haunting his sage eyes. I'm tired of fate and dreams and destiny.

The back of my mind agreed and reminded me that no one would fault me for deserting Tarana at the other end of the world, especially not now, considering recent events. It was imperative to bring word to the king of dangers yet to come so that he would have time to take action . . . perhaps to the extent of having to defend the realm. After all, if one of the aliens would attack us, perhaps others might, too. And if this necessity inadvertently left out Tarana, her sacrifice was just fickle Luck's whim . . . and mere coincidence that Academe's plot to be rid of her would be served. I wasn't murdering her in the strict sense of the word. I hadn't lifted a hand against her. Uneasily, I ralized that the back of my mind could rationalize the need for an immediate audience with the king to everyone's satisfaction except mine. I shook my head.

"We must go back for Tarana," I said.

Baltsar looked at me strangely. "Academe . . ."

"Academe needs a living sign, too," I said. "If Academe decides one year that there is no place in society for Tarana, whom might they turn against next year?" I looked at Teon, who was standing by the engineers at the controls, hands empty. When I saw him next, would it be with plow? Or with sword? I wondered. Slowly I turned back to Baltsar. "The deaths of three martyrs should be sufficient to remind intelligent men and women that if truth is worth dying for, it is also worth living for. We don't need another death."

"The truth is that there is something new to consider," Baltsar said angrily. "These . . . renegade slaves are more dangerous than all academians and guardians in the world run amok!" He sighed. "I'd rather leave the witch to her fate, but then I'd have to watch for new ones, springing up to take her place." He tugged thoughtfully on his whiskers and his tail twitched. "It's not easy being with you, Heao. Your sense of fairness and justice are selfless and have led me down many a strange path. But I'm learning to trust you. Let's go back for Tarana."

It was no command of fate that made me put my arm around him just then; nor was it destiny guiding my gaze to meet Teon's somber eyes. It was my own act, for which I will always take complete responsibility.

Epilogue
HEAO'S WORLD

IN A fashion, Tarana's destiny was unchanged from the one in her dream. She returned to the tablelands with us in the flying machine. She was often seen wandering about the city in what must have seemed to her to be the darkness of the Evernight Mountains, for she never regained her sight. In her faith, her personal tragedy was a stroke of order, a kindness I will never believe she deserved.

The King-conqueror had to deal with each of our versions and opinions of what had transpired on the expedition and how the strangers at the edge of the world would fit or not fit into our society. And then he had to deal with the aliens themselves and a new concept they called *insurance*, which replaced the bridge Adriana had destroyed, at no cost to the king. That gesture of goodwill did not indemnify them from the king's wrath, however, for he sent an army of warriors to contain the construction site while he pondered the choice between coexistence and conquest. He wasn't so rash as to believe that his warriors could overpower their lasers and complicated machinery; more likely, it was a ploy for time to gain the knowledge of how to turn the alien's own laws to the realm's advantage. Why else would he have sent me and Baltsar along with Mussa's warriors to engage the Board's representative to our people?

I see Teon from time to time, dressed alternately in the

alien glitter and native spidersilk, exported by Baltsar to trade for glowlamps, and heatpacks, and tools . . . nearly anything loose and portable that Teon can find a way to move. And having served Baltsar for many a year, the cleverest merchant of them all, Teon can move nearly anything from the steadily rising structures, including the entire chummery, in which Baltsar, the twins, Sema, and I now reside. My more-than-friend has effectively monopolized trade by virtue of being bilingual. Other ex-slaves are joining him, ones quietly freed by Baltsar and the King-conqueror, even while Academe still ponders the question of how to free them all without undermining the economy of the entire realm. I hope a plan will be implemented before the aliens recover from their confusion and implement one of their own.

It remains to be seen if the aliens' technology will overwhelm us, as Sergi predicted, or if, as I believe, Academe's precept of exploring change and causing it to happen in an orderly fashion is merely being fulfilled once again, as it has been fulfilled throughout time.

Glossary

HEAO'S WORLD

Academe A cult of truth-finders, temporal puzzlers, and speculators who deal in facts.

Academian A member of Academe.

Luck A fickle god. An aspect, sometimes fortuitous, sometimes not.

Duskglow A hearty light on the horizon just before night.

Dawnglow A brilliant glow on the horizon just before twinight.

Flametender God of fire, the hearth, and the forge. Associated equally with war and peace, since weapons and plows alike are fashioned in his flames. He is said to herald the spring by building a great fire at the upcoast feet of the skybridge.

Godsfire The fire Flametender builds at the upcoast feet of the skybridge, resulting in an especially brilliant dawnglow during spring.

Perspicuity A goddess. Also an aspect of clarity, understanding, and truthfulness.

Skybridge An arc through the sky. A dark arc visible in the sky during cloudless times. Gods are said to have written messages underneath for humankind to perceive, if only they were perfect enough to see. It is also said that the gods tread the skybridge, and that Raingiver frequents it often to empty his water jugs over the side.

Raingiver God of rain.

Temple The religious cult and/or the religious gathering place.

Temple guardian A special sect who claim to serve the gods, tend the lexicons, and guide the non-secular community to righteous paths by means of minor witchcraft (trickery and hoaxes) and by preying on primordial fears. Guardians are celibate, living apart from the community in the temples. Individuals are often associated with specific noblepersons.

Twinight The time between nights when the air glows and the does leave their hutches to browse.

THE YEARS OF THE DREAMS

Godsfire It appears to have a geocentric movement, but this is apparently open to question.

Skybridge The planetary ring. A broken-up satellite. Dust and debris orbiting the world with a definite geocentric affinity.

Shadowland The land around the equator that is in the umbra and penumbra of the shadow cast by the planetary ring/skybridge.

East Upcoast direction.

West Downcoast direction.

North A direction that bisects Shadowland.

South Another direction that bisects Shadowland.

Window A transparent portal.